Sign up for our newsletter
about new and upcoming relea.

www.ylva-publishing.com

Other Books by
Rachael Sommers

Fool for Love
Never Say Never

Chemistry

Rachael Sommers

Acknowledgments

First and foremost, thank you to Astrid and everyone at Ylva publishing, because without them, this book wouldn't be a possibility.

Thanks to my beta readers Gane, Danna, Miira and Sarah S. Particular thanks go to Yan for being my sounding board and helping me make improvements to draft after draft. Sarah P—thank you for helping me sound American, and for all your input on the U.S. school system. You've taught me a lot, and I hope I've done it justice.

Huge thanks to C.S. Conrad for being such an amazing developmental editor, and for helping me out with a lot of the sensitivity issues in this story. Thanks to Sheena Billett for being my copy editor and catching any English words that fell through the cracks.

Finally, Laura, thank you for everything you do for me. I'm sorry for annoying you by pronouncing everything the American way when I was writing this book. I can't promise it won't keep happening, but we all have our flaws. Love you!

Chapter 1

Lily stared with a sense of resignation as the departure time of each flight listed on the board changed to the same word:

CANCELED.

This was not good.

"Excuse me?" The woman standing in front of her in the check-in line stepped toward the nearest member of airport staff. "My flight is canceled?"

"All of the flights are canceled, ma'am." He looked like he'd rather be anywhere else, and Lily didn't blame him. He was about to say the same thing a hundred times over.

"But why?"

His gaze flitted to the windows of Miami International Airport. The panes were streaked with rain, and the palm trees in the distance were bent in half. "Have you seen the weather, ma'am?"

She waved a hand. "It's just a little rain."

Lily snorted. She wouldn't call a category three storm "a little rain". The woman turned to throw Lily a haughty glare.

"I'm afraid there's not much we can do. We have to wait for it to pass."

Lily sighed. It had been a risk to travel to the airport—she'd been keeping a careful eye on the news for the past few days—but it wasn't like she had much choice.

She'd given the keys of her apartment over to its new owner that morning.

Curling a hand around the handle of her suitcase, Lily stepped out of the line. There was a hotel somewhere in the central terminal, and if she was quick, she might be able to grab a room before everyone else had the same idea.

Trying to re-book a flight for later in the week would be much more fun if she could do it sprawled on a double bed with room service.

As she walked, Lily pulled out her phone and dialed her sister's number.

"Christ, Daisy." Lily jerked the phone away from her ear when greeted with the sound of a wailing baby. "I think I've gone deaf."

"You've gone deaf? Try being in the same room. She has the lung capacity of an adult human."

"What did you expect marrying someone who's six four?"

"Don't. She's already doubled in size since she was born. She's going to be a giant." Emma's crying lessened, and Daisy's sigh of relief was audible. "Are you all right? Is your flight on time?"

"My flight is canceled."

"What? Why?"

"Have you not seen the news?"

"I have a six-week-old baby, Lily. I haven't watched anything."

"There's a storm. All flights are grounded until further notice."

"Shit."

"Yeah." Lily's black Vans squeaked on the marble floor as she weaved her way through the people scattered throughout the terminal. "I'm going to see if I can get a room nearby to hole up for the night."

"Do you think you'll be able to get here tomorrow?"

"I don't know." Lily shot a baleful look at the black sky through a nearby window. "Right now, I doubt it. Which means I'm probably going to miss the first day of my new job, and then they'll fire me, and I—"

"Okay. Stop." Daisy cut her off mid-spiral. "They're not going to fire you, even if you do miss your first day."

"They might."

"They won't."

"It doesn't make a good impression though, does it? I knew I shouldn't have booked a flight so close." Not that she'd had much choice. The move back to her hometown hadn't exactly been planned and selling her apartment and packing up her things—as well as finishing up her last two weeks at work—had meant cutting it fine.

"It's not your fault. You couldn't have predicted this."

"Should've. It is hurricane season."

"True. You did abandon us for the sunshine of Florida."

"Not for much longer." As nice as it would be to be back around her family, Lily would miss Miami. It had been where she'd found herself, her place in the world, and she'd be sad to leave it behind. "Can you call Mom and let her know?"

"'Course."

Lily spotted a sign for the MIA Hotel and quickened her pace, ducking around a group of British tourists arguing about the best way to proceed. "I hope she'll be okay watching Hades for a while longer."

"Please. She loves having a cat in the house again. You might not get her back."

"She's welcome to cat sit whenever she likes." Lily stepped inside the hotel and joined the back of the line snaking from the check-in desk. It wasn't too long; she hoped they had enough rooms left for the handful of people in front of her. "Right, I'd better go. I'll call you later."

"Bye!" Daisy hung up, and Lily tapped her foot as she waited to reach the front of the line.

"Do you have any rooms free for the night?" Lily said, when she could finally step up to the desk.

"You're in luck," the clerk said with a tired smile. "There's one left."

Lily didn't feel particularly lucky as she forked out a hundred and twenty dollars for the luxury of not having to sleep on the airport floor.

But at least Lily was inside. And the room was nice enough, a queen-sized bed in the center and a comfortable-looking red leather armchair tucked into the corner.

Sinking onto it, Lily abandoned her suitcase by the bed and pulled out her phone. She had a call to make.

Lily hoped her new boss would be forgiving.

"Look who finally made it!" Lily was greeted by Daisy, her face alight with a broad grin, outside Arrivals at O'Hare. Lily was swept into a tight hug as soon as she was within arm's reach, and nearly inhaled a mouthful of her sister's hair.

When they were younger, they'd often been mistaken for twins with only a one-year age gap between them. They had the same dirty blonde hair and blue eyes, a spattering of freckles across white cheeks that were easy to redden. Lily was an inch taller—and never let Daisy forget it.

"Glad to be back?"

Lily squeezed her sister tight. "You have no idea." Her bank balance sure was—one night at the MIA Hotel had turned into three while she waited for a space on a flight to Chicago to become available.

"How's my favorite sister-in-law?" Alex stood beside Daisy, a baby carrier in one hand.

"I'm your only sister-in-law," Lily said, feeling tiny standing in front of him. "And I'm good." Lily glanced inside the carrier; Emma slept soundly within. "I see she's stopped screaming."

"Don't jinx it. This is the longest she's slept this week." Daisy started off toward the exit. "I'm guessing you still have a job?"

Lily rolled her suitcase behind her, squinting in the late afternoon sun as they stepped outside. She regretted her decision to pack away her sunglasses. It was a warm day, and though it didn't compare to the Miami heat, she couldn't complain.

"I do. They were understanding."

"I told you." Daisy nudged Lily with her shoulder. "Wasn't it an institute day you missed anyway?"

"Yeah, but still. It was supposed to be my chance to familiarize myself with the school and the staff." Which she'd have to do between classes on Monday morning.

"You'll be fine."

They reached Alex's Volvo, and Lily put her case in the trunk while Daisy secured the baby carrier on the backseat.

Alex slid behind the wheel and Daisy into the passenger seat, leaving Lily in the back beside her sleepy niece.

Daisy turned to glance at Lily over her shoulder. "Want to go to Mom and Dad's or your new place?"

"The new place, I think." As much as she'd like some of her mom's cooking, Lily wanted to settle in as soon as possible.

Especially if she only had a day before working full time.

"I'll let Mom know they can meet us there if they want." Lily fired off the text and then leaned her head against the back of the seat.

She was exhausted. It had been a hectic few months between her career change and moving halfway across the country, but it felt right, and she couldn't wait to get started on her new life.

In an old haunt.

As Alex pulled onto the highway, Lily glanced out of the car window. It had been ten years since she'd left Illinois for college. Returning only for holidays since, she was back—possibly for good.

Lily had worried it would feel like a step backwards, but instead she felt content. Her new place wasn't quite in her hometown of High Grove, but it was only a half-hour drive—so, as her mom had said when Lily had told her she was coming back, she had no excuse not to visit.

It was small for a house but compared to the apartment she was used to in Miami it was spacious. And—most crucially—here, she'd be living on her own.

Not with her cheating ex.

Plus, it was a five-minute drive to the high school where Lily would start teaching on Monday. Which, as she struggled to get out of bed in the morning, was an added bonus.

"Looks like they beat us here," Alex said, as he pulled onto Lily's street.

Her parents' Accord was parked behind her Corolla, abandoned in the driveway since she'd driven it up a few weeks ago with as many of her belongings she could fit inside it.

They stepped out of the car as Alex pulled in behind them, and Lily was swept into her mom's arms before she was properly out of the car.

"Give her a chance to breathe, Mom," Daisy said, unbuckling Emma from the car seat when she fussed.

"I can't help it. I've missed her."

"I've missed you too, Mom."

"What about me?" Her dad said, and Lily hugged him, too.

"And you." Lily heard a yowl from inside her parent's car and peered through the rear window. A cat carrier sat on the backseat, and Lily caught a glimpse of a black paw trying to bat at the latch, green eyes glimmering from within. "Has she been living up to her namesake?"

"She's been wonderful," her mom said, a fond look on her face. "But I'm sure she's eager to explore her new home."

Lily was, too. She grabbed the carrier and led the way to the front door.

"I hope you don't mind," her dad said as she slid her key into the lock. "But we've done some work on the place since you were last here. Wanted to help you settle in—especially with the delay."

Curiosity burning, Lily let herself inside.

The cream wallpaper she'd chosen to replace the dingy gray in the hall had been hung, and the carpets lining the stairs looked like they'd been deep-cleaned. A glance into the living room revealed her new couch had arrived safely, and the flat pack furniture had been assembled, a TV stand and a bookcase pressed carefully against the wall. It was still bare—the price of having to start all over again, her old furniture tainted with memories she'd rather not re-visit—but at least it was all hers.

Lily suspected the same sight would greet her upstairs, and the knowledge she wouldn't have to spend hours assembling her bed before she could go to sleep made her want to cry.

"Obviously, you can move it all around," her dad said. "But we wanted to make life as easy for you as possible."

"You did all this for me?" Lily said, her throat feeling tight.

"We all did," Daisy said, knocking Lily's shoulder with her own. "Welcome home, sis."

Lily's footsteps echoed in the empty hallway, devoid of the sound of lockers clattering open. In an hour, this place would be heaving with teenagers fresh from their summer vacation, and Lily reveled in the calm before the storm.

"I'm sorry, again, for not being here on Friday." Lily turned to her new boss—the head of Greenfield High School's science department—and was promptly waved off.

"Please don't apologize," Alisha said, her heels clicking against the floor. "It was out of your control. And you're here now. That's the most important thing." A tall, Black woman with warm brown eyes in her late-forties, Alisha Woods struck Lily as straightlaced and intimidating, but her smile as she ushered Lily into a classroom was kindly. "Here we are. This is your room."

Lily stepped inside and glanced around, taking it all in. It was bright and airy, the windows along the rear wall offering a view of the sports fields at the back of the building and letting in plenty of the early morning sun. Wooden benches pointed toward the white boards at the front of the room, with green stools neatly tucked underneath.

"It's perfect." The walls were bare, but Lily could work with that. She set her bag on the teacher's desk—her desk—and ran her fingertips across its surface.

"I'll give you a quick tour of the rest of the department while it's still quiet," Alisha said, turning toward the door and leaving Lily hurrying to catch up. "We have four other science teaching staff. Andrew is physics, Mei is earth and physical science." She pointed at their classrooms as they passed, the lights within dim. Alisha seemed to be the singular early riser.

"Brandon does a bit of everything across the whole school, so he's often not around, and Eva…" Alisha trailed off, glancing at the room at the end of the hall. It was the only one bearing a name; Dr. Eva Thomas was engraved on the plaque.

Lily tried not to think it was pretentious. She'd reserve her judgment until she'd met her.

"Eva is our resident biologist. I should warn you now—she can be prickly."

"Prickly?"

"Yes. I'd give her a wide berth. Most other people do."

Well, that didn't sound encouraging.

"This is my room." Alisha propped open the door to let Lily see inside, the walls plastered with an array of brightly colored posters. "If you ever need anything, please don't hesitate to ask. I've been teaching for years, but I still remember how overwhelming my first year of it was. I don't know if you've had a chance to look at your schedule yet, but you have first period free today, so you have a chance to settle in before you get thrown in at the deep end."

Their next stop was the teacher's lounge. "There is one over in the main building, but everyone tends to use this one. It's cozy." It was smaller than Lily had been used to at the school where she'd finished her training, with a few padded chairs placed around a large wooden table in the center of the room. A fridge sat beside a sink along one wall, and Lily was delighted to see a Keurig coffee machine on the counter.

"Feel free to help yourself," Alisha said, noticing the direction of Lily's gaze. "There's a monthly contribution toward keeping it stocked, or you can bring in your own if you wish. There's a toaster and a microwave, too. All I ask is you clean up after yourself—which doesn't stop half of the department from leaving a mess behind. This might be the cleanest you'll see the place."

"I think it's a requirement for every department to have a serial slob."

"That's been my experience." Alisha's smile eased some of the nerves that had been somersaulting around her stomach all morning.

Lily had yet to meet any of her students, but at least Alisha had offered her a warm welcome.

"I'll leave you to get yourself settled." Alisha glanced at the silver watch around her wrist. "There's still forty minutes until classes start if you want to explore the rest of the school, and I'll see you later. I hope you settle in okay."

"Thanks, Alisha."

Alisha disappeared down the hall, and Lily returned to her classroom to fetch her lunch so she could put it in the refrigerator. She grabbed her trusty mug, too, a present from the students she'd spent her last few weeks of teacher training with. Miss Cross, was written on the side using symbols from the periodic table.

Lily was filling it with coffee when the door to the teacher's lounge opened behind her. A white man who appeared to be in his early thirties joined her.

"Oh, hi." He pushed square-framed black glasses up his nose before stretching a hand toward her. "You must be Lily. I'm Andrew."

If pressed, that was what Lily would have guessed—something about his skinny frame, glasses and tweed suit screamed physicist.

"That's right, it's nice to meet you." Lily shook his hand.

"How are you feeling?" He leaned past her to put a salad in the refrigerator. "Alisha said this was your first job."

"Nervous, but excited to get going."

"Good, good. The kids aren't so bad here. They'll try and test you, but as long as you're firm with them I'm sure you'll be fine. I know Alisha will have already offered, but if you need anything, please ask."

"Thank you." Coffee in hand, Lily retreated to her classroom, settling behind her desk and pressing the power button on her new staff-issued laptop. She spent a few minutes familiarizing herself with the system, relieved to find it was similar to the ones she'd used before—the last thing she needed was to be plagued by IT issues on her first day.

That wasn't the way to win over her classes.

Lily glanced at the clock on the wall. It was seven thirty, which left her with twenty minutes before the building would be flooded with kids. Already she could see them gathering outside, eager to catch up after their summer break.

Deciding to leave exploring beyond the safety of her own floor for another time, she went in search of the nearest staff toilets, instead. On her return, Lily paused in the hallway to read a poster on the wall detailing the science and STEM clubs the school ran as extracurriculars.

Lily failed to notice the door opening behind her and didn't realize she was blocking the doorway until someone collided with her back, jolting them both.

"Oh, gosh, I'm sor—" Lily turned to apologize, but the words died in her throat because the woman glaring at her was drop-dead gorgeous. Short dark hair framed a strong jawline, black-rimmed glasses sitting on her nose above sharp cheekbones, her white skin flawless.

A dark stain was spreading across the front of the woman's white blouse, drips of coffee from the mug gripped in her hand splashing onto the floor, and Lily gulped.

"I'm so sorry." The blouse looked expensive, and this was not the way to make a good impression on her new colleagues. "Is it hot? Let me help."

"Of course it's hot!" Her voice was as cool and steely as the gray of her eyes, her expression morphing to disgust as she glanced down at herself. "Why are you standing there?"

"I-I was reading the posters." Lily waved toward the wall, trying not to quail beneath the weight of the woman's gaze as she stared down at Lily's black slacks and floral blouse. "I'm Lily. Lily Cross, the new chemistry teacher. I hope you aren't hurt, and I'll pay for your blouse to be dry cleaned."

Lily stretched out a hand, glancing over the woman's shoulder and realizing she was outside of Eva's room.

Eva looked at her hand, lip curled in distaste, and Lily let it drop back to her side. Lily thought of Alisha's earlier warning—she hadn't realized that prickly was code for extremely rude. And a little scary.

On the plus side, Eva's attitude made her instantly less attractive.

"I'll be surprised if you last the week." Eva brushed past Lily in the direction of the staff toilets, leaving Lily staring after her.

A low whistle caught her attention, and Lily turned to see an Asian woman exiting the classroom opposite Lily's, dark curls framing a smiling face. "Damn, newbie. You're lucky you're still alive."

Lily groaned. "Not the first impression I hoped to make. Or be greeted with."

"Eh, I wouldn't worry about it. She wouldn't like you anyway." She said it so cheerfully Lily had to laugh.

"You're Mei, right?"

"Yeah. Welcome to the madhouse. I promise no one else will be as unwelcoming."

"Even the kids?"

"Oh, the kids are a breeze compared to her. Trust me."

The shrill sound of the bell echoed in the hall, and Lily jumped.

"Here they come," Mei said, as shadows started to approach from the building's entrance. "Good luck."

"Thanks."

"Good morning," Mei said to her students, receiving a few grunts in response. "I see we're not awake yet. You've had the whole summer to catch up on sleep! Look alive, people."

Lily spent first period decorating. She hung a large periodic table on one wall and some posters about different educational styles on another. Her desk remained bare, but she was sure after a week or two it would be covered—she would never be one of those teachers who managed to keep an immaculate workspace.

Having printed off her schedule, Lily sat to study it. All her classes were sophomores, and it would be their first taste of chemistry since middle school. Lily knew most of them dreaded it—it involved a lot of math, and not nearly as much lab work as they'd prefer—but she was looking forward to trying to change their minds.

Forty-five minutes passed quicker than Lily expected, and when the bell rang, she climbed to her feet and smoothed out the creases in her blouse as she waited by the door for her new students.

They arrived in dribs and drabs, and Lily ushered them inside. She let them sit where they wanted, though she wouldn't hesitate to shift them around if she found some didn't work well together.

Once all the seats were filled, Lily took a deep breath and moved to the front of the room. She leaned back against her desk and willed her fingers not to shake as she wrapped them around its edge. "Welcome. I'm Miss Cross, and I'm going to be your chemistry teacher for the next year. I thought we could start by going around the room and have each of you give me a chemistry fact."

Lily saw a few eye rolls but didn't let it discourage her.

"Let's start here." She moved toward the first desk on the front row, where a kid with a mop of dark curls sat. "What's your name?"

"Luke."

Lily made a note on a piece of paper, knowing she'd never remember their names if she didn't write them somewhere.

"Okay, Luke, can you think of a fact for me? It can be anything you like."

"Uh…" Luke paused, pen twirling. "Technetium was the first ever man-made element."

Lily hadn't expected that from a fifteen-year-old. "Wow, that's right. Who's next?" Lily glanced at the next student along.

"Marie Curie is the only woman to win a Nobel Prize in two different sciences."

"Great, and you are?"

"Amanda."

Lily remembered the (they/them) pronouns from the class list she'd been given and made a mental note not to slip up when referring to Amanda in future classes. "And sitting next to you is…?"

11

"Macie. Bromine and mercury are the only elements liquid at room temperature." Macie offered the fact without being prompted, and Lily smiled.

Lily made her way around the room. Whether they knew it or not, the fact they chose told her a lot about them, and by the time she reached the end Lily felt the last of her nerves fade away.

Macie raised a hand as Lily returned to her desk.

"Yes, Macie?"

"Do you have a fact, Miss Cross?"

Thankfully, Lily had anticipated someone asking and had a few prepared. "How about the fact that while oxygen gas is colorless, its solid and liquid forms are blue? Or the human body contains enough carbon atoms to provide graphite for nine thousand pencils? There's one letter of the alphabet that doesn't appear on the periodic table—can anyone tell me what it is?" Several pairs of eyes flitted over to Lily's poster, and she smiled. "Preferably without cheating."

"Z!"

"X!"

"J!"

"K!"

"No, that's potassium, you idiot—"

"While I appreciate the enthusiasm"—Lily raised her voice to cut through the noise—"let's not all shout out at once, okay? And let's not call people idiots, either." She looked pointedly at the culprit.

"Sorry, Miss Cross."

"I did hear the right answer in there somewhere, though. Who said J?"

Luke's hand raised.

"Well done, Luke. Now, I know sometimes it can be hard to speak in front of the class, so here's some incentive." Lily reached behind her desk for the box of candy she'd bought the previous day, trying not to laugh at the widening eyes of her class. "No one has any allergies, do they?" She'd glanced over the medical information for all her students and didn't remember any, but she wanted to be sure. When there were no nods, Lily held the box toward Luke. "If you answer a question—right or wrong—you get candy. But you have to raise your hand rather than shout out. Sound good?"

She was met with vigorous nods.

"Let's test it out, shall we? Who can tell me what the smallest unit of matter is?"

Several hands shot into the air, and Lily chose at random.

"An atom."

"Correct." Lily offered Ben the box. "And what is the center of the atom called?"

Again, she had a few students to choose from.

"The nucleus."

"Which consists of…?"

Lily continued to build the questions until they'd all gotten a piece of candy, impressed with their base level of knowledge and confident she had a bright group of kids.

Time flew by, and when the bell rang and signaled the end of her first class, Lily felt good, amped up for her next and ready to do it all again.

Chapter 2

THE FIRST DAY OF THE semester was always Eva's favorite, but today she couldn't enjoy it as much as she usually did.

Five minutes of scrubbing at the stain on her blouse hadn't been enough to get it out entirely, and she'd had a question about it from every single class she'd taught. And as for the woman who'd caused it in the first place… well, that was like looking at a ghost.

It had been two years since Eva had last laid eyes on her ex, but Lily and Victoria seemed to share some similarities. Blonde hair, bright blue eyes, pale white skin and a full figure. Victoria would never be caught dead in a shirt like Lily's, but it had still been enough to make Eva do a double-take. Enough to make Eva react more viciously than she might have done were it anyone else.

No matter. Eva refused to let their encounter ruin the rest of her day.

Eva knew she had a reputation for being one of the toughest teachers in the school, yet that didn't stop those students she'd never taught from testing her limits, seeing how far they could push things before she snapped.

It was her fourth class of the day, and she'd handed out six detentions.

More were brewing as she watched her freshman honors students file into her room, talking animatedly with one another. If they thought Eva was going to give them an easy ride because she had them the period before lunch, they were sorely mistaken.

"Quiet, please." Eva rarely needed to raise her voice to take command of a room, and silence fell when she stood in front of the board. "I am Dr. Thomas, and for the next two semesters, we will be studying the four pillars of biology: cells, genetics, ecology, and evolution. A lot of people consider biology to be the easiest of the sciences"—an opinion not helped by cramming the entire biology syllabus into their freshman year—"but I think you'll soon learn it's not the case."

A hand raised at the front of the class.

"Yes?"

"What is the easiest? In your opinion?"

Eva wasn't going to be drawn into a debate within the first five minutes. "They're all on equal footing, but if any of you consider this class an easy ride, you're in for a rude awakening. You've been placed in an honors class based on placement tests and teacher recommendations but make no mistake: if you don't pull your weight, you will be moved. I don't tolerate slackers. Understood?"

Twenty heads bobbed in unison.

Eva slipped her glasses onto her nose to take roll call, noting where each student was sitting as they answered. She prided herself on learning their names—and identifying any potential troublemakers—quickly.

"Another thing I don't tolerate is people talking when I am," Eva said when she was finished, leveling a glare at two kids in the back row of seats. One of them dropped their head, looking at the desk with pink cheeks, but the other stared right back at Eva.

Her first problem student.

Eva refrained from rubbing her palms together.

"Francesca, is it?"

"Yes."

"That's 'Yes, ma'am', or 'Yes, doctor', if you prefer." Eva hadn't spent six years slogging through a PhD program not to use the title that came with it, but she didn't always use it in the classroom.

"Yes, ma'am."

"Do I need to move you elsewhere, or do you think you can manage to keep your mouth shut for the next forty minutes?"

"I'll try my best." Francesca smirked, leaning back in her chair like she was sitting at a restaurant with her friends. The logo of her jacket caught Eva's attention—Gucci and Eva tried not to generalize but her most difficult, entitled students were usually the ones with the richest parents.

"If you can't manage it, you can spend an hour with me after school practicing." Eva rose to her feet to stand beside the board, her PowerPoint presentation for the introductory lesson already on the screen. "Now, let's get started, shall we? Who can give me the definition of a cell?"

Eva kept a close eye on Francesca throughout the rest of the class, expecting some pushback, but to her surprise, none came. Her dressing-down seemed to have scared her classmates, too, and Eva didn't issue a single detention for the remainder of the period.

When the bell rang, Eva followed her students out into the hall. Lunch duty wasn't something she particularly enjoyed, but it was a necessary part of the job. Eva garnered a few curious looks over the state of her shirt, and she folded her arms across her chest to hide the worst of the brown mark, a glare enough to silence any snickers sent her way.

Several other members of staff stood huddled together in groups, but Eva skirted around them. She didn't make a habit of engaging in idle chit-chat with her colleagues, and was purposefully standoffish, careful to cultivate an attitude of do-not-approach to students and staff alike.

Eva was happiest on her own—had never seen the point in forming relationships with others when they always inevitably ended, leaving her lost and disappointed and wondering why she'd ever bothered in the first place—and made sure everyone else knew it.

She was on her third loop when another teacher joined the fray. Eva recognized the blouse of her department's newest hire and rolled her eyes, because of course she shared a duty with Lily.

Just her luck.

Lily looked lost and out of place, hovering inside the doorway. Nerves showed in the way she wrung her hands as her eyes darted around the room. Young and fresh-faced, she didn't look like she'd be the sternest, and the way she'd quailed under Eva's glare earlier didn't bode well for her.

When her eyes met Eva's, a flicker of recognition passed across Lily's face, but surely after their previous meeting she wouldn't be stupid enough to approach.

Would she?

Eva watched and waited, adopting an air far from welcoming.

It didn't have the effect she was hoping for, because much to her horror, Lily approached with a spring in her step and a hesitant smile on her face.

"I think we got off on the wrong foot before," Lily said, coming to a stop by Eva's shoulder. "I—"

"I don't think we did, actually." Eva chose to examine her nails rather than meet the other woman's gaze. It was a behavior more reminiscent of her students than of a thirty-five-year-old, and sure, Eva could entertain her, but Eva didn't need a friend—especially one who reminded her of her past—and if she humored Lily on her first day, she'd talk Eva's ear off in the weeks to come.

"Oh."

Eva glanced up. Lily looked crestfallen, but Eva refused to let it bother her. "If that was all...?" Eva raised an eyebrow and watched Lily's throat work as she swallowed.

"I'm sorry again about your blouse. Like I said before—I'll pay for the cost of dry-cleaning."

"I think you've done enough already, don't you?" A scrub with vinegar and a few rounds in the washing machine and Eva was confident it'd look as good as new. And it meant she wouldn't have to talk to Lily again.

"O-okay, then. See you around, I guess." Lily walked away, and Eva tried to ignore the defeated slump of her shoulders as she approached a different group of teachers.

She'd bounce back. Eva had met her type before: bright with enthusiasm and eager to please, but Eva didn't have the time nor energy to deal with it.

Not with what awaited her at home. Any nurturing or patient instinct—of which, admittedly, she already had little—was reserved for her mother, and the role of carer Eva had stepped into when she'd moved to High Grove from Washington D.C. two years ago.

She worked to pay the bills for them both, and that was all.

If the new hire thought she was going to change that, well.

She was mistaken.

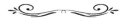

Downtrodden after her attempt to make amends with Eva, Lily tried to shake off the memory as she slipped into the teacher's lounge, her stomach rumbling.

Inside, Mei and Andrew sat at the table, both smiling at Lily as she approached the refrigerator.

"How's your first day going?" Andrew said, once Lily had grabbed her pasta salad and joined them. "The kids behaving themselves?"

The kids weren't the ones she was having an issue with. "Yeah, they've been great. A few of them have tried it on, but I haven't had to hand out any detentions yet."

"Speaking of detentions," Mei said, sipping from her mug of coffee. "We're having a wager on how many kids Eva is going to keep after school tonight if you'd like to join. It's five dollars, winner takes all. We have guesses of five, seven and eight."

"So many?" Lily was shocked. "It's the first day."

"Oh, you're adorable." Mei patted the back of her hand. "You can go lower if you want."

"But I wouldn't," Andrew said. "It's usually high. She likes to set a precedent."

Lily could barely comprehend it. The most she'd ever had to keep behind was four. Then again, based on what Lily had seen so far, she wouldn't be surprised if Eva handed out detentions if the kids dared breathe too loudly. "How does she get away with it?"

"Because it works," Andrew said around a mouthful of his salad.

"Yeah, cause they're too scared of her to step out of line again," Mei said.

Andrew shrugged. "It's not my style, but you can't argue with the results. She doesn't have any issues with behavior, and we've had the best biology grades in years since she's been here."

"I know. It's annoying." Mei sighed, before turning her attention back toward Lily. "So, what's your guess?"

"Uh, twelve." If it seemed outlandish, neither of them commented. Mei made a note of it in her phone as Lily reached into her bag to see if she had a five-dollar bill in her purse. She did, and as she was handing it over the door opened behind her.

"Are you betting on detentions again?" Alisha said, making a beeline for the coffee machine. Lily felt her cheeks warm and wondered if this was supposed to be a secret, not wanting to get on the wrong side of Alisha on her first day.

Mei seemed nonplussed. "Uh-huh. What's your guess?"

"Considering I've heard her chew out at least six different kids, and we're not yet halfway through the day... Let's go with twelve."

"You're out of luck, boss, Lily already took that."

"Good guess," Alisha said, nodding at Lily. "I'll have thirteen, then. How are you finding things, Lily?"

"Fine." Lily knew it was still early, but she was enjoying her day so far. The kids were good, seemed eager to learn, and she was excited to dive in.

"How did you get into teaching, anyway?" Mei asked. "Was it always the plan?"

"Far from it. After I finished my degree I worked in industry for a while, at a pharmaceutical company."

"Wow, that's a change of pace. Why'd you switch careers?"

"I didn't feel fulfilled, I guess. I always wanted to do something to make a difference, and I thought that job would, but... It's disheartening to dedicate so much time to developing a drug with the potential to help thousands of people for it to fail at the first hurdle or get sold at extortionate prices so only the richest can afford it. I enjoyed being a tutor when I was at college, loved seeing students succeed, and I guess it spiraled from there. What about you all?"

Lily wasn't surprised Mei answered first—she seemed the most talkative of the lot. "I always wanted to teach. Got my master's in education and never looked back. Specializing in earth and physical sciences wasn't part of the plan, but"—Mei shrugged—"it's the way things worked out."

"What did you want to teach?"

"I started out in elementary school, believe it or not."

Lily scrunched her nose. High schoolers could be a nightmare, but she did not have the patience for younger kids. Plus, they were brutal.

"Yeah, I didn't last long," Mei said, lips twitching. "I was already certified to teach high school, so when a job for an earth and physical science teacher came up, I took it."

"How long have you worked here?"

"God, too long." Mei grinned as Alisha mock-glared at her. "Five years I think?"

"Yep." Alisha joined them at the table, mug held between her palms. "I've been here ten, and Andrew you're on your fourth year now, aren't you?"

"Uh-huh."

Lily was impressed. At the school where she'd done her training, the longest anyone had stuck around was two years. "You have a high staff retention rate."

"It's all due to Alisha," Mei said, and Andrew nodded in agreement. "Once you sign your contract, she never lets you leave. You're stuck here forever now, Lily."

"From what I've seen so far—which admittedly isn't much—I think I'm okay with that."

"We'll change your mind soon enough."

"Don't scare her off," Alisha said, but it was good-natured. "And don't remind me how long I've been here, either. It makes me feel old."

"You're hardly old," all three of them chimed in unison.

"Tell that to my creaky joints."

"How did you become a teacher, Alisha?" Lily was eager to learn about her new colleagues—and to take some of the attention away from herself.

"I was a social worker for a few years. Spent a lot of time with a lot of different kids and seeing how many adults in their lives let them down—I don't know. It's like you said, Lily, about wanting to make a difference. To give them something stable. I went back to school to get my teacher's license. They needed science teachers, so I became one."

"My story isn't as interesting," Andrew said, when Lily moved her gaze to him. "I was working at an energy company and hated it. My brother was a teacher and seemed a hell of a lot happier than I was, so I looked into it, and here I am."

"Here we all are," Mei said, leaning over to throw her trash away. "What made you choose Greenfield, Lily? Are you from nearby?"

"I grew up a few towns over. I left for college, but my family never moved so when I found this job listing it made sense to move back. My sister recently had a baby, too, so it means I'll be able to spend more time with them." They didn't need to know the other reason she'd wanted to leave Miami—to escape the memories of the woman she'd thought she was going to spend the rest of her life with.

"That's sweet. Do you have kids of your own? A husband?"

"Uh, no to both." A forever no, to the husband, but she wasn't sure she was ready to out herself to her new colleagues yet.

"Give the poor woman some time to breathe without being interrogated, Mei," Alisha said, and Mei flushed.

"Sorry. It's been a while since we had any fresh blood in the department. Eva was the last, and you can guess how well my questions went with her."

"Like a lead balloon?" Lily said.

"It's been two years and we still don't know anything about her. If the kids didn't need to know her last name, I think that would be a secret, too. The only thing we do know is she used to be some hotshot professor at Georgetown."

Lily's interest was piqued. "And she teaches here?"

"Uh-huh. There are all kinds of rumors about how it happened, but no one knows for sure. Or if they do"—Mei glanced toward Alisha—"they won't say."

"I've told you a million times: I have no idea why she left Georgetown."

Lunch passed too quickly, and soon Lily was back in her classroom and welcoming her final class of the day.

Once it had finished, Lily relaxed back in her chair, revitalized after her first proper day of teaching. All the students she'd met so far were lovely, and Lily was looking forward to getting to know them better as the year wore on, ready to challenge them and watch them succeed.

A light knock sounded on her door, and Lily turned to see Mei. "Hey. We're about to see who won our bet if you'd like to join us."

Lily had forgotten all about it in the excitement of atomic structure. She followed Mei out the door and found Andrew and an older white man she assumed was Brandon standing in the hall.

"Okay, I'm going in," Mei whispered, tiptoeing toward the classroom at the end of the hall, and Lily pressed her lips together because she looked ridiculous.

Lily edged closer with everyone else, and when Mei reached Eva's door, she ducked to one side, her lips moving as she counted the kids within through the glass panels.

"Damn," Mei said when she'd finished, before retreating to the safety of the group and reaching into the pocket of her blazer. "Okay, the grand total is…twelve, so, newbie, you win."

Mei handed Lily an envelope, and Brandon clapped his hands together.

"Beginner's luck." He had a wide smile, his beard peppered with gray. "Nice to meet you, by the way, seeing as no one is going to introduce us."

Mei pulled a face. "We had more important things to attend to! And that's Alisha's job, anyway. It's not my fault she's in a meeting. What're you gonna spend it on, Lily?"

Lily glanced at the envelope. "No idea. Treats for the department, maybe?"

Brandon grinned. "I like you—you're going to fit in great around here. Right." He slapped his hands against his thighs. "Speaking of treats, I'd better get going. There's cake in the math office with my name on it."

"They always have cake over there." Mei was remorseful as she watched him go. "And we never have any."

"You know, if you bought some there would be," Andrew said, and Mei elbowed him in the side.

"Stop making sense."

Lily smiled at their bickering, and, as she slipped her winnings into the pocket of her slacks, she hoped Brandon was right: she did want to fit in.

Twelve students were forced to spend an hour in silence with Eva at the end of the first day.

None were happy about it, but no one dared miss it, not wanting to face her wrath. Eva was satisfied, as she watched the last of them hurry out the door, she'd well and truly set a decent precedent for the year ahead.

She was quick to follow them out. A teacher's work might never truly be done—with something to grade, parents to call, or lessons to plan—but she was needed at home, and there was no reason she couldn't do it there.

Eva was the first of the department to leave, the lights on in all the other classrooms as she stepped out into the hall. A janitor mopped the floors near the main entrance, and Eva nodded to him, skirting around the edge of the wet floor and swiping her badge to exit. Eva slid behind the wheel of her Mercedes and the engine purred to life.

Home was forty minutes away, but Eva liked the drive, using it to clear her mind. Listening to true crime podcasts passed the time, and Eva was soon pulling into her driveway. The lights were on in the front room, the sound of the television filtering into her ears as she unlocked the door.

A black Spaniel rushed to greet her, and Eva bent to scratch behind his ears. "Hi, Franklin." His tail thudded against the wall, and he followed Eva closely when she stepped into the living room. "Hi, Mom."

"Hi, sweetheart. How was your day?" Her mother was in her favorite position—in front of the television, with Jeopardy! Eva pressed a kiss to her cheek.

"Same old, same old." It wasn't an overly enthusiastic response, but she didn't find teaching high schoolers to be particularly stimulating. She liked the hours, though—not many other jobs would allow her to be home by four. "How was yours? How's your pain today?"

"So-so."

Eva searched her face, knowing her mother had a tendency to downplay her condition.

"I had my PT with Jennifer today which went well."

"Good. Did she give you some more exercises to do?"

"Yes."

"And are you going to do them?"

Her mother glanced at Eva from her wheelchair, twinkle in her eye. "Yes, nurse."

"If I was your nurse, I'd be a hell of a lot sterner with you than your current ones are. They let you get away with too much."

"And you worry about me too much."

"Someone's got to."

"What happened to your shirt?" Her mother frowned, plucking at the stain with her fingers.

"I spilled coffee on it. It'll come out." Eva would make sure of it. "Are you hungry, or can dinner wait until after I've been for a run?"

"I can wait. Or I can start it without you."

"And set the house on fire?"

Her mother huffed. "I managed without you living here for seventeen years, you know."

"Yes, and I have no idea how you survived. Besides, I like to cook."

"But you do so much for me already."

Eva squeezed her mother's shoulder gently. "You know I don't mind. How about we cook together tonight?"

"Okay."

"I'll be back soon—do not start without me." Eva gave her one last squeeze before jogging up the stairs, swapping her pencil skirt and stained blouse for leggings, a sports bra and a loose-fitting top.

Back downstairs, she pulled on her trusty running shoes, lacing them with Franklin peering at her hopefully. "Come on."

Eva reached for his harness, and she slipped it onto his wriggling frame with practiced ease. Her earbuds sat on the table by the front door, and, once they were in and connected to her phone, her carefully curated running playlist sounding in her ears, Eva stepped out the front door with Franklin at her side.

She shivered as the cool air hit her skin, but Eva knew she'd soon be grateful for it. Once they were at the end of the street Eva broke into a light jog, enjoying the wind on her face. Eva pushed herself faster, until her lungs were burning. Running had always been her release, the sound of her feet pounding on the sidewalk bringing her a sense of calm nothing else could.

Wary of staying out too long, she turned back after fifteen minutes. Her mother was still by the television when she returned, but soon joined Eva in the kitchen, the wheels of her wheelchair squeaking on the linoleum.

"What do you want?" Eva poked her head into the refrigerator. She needed to go shopping—the shelves were getting bare. "Salmon pasta?"

"Sure."

Eva passed her mother the bag of fusilli and tried not to be obvious about keeping an eye on her when she moved out of her chair to stand at the counter, checking how steady she was on her feet.

"I'm not fragile, you know. I'm not at the point where I can't stand yet."

Clearly, Eva hadn't been subtle, and she averted her gaze, concentrating on preparing the salmon. "And hopefully you never will be." Her mother's multiple sclerosis had worsened in the two years since Eva had come to help look after her, but the doctors were optimistic about her long-term prognosis.

Something her mother found hard to share.

And Eva understood it. The two of them were similar, particularly when it came to their independence, and Eva, too, would hate becoming reliant on another person. Her mother had vehemently resisted the idea of Eva moving back in—but they shared their stubbornness, too, and Eva had given her little choice in the matter.

Moving from Washington D.C. to the suburbs of Chicago—giving up her dream job and her girlfriend in the process—had never been part of her grand plan, but Eva didn't regret it.

She'd missed her mother when she'd been across the country. Missed nights like this, a pan sizzling on the stove, her mother chattering away about her day while Eva stirred with a wooden spoon.

"Angela has a neurologist appointment on Thursday so she's coming over tomorrow instead," her mother said when they sat to eat. "You can stay late at school if you like."

"Okay. Are you going out somewhere?"

"No, there's a new Netflix show we want to watch."

Eva shook her head. She worried about her mother spending too much time indoors, growing more reclusive as she deteriorated. Joining an MS support group was supposed to help, not encourage it, though she was glad her mother was making friends.

"Will you remind me how to set it up again before you go to bed?"

"I've shown you a million times, Mom."

"I know, but I always forget."

"Want me to write you some instructions? Step by step, like I give my students when they're struggling with a problem?" Eva said, laughing as her mother's eyes narrowed into a signature Thomas glare. "I'll take that as a no."

"As you should. Anyway, you can't get on my case about not getting out more. When was the last time you went somewhere other than work?"

"I got those new toys for Franklin at the weekend."

"I meant with another person, Eva."

Great. This again.

"You've been here for two years, now, and as far as I'm aware, have only spent time with me. When's the last time you went on a date?"

"Mother—"

"And what about friends, Eva? You used to be out every night."

"When I was a teenager. Things are different now."

"Still. I don't need a babysitter twenty-four-seven. You need a life, Eva." She had her best no-nonsense voice on, and Eva blinked at her across the table, forgetting all about her half eaten pasta.

This was not the dinner time conversation she'd been expecting.

To be honest, it wasn't one she'd ever been expecting—her mother wasn't usually this pushy.

Eva knew she shouldn't have let her mother and Angela watch *Love Is Blind*.

"I know you don't. But I'm happy with the way things are, Mom. I don't need more than I already have."

"But aren't you lonely? How long has it been since Victoria?"

Her mother knew exactly how long it had been since her last breakup, considering it was the distance when Eva had moved to Chicago that had been their demise.

It was the second time in one day Eva had thought of Victoria, and it made her lip curl. Instead of answering, Eva turned the question on her mother. "And what about you? It's been thirty years since Dad left." And never came back. Was bringing it up a low blow? Yes, but Eva wanted to end this conversation as quickly as possible. "Aren't you lonely?"

"That's different."

Eva raised an eyebrow, and her mother sighed.

"It is, and besides, I have friends. People to talk to."

"And I have work." Sure, teaching teenagers about the wonders of biology wasn't the same as venting to a friend over cocktails, but it worked for her. "I'm fine with the way things are, Mom." Eva reached across the table to pat the back of her hand, trying to ease the frown on her mother's face. "I am. So can we drop this please?"

"Fine."

She didn't look particularly happy about it, though.

Somehow, Eva doubted she'd heard the last of it.

Chapter 3

IF EVA HAD BEEN IN charge of the school schedule, she'd strike off homeroom completely. The fifteen minutes she spent taking attendance and making announcements could be put to much better use—or easily incorporated into the first class of the day, which was how they'd used to do things when she was in high school.

Unfortunately, her opinions on the timetable would never be sought after. At least she had a decent mix of kids in front of her—twelve sophomores, all of whom she'd taught the year before and knew exactly how she liked things.

When the bell rang, they all scrambled to gather their belongings, ready to disperse across the school for a day of learning.

"Could you wait behind, Carly?" Eva called over the sound of books being shoved into bags. "I'd like a word."

"Ooh, you're in trouble."

"That isn't a helpful comment, Sean," Eva said, and Carly laughed when his cheeks turned pink. "Would you like to be in trouble?"

"No, ma'am." Sean ducked his head and slouched to the door, and Eva waited until it had closed behind him before turning her attention to the young woman at the front of the room.

"Is there anything you want to tell me?" Eva said, folding her arms across her chest and watching Carly scowl down at the floor. "Your whereabouts after school tonight, for example?" Silence. Eva sighed. "It's the second day of the semester, Carly. Detention already?"

"Didn't you have like, twenty kids in detention last night?" Carly fired back, glancing away from the floor to offer Eva a look of defiance.

Eva pinned her with a glare—an attitude wasn't something she tolerated, which Carly knew all too well.

"Sorry. Still got my back up, I guess."

"What did you do?" The e-mail asking Eva to have a quiet word hadn't given her any specifics, but for a weeks' worth of detentions, it must have been bad.

"Told Mr. Mayhew to shut the eff up."

Eva pressed her fingers to her temples. "I know you have an issue with him." And most men, in truth. After spending ten years of her life living under the thumb of a physically and emotionally abusive father, Eva didn't blame Carly. But Greenfield High had rules—rules that meant disrespecting members of staff had severe consequences. "But you can't go around saying things like that."

"He wasn't supposed to hear me. Got goddamn bat ears, doesn't he?"

"Carly, you're a sophomore now. They won't be tolerant of your behavior for much longer." The only reason she hadn't been expelled already was because Eva kept going to bat for her. As something of an expert on shitty fathers—though nowhere near to the same extent as the things Eva had read in Carly's file—Eva had something of a soft spot for Carly, a desire to protect her and see her succeed. If Eva could offer Carly a safe space, a comforting presence in a world that had been so cruel, make a difference in someone's life, then this job was worth it.

"I know. I'll try and be better."

"Good."

Carly turned to leave, but Eva stopped her after a quick glance at the clock. They still had two minutes before the first class of the day officially started.

"Ah, ah, not so fast. Why'd you do it?"

"Because he was annoying me. Asked me a question and I didn't know the answer. Apparently, that was unacceptable, so..." Carly shrugged, staring at her shoe as she scuffed it along the floor, and Eva suspected there was more to the story.

"How was your summer?"

"Fine." A pause, Carly shifting her weight from one foot to the other. She bit at her bottom lip, something weighing on her mind, and Eva waited, hoping Carly trusted her enough to know she could speak freely. "My mom moved her new boyfriend in."

Ah, there it was. The reason for the sullenness and attitude problem. Not that Eva could blame her. Carly clung to routine and consistency and having a new man inside the home couldn't be easy for her.

"What's he like?"

Another shrug. "He's okay, I guess." Well, it wasn't exactly a glowing review. "Better than my sperm donor." Her face creased into a scowl. "But I wish he wasn't always around."

Eva's protective streak sparked to life. "Is he making your life difficult?"

Carly shook her head.

"Are you still seeing the school counselor?"

"Twice a week."

"And they know what's going on at home?"

Carly rolled her eyes skyward. "I'm not stupid. I wouldn't keep something like that from them."

"Good." Eva made a mental note to follow up with the counselor anyway—if she didn't report her concerns and something bad happened later down the line, she'd never be able to forgive herself. "And you know you can come to me about anything, yes?"

Carly offered Eva a rare smile. "I know."

"Let me write you a note to let your next teacher know why you're running late." Eva scrawled one quickly, handing it over as the bell rang. "Take care, Carly."

Carly hurried out of the room, and Eva watched her go.

She'd been Eva's brightest student the previous year, persevering despite the bad hand she'd been dealt, and Eva wasn't going to let her slip because she no longer taught her. She'd just have to make more effort to keep up with her progress.

Lily's first week flew by.

Aside from one or two kids who decided to test her limits, she'd had few problems. When the bell rang at the end of Friday last period, Lily watched her students scramble for the exits before leaving her room, planning to grab a coffee to take with her to the mandatory department meeting starting in five minutes.

When she pushed open the door of the teacher's lounge to be faced with Eva's back, Lily nearly reversed out the room. Aside from brief glimpses of her in the hall, Lily hadn't seen Eva since their lunch duty on Monday. She didn't know if that was normal, or if Eva was avoiding Lily in particular, but considering her aversion for human interaction, Lily wouldn't be surprised if it was the former.

Eva didn't notice her until she'd finished stirring her coffee, turning around with her mug between her palms. Lily could usually tell a lot about a person from the mug they chose, but Eva's—plain black—didn't tell her much at all.

Lily supposed, considering her blank expression and the coolness of her gaze, that made a lot of sense.

Lily didn't realize she was staring, or blocking the exit, until Eva paused in front of her, arching a perfectly sculpted eyebrow. "Do you make it a habit to stand in doorways? Do you want to splash this coffee on me, too?"

"Oh. Sorry." Lily shuffled out of the way, and Eva stormed past her without another word. "Always a pleasure," Lily said once the door had shut behind her. She hurried to pour her own coffee, not wanting to be late for her first proper meeting.

Alisha wasn't there when Lily shouldered open the door of her room, notebook tucked under one arm and mug held in her other hand. Andrew, Brandon and Mei sat together on one end of the front row, and Eva sat alone at the other, laptop open as she typed furiously.

Mei smiled warmly, and Lily slipped into the seat beside her.

"Hey, newbie. You made it to the end of the week—congratulations."

"Thanks."

"Hate it here yet?"

"I've had a good week."

"Give it time."

"What have I told you about scaring her off?" Alisha said, overhearing their conversation as she entered the room. Lily was surprised when she dropped into the center seat of the row, instead of sitting behind her desk. "I promise it'll be a quick one today."

Lily grabbed her pen, ready to take notes.

"First and foremost, I've been told to remind you all about the training opportunities the school runs. They're on the staff portal and can be accessed any time. Also, you all need to familiarize yourself with the special education needs profiles of every student you teach, so you know the best way to support them. If you think something needs to be added, please bring it to my attention. Same if you have any other concerns about a student. In addition, we've had a number of students express the desire to use gender-diverse pronouns. This is a gentle reminder to take care when addressing your classes, and to check if anyone you teach would prefer to be addressed with the gender-diverse pronouns of their choice. There's a list of students on the staff portal."

No one else seemed to be writing anything, but Lily didn't let it deter her. She'd rather be prepared.

"We need to work out a schedule for the STEM and science clubs starting in two weeks' time. STEM won't be each week, but science will be every Wednesday. Does anyone want to volunteer for the first session?"

"I will."

If anyone else was surprised by Eva's offer, they didn't show it. Maybe she wanted to get it out of the way.

"Okay." Alisha made a note on a piece of paper.

"I'll do the one after," Mei said. "I thought of some fun things for them to do over the summer."

"I can do a week." It wasn't something Lily had done before, but she wanted to throw herself into her role at this school with both feet. "Would I be able to run my ideas by you first, though?"

"Of course you can." Alisha's smile was reassuring.

"I wouldn't worry too much," Mei said, chewing on the end of her pen. "Your predecessor made the poor kids copy out of a textbook on chemistry weeks."

"I can think of something more fun than that."

"Not too fun," Alisha said. "I don't want them doing anything dangerous. Or messy."

"You made a giant mess one time," Mei muttered under her breath, and Lily decided she was going to get the story about that later.

Alisha swiftly got them back on track, filling in the rest of the schedule with everyone else's names. "That's all the official business we needed to get through. Is there anything else anyone wanted to add? Any issues, behavioral or otherwise?" She paused. No one answered. "Okay, well if anything comes up you know where to find me. I think we'll leave it there—I told you it would be a short meeting."

They gathered their things, and Lily wasn't surprised when Eva was the first to leave.

"Has Mei told you about our unofficial Friday tradition, Lily?" Alisha asked, moving to the front of the room to slip her laptop into her bag.

"After-work drinks? She did, but I've already agreed to go to my mom's for dinner tonight. I'll join you next week, though."

"All right, have a good weekend."

"You too." Lily waved good-bye to Alisha and the others. "I'll see you all on Monday."

Returning to her own room, Lily was about to pack away her things when she noticed a missed call on her phone. Lily swallowed when she read the name. Being so busy with the new job and putting the finishing touches on her new home had meant she hadn't had much time to dwell on the past, and the woman she'd left behind in Miami.

Now it all came flooding back in a rush of memories, her heart feeling like it was caught in a vice. She and Sophie hadn't spoken in nearly two months—what was she doing calling her now?

And more importantly—was curiosity enough for Lily to call her back?

To hell with it. Lily lifted the phone to her ear. It might be important.

"Lily." Sophie saying her name didn't fill her with the same warmth it used to. "I thought you were ignoring me."

"Thought about it." Lily dropped into the chair behind her desk and worried at her bottom lip. "What do you want?"

"You moved."

Not an accusation, exactly, but there was an undertone to Sophie's voice that made Lily bristle. "Yeah, I did."

"You loved that apartment."

Lily closed her eyes and leaned her head back, trying not to remember the shape of Sophie's face, the way her brow crinkled when she frowned. "Yeah." It had been her first place, and she'd made it her own, and now she had to start all over again. "But I couldn't stay there. Not after…" Lily trailed off, still struggling to think about the demise of their relationship, the new "friend" Sophie had made at work that she insisted Lily was crazy to be jealous of. "How do you even know?"

"I ran into Jessica yesterday. She told me you quit your job and sold your place. I—I'm sorry, Lily." It wasn't the first apology Lily had heard, but it was the first time Sophie had actually sounded contrite. "I didn't—I didn't mean to hurt you."

Lily scoffed, even as she was blinking back tears. "If you didn't want to hurt me, you wouldn't have done what you did."

"I know. I fucked up, okay? I really am sorry."

"If you're expecting my forgiveness, you're not going to get it."

"I don't. I just…I just wanted to know you were okay. And I know I don't have any right to know, and I shouldn't have called, but I—I miss you."

"Don't," Lily said, voice sharp as a tack. "You made your bed, Sophie. You have to lie in it." Lily glanced at the time—she really ought to be going, or she'd be late for dinner. "I'm fine, and I'm happy where I am now."

Happy to be away from Sophie. Away from any painful memories. A fresh start was exactly what Lily needed. "Please don't call me again."

Lily hung up before Sophie could reply, her breaths coming quick and fast. Closing her eyes, Lily concentrated on the ticking of the clock and tried to calm herself down. She hated that another person could have this effect on her—someone she trusted, someone who had promised, on late nights tangled up in the sheets, that they'd be together forever.

But she refused to let Sophie have any power over her anymore. Lily shoved her things into her bag and headed for the car. Eva's classroom door caught her eye as she stepped into the hall, and Lily wondered what Eva would do in her situation.

Not let Sophie walk all over her, for one. Eva wouldn't entertain her in the slightest, and maybe Lily could do with taking a page out of Eva's book. Determined, Lily pulled out her phone and blocked Sophie's number, just in case she did call again, and tried to push all thoughts of her ex from her mind as she slid behind the wheel of her car.

The forty-five-minute drive gave her time to clear her head, and Lily felt better once she'd parked in the drive behind her sister's car.

Pulling open the door to her childhood home, Lily was greeted by the smell of cooking. She followed the sound of quiet voices into the kitchen. Her mom stood at the stove stirring a pot, and Daisy sat at the table with baby Emma cradled in her arms.

Her mom dropped her wooden spoon in favor of wrapping Lily in a hug. "Hi, sweetheart. How are you? How's the new house? Did your first week go okay?"

"Jesus Christ, Mom. Give her a chance to sit before you start the inquisition." Daisy rolled her eyes, and Lily kissed her sister's cheek.

"I'm excited to see her, is that a crime?"

"You saw her like five days ago," Daisy said, and Lily grabbed a glass of water before settling into the chair next to her. She waved at Emma, who was watching her with wide blue eyes. "You're never this excited to see me."

"I'm always equally excited to see both of you."

"How come you never show it?" Daisy winked at Lily, enjoying watching their mom get more flustered.

"Enough." Their mom pointed at Daisy threateningly with her wooden spoon. "I'm still waiting for an answer, Lily."

"I'm fine, the house is fine, and work is—"

"—fine?" Daisy said, and Lily elbowed her in the side.

"Work is great, I'm enjoying it."

"Good. Your colleagues are nice?"

Lily thought of Eva's cold indifference and was glad she was the exception and not the norm. "Most of them. I think I'm going to fit in well there."

"You look happy," Daisy said, once their mom had turned away to tend to the food.

"Yeah, I am." Lily finally felt like she was where she belonged, fulfilled, professionally, in a way she hadn't before. "How are you, anyway?"

"I'd be better if this one"—she poked Emma's nose—"would sleep through the night. But otherwise, I'm good. I joined a mommie's group so I can have some adult conversation during the day. Would you mind holding her for a sec? I need to pee."

"Sure." Emma was placed carefully into her arms. She stared at Lily with her fist in her mouth. "What's for dinner, Mom?"

"Chicken casserole. It'll be ready when your father gets home, which should be any minute."

"Is the garage still doing okay?" Neither Lily nor Daisy had ever had a penchant for the family business, but she had fond memories of helping out at the weekends.

"Business is booming."

Daisy rejoined them and set the table. "Have you told Lily about the new mechanic yet? She's hot."

"After what happened the last time you tried to set me up, I think I'll keep my distance."

"Okay, that was an anomaly. Izzy seemed perfectly normal—how were we supposed to know she was a stalker?" Daisy said, and Lily shook her head. "Anyway, that was years ago. My matchmaking skills have improved."

"Have they?"

"Yes. I've set up two of my friends in the last few months."

"And neither of them has been murdered yet?"

Daisy smacked her on the back of the head.

"Ow! I'm holding your daughter here, you know, you should be more careful."

"Please, she's fine. Aren't you, my little angel?" Daisy leaned in and blew a raspberry against Emma's cheek. "Your auntie Lily wouldn't dare drop you. I'd never let her hear the end of it. And we've gotten off-track— we were talking about the hot mechanic."

"No, you were talking about the hot mechanic, and I was—"

Daisy spoke right over her. "She's called Anna. She's thirty. I know you like older women—"

"Two years is hardly an older woman, Daisy."

"Still."

"I don't need a date." Lily still felt raw from what had happened with Sophie. There was no way she was ready to put herself back out there yet.

"I beg to differ. You know what they say about the best way to get over someone." Daisy wiggled her eyebrows, and Lily shook her head.

"I am over her."

Daisy didn't look convinced. "Sure you are."

"Oh, girls." Their mom came to stand between them, resting a hand on their shoulders. "It's so nice having you both home. I was starting to miss the constant bickering."

"You love our constant bickering," Daisy said, sitting beside Lily. "It keeps you young. You got any plans for the weekend, Lily?"

"I don't want to meet the mechanic."

Daisy rolled her eyes. "That's not why I was asking. Alex doesn't get back from his business trip until Sunday, so do you wanna keep me company tomorrow?"

"You mean help you look after the baby? Yeah, sure." It wasn't like Lily had anything better to do.

The front door opened, heavy footsteps sounding on the wooden floor a moment later, and their father appeared in the kitchen doorway, his face streaked with grease. "Well if it isn't all my favorite women in the same room."

"Flatterer," her mom said, fond smile on her face. Lily loved that after thirty-five years together they still looked besotted by one another.

"That's me. Hi Daisy, Lily." He bent to kiss their cheeks. "Have I got time to shower before dinner?"

"As long as you're quick."

"I always am." He trudged toward the stairs, and Lily handed Emma over to Daisy so she could settle her in her carrier while they ate. Lily helped her mom plate their food, then sat between her mom and her sister. Her dad soon joined them, and the night flew by, Lily reveling in the familiarity of being home.

"Do you want wheat or rye bread?" Eva glanced at the bakery selection with her hands on her hips. Receiving no answer from her mother, Eva nudged the back of her mother's chair. "Mom?"

"Hmm?"

Eva turned to look at her, finding her attention was elsewhere, fixed on something further down the aisle. "Wheat or rye? What are you looki—" Eva froze when she followed the path of her mother's gaze.

Lily Cross stood a few feet away, looking like a deer in the headlights when her eyes met Eva's.

Lily's thumb was trapped by the tiny fingers of the baby strapped to her chest. At only a few weeks old, there was no way she could be Lily's. Her niece, maybe, based on the similarities between Lily and the woman who was pushing a cart next to her, chattering away and seemingly oblivious to Lily's sudden silence.

"Do you know that woman?" Eva's mother said, cutting through her thoughts. "She keeps looking over here and I don't recognize her."

"We work together," Eva said, her words curt, and she shoved a loaf of rye bread into the shopping basket, tired of waiting for an answer.

"You do?" Her mother looked elated, and Eva smothered a groan. "Let's go and say hello."

"Let's not." Eva grabbed the handles of her chair, keeping her in place, when her mother tried to wheel away.

"Why?"

Eva sighed, regretting the decision to take her mother to the grocery store with her. She thought it would be good for her mother to get out of the house—now Eva wished she'd left her at home. "Because I don't want to."

"Very well."

Eva steered them back the way they came to avoid Lily—and to ensure her mother couldn't involve herself in Eva's business—but they ran into her on the next aisle, and the next, the woman damn near inescapable.

It was the first time Eva had ever seen someone from work—student or otherwise—off-campus. The reason she hadn't chosen a school closer to home had been to avoid a situation like this, a run-in with someone while Eva was out minding her own business.

Especially Lily.

Eva couldn't pinpoint what, exactly, it was about the other woman that grated on her nerves, but she'd been avoiding her all week. Successfully. But there Lily was, at the other end of the coffee aisle, laughing at something her sister said.

Did she live nearby? Did her sister? Was this going to become a regularity? Running into Lily at the grocery store, or at the pharmacy, or at the gym?

Eva hoped not.

Her skin itched with the feeling of being watched. Eva wondered, as Lily's sister glanced over at her, what Lily was saying. Was she telling her all about the demon biology teacher at Greenfield? Was she trying to work out why someone so heartless would spend their weekend wheeling a woman around a grocery store?

"Eva!" Her mother sounded annoyed, and Eva suspected it wasn't the first time she'd tried to get her attention.

"Not nice being ignored, is it?" Eva winced when her mother rolled over her foot in response. "What did you say?"

"I was asking if you would get me a pack of those caramel lattes." Her mother pointed to one of the top shelves. "But you seemed too busy staring at that young lady over there to hear me."

"Will you lower your voice?" Eva glanced toward Lily, but she appeared to be well out of earshot.

"I'm just saying. You seem awfully distracted."

Eva ignored her in favor of leaning on her toes to reach for the coffee her mother wanted.

"She's pretty."

Eva nearly brought the whole display down on top of her. "What?"

Her mother blinked innocently at her as Eva dropped the coffee into the cart. "Don't you think so?"

"I hadn't noticed."

"Looks a bit like Victoria."

Eva sighed, because she'd been trying hard not to remember that. Though the more she saw of Lily, the less she saw the similarities. Physically, yes, but everything else? The bright-eyed innocence and boundless enthusiasm? They couldn't be more different.

"If you squint, I suppose." Eva glanced at her shopping list to avoid her mother's probing gaze. "I think that's everything, unless you thought of anything else?"

Eva was relieved when her mother shook her head. It meant they could go to the checkout, and her unexpected Saturday morning torture would come to an end.

Lily ended up on the checkout next to them.

Eva ground her teeth.

Was the cashier being purposefully slow? Were they aware Eva was in a hurry?

It felt like it took an age for them to scan everything, and Eva willed the worker packing their bags to go as fast as humanly possible. She relaxed once they were outside. It was a beautiful day, and Eva wasn't going to let her mother get away with spending the rest of it indoors.

Chapter 4

ON MONDAY MORNING, LILY ARRIVED at lunch duty with a cup of coffee in each hand.

She knew trying to win Eva over was more than likely an exercise in futility, but she was still going to try. Call it a character flaw, but Lily was a people-pleaser, and she hated knowing someone didn't like her. Plus, wouldn't things in her new job run smoother if she could get Eva on her side?

Lily sought Eva out in the crowded cafeteria. She patrolled the perimeter, eagle-eyes scanning the room, waiting to pounce on any poor unwitting soul that stepped out of line.

Eva didn't acknowledge Lily until she was right in front of her.

She received a glare, and no greeting.

Lily's first clue this was a bad idea.

"I, um, brought you a coffee." She held the disposable cup toward her, and Eva looked at Lily's outstretched hand with distaste. "It's not poisoned."

Eva didn't crack a smile.

"Uh, do you not want it? It's the same brand I saw you using the other day."

Eva folded her arms across her chest and tilted her jaw. "Have you been stalking me?"

Lily snorted, but her amusement faded as she watched a sculpted brow inch toward Eva's hairline. "Of course not. Is this because I saw you over the weekend?" Seeing Eva while running errands with Daisy hadn't been how Lily had expected her Saturday to go, although she felt like she knew

Eva better. Mei had said Eva was notoriously private, but Lily had learned three things in a single week.

One: Eva liked strong, bitter coffee with enough caffeine in it to incapacitate a small child, which Lily didn't find too surprising. Two: when she wasn't at work, she still dressed like she worked for a fashion magazine. The pantsuit she'd been wearing at the grocery store wouldn't have looked out of place in a photoshoot, as did today's black and white patterned dress. Three: she wasn't completely soulless, bantering with the woman she'd been with, a fond look in her eye. Lily assumed it was her mother, and she wondered if she had anything to do with the reason Eva had swapped Georgetown for Greenfield.

Not that she'd ever dare to ask, considering Eva was giving Lily daggers over a beverage.

"Yes. And you're offering me weirdly specific coffee."

"I didn't realize it was weirdly specific to notice things about other people," Lily said. "Of course I'm not stalking you. I thought it would be a nice gesture—"

Eva cut her off. "It's not. It's weird."

"Right. I'll take this coffee and be on my way, then."

"By all means."

"Have fun spending another lunch alone." Lily spoke more viciously than intended and had to bite back the apology that threatened when Eva blinked at her in surprise. Turning on her heel, Lily retreated to the safety of the other side of the cafeteria. Not wanting to let the coffee go to waste, she drank from both cups as she watched the kids, washing the bitter taste of Eva's away with a sip of her own.

Lily wasn't alone for long, soon approached by two members of the English faculty she'd briefly spoken to the previous week. If she remembered correctly, Steph was the older of the two white women, her hair streaked with gray and large square-framed glasses perched on her nose, and Paige was the blonde with a shy smile.

"You're a braver woman than I am," Steph said, coming to stand at Lily's shoulder. "No one else would dare approach her."

Lily followed the path of Steph's gaze to Eva. She was pacing the opposite wall of the cafeteria, arms still folded across her chest and her jaw clenched, and Lily felt sorry for the next person to cross her path. Her gaze was drawn to Eva's legs, long and shapely beneath the black pantyhose, and Lily hated herself for noticing.

How could someone with such an acidic personality look so good? It wasn't fair.

"She's not so bad." Lily tore her gaze away and was met with disbelief from her companions.

"Are you ser—" Paige paused when they heard a commotion from across the hall, the cafeteria falling silent as everyone turned toward the noise. A few feet away from Eva, a student was on the floor, another two standing nearby sneering.

The quiet meant the whole room heard the words that followed.

"Watch where you're going, dyke."

The student who had fallen scrambled to their feet, cheeks pink and their eyes glossy with tears, and Lily recognized Macie from her sophomore class.

As the closest member of staff, Eva sprang into action, a chill in her voice that could freeze blood in a vein. "What did you say?" Eva stepped toward the two sneering students, her face white with fury and her eyes stormy. When no reply came, she snapped her fingers in front of their faces. "I asked you a question."

Macie used the opportunity to hurry from the room, her gaze fixed on her shoes, and Lily didn't think before following her.

"Macie!"

Macie paused at the end of the hall, swiping at her wet cheeks with the back of her hand.

"I was going to ask if you were okay, but that's a dumb question. Do you want to sit in my room for a while? Get yourself together?"

"I..."

Behind them, they heard Eva's voice through the closed doors. "Both of you outside now."

"Okay," Macie said, sniffling as Lily reached her, escorting her toward science with a gentle hand on her elbow. "Thank you."

"Has this kind of thing happened before?" Lily was hesitant to ask in case Macie didn't want to talk about it, but if it was a recurring issue it needed to be reported.

Lily opened her classroom door and ushered Macie inside when she nodded. She sat in her usual seat on the front row, and Lily offered her a tissue from the box she had on her desk. "How often?"

Macie shrugged. "Every once in a while. I wasn't...I wasn't ready to come out, but I got caught kissing a girl at a party last year. I was stupid."

"No, Macie." Lily's voice wavered—kids could be so cruel. "No one deserves to be outed before they're ready, and it's not your fault it happened to you. I'm sorry it did." The words did little to comfort Macie, and Lily made a quick decision. "You know, I was outed when I was in high school."

Macie's head snapped up.

"It was no picnic. I want you to know that I know how serious this is, and I'm going to make sure it's dealt with." Lily was sure Eva would, too. A part of Lily was sad she hadn't been able to stick around to hear the show, but Macie's wellbeing was more important.

"Thanks, Miss Cross. Can I go and use the bathroom before my next class?"

"Of course you can." Macie looked brighter when she climbed to her feet.

Lily hoped she'd helped. "Let me know if something like this happens again."

"I will. And don't worry—I won't tell anyone about you."

"Thank you, Macie." Lily wasn't worried about her sexuality getting out—she wasn't ashamed of it—but she knew there might be a parent or two out there who would object if word got back to them a lesbian was teaching their child. "I hope you feel better."

After shooting off a quick e-mail summarizing the events in the cafeteria—and what Macie had disclosed to Lily in the safety of her classroom—to the relevant people, Lily wondered whether she should return to her lunch duty. The bell rang, making the decision for her. Lily was glad she had a break before her next class, needing some time to recover from the excitement. She hoped it wasn't the start of a trend—she'd enjoyed her uneventful duty last week.

Mei stood beside the microwave in the teacher's lounge, her eyebrows twitching when she saw Lily's face. "Rough day? Don't tell me this place has gotten to you already."

"Not yet." Lily had brought a sandwich for lunch, and she sat in the chair she'd claimed as her own at the table. "There was an incident in the cafeteria."

Mei joined her, a mug of steaming soup in her hands. "Tell me more. Did you and Eva get into a fist fight?"

Lily snorted. "You think I wouldn't be left with scars if that happened?"

"You're right. Eva is too feisty—you wouldn't stand a chance."

"Hey!"

Mei patted the back of her hand. "No offence. You're too nice, Lily. She'd eat you alive."

"I can be feisty." Sure, she'd never been in a fight in her life, but she worked out.

Sometimes.

"So, if you and Eva didn't start trading punches, what did happen?"

"Just some sophomores being assholes." Lily didn't want to go into too much detail, especially not at Macie's expense.

"They tend to do that. Did you sort them out?"

"I left that to Eva."

"A smart choice."

Eva's fury carried through the rest of the day.

She may have only taught her classes a handful of times, but one look at Eva's face as they entered her room, and her students were silent for the remainder of the period. None of them dared to push her, and Eva's singular complaint was their reluctance to answer any of her questions, as though they were scared simply opening their mouths to reply might earn them an immediate detention.

No one mentioned the scene from the cafeteria, though Eva had little doubt it would have spread around the whole school by now. She hadn't held back as she'd ripped the two troublesome sophomores a new one before marching them to the principal's office, and she'd expected whispers to sound whenever her back was turned.

They seemed to have collectively thought better of it, and the rest of her day passed without incident. After her last class of the day had filed out the door, Eva was preparing to gather her things together when she heard a light knock. Frowning, Eva raised her head, wondering who dared to disturb her.

Seeing Lily's uncertain face through the glass, Eva supposed she shouldn't be surprised. No one else would be so stupid.

She toyed with the idea of ignoring her, wondering if Lily would be brave enough to enter without Eva's permission, but that would be childish, and Eva had had enough of that kind of behavior for the day. She beckoned Lily inside. Lily's hands were empty, buried in the pockets of her slacks as she leaned against the door to close it.

"No coffee this time?" Eva couldn't resist the barb, not knowing what had possessed Lily to come at her with a peace offering.

"What, after it went so well before?" She'd let her hair down since Eva saw her last, messy blonde curls framing her face. Lily looked tired, and Eva wondered if this job was taking a toll on her already. If it was, it didn't bode well for her making it to the end of the year. "You have a shit taste in coffee, by the way."

Eva rolled her eyes, turning her gaze away from Lily. She shoved her laptop into her bag. "Thanks, I really value your opinion."

"You're welcome."

It had been so long since anyone had bantered with her, challenged her instead of backing away, and Eva told herself she didn't find it to be a refreshing change of pace.

Annoying. It was annoying.

"Was there a point to this social call? Or do you just like irritating me?"

"I'm irritating? Have you met you?"

"Have you met you?"

"At least I'm not—" Lily paused, taking a deep breath and seeming to think better of whatever it was she'd been about to say. "I didn't come in here to argue. I wanted to talk to you about what happened at lunch."

"About you offering me unsolicited cups of coffee?" Eva purposefully played dumb, enjoying the flush of anger on Lily's cheeks. "Yes, I'd like to talk about that too. Never do it again."

"I think I've learned my lesson, thanks. Excuse me for trying to do something nice."

"Is it nice, if I didn't ask for it?" Eva leaned back in her chair, lips pursed.

"Anyway. Lunch. I had a conversation with Macie, the girl who was being bullied."

That explained where Lily had disappeared off to—Eva hadn't been watching her, but she had noticed she was nowhere to be found when Eva had escorted the sophomores from the room.

"She told me this isn't the first time something like this has happened. I wanted to make sure the culprits were suitably punished."

"I see." Eva studied Lily, wondering why she cared. "And you don't trust I did that? Because I've been doing this for a while, you know. I know how to discipline students."

A muscle twitched in Lily's cheek. Eva was getting to her. "I wasn't implying you didn't."

"And yet you came in here to see how I handled it because…"

"Because I wanted to let Macie know what happened to them."

"Right. Well, you'd be better off asking the principal. I recommended several days of suspension but based on who their parents are I wouldn't be surprised if they were back in tomorrow morning." Both girls had been in Eva's freshman class the year before, and they'd been a nightmare. After speaking to the parents, Eva had begun to understand their behavior.

"That's not fair."

"Life rarely is." If only she were teaching them again this year—they'd be staying behind after school for the slightest infraction. "But I'm afraid there's nothing else to be done for now."

"That's bullshit."

Eva raised an eyebrow, impressed by the sudden fire in Lily's blue eyes. "Strangely enough, I agree with you. But there's not much else we can do other than keep an eye on the situation. Which I will be doing." She was going to watch them like a hawk the following Monday. "Is she all right? The girl?"

Eva didn't know why she asked. Perhaps it was a remnant of her own high school days, the whispers she had pretended not to hear.

"Careful, Eva." Lily's eyes glinted, a smile playing around the edges of her lips. "You don't want people to think you care."

Eva ground her teeth.

"And she's as okay as she can be, I think."

"Good. You can go now." The dismissal lacked bite, and Lily was still smiling when she pulled open the door.

"Good-bye, Eva."

Eva didn't acknowledge her leaving. She'd rather not acknowledge Lily at all.

Lily's easy ride to the beginning of her teaching career was brought to a grinding halt in its third week when two kids started arguing at the back of her honors class.

She'd had a few problems with one of them already—Denny Marshall could be disruptive and talkative, but Lily had always managed to dial it back before it escalated.

Until today.

"Give it back!"

Lily was surprised by the shout. Carly Adams barely said a word in class, staunchly ignoring Denny's antics despite sitting beside him.

Lily was even more surprised by the shove—so strong it nearly knocked Denny off his stool. As anger washed over his face, Lily didn't want to see what he might retaliate with.

"Carly!" The shout—the first time she'd had to truly raise her voice—silenced the whole class, several shocked faces turning toward her. "Outside. Now."

Carly threw Lily a poisonous look, but she complied, stalking to the door and making sure to slam it shut behind her.

"Denny, would you come here please?"

His stool screeched against the floor as he shoved himself to his feet and approached her desk.

"Do you want to tell me what that was all about?"

"She said I could borrow a pen."

"Did she? Because it sounds like you stole one."

"Okay, fine, I took it, but she didn't have to act like such a psycho about it."

"I don't think that language is appropriate, do you?" Lily met his gaze, and Denny's cheeks reddened.

"Sorry, Miss Cross."

"Consider this your warning—any more trouble from you, and you'll be in detention after school. Go back to your seat."

Denny nodded, ducking his head as he returned to his seat. Lily watched him go before rising from her own, intending to seek out Carly and give her the same speech.

"What are you doing out here, Carly?"

Lily heard the question as she stepped into the hall and did a double-take when she realized who was speaking. She'd never heard Eva sound like that—soft, almost fond—and Lily watched as Eva stopped beside where Carly leaned against a row of lockers.

"Miss Cross sent me out." Carly was sullen, her head bowed.

"What for?"

"Pushing Denny Marshall."

Eva groaned, pinching at the bridge of her nose. "What have I told you about being careful, Carly?"

Lily debated leaving Eva and Carly to it and edging back into her classroom—after all, it felt wrong to eavesdrop like this, but was it really her fault if Eva hadn't heard her approach?

"It wasn't my fault!" Carly's voice was laced with indignation. "He was being a dick, and I hate sitting next to him, and—"

Eva cut her off. "Did you try using your words? Asking Miss Cross if she would move you, perhaps?"

Carly's chin sank to her chest. "I didn't want to speak to her. Didn't want her to think I was being awkward. Then she might not like me like some of the other teachers."

Lily's heart ached at Carly's words—at the thought she might have made someone feel that way in her class, at discovering Carly was struggling to this extent and Lily had been none the wiser.

"Hey." Eva's voice turned impossibly softer. "That's not true. And I have a feeling Miss Cross isn't like that."

Knowing she'd already been standing there too long—and overheard too many things she shouldn't have—Lily made sure to rattle the handle on her classroom door as she stepped further into the hall.

Both Carly and Eva whirled to face her.

"You can come back in if you've calmed down, Carly." Lily was relieved her voice didn't waver as Eva's gaze landed on her face; she had the distinct feeling she was being assessed, and she hated every moment of it. "If you and Denny are having issues, feel free to move to a different seat. There's an empty one on the front row. And it goes without saying, but if you ever pull anything like that again you'll be in detention with me after school."

"Yes, Miss Cross." With her head lowered, Carly scurried past Lily and back into her classroom.

Lily was about to follow her—she'd left her students for too long already, and God only knew what mischief they'd gotten up to while she'd been gone—when Eva's voice stopped her.

"How much of that did you hear?"

How did Eva manage to make herself sound so much colder? And those eyes—they could give Medusa a run for her money.

"I don't know what you're talking about."

"You are a terrible liar."

Lily chose not to dignify that with a response. What did it matter, anyway? Lily pushed away the guilt as she returned to her desk. Eva was probably just worried Lily thought she might have a heart, after all.

Glancing at Carly—now situated in the seat Lily had suggested, on the front row and away from everyone else—and remembering the look on Eva's face when they'd been speaking, Lily was starting to think that might not be so far from the truth.

Chapter 5

Alisha peered around Eva's open classroom door, and Eva waved her inside. She hadn't seen much of Alisha since returning from their summer vacation, and she'd been expecting a catch-up sooner rather than later. As the second in the department, Eva was waiting for some more work to be dropped into her lap—Alisha's to-do list was never-ending, and Eva was happy to help lighten the load.

"Got a minute?" Alisha perched on the edge of one of the student desks. "There's a few things I wanted to run by you." As much disdain as Eva held for this place, she had a lot of respect for Alisha. She was in charge, but she didn't rule with an iron fist and was happy to listen to suggestions and take on board other people's opinions, never forcing her time on anyone else.

"Sure."

"I've been given the department's budget for the year, so we need to find some time to go over it and figure out what we need to buy. Maybe after Friday's department meeting? Have a think if there's anything you want to put on the list."

Eva wondered if "a whole new laboratory" would be an acceptable answer. The school wasn't ancient, but it wasn't ultra-modern by any means. When Eva thought about the equipment she'd been used to at Georgetown—and how much she could enrich the biology syllabus if she had access to even an eighth of it—she wanted to weep.

"I've been asked if we want to run extra support classes after school. I'm going to speak to Andrew about offering it for physics, but if you want to run some for biology let me know."

"I'd be happy to." Whether those who needed them would use them was another matter, but no one could ever say Eva didn't put everything on the line for those kids.

"Great. Oh, and one last thing. Would it be okay if Lily shadowed your science club session after school tomorrow?"

It wasn't a question Eva expected to be asked, considering the other topics of conversation, and she wasn't quick enough to school her expression, her nose wrinkling in distaste.

"I'd like her to get an idea of how we do things, seeing as she's never done one before," Alisha said, and Eva wondered about the politest way to say, "No way in hell."

"What about Mei's next week?" The two of them seemed to get along swimmingly—Eva was sure Lily would rather spend an hour with her, and Eva certainly would prefer it. She enjoyed science club sessions; having Lily there would sour her mood considerably.

Alisha looked at her in disapproval.

"You know I don't work well with others."

"I'm not asking you to work with her, I'm asking you to let her sit there and watch. Your sessions are the best, so she'll get the most out of them." Flattery was a fine way of getting Eva on her side, and Alisha knew it. "It's one hour, Eva. Is that so bad? You know what?" she said, as Eva opened her mouth. "Don't answer that."

"Am I allowed to say no?" Eva might like to act like she ran the place, but she knew who was in charge. Alisha wasn't afraid of throwing her weight around to get things done, and as much as she might resist, Eva respected that.

Alisha smiled. "You can, but I won't be happy about it."

Eva sighed. She didn't have to be happy about it, either. "Fine."

"Thank you. We'll talk Friday about the budget." Alisha pushed herself off the desk and left, allowing Eva to return to her e-mails. Not that she felt like she could get much done, with irritation thrumming below the surface of her skin.

Lily eyed Eva's ajar classroom door with trepidation churning in her stomach. When she'd asked Alisha for more details of the science club, Lily hadn't expected Alisha to say she should spend an hour of her Wednesday watching Eva run a session.

But Lily hadn't known how to say no, and Eva had agreed—though she didn't look happy to see Lily when she stepped into her room, notebook clutched to her chest like a shield.

"Um, hi." Lily paused beside Eva where she leaned against her desk, because it would be rude to waltz inside without saying anything. "Thanks for doing this. Can I help you with anything?"

Eva shook her head. "Sit wherever you like."

Lily dragged a stool over to the side of the room, trying to stay out of the way as much as possible as more students arrived.

Eva let a few minutes pass before she began, and Lily did a quick headcount—twenty-five kids were crammed into the room, and Lily wondered if this was the usual level of turnout.

"Welcome," Eva said, silence falling the moment she opened her mouth. "I see some familiar faces but a lot of new ones, too. Let's start by learning everyone's names." She wrote them on a piece of paper as they went around the room. Lily didn't recognize a single one from any of her classes. "Okay, for those of you who haven't been here before, I'll explain how things work. You'll have a different teacher each week, and as those teachers have a different specialty, you'll be doing all kinds of different things. I'm a biologist, so that's what we're going to be doing today. Let's get started, shall we?" Eva reached for a model on her desk. "Can anyone tell me what this is?"

Eva waited, eyes scanning around the room, for a brave soul to raise their hand. "Yes, Madison?"

"It's DNA."

"Right, and what's the structure of DNA? James."

"A double helix."

"Correct. Who knows what DNA stands for?" Silence. "No one want to hazard a guess?" Eva's gaze flickered over to Lily. "Miss Cross, perhaps?"

Lily tried not to scoff. Of course Eva would try and put her on the spot. Did she want to embarrass Lily in front of the kids, as some form of payback for daring to infringe on her time?

Well, it wasn't going to work. Lily may be a chemist, but biology had been another one of her favorites when she'd been at school. She set her jaw and made sure to meet Eva's eye. "Deoxyribose nucleic acid."

If she was impressed, Eva didn't show it. "Thank you. Now, on your desks you have some toothpicks and different types of candy. In groups, I want you to make me an accurate DNA model. You have five minutes, and the best one will win a prize. Go."

They sprang into action, the room soon filled with noisy chatter. Lily was surprised Eva didn't shush them as she stalked around the perimeter. And stalked was the only name for it—Eva had an easy grace, her heels clicking against the floor, her posture perfect. She possessed a confidence Lily could only dream of one day having.

Once she'd done a circuit of the room, Eva paused beside her, and Lily tried not to tense. Why did she suddenly feel like a naughty kid?

"Want to warn me next time you plan on throwing a question my way?" Lily said, glancing away from her notebook.

Eva smirked. "Where's the fun in that?"

"You're disappointed I got it right, aren't you?"

Eva kept her voice low. "That sounds like a challenge."

Lily didn't get a chance to reply, as the students' time was up, and Lily blinked when Eva clapped her hands to get their attention. Was she imagining things or had that sounded flirtatious?

Lily shook her head.

Definitely her imagination.

"Whose is this?" Eva lifted one of the models. Three shy hands raised at the back of the room. "Well done. Stay behind at the end for your prize."

After a quick rundown of what the other groups could have done better, Eva moved to their next activity. When she dumped several containers of strawberries onto the front desk, Lily wasn't the only one who appeared to be confused.

"You have all seen a strawberry before, right?" Eva folded her arms across her chest. "You're going to extract some DNA from them, using things you'd find at home."

Lily watched as confusion turned to interest, Eva easily captivating their attention as she ran through the procedure and let them loose. The rest of the hour flew by, Lily preoccupied by this different side of Eva she was seeing. She seemed lighter when she was teaching, happy to answer any questions directed her way—sometimes with a smile. Eva was the polar opposite persona to the one Lily had been subjected to, and she marveled at the difference.

All the kids left with a smile on their face, chattering about what they'd done. Once they were alone, Lily helped Eva tidy everything away.

"I hope that was useful to you," Eva said.

"Yes, thank you, it was interesting." Both the subject matter and the insight into the secretive Dr. Thomas. "You're good with them."

"Why do you sound so surprised?" Eva moved to her desk, tossing her glasses onto it and rubbing her hands over her eyes. "It's not like I'm new at this."

"I know. You used to be a professor, right?"

Eva eyed her warily, and Lily wondered if she was about to be accused of stalking again. "I did."

"Must be different, going from college kids to high schoolers."

"In some ways. In others…not so much. Regardless, my role is the same—to make sure they have the knowledge they need to get to the next stage of their lives."

And Eva was good at it, too. Alisha had said Eva was the best in the department at what she did, and Lily could see it now. Not that she was going to tell Eva that—she didn't need her ego inflating any more than it already was.

"If that's all," Eva said. Lily could practically see a shutter going down, Eva closing off any further questions, "I have to get going."

"Right, of course. Thanks for…everything."

Eva grunted in response, and Lily fled from the room, feeling like they'd had something of a breakthrough. Sure, they weren't going to be going for after-work drinks together any time soon, but they'd managed to spend a whole hour together without ripping each other's throats out.

Lily counted that as progress.

Silence greeted Eva when she opened her front door.

Frowning, she stepped inside and heard Franklin's claws skittering on the wooden floor of the landing as he raced to the top of the stairs before bounding down them to greet her. "Hey, buddy," she said, giving him a pat when she met him halfway up. "You keeping Mom company?"

He followed her back up the stairs, and Eva knocked lightly on her mother's ajar bedroom door. She was curled up in bed, the TV playing low, and Eva could tell from one look at her it hadn't been a good day.

Still, she tried to put on a brave face. "Hi, sweetheart. How was work?"

"Fine." Eva kicked off her shoes and padded inside, weaving around her mother's wheelchair as Franklin launched himself onto the bed and snuggled into her mother's arms. "How long have you been in bed?"

"Most of the day." Of all the symptoms her mother suffered with, fatigue was often the most debilitating. She could adapt to the walking difficulties, muscle weakness and vertigo with the help of her chair, but it was hard to overcome anything when climbing out of bed required herculean effort.

"Have you eaten?"

"Not since breakfast."

"Mother." Eva ground her teeth. "Why didn't you call me?"

"Because you had your club, and I know you'd have rushed home. I'm fine, Eva."

"You're not." Admitting needing help didn't come easy to the Thomases, but at times like this, Eva really wished it did. "I'll make you something. What do you want?"

"I'm not hungry."

"Tough." Eva adopted her best teacher-voice. "You have to eat."

"Take Franklin out first."

"We'll go out after—another hour won't kill him. What about matzo ball soup? We still have some leftovers from the weekend."

"All right."

Eva made her way to the kitchen, adding a generous helping of soup to a pan on the stove. Her phone rang while she waited for it to boil, and she smiled at the name flashing across her screen. "Hey, stranger."

"Hi, Eva." Kate's voice was familiar in her ear. "It's been a while. How you doing? Bored of small-town life yet?"

"I was bored of small-town life the day I moved here." Eva stirred the soup with a wooden spoon. She'd always been more of a city person, had loved spending her weekends exploring museums or finding the best local spots to eat. Chicago was nearby, but she didn't like being too far away from her mother. Especially after a day like today. "I miss D.C."

"D.C. misses you, too. And by D.C., I mean me."

"Naturally. How are things over there?"

"Same as ever. You know nothing exciting happens here. What about you? Got anything fun planned for the rest of the day?"

Eva glanced toward the hall, where she'd left the pile of papers she had to grade.

"Grading AP biology homework."

"Exciting."

"Oh it's thrilling."

Kate chuckled. "We can swap if you want. I'm currently sitting in my office with a stack of essays on nanoparticles, and a thesis to read through before the end of the week."

"Unfortunately that's outside of my range of expertise."

"Are you telling me there's something the great Eva Thomas doesn't know?"

"Fuck off," Eva said, but she was smiling. Kate was the one person she'd tolerate teasing from. "And stop telling me about your office. My office is my bedroom. I have a delightful view of my elderly neighbor's hot tub."

"Aren't you lucky? I have a view of campus. It looks lovely in the sunset."

"I hate you."

"Well, that's rude. I'm not going to come and visit you."

Eva paused, cradling the phone between her ear and her shoulder as she reached for two bowls. "What?"

"It's why I called. There's a conference in Chicago next month, and yours truly is one of the guest speakers. I thought we could meet up while I'm in the area."

"I'd like that." She'd seen Kate on a visit to Georgetown with the school before summer, but Eva would never turn down the chance to reconnect with a part of her old life. It would have the bonus of getting her mother off her back for having no social life, too.

"Great. I'll call you closer to the time and we can set something out. I'd better get back to my own grading or I'm going to have fifty angry kids writing me complaints."

That was one thing Eva didn't miss. She might teach more classes now, but the assignments were much less time-consuming to grade, and the deadlines weren't as tight. "I'll see you soon. Bye, Kate."

Eva had a spring in her step as she returned to her mother's bedroom, carefully carrying both bowls and making sure not to spill a drop. She was exactly where Eva had left her, and Eva put the bowls down to help her mother sit up before curling up beside her.

"Thank you," her mother said, sipping delicately at her soup. "But you don't have to join me. I know not eating at the table offends you."

Eva swallowed her bite of matzo ball. "I'll make an exception for you. Do you want me to come home early tomorrow?" Thursdays were usually spent squirreled away in her classroom until night fell, her mother busy with Angela, but Eva wouldn't hesitate to change her plans if she was needed.

"No, it's okay. Angela's still coming over. We can watch Netflix in here if I'm not up to moving. And you know she'll make sure I eat."

"True." Angela was almost as protective of her mother as Eva was, for which she was endlessly grateful. "But promise you'll call me if you need me?"

"I promise."

"Okay."

Their soup finished, Eva kissed her mother on the cheek and cleared up their dishes. She whistled for Franklin to follow her out and shut the bedroom door gently behind them, leaving her to rest.

"Ready for a walk, rascal?"

Franklin's ears perked up, and he raced past her down the stairs so fast it was a miracle he didn't topple over.

Chapter 6

LILY STRETCHED HER ARMS OVER her head as the last of her students left the room, relieved to make it to the end of another week. The department meeting awaited her, and Lily was the last to arrive, sliding into her usual seat and opening her notebook in front of her.

"It should be another quick one this week," Alisha said, and Lily made notes as she went through the agenda. "Before I let you go, there's one last thing we need to do. As I'm sure you're all aware, Homecoming is fast approaching, and as always, teachers are being drafted in as chaperones." Groans echoed around the room, and Alisha turned to Lily. "They expect a few representatives from each department at each dance. We usually send two, and we draw straws for it. Red is for Homecoming, blue for Winter Formal and green for Prom. Sound fair to you?"

Lily nodded, and Alisha let her pick first from the straws she produced from her bag. When they revealed them, Lily didn't know whether to laugh or cry. She and Eva both held blue straws.

Did the universe have it in for her? While science club hadn't been the disaster she'd feared, Lily wasn't sure they'd be able to survive an awkward night of chaperoning teenagers together.

She glanced at Eva and found her glaring at her palm—Lily wasn't the only unhappy one.

"So, we have Mei and Andrew for Homecoming, Lily and Eva for Winter Formal, and Brandon and I for Prom."

Alisha soon adjourned the meeting, and Mei patted Lily on the back as they were leaving the room. "Commiserations."

"You don't want to swap?"

"No thank you. Although Eva is funny. I did Homecoming with her last year, and she gleefully separated students who were dancing too close together."

"Sure I can't persuade you?"

"Sorry, kid. You're on your own. But good news—it's home time. Or bar time, I suppose. You are coming, right?"

"Wouldn't miss it."

Lily fell into step beside Mei as they walked to the parking lot, the others promising to meet them there once they'd finished a few last things.

It was Lily's third time going to the bar, but she still followed close behind Mei's Subaru, not having managed to remember the way yet. It was tucked between an Indian restaurant and a convenience store, and the smell of spices never failed to make Lily's stomach rumble.

Inside it was quiet, the early evening rush yet to start. Booths stretched along one wall, black leather illuminated by low level lighting and sports commentary filtered through the speakers for the football game playing on the TVs mounted on the wall above the bar. The solitary bartender smiled when he saw them.

"The usual?" he said, reaching for two glasses.

"Yes please."

"Coming right up." He mixed Mei's frozen daiquiri and Lily's gin and tonic with practiced ease. Once they were ready, Lily followed Mei to their usual booth toward the back of the bar.

"God, I'm glad it's the weekend," Mei said, taking a sip of her drink. "I can't believe we've only been back for a month. It feels like three. How are you finding it?"

"Good." Aside from her honors class. Denny was still trying to push her boundaries whenever the opportunity presented itself—but Lily didn't want to talk about work too much tonight. "Any plans for the weekend?"

"I have a date tomorrow night, so if I don't come to work on Monday morning I've been kidnapped and murdered."

Lily nearly inhaled her gin. "Do you usually attract serial killers?"

"I usually attract weirdos, so it would be on brand. It's the first time I'm meeting anyone from a dating app."

"Oh, I know the feeling. Make sure you have an exit strategy in case he is a serial killer."

"Noted. You got any horror stories?"

"Not really. But I wouldn't meet people until we'd been speaking for a while."

"Anyone turn out not to look like their pictures?"

Lily shook her head. "Have you been watching *Catfish*?"

"...Maybe."

"I'm sure it'll turn out fine."

"I hope so. My ex was a cheating asshole, so I feel like I'm due for some good karma." Behind Mei's head, the door opened, and Lily waved as Alisha and Andrew walked through it, pausing at the bar to get their drinks. "Did dating apps work out for you?"

"Uh, no. My last ex was also a cheating asshole."

"Shit, I'm sorry. Cheers, I guess?" Mei clinked her glass against Lily's. "Have you been thinking about getting back out there?"

Lily tapped her fingers against the stem of her glass. "Sometimes." Lily didn't know if she was ready, but she wasn't used to living on her own. It'd be nice to have someone to talk to, even if it didn't go anywhere. Lily wondered how likely finding a woman who just wanted to be friends would be. "Aren't dating apps something of a minefield, being a teacher?"

Lily wasn't sure she could handle the mortification of a student or one of their parents examining her dating profile.

"It can be. It's why I used the one I did. It's called CuteMeet. It lets you stay anonymous until you exchange digits. You use usernames, no identifying photos if you don't want to. You can put as much or as little on your profile as you want."

"Huh." It was an interesting prospect.

"Of course, it means the likelihood of meeting a murderer is increased, but..."

Lily laughed. "Well, I might check it out. Anything to get my sister off my back. She keeps trying to set me up with people."

"I hate when people do that. Like, if I wanted a date I could get one myself, thank you."

"Exactly! Plus she has terrible taste in women." Lily froze as soon as she said it—she hadn't intended on casually coming out over drinks in her first month of the job, but it was too late to take it back now.

To her credit, Mei was unfazed. "Well, if you ever need a fake date to get them off your back, let me know."

Alisha was the first of the other two to join them, sitting with a glass of white wine. "Good to see you here again, Lily. Although I would like to point out it's not mandatory."

"Please say it is, somewhere in Eva's vicinity." Mei smiled at the thought, and Andrew chuckled when he perched beside her with a bottle of Corona. "I'd love to see her face."

"You are free to say it, but I will not."

"Boring. Could Brandon not make it this week?"

"It's his wedding anniversary so he went straight home," Alisha said. "They've made it to thirty years."

"Why do you sound impressed?" Mei asked. "Aren't you and Darius closing in on that?"

"We've managed twenty-two. Although we've been together for almost thirty." Alisha glanced at Lily. "It took him eight years to propose."

"You did meet when you were like twelve."

Lily listened to them bicker with a smile. "You were high school sweethearts?"

"We were. Andrew, you must be thinking about proposing soon, no? You and Kerry have been together for ages."

"I feel like I'm at my mom's." Andrew grinned around the rim of his bottle. "We're waiting until we've bought a house—which will hopefully be soon—but then, yeah."

"Here's to being single," Mei said, tilting her glass toward Lily's and clinking them together. "At least it's not just me anymore."

"You never know, this guy you're meeting tomorrow might be the one."

"I'm not getting my hopes up."

"You haven't shown me a picture," Alisha said, leaning her elbows on the table. "I want to see what he looks like."

Mei reached for her phone, tapping at the screen and showing them all a photo of a grinning white, sandy-haired guy, a black and white cat curled around his shoulders. "Here he is. His name is James."

"He's cute."

"He seems...nice."

Lily smiled at the two different responses, agreeing more with Andrew than Alisha. "He doesn't look like a serial killer," she said, and Mei laughed.

"Well, I'm glad he has your seal of approval."

They chatted until their glasses were empty before going their separate ways. Lily drove home content, her cheeks hurting from smiling, feeling like she finally belonged.

Lily checked and rechecked the PowerPoint she'd made for her first science club three times while waiting for her classroom to fill, students trickling in from classes they'd had in other parts of the school.

There was no reason for her to be nervous. She had four weeks of teaching under her belt with no disasters, but this felt different. These weren't all kids she was familiar with, for one, although she did recognize several of the faces settling at the desks in front of her. Macie was one of them, smiling shyly when Lily made eye contact with her.

These were kids that were really interested in science, and she wanted to win them over, nurture the curiosity within them—and do a better job than the teacher she'd replaced. According to Mei and Alisha, she wouldn't have to try hard to achieve that, but still.

Lily waited five minutes after the bell to start, giving everyone time to arrive, and wiped her sweaty palms on her black slacks as she rose to her feet to stand by the board.

"Welcome, everyone. For those of you that haven't met me before, I'm Miss Cross. I don't know how many of you are familiar with chemistry, but for those of you that are, these sessions won't contain nearly as much math or theory as you're used to. I want to show you how many different things chemistry can do, and more importantly, I want you to have fun. Is that okay with everyone?"

"Yes, Miss Cross," sounded as a chorus, and Lily relaxed.

She took a leaf out of Eva's book and noted down the names of everyone in the room, making her own cheat sheet for when she asked them questions, and then Lily dived right in.

"I want to start with some friendly competition. I have a task for you to do in groups, and the group to get the best results will win a prize." She tapped a box of chocolates on her desk, grabbing their attention. Another trick taken from Eva, maybe, but Lily wasn't going to give her credit. She'd been handing out candy for answers since she'd started teaching.

"Your task is to make me copper sulfate crystals from copper oxide and sulfuric acid. On your benches is all the equipment that you need to use—you have ten minutes to brainstorm with your group members and write me a method. Each group can ask me up to three questions, but no more, and there will also be a prize for the best method. Once you've shown it to me, you can get started. Your time starts…now."

They scrambled into action, hushed whispers filling the room, and Lily watched them from her perch on her desk. She gave them a few minutes before she wandered around, knowing they were more likely to ask her something if she was passing by.

"Miss Cross?" Sure enough, a timid voice from the back desk called out as she was making her second pass. "The acid has already been measured out for us, but how much copper oxide should we use?"

Lily glanced down at her sheet of paper. "Good question Jonathan. What do you think?"

"Uhm…not a lot?"

"Are you asking me or telling me? Because if you're asking me, that counts as another one of your questions."

"Not a lot," Jonathan said with more confidence.

"Right. But you do need to add it in excess, or you won't get any crystals. Do you know what that means?"

An answer came quicker this time. "Keep adding it until it stops dissolving."

"Good. Let me know if you have any more questions." Lily continued her loop of the room, stopping to talk to some of the other groups. One seemed reluctant to ask her anything, even when Lily pried, but she couldn't do much to help them if they didn't want it. Hopefully they'd start to relax once they got to know her better.

Jonathan's group won the prize for best method, but it didn't mean they would make the best crystals. Lily wouldn't be able to choose a winner until the following week, but that didn't dampen the enthusiasm of her students as she set them off on the lab task.

Lily liked every part of teaching, but labs were always her favorite. The kids loved them, and it was a good opportunity to engage those of them who struggled with the theory. Watching understanding bloom behind their eyes when they put what they'd learned together with the task they were doing was always a highlight.

Lily couldn't let them have fun for the whole hour, though. Once they had a dish of copper sulfate to be left to evaporate, she called them to attention. "Now that we've done the experiment, let's go back a step and find out why."

The remainder of the hour passed quickly, and Lily was pleased as her room emptied out, already looking forward to her next week in charge. One student lingered, and Lily smiled at Macie when she hesitated by her desk.

"Is everything all right, Macie?"

"Y-yeah, I wanted to ask you something." Macie fiddled with the sleeves of her shirt, eyes focused on her sneakers, and Lily waited to hear whatever she was struggling to say. "I've been talking to a couple of other students over the past few weeks, and we want to set up a gay-straight-alliance, but we need a teacher to like, oversee meetings and be in charge, and I was wondering if you'd be interested in doing that?" The words rushed out of her, and Lily struggled to keep up. "You don't have to, because I know you're busy and everything, but I thought I'd ask."

"I'll have to check with Mrs. Woods first," Lily said, not sure if Alisha would want Lily signing up for extra work when she was still new to the faculty. "But I'll let you know what she says, and we can talk about it more on Friday. That's when I see you next, right?"

Macie nodded. "Thanks." She hurried away, and Lily went to see if Alisha was in her room. The lights were on within, so Lily rapped her knuckles on the smooth wood of Alisha's door.

"Come in!" Alisha said, and Lily found her sitting behind her desk with a pile of books. "Lily, hi. How was science club?"

"Great. I enjoyed it and I think they did, too."

"Good."

"Have you got a minute to talk about something?"

"Absolutely." Alisha gestured toward the front row of seats, and moved to sit beside Lily, turning to give Lily her full attention. "Is everything all right?"

"Everything's fine. I had a student ask me about something and I wanted to run it by you. She'd like to set up a GSA. They need a teacher to run it, and she asked if I'd be interested."

"And are you?"

"Yeah, I am. I think it's a valuable resource. It could make a lot of difference to kids who might feel like they don't have anywhere else to go." Lily wished there had been something like that in place when she'd been a teenager. "But I didn't want to say yes without talking to you first."

"That's understandable. I'm not against it—in fact, I actively encourage all members of the department to get more involved in school life. Perhaps not so early into their career…" Alisha said, lips quirking into a smile, "but from what I've seen from you already, I don't doubt that you'll be able to handle it."

Lily's cheeks felt hot. "Thanks."

"They'll have to fill out the relevant documentation. If they need any help, you can send them to me. I had to do it when we started the science club. And we used to have a GSA, so the framework should already be in place."

"How come it stopped?"

"Mostly a case of bad timing. The teacher running it left the same year that a lot of the older members graduated. No one stepped up once they'd all gone."

"Oh." Lily hoped that wasn't an indication of the school community's overall attitude toward LGBTQIA+ issues. "That sucks for the younger kids."

"It does. Which is why I'm happy for you to start it back up again."

"Do we need to get the principal involved?"

"You'll need his approval, so I'd recommend sending him an e-mail telling him you want to do it. Let me know if there's anything I can help you with."

"I will, thank you." Lily rose to her feet, already drafting an e-mail in her mind.

"And Lily?" Alisha's voice brought her to a stop halfway through the door. "Keep doing what you're doing. You're clearly winning over the student body, and I'm impressed by what I've seen from you so far. You're settling in nicely. I can't wait to see what more you can do."

The second compliment had the same effect as the first. "Thank you." Lily escaped before Alisha could make her flush any further, a spring in her step as she retreated to her own room.

"Come in!" Lily said in response to someone knocking on her door. She didn't look up right away, too busy focusing on updating her lesson plan for the following day. She expected Mei—a near-constant fixture in her room at the end of the day—or Alisha, who often swung by to check everything was going okay. Even Eva, storming in to argue with her about something would have been more likely than the man clearing his throat at the front of her classroom.

"Principal Blake!" Lily set down her pen and straightened in her chair, wondering if she should get to her feet or shake his hand. "Sorry, I was miles away."

"Please, call me David."

Lily had only spoken to him a handful of times since she'd been hired, but he seemed pleasant enough. At around fifty years old, his hair was starting to speckle with gray, a no-nonsense aura exuding from him that Lily suspected had gotten him to the top of the ladder.

"Is everything all right?" Lily said, wondering what had prompted a visit from the principal on an otherwise unremarkable Monday afternoon.

"Fine, fine. I just thought I should check in. See how things are."

If it was an official visit, Lily knew Alisha would have warned her ahead of time. Lily doubted he'd stop by "just because" and waited, with tension held in her shoulders, for the other shoe to drop.

"Some paperwork landed on my desk with your name on it," he said, and realization dawned. "You want to set up a GSA?"

"Not me personally." Lily picked up her pen so she had something to do with her hands. "One of my students approached me about it."

"And you think it's a good idea?"

Lily blinked, taken aback by the question. "I think it's a wonderful idea. Don't you?"

"I just…" David sighed as he tucked his hands into the pockets of his suit jacket. "I don't know if it's an acceptable use of school resources."

Lily squeezed the pen so hard she felt the plastic crack, but better that than let her mouth run, better that than reaching out and strangling David with his tie. She rescinded her earlier assessment—there was nothing pleasant about him at all.

"Or your resources," David said, seemingly oblivious to the anger simmering beneath Lily's skin. "We don't want you to burn yourself out during your first year."

Lily wondered who the 'we' was in that equation. "Alisha doesn't have a problem with it," she said, trying not to grit her teeth. "And I know I can handle it."

"Right. But—"

"I think it would be good for this school," Lily said, speaking over him, letting her anger carry her words forward. "Because I've not been here long, but it's long enough for me to notice there appears to be a problem with homophobia."

Lily didn't say she was starting to see where it might come from—she had a feeling that wouldn't go down well, and she wanted to keep this job. "Out of interest, what happened to the two girls bullying Macie Taylor?"

"They were suitably punished." Gone was David's easy-going smile, his lips pursed and his eyes narrowing. "Is this something that's important to you?"

Lily knew the real question was: is this the hill you want to die on?

In any case, her answer was yes. These kids needed someone to fight for them, and Lily wished there had been someone in her corner back when she'd been in their shoes. "It is."

"I'm concerned about pushback from parents."

Lily tried not to scoff. "Well, my only concern is for the children, and the message it would send if this was stopped. That they don't matter. That parents' opinions are more valued than their wellbeing." Her heart was beating in her ears, because, despite how she sometimes acted around Eva, Lily hated conflict. Lily tried to inject that same steel she had whenever they argued into her voice, so she didn't quail under David's stare. "Also, technically speaking, preventing a GSA from forming is against the law under the federal Equal Access Act." She'd done her research, hoping she wouldn't have to use it.

"I see." David regarded her for one long, charged moment. "Well, I'll consider it."

He strode from the room, and Lily let out a sigh, dropping her forehead onto her desk. Why did everything have to be so difficult? It wasn't like Lily had expected this to be easy but having some support from her superiors would go a long way.

No matter. Lily didn't need anyone else to make the GSA a success—she was determined enough to do it all alone.

Resolved, she lifted her head, and noticed a notification on her phone. Curiosity and boredom had led to her download the CuteMeet app at the weekend—she had a match.

Lily opened the app and found a reply from the cute blonde she'd messaged last night waiting for her.

Smiling, Lily typed a response, hoping the conversation wouldn't stall like it had with the handful of other women she'd messaged with.

Chapter 7

As the only redhead in attendance, Kate was easy to spot in the hotel bar. "Finally! I thought you were standing me up."

"Sorry." Eva slid into the seat opposite Kate and leaned forward to press a swift kiss to Kate's cheek. "Traffic was terrible."

"I ordered you a drink." Kate nodded to the cocktail on the table.

"Thank you." Eva took a sip of the martini, humming in contentment as the gin hit her tongue. Kate's drink was half empty—Eva had some catching up to do. "How was the conference?"

"Incredibly boring."

"Including your presentation?"

"Naturally, mine was the only highlight."

"I'm sure." Eva chewed on the end of her straw and cast her eyes around the room. "It's a fancy hotel they've put you up in." The gold painted ceilings were high, and marble arches separated the bar from the main lobby. Large windows looked out onto the street beyond, where Chicago was beginning to come alive as the sun sank on the horizon.

"Yeah, it's not too shabby. Only got one bed, though, so it looks like we're sharing later."

"As long as you don't snore."

"I don't."

"You do. You kept me up half the night when we shared a room at that biotechnology conference in London."

"Lies." Kate raised a hand to signal a server as she finished the last of her drink. "You want another?"

"Yes, please." Eva hadn't been out for so long—she was determined to enjoy the freedoms that came with a night on the town. "I'll get this round."

Kate waved her off as she ordered two refills. "Don't worry about it. I've got a fifty dollar a day allowance to put on my room tab, and I've yet to use any of it today."

"God, I miss being a professor." Eva tilted her head back in a groan, and Kate patted her hand.

"You could always come back. Gordon would love to have you. All he talks about is how good you were."

"He does not."

"Oh, he does. Whenever any of us do anything wrong, you can tell he's thinking: Eva wouldn't do this to me. I'm surprised he hasn't called, begging for you to return. He's retiring soon. There'll be a department-head spot."

"Like they'd give it to me after two years away. Teaching high schoolers the difference between mitosis and meiosis doesn't exactly bulk out my resumé. You'd have more chance than me."

Kate scoffed. "Please, they'd never choose me, I'm too disorganized. I wouldn't want it anyway—too much extra work, and you know how I feel about that. Carter will get it, I think."

"He'd do a good job." Eva finished the last sip of her martini as another was set in front of her. "Not as old fashioned as Gordon."

"Because Gordon's pushing seventy, and Carter's barely forty."

"True. How are the others?"

Kate's shoulders lifted. "I told you—not much has changed. Except everything is more boring without you."

"I find that hard to believe."

"It is! Will you ever come back east?"

"I don't know. Not any time soon. As much as she insists she doesn't need me, I can't leave my mother. And I can't ask her to move just for me." Greenfield had been her mother's fresh start when Eva had gone to college, and Eva couldn't bear to ask her to give it up, no matter how stuck she might feel sometimes.

"Even though you moved for her?"

"It's different." Eva stared at her drink, swirling it with her straw. "My dad walked out when I was five, and we...we struggled. My mother busted her ass to give me everything I needed. To put me through college and grad school. She worked overtime and double shifts so I could graduate without thousands of dollars of debt, and she never asked for anything in return. But she needs me, and I should be there for her. I want to be."

"You don't have to explain yourself to me." Kate reached for Eva's hand again. "I get it. I just... Are you happy here?"

"Who says I was happy at Georgetown?"

"How could you be sad with me around?" Kate said, batting her eyelashes, and Eva chuckled.

"I'm okay here," Eva said. "But I do miss you."

"I miss you, too. We should do this more often."

"You're welcome to visit anytime. Although something tells me you'll be less inclined if you have to pay for yourself."

"It's a sacrifice I'm willing to make. How is your mother, anyway? Is she still managing okay?"

"She has good days and bad days." Though the bad seemed to outnumber the good, lately. "She has more independence since she got her wheelchair, and the support group she's joined has been helping, too."

"Good. As long as you remember to look after yourself, too."

"I always do."

Kate's phone buzzed on the table, and she heaved a sigh when she read the notification.

"Everything all right?"

Kate took a hefty sip of her Manhattan before answering. "Dan and I are...having some trouble."

"What? How come?"

"We've been arguing a lot lately. He started a new job, works longer hours. Some days we hardly see one another. Some days it feels like he prefers it that way." Kate ran a hand through her hair, a faint tremble in her fingers. "I...said things I'm not particularly proud of before I left for this trip."

"God, I'm sorry. I hope you manage to work things out."

"Me too." Her smile was tinged with sadness. "I think we're going to start couple's therapy when I get home, which sounds like a nightmare, but..." Kate shrugged.

"Just ask Victoria. She turned into a therapist toward the end." Eva tried not to sound bitter. "Not long after I moved out, she said I wasn't putting enough effort into things. That I was 'pulling away because of my abandonment issues'." Eva parroted back the words, one of their last arguments burned into her memory. "So that when we broke up it wouldn't be as painful."

"I mean...you do have abandonment issues," Kate said, grinning when Eva glared at her across the table. "But you were too good for her anyway. And I don't want to talk about Dan tonight. Distract me with details of your own love life."

"I'm afraid there are no details to report."

"None? Nothing since Victoria?"

"Nope."

"Unacceptable." A spark bloomed in Kate's eyes, and Eva's stomach twisted. "That's the rest of our night sorted, then. I'm going to be your wing woman."

"I don't need a wing woman."

"Why not? I'm great at it. I have an exemplary track record."

"You've only been my wing woman once."

"And you dated the woman I set you up with for three years afterwards, so...proven winner, right here." Kate tugged at her collar, and Eva rolled her eyes. "It's time for me to make it two out of two. Are there any gay bars around here?"

"Again, I don't need a wing woman. And I don't know—I don't come into the city much."

"Then what do you do for fun around here?"

"With my working hours, there's not much time left for fun."

Kate scoffed. "With those vacation days? You can't tell me it's more work than being a professor."

"It's close."

"Bullshit. Are you telling me you don't have a life here?"

"God, you sound like my mother." Eva rubbed a hand across her face. "She's forever telling me to get out of the house. You should've seen her face when I told her I'd be spending the weekend with you. Anyone would think she didn't want me around."

"She's probably just worried about you. She knows you moved back here for her—she doesn't want you to hate it."

"But I don't. Yeah, it's not D.C., but…it's not terrible, either."

"You're not lonely?"

"Sometimes. But it's not like I live alone, and I don't miss being in a relationship."

"Not even the sex?"

Eva hesitated, and Kate's eyes lit up.

"I knew it! Okay, give me your phone."

"What?"

"If you're going to refuse to let me take you to a bar tonight, then I'm going to find you someone another way. There's this new dating app doing the rounds. I'm signing you up for it."

"No way in hell."

"Come on. It'll be fun. We can spend the night swiping through profiles."

"That sounds like hell on earth."

"What if your perfect woman is on there, waiting for you?"

"I told you—I don't want a relationship."

"But you do want a hook-up, and apps are the easiest way to do that right now. Step into the twenty-first century, Eva."

"I'm thirty-five, not a hundred-and-five," Eva said, staring resentfully at her empty glass—she would need way more alcohol to get through this night alive.

"So live like one."

Kate reached for something under the table, and Eva realized too late she'd grabbed Eva's bag. Kate plucked her phone from its depths. "Don't you dare."

"Let me sign you up," Kate said, leaning back when Eva tried to lunge for her. "Where's the harm in that?"

"There's a lot of harm in that." Eva got to her feet, but so did Kate, keeping the table between them like a buffer as she typed something in.

Eva regretted her decision to keep her passcode as her birthday.

If she'd changed it, she wouldn't be in this mess right now.

Circling the table, they looked ridiculous, and the only reason Eva wasn't breaking into a run was because she didn't want to be thrown out. Already, they were garnering curious glances from patrons at nearby tables.

"Kate, please."

"Let me be in charge of it for one night," Kate said, holding up a finger. "Give it a try. And then once I've gone tomorrow you can delete it."

Eva didn't want to accept the offer, but she knew if she refused they'd only argue for another few hours, and she wanted to enjoy the night. Besides, if Eva played nice now—and got Kate drunk enough—she might be able to swipe the phone from her and delete it without her noticing.

"Fine." Eva sighed as she dropped back into her seat. "One night."

"Yay!" Kate threw her arms around Eva's neck. "This is going to be so fun."

Eva woke with a groan.

Either she or Kate had neglected to draw the drapes of the hotel room, and sunlight streamed through the window. Eva rolled over, pulling the pillow over her head and burrowing further into the covers.

Her head pounded, making it impossible to go back to sleep. A cursory glance at her watch told her it was ten past eight—far too early to be awake, considering they'd only gotten back to the room at 4 a.m.

As she pushed herself out of bed and stumbled to the bathroom, a hand over her eyes to ward off the blinding sun, Eva vowed to never go out with Kate again. With the door shut, the room was blissfully dark, and Eva didn't reach for the light switch.

She splashed some cold water on her face in the hope it would ease the throbbing behind her eyes. All it served to do was jolt her even further awake.

Peeking out of the bathroom door, she discovered Kate was merely a lump of blankets on the bed, a shock of red hair just barely visible on the pillow. Eva was debating whether to slip back beneath the covers or to start getting dressed when a raspy voice called across the room.

"Why are you awake at such an ungodly hour?"

"Don't lectures start at eight?"

"Yes, but not on a Sunday. Sunday is for sleeping."

"Well, I can't sleep, because my head feels like it's going to explode." Eva opted to get back into bed, not yet ready to face the day, and sat with her back against the headboard.

"Join the fucking club."

"You were the one who wanted to get wasted."

"A decision I well and truly regret."

Eva reached for her phone, frowning when she saw several unfamiliar notifications on the screen. "What did you do last night? Why do I have a load of notifications from something called CuteMeet?"

"Oh my God." Kate sat up—too quickly, based on her grimace. Her hair stuck up in every which direction, last night's make-up smudged all over her face. Eva doubted she looked much better. "You have matches already?" Kate grabbed the phone.

"Give that back!"

"It's for your own good, Eva. Trust me on this."

"I trust you on very little."

"Let's see what we've got, shall we?"

Eva leaned over her shoulder as Kate opened the app.

"Four likes and two messages. See? Being mysterious on these things works. Should we message one of them back?"

Eva lunged for the phone, because knowing Kate, she'd say something sexually suggestive and make Eva's cheeks burn. "Neither of them appears to be stunning conversationalists." Both messages simply read 'hi'. "Where's the creativity?"

"They're leaving that up to you."

"Well, they'll be waiting a long time."

"Come on, Eva! Live a little. You might find someone you like on there."

"Unlikely." Eva swiped the app away with her thumb. "What time is your flight?"

"Twelve."

"Enough time for breakfast, then." Rousing Kate was no easy feat, and Eva helped by packing Kate's suitcase while she showered. By the time they were stepping out of the hotel lobby, shivering at the bite in the air, it was nine thirty.

"There's a café down the street that does good pancakes," Kate said, and Eva was happy to follow her lead. The smell of coffee and bacon hit Eva's nose when Kate pushed open the door, revealing a cozy café with a handful of tables, a counter filled with mouthwatering pastries set against one of the walls.

"Everything sounds amazing," Eva said, reading the menu on the table they were shown to. "How did you find this place?"

"Someone I met at the conference recommended it. In the last few days I've been here more often than I care to admit."

Kate ordered maple bacon pancakes, and Eva asked for blueberry and an espresso, needing a healthy dose of caffeine to ward off her hangover. The first sip had her sighing in contentment, and she relaxed in her chair.

"How far away do you live from here?"

"About an hour and a half."

"So two hours for a normal person?"

"I don't speed that much."

"Tell that to my blood pressure, which rises significantly when you're behind the wheel."

"Funny, I feel the same whenever I'm in your car."

"Rude."

Eva set down her empty cup. "You don't want a ride to the airport, then?"

"I won't turn one down," Kate said, her grin cheeky, and Eva rolled her eyes as their food was placed in front of them. The pancakes were delicious, the sharpness of the blueberries sweetened by the syrup she'd poured over them.

Once they'd eaten, they returned to the hotel parking lot. "Last chance to hail a cab," Eva said, as she opened the trunk of her Mercedes for Kate's suitcase.

"That'd be just as bad for my blood pressure."

"You are ridiculous."

"So is your taste in radio stations." Kate fiddled with the dials, and Eva allowed it, even though the one she settled on was terrible.

The drive to O'Hare was only around twenty minutes, but it was long enough for Kate to doze off, her cheek pressed to the passenger side window when Eva pulled up to departures.

"Wake up." Eva prodded Kate in the side. "You are awful company."

"Please, I am delightful."

Eva got out of the car to hug Kate good-bye. "Thank you for this weekend, it's been fun."

"Yeah, it has. Don't be a stranger, okay?"

"I won't," Eva promised. "I hope you and Dan manage to work things out."

"Thanks. I'll see you soon." Kate squeezed Eva one last time before grabbing the handle of her bag. Eva watched until she melted into the crowd and then got back into her car for the long drive home.

The TV was playing when Eva arrived, her mother sitting with her beloved Netflix, a pair of knitting needles in her hands. Franklin bounded over to greet Eva like he hadn't seen her in weeks.

"Hi, sweetheart. Did you have a good night?"

"I did. Were you okay without me?" Eva knew her mother had probably loved it. Eva tried not to be too overbearing, knowing how much her mother valued her independence, but sometimes it was hard.

"Franklin and I were fine."

"I'm going to hop in the shower."

"Good. You smell like a brewery."

Eva chuckled, not doubting it. She'd had a lot to drink, but she'd had fun.

Not as much fun as Kate had at her expense, Eva remembered, stepping out of the shower to find a notification waiting for her. Sighing, Eva opened the app, fully intending to delete the damn thing, but curiosity had her opening the message thread, instead.

Cute dog, the message, from MollyCule13, read. *What's his name?*

For a moment, Eva was startled. Had someone hacked her phone? Could they see the Spaniel staring hopefully at her from the foot of the bed?

And then she remembered—Kate had used a photo of him as her profile picture.

Well, it wasn't a 'hi', but it still wasn't terribly original.

Is that the best you can come up with?

Eva typed, fingers moving before she could stop them. She didn't expect a reply, but the buttons indicating typing popped up along the bottom of her screen mere seconds after she'd pressed Send.

Oh, you want a cheesy opening line? All right. We're not socks, but I think we'd make a great pair. If I could rearrange the alphabet, I'd put 'U' and 'I' together. I'm no photographer, but I can picture you and I together.

Eva shook her head as the messages kept coming, each one worse than the last.

Do you have a pre-made list of these? Eva wrote, unable to ignore the fact she was smiling down at her phone.

No. I'm using Google. Want me to keep going?

Eva snorted despite herself. *I think I've heard enough.*

Have I earned your cute dog's name yet?

Eva pursed her lips—she was supposed to be deleting the damn thing, not entertaining random strangers online. And yet—maybe Kate was right. What harm could it do?

It's Franklin.

Franklin? That's an unusual name.

That was a response Eva was used to getting. Though considering some people named their pets Princess Tinkerbell the Third, Eva didn't think there was anything wrong with Franklin.

It's after Rosalind Franklin.

I've never known a dog named after a scientist before. Is she your favorite one?

Eva raised an eyebrow. She'd never been asked that before, and she certainly hadn't expected to be asked that on a dating app, of all places.

I've never really thought about it, but I suppose so. I admire her for preserving in a difficult environment. For having her work scrutinized. And for being robbed of a Nobel Prize, and the recognition of the crucial role she held in the discovery of DNA structure.

Aware she was straying close to giving a lecture, Eva ended with a question: *Who's yours?*

Marie Curie, came the quick reply. *For similar reasons. I didn't name my cat after her, though. Maybe I should change her name?*

From what?

Hades. Attached was a photo of a grumpy-looking black cat, and Eva smiled.

Don't change it. It suits her. Besides, I wouldn't want Franklin to feel like he wasn't special.

Me either. He's gorgeous. As, I'm sure, is his owner.

Eva shook her head. Molly clearly thought of herself as a smooth talker.

You're not getting a photo out of me that easily.

Who says I was trying to? Isn't that the fun of this thing? Getting to know someone without knowing what they look like?

I suppose. You're going to have to work hard, though. I value my privacy. Something of an understatement to those that knew her.

I've always liked a challenge. How about this: we don't give out any identifying details whatsoever. That way, we don't let any outside influences color the way things develop between us.

It was an intriguing offer. Just enough to pique Eva's interest, just enough to have her second-guessing her decision to delete it. *All right*, she wrote, smile still firmly in place. *I'm in.*

Lily smiled at the message thread with QueenElsa35. She hadn't talked to many people on the app—hadn't used it much at all, in truth, only scrolling through when she was bored—and this was the first time Lily felt like it was going well.

Too often, conversation faded after the initial hello, both counterparts scrambling for something to say, something to catch the others' attention— made even more difficult when there wasn't much public information on some of the profiles.

But this one seemed to be going well, if she did say so herself, and pulling Lily's attention away from the term papers open on her coffee table, calling out to be marked.

Big Disney fan?

Lily hoped her replies weren't too fast, that she didn't seem too eager— and hated herself for second-guessing things the second she'd sent the message.

That was what Lily hated the most about dating: the uncertainty of it all. At least talking to people online omitted the crushing feeling of rejection when someone turned you down face-to-face. With this, only Lily would know if things went terribly wrong.

Disney?

Your username. Elsa? From Frozen?

Lily wasn't much of a Disney fan herself, but even she knew that movie, advertised to within an inch of its life a few years ago.

Oh. No, came the reply. *My friend set this profile up for me and thought it was a hilarious username for me.*

Lily was intrigued.

Because?

She calls me an ice queen.

And are you?

It's not an inaccurate statement.

Strange, what you could decide about another person by the words they strung together. Elsa seemed well-educated—especially in the sciences, if her comments on Rosalind Franklin were anything to go by. Maybe on the older side, though her age wasn't listed.

I bet I could get you to melt.

Strange, too, how confident Lily could feel, typing on a screen. Lily was never so self-assured when trying to chat up women in real life, but with the protection not having to look them in the eye offered, she felt invincible.

You are full of lines, aren't you?

Oh, I'm just getting started, Lily replied, smile pulling at the corners of her mouth. *Unless you'd like me to stop.*
Lily held her breath as the bubbles appeared, hoping Elsa wasn't about to turn her down.

When I opened this app, I was going to delete it, read the message, and Lily felt her stomach plummet. *But I suppose I can stick around. See you make a fool out of yourself for a while longer. I should warn you, though: I'm not looking for anything serious.*

What are you looking for?

I don't know.

Well, Lily typed, feeling lighter than she had in a long, long time. *How about we start out as friends, and see how things go from there?*

I suppose I could use a few more of those.

Chapter 8

"Can someone give me one difference between covalent and ionic bonding?" Lily glanced at her watch—two minutes until the bell was due to go. "Quickly, please." Her gaze darted around the room, waiting for someone to take pity on her. She was unsurprised to see a hand on the front row shoot into the air. "Yes, Imogen?"

"Atoms share electrons in a covalent bond. Ionic bonds transfer electrons."

"Thank you." The bell rang, excitement thrumming in the air, and Lily's voice was nearly drowned out by the sound of her students packing away their things. "Remember you'll have an exam next week!"

Her room emptied in seconds, everyone eager to get down to the football field or to get ready for the Homecoming dance, and Lily breathed out a sigh once they were gone. Work was starting to pile up, and she was looking forward to a relaxing bath at home before getting on with it.

Lily grabbed her phone from her desk drawer and pulled up her thread with Elsa. She tended to shoot her a message when she was done with her workday, her evenings now incomplete without a conversation with Elsa—no matter how random.

Would you rather twenty butterflies appear every time you sneeze, or an angry raccoon appear every time you cough?

The reply came quickly, and Lily chuckled.

What kind of question is that?

Well, I've got to keep you on your toes, Lily wrote. *Can't have everything be serious.*

And that's where your mind goes? Should I be concerned?

Nah. And you haven't answered.

A knock sounded on her door, and Lily tore her attention away from her phone to see Macie hovering in the doorway. Another student Lily didn't recognize stood at her elbow. Lily beckoned them both inside. "We got approval!" Macie said, waving a piece of paper in front of her, and Lily's lips curved into a smile to match the ones on their faces. Relief flooded through her—she'd been dreading the thought of another battle with David had he turned them down and was glad she hadn't fucked it up.

Lily might have to watch her back, might have to deal with parental opposition once they were up and running, and they'd no doubt be scrutinized to high hell, but still. It was progress.

"That's great news! What's next?"

"We're going to start putting together posters to put around school so people know when we're meeting. Are you still okay to do every Thursday?"

"Absolutely. How many members do you have so far?"

"Six, but we're hoping to get a few more." It was the most animated Lily had seen Macie, her hands gesticulating wildly as she spoke. "Sara is one. She helped me set everything up." Lily glanced toward her friend. "And we have a couple of juniors on board, too."

"Good. Let me know if you need help with anything."

"We will. Thank you again for helping us do this."

"You don't need to thank me, Macie. I'm happy to do it. Are either of you going to do the dance?"

They both shook their heads. "Dances aren't our thing."

They weren't Lily's either, and she was glad she had another few months before she'd be forced into chaperoning. "Have a good weekend then, and I'll see you next week for our first meeting."

"Bye!" They turned to skip away and nearly ran straight into Mei, who deftly stepped out of the way.

"Knock knock," Mei said, perching on the front desk of Lily's room. "What was that about? No student has ever been that happy leaving my class after school."

"Our GSA has been approved."

"Sweet. Look at you, already setting up extracurriculars. You're making the rest of us look bad. Alisha's going to start using you as an example to tell me I'm slacking."

"Hardly. I haven't had to do anything yet. They did all the paperwork themselves, and I think my supervisory duties are just going to be letting them use my room for meetings and making sure they don't argue."

"Still. It's cool that you're doing it. They need a safe space, and I can't think of anyone better to run it than you."

"Why? 'Cause I'm gay?"

"I was going to say because you're kind and welcoming, but that helps too." Mei grinned, and Lily rolled her eyes. "You coming to the game? We're going to be late."

Lily's nose wrinkled. "It's not my idea of fun."

"Where's your school spirit?"

"I'd prefer to show it in ways other than watching high schoolers trying to throw a ball as far as possible."

Mei snorted. "Come on, it won't be that bad. What are you going to do instead?"

Lily glanced toward the huge pile of work on her desk.

"Nope, no working on a Friday night."

"But—"

"No buts." Mei marched over and seized her wrist. "At least watch the first quarter."

"Fine." Lily shrugged on her coat and let Mei drag her from the room. She'd never been down to the football field, and they followed the steady trickle of latecomers past the tennis courts to the bleachers, the field illuminated by floodlights though the sun had yet to set. Andrew waved at them from a seat near the front, and Mei and Lily squeezed into the space beside him.

"Hey, Andrew. How's it going?"

"Not bad." He tightened the scarf around his neck before digging his hands into his pockets. "Better once the night is over."

"You mean you're not looking forward to spending the night with me?" Mei feigned outrage. "How rude."

"It's more the dance I object to," he said, grinning. "Nothing to do with your company."

"I promise to try and make it entertaining."

"At least you aren't stuck with Eva," Lily said, thinking Winter Formal would be much more fun if she had Mei as company.

Mei gave her a gentle pat on the back.

Shouts rang out as the cheerleaders took to the field, and Lily glanced around the stands. It was a sea of the emerald-green school colors, the crowd chanting along with the cheerleaders.

Lily's breath fogged in the air. "Is the team any good?"

"They're all right," Andrew said. "Not going to win any championships, but they're not at the bottom."

Lily recognized a few of the cheerleaders and some of the team from her classes—by face, if not by name. It at least gave her something to watch, because she didn't know the rules well enough to follow what was happening. She copied the reactions of those around her, cheering and booing at what she hoped were the right moments.

"See, it's not so bad, is it?" Mei said after Greenfield scored their first touchdown. "Admit it, you're having fun."

"I'd be having more fun if I was relaxing in a bath right now."

"I take back what I said before about you being kind and welcoming." Mei knocked Lily's shoulder with her own. "Is Eva rubbing off on you?"

Lily threw her a look, and Mei grinned.

"Any plans for the weekend?" Lily was eager to change the subject. "Are you seeing James again?"

"For dinner and a movie."

"I'm glad it's going well. Now I'm going to be the only single one when we go out for drinks."

"I've done my time—it's someone else's turn," Mei said. "Have you not had any luck with the app?"

Shit. Lily had left her phone on her desk, abandoning Elsa mid-conversation. Hopefully she'd be forgiving. "I've messaged a couple of people, but only one of interest."

"Oh yeah? Tell me about her."

"Not much to tell." Not without sounding crazy. Lily knew what brand of cereal Elsa ate in the morning, but not her real name. "She takes the whole anonymous thing seriously."

"Ah, so she's mysterious."

"A closed book," Lily said, although she'd managed to crack open a few of the pages. And she couldn't deny it being part of the thrill for her. "I doubt it'll ever go anywhere, but at least it gives me something to do when I'm home alone."

A loud cheer cut through their conversation as Greenfield scored another touchdown, and Lily smiled, enjoying herself more than she thought she would. She'd rarely gone to her own school's games when she'd been younger, and while it was strange to be on the other side of things, it was fun.

Starting to lose feeling in her feet, Lily ducked out at halftime, waving good-bye to Mei and Andrew before making her way back to her classroom. Night had fallen, and only a few windows in the school were alight.

Her phone sat where she'd left it, and she felt a stab of guilt when she saw a message had been sent over an hour ago. Lily hadn't realized she'd stayed at the game so long.

A raccoon would be easier to deal with, I suppose.

Even though it's angry?

Lily packed away her things as she waited for a reply—her bath was calling out to her, and she'd spent far too many hours in her classroom that week. Her phone buzzed as she was locking the door behind her.

You'd rather have a horde of butterflies flying around your head?

A horde? How many times a day do you sneeze?

More than I cough.

Lily chuckled, drawing her jacket tighter around her body as she stepped outside. In the distance, she heard cheers from the football field—the game must be back on.

Looking forward to the weekend? Lily typed as she made her way to her car. She knew she was. Christmas break couldn't come fast enough.

The parts I won't be spending at my desk, yes.

Not for the first time, Lily wondered what Elsa did. It could be anything—there were dozens of jobs that involved taking work home. She could be a lawyer, or an IT expert. Hell, she could even be a teacher like Lily. Wouldn't that be weird?

Ah, yes, I forgot. A queen's work is never done.

The response was nothing but a string of middle finger emojis, and Lily laughed as she slid behind the wheel.

"Don't forget your essays on the history of the atom are due next week!" Lily called over the rustling of jackets and bags as her students packed away at the sound of the bell. "Late submissions automatically get a zero."

Once they were gone, she hurried to the teacher's lounge with her coffee mug, in need of some caffeine to make it to the end of her first GSA meeting after a late night of exam marking. Rainbow posters were plastered periodically along the hallway, reminding people of the date, and Lily wondered what kind of turnout they were going to get.

A relatively small one, by the looks of the group hovering outside of her door when she returned. Macie was at the forefront, and Lily smiled as she ushered them inside. Five in total, but more could be on the way.

Two turned up a few minutes later, flushed and out of breath. "Sorry we're late," one of them said, tall with a shock of jet-black hair. "Math let out late."

"It's all right, come in, take a seat." Lily leaned back against her desk and studied the group sitting in front of her. "I'm Miss Cross, for those of you I haven't met yet. I've volunteered my room and my time, but this club is all down to Macie and Sara, and they're in charge here." Lily glanced toward Macie, whose cheeks tinged pink. "I can be as involved or uninvolved as you want me to be. I can't leave you unsupervised, but I can sit and pretend I can't hear a thing if that would make you all more comfortable."

A beat of silence, all seven of them glancing at one another, waiting for someone to speak up, clearly not used to a teacher letting them make their own decisions.

"Seeing as our whole message is to be inclusive, it wouldn't be fair of us to exclude you, Miss Cross," Macie said eventually, and the rest of the group nodded.

"Okay, then. What would you like to do today?"

"I thought we could start with introductions." Macie glanced at the folder she'd brought with her, spine straightening. Lily hadn't thought of Macie as a natural leader, but she seemed to be growing in confidence with every passing minute. "I'll start. I'm Macie, I'm a sophomore, I'm a cisgender girl, I identify as a lesbian and my pronouns are she/her."

"I'm Sara, also a sophomore, cisgender girl with she/her pronouns. I identify as bisexual."

The kid who had come late from math class spoke next. "Mark, junior, cis male, he/him, and I'm gay."

"I'm Hannah. Junior. My pronouns are they/them, and I identify as a non-binary lesbian," said the other latecomer.

"Hi, I'm Kelly. She/her. I'm a freshman, cis bisexual girl and I also identify as asexual."

"Jordan. Also a freshman. I identify as non-binary and use they/them pronouns, and I'm pansexual."

Lily made a mental note of everyone's names and pronouns as they went around the group, trying to come up with a way to identify them all. Jordan's hair was buzzed short and dyed a brilliant shade of blue. Kelly's auburn hair, scraped into a ponytail, fell down to her waist. Hannah had a streak of pink through their blonde hair. Lily repeated their names in her head in an effort not to forget them.

She recognized the final member of the group from her honors chemistry class. Charlotte was one of Lily's quietest students, usually sitting huddled in the back corner of the room, and Lily didn't know if she'd ever heard her speak before. The response to Lily asking if she was all right was usually a quick nod, but Charlotte always scored highly on every homework. "I-I'm a sophomore. Most…most people know me as Charlotte, but I've started to ask my friends to call me Jude." Jude took a deep breath. "My pronouns are he/him. I identify as trans and pansexual."

Macie gave Jude a pat on the back, and he managed a weak smile. Lily felt awful for misgendering Jude all this time, even though she hadn't known any better.

Seven pairs of eyes turned expectantly to her, and Lily realized it was her turn to introduce herself. "You already know I'm Miss Cross, and I'm a teacher." That earned her a few chuckles. "My pronouns are she/her, I am a cisgender woman, and I…I'm a lesbian." She'd debated how open to be with them, but Lily wasn't interested in hiding her identity in an environment that was supposed to be supportive. It was worth it for the wide-eyed looks on their faces, for that sense of familiarity.

"Now that we all know more about each other," Macie said, attention returning to her folder. "I thought we could start discussing what we want to achieve over the next year. Brainstorm ideas, set goals, that kind of thing. See if there are any events or campaigns we want to be a part of."

Lily let them chat among themselves for a while, settling behind her desk and pitching in when they asked her for advice. They seemed like a good group of kids with a lot of ideas, and she couldn't wait to see what they managed to do over the next few months.

Once the hour was up, they started heading for the door, a bounce in their steps and a smile on their faces, exchanging social media information so they could set up a group online.

"Jude?" Lily called out before he could reach the door. "Could I have a quick word?"

"O-okay. I'll catch up with you later," Jude said to Macie and Sara. He approached Lily's desk with his head down, eyes fixed on his sneakers. "Am I in trouble?"

"Of course not. I just…I realize that I've been using the wrong name and pronouns for you in class, which might have made you uncomfortable."

"Oh." Jude lifted his head. "Um, it's okay. There was no way for you to have known."

"No, but there could be. There are procedures in place for students who want to change their name. I could kickstart that process if you'd like me to."

Jude chewed at his bottom lip. "I…I don't think I'm ready for that yet. I haven't even told my parents." His gaze fell to the floor again, and Lily's heart clenched to see him look so defeated.

"That's okay. There's no timeline on coming out—you do it whenever you feel comfortable and safe, and it doesn't matter how long it takes you. But if there comes a point where you do want your name changed, let me know and I'll make sure it happens. And I won't out you by calling you Jude in class, either. I will try and limit my pronoun uses for you, though."

When Jude raised his head there were tears in his eyes, blinked swiftly away. "Thank you. It means a lot."

"If there's anything else you need, let me know."

Jude nodded before hurrying from the room. Happy with the way her evening had gone, Lily's good mood faded when she glanced at the pile of work she'd neglected. She had just two days to grade the pile of exams—and she hadn't even started yet.

If Lily stayed for an hour or two longer—without the distractions that awaited her at home—she could get the majority of them done and finish the rest tomorrow afternoon.

But first, she needed more caffeine.

Lily dreaded to think what her doctor would say if he knew her daily level of coffee consumption.

She made her way to the teacher's longue for a refill and found Eva standing by the machine.

"What are you still doing here?" Lily said before she could stop herself, and Eva raised an eyebrow.

"I didn't realize there was a time limit on how long I could stay for."

"There's not. You're just…not usually here that late. That's all."

"Are you tracking my movements? Do I need to get a restraining order?" Eva poured her coffee and made no effort to move, hands curling around her mug and blocking Lily's access to her beloved caffeine. "I didn't realize

I needed a reason to be here after hours," Eva said, voice a low drawl. "Do you have one?"

"I do." Lily folded her arms across her chest. "I'm running a GSA on Thursdays. Have you not seen the posters?"

Eva tilted her head to one side as if Lily were a problem she was trying to solve. "Why?"

"Because some kids asked me to and I think it's important for LGBTQIA+ kids to have a safe space in school when they might not have one at home. It's especially important here in light of what we saw happen to Macie."

"A GSA isn't going to magically solve homophobia."

"Well, obviously not, but that doesn't mean we shouldn't have one. It could help. I know it would've helped me a lot when I was in high school." Lily watched understanding flicker across Eva's face. "Anyway, I don't expect you to get it, so—"

"Why's that?"

"Um. Just that…you know." Lily waved a hand toward her, knowing she was digging herself into a hole and not sure how to stop or pull herself out. "You know what? Never mind."

"Oh no, please continue. Or should I fill in the blanks?" Eva raised one of her sculpted eyebrows. "I can't possibly understand the impact of homophobia because I'm straight, is that it? Surely the first thing you should be teaching in your little club is to not make assumptions, hmm?"

Lily's stomach lurched. Was Eva saying what Lily thought she was saying? Had Lily read her wrong? Not that Eva was easy to read in any respect, but Lily had never gotten any kind of vibe from her. "I…" Lily's mouth opened, but she had no idea what to say. "I, um, I didn't realize."

"That's the thing, isn't it? There is no way to know. Maybe that should be your next topic of discussion." Eva brushed past her, freeing up the coffee machine, but Lily didn't feel like drinking anything anymore.

What the hell had just happened?

Eva dropped into her desk chair with a huff.

She hadn't planned on outing herself to Lily Cross across the teacher's lounge on an otherwise quiet Thursday evening, but she'd had to pick a fight, hadn't she? Eva couldn't control herself around Lily, she should know to keep her head down and not engage, and yet…

And yet she hadn't, but instead had let herself get annoyed about Lily assuming she was straight, even though she'd never once revealed anything so personal at work. Even at Georgetown, Kate had been the only exception.

Eva glanced at the clock hanging on the rear wall of her classroom. Five thirty. She didn't have to pick up her mother from Angela and Tom's until seven, and Eva refused to let her confrontation with Lily get in the way of the work slowly piling up around her. Eva had earmarked this time to get ahead while she wasn't needed at home, and she wasn't going to let it go to waste.

Focusing her attention on finalizing her lessons for the next few weeks, Eva pushed all thoughts of Lily Cross from her mind. Which became impossible to do when the woman knocked on Eva's door.

Eva bit her tongue, aware of the possibility that a fuck off might slip out were she not careful. "Can I help you?"

Lily wrung her hands as she slipped into the room and closed the door behind her. Eva opened her mouth to protest, but then footsteps sounded in the hall, and Eva understood. The janitors were some of the biggest gossips in the school—Eva didn't want to be overheard either.

"I wanted to apologize." Lily took a few halting steps forward, but paused shy of Eva's desk, plucking at a loose thread of her sweater. "I shouldn't have assumed anything, and I'm sorry."

Eva kept her on the hook for a moment, lips pursed. "Okay." Meant to be a dismissal, her gaze returned to her laptop screen.

Lily didn't take the hint. "And I…I won't tell anyone."

"Tell anyone what?"

Lily's laugh was nervous. "Right. Cause I'd never out someone. Especially not…well. I know you're a private person, so. I wouldn't."

"Yes, I believe we've established that."

"Who'd have thought you and I had something in common?"

Eva pulled off her glasses, and Lily turned fuzzy around the edges. "Certainly not me." If Lily expected comradery, or a shift in Eva's demeanor, she was sorely mistaken.

Why would it? Lily was still infuriating, still invading Eva's space at every opportunity.

Which she was doing right then, lingering when surely there was nothing else to say, her eyes on Eva's face. "Was there something else?"

"Um, no, I guess not." Lily buried her hands in the pockets of her slacks and turned toward the door. "Goodnight, Eva."

Eva didn't return the greeting, slipping her glasses back onto her nose as she watched Lily leave. The door clicked shut as Lily's footsteps retreated down the hall, and Eva's attention returned to her lesson plan.

One more, and then she was free.

Half an hour later, she locked the door of her classroom, twirling her keyring around her fingers as she made her way to the exit. The light in Lily's room was still on, and Eva didn't know why but she found herself glancing inside through the glass panes of the door.

Lily sat behind her desk chewing on a pen, music playing loudly enough for Eva to hear it in the hall. She couldn't make out the words, only the thump of the bass, a world away from the Vivaldi Eva had been listening to when Lily had interrupted her. A frown crossed Lily's face, her head shaking as she read the page in front of her, and she scrawled something furiously with the pen.

The movements were familiar to Eva from when she was grading, because some of the answers they managed to come up with made her wonder if she'd been in the room teaching them all at.

Another thing they had in common, Eva mused, though their similarities were vastly outnumbered by their differences.

Blonde hair fell in front of Lily's eyes, and when she raised a hand to brush it away, she glanced toward the door, as though she could feel Eva's presence. Eva ducked away, her heart thumping in her chest, praying she hadn't been caught, because what on earth would Lily think?

Nothing good...why would she? Eva had made sure not to give Lily any reason to.

Chapter 9

LILY STRETCHED HER ARMS OVER her head and smothered a yawn. Just one more exam to grade, and then she'd finally be finished with the pile of papers that had been sitting on the corner of her desk for the past week.

Opening the first page, Lily frowned. Half of the questions hadn't been answered—and most of those that had bore the same three words: *I don't know*. Lily glanced at the name on the front of the paper and sighed.

She should have known.

Carly had been quiet as a mouse since moving to the front of her classroom, but Lily had noticed her attention waning in class, her reluctance to verbally answer any questions—even for candy—extending to exam papers. Lily had tried talking to her after class, offering tutoring sessions and pointing Carly in the direction of resources to help bolster her understanding of what they were studying, hoping she'd see an improvement on this exam, but Carly had barely scored any marks at all.

Students in an honors class required a certain GPA to continue, and Carly was close to toeing the line. It was time for Lily to take more drastic steps to intervene, because there was no way she was letting Carly fail out of her class.

Lily would never give up on a student without pursuing every possible avenue.

Alisha was Lily's first port of call. She smiled and waved Lily inside when she knocked on the door of her classroom. "Something on your mind? You don't usually look so serious."

"I'm worried about a student." Lily held out Carly's exam, letting Alisha leaf through the pages. "I don't know what to do to help her. I've tried offering her extra help, asking her if there's anything I can do, anything she needs, but...I don't get much back."

"You won't," Alisha said, twirling a pen between her fingers. "Carly's a unique kid. I don't know how much of her file you've read...?"

"All of it." Lily taught a lot of kids, but she did her best to familiarize herself with anything that could help her teach them better. Some had ADHD, some had memory problems that meant things like homework and lab instructions needed to be repeated several times, others had medical issues that sometimes required sensitivity. And then there were the kids like Carly, the ones who had been mistreated and abused by the people who were supposed protect them. "I know she has problems with men, and sometimes with authority, but she's never shown that with me. She keeps her head down, for the most part."

"Because she doesn't want to cause any trouble."

Lily remembered overhearing Carly's conversation with Eva in the hall. That sounded right, but how could Lily assure Carly she wasn't like some of the other teachers she'd come across?

And how the hell had Eva, of all people, gained Carly's trust?

But then Lily thought of Carly's attitude that day with Denny—quick to anger, reacting first and thinking later—the way she always seemed to keep to herself, and maybe it made sense after all.

And maybe Eva had the answers Lily was seeking.

Lily just hoped Eva would be willing to share them.

"I think I have an idea," Lily said, beginning to back toward Alisha's door. She hoped Eva was still around. "Thanks for your help."

"I don't feel like I really did anything," Alisha said with a chuckle. "But you're welcome, all the same."

Lily breathed a sigh of relief when she noticed the lights were still on in Eva's classroom. She knocked on the door, and Eva glanced away from her laptop, surprise flickering across her face when she saw Lily.

"Can I talk to you?"

Eva waved her inside. "If you must. What's wrong?"

"It's Carly. I don't know how to get through to her."

"And you think I do?" Eva leaned back in her chair, tapping a pen against her thigh as she observed Lily hovering at the front of her room.

"I've seen you with her. She listens to you, and you seem to understand her. If there's something I could be doing better, some way I can bring out the best in her I'd like to know."

Eva looked delighted to have Lily come to her for advice, and Lily tried her best to ignore the gleeful expression on her face. "What's the problem?"

"She's struggling. Barely pays attention in class, does the bare minimum on her homework. On the latest exam she wrote *I don't know* for most of the questions. She's one bad grade away from being kicked out of the class."

Eva frowned. "That can't be right. She was my brightest last year."

"See for yourself." Lily placed the exam on Eva's desk, watching her frown deepen as she flicked through the pages.

"This isn't like her. Does she ask for help?"

"No, and she doesn't want it when I offer it, either. It's like she doesn't care. I don't know how to change that."

"Leave it with me," Eva said, thoughtful look on her face. "I'll have a word with her and see if I can help."

"Okay. Thank you."

Had they just managed to be civil for an entire conversation?

Eva's phone buzzed two times in quick succession in her lap.

It earned her a curious look from her mother, sitting beside her on the couch, a bowl of popcorn nestled between them, and Franklin curled up on her knee.

"Someone's popular tonight," Eva's mother said, turning her attention away from the TV screen. "You've been on that phone a lot lately."

A lot seemed like an exaggeration. Sure, Eva had been using it more often than usual, thanks to a certain app. Not that Eva was using it as intended. She didn't scroll through any profiles, only ever using it to message Molly. And it wasn't that frequent—a message here and there every couple of days—so she didn't know how her mother had noticed.

"It's Kate," Eva said, because if her mother ever found out about the app, Eva would never hear the end of it. She want to know every single detail about the mysterious MollyCule13.

Thankfully, Eva's mother accepted the lie without question, turning her attention back to the screen as Eva turned hers to the phone in her hand.

The first message was a picture of a black cat curled into a tight ball in a bathroom sink, one green eye staring at the camera.

I spent an hour looking for her. Thought she'd managed to escape. Want to swap pets?

Not really, Eva replied, snapping a quick picture of a sleeping Franklin and sending it in the message thread. *He's keeping me warm.*

He's adorable. Mine is a little shit. I just had to wash my hands in the shower because she refused to move.

That's what you get for having a cat.

I can't get a dog with the hours I work.

Eva refrained from asking the obvious question, because it risked breaking their golden rule. She liked thinking of Molly as a puzzle that needed to be solved, liked trying to work out little things about her from the snippets she revealed each day, sharpening the fuzzy impression Eva had of her in her mind.

Like the photo of the cat. A cursory glance didn't reveal much, but a second look showed Molly favored bright decoration—the tiles behind the sink were light blue, the collar on the cat yellow, and the toothbrush sitting beside the tap bright pink. She also seemed to be messy. A sliver of the bathtub was visible, the side of it covered with products—a stark contrast to Eva's bathroom, where everything was tucked neatly away.

Eva glanced at the photo she'd sent of Franklin and wondered what conclusions Molly might draw about her. That she was a neat-freak, the couch covered in a gray throw to protect it from dust, scratches and spills. The scant few inches of the floor on the photo were clear of any obstacles, the edge of the coffee table containing only a coaster and one of her mom's knitting patterns.

It showed her legs, half-hidden by Franklin's furry body, and clad in the blue sweats she wore to lounge around the house in. Sweats Eva wouldn't be caught dead in outside—sweats anyone who knew Eva would be shocked to find out she owned—so perhaps the photos were misleading, as well as informative.

Not everything was always as it seemed, Eva reminded herself. Molly could be anyone. And Eva shouldn't become too attached to a ghost, no matter how fun talking to her might be.

What are you doing?

Watching Star Wars.

The new ones?

The old ones. Though Eva hadn't seen the new ones, either. *My mother tried to get me to watch them when I was younger, but I wasn't interested. I promised to give them a try. She thinks it's a tragedy I've never seen them.*

You've never seen them? Molly seemed as outraged as everyone else always was when Eva admitted that fact. *That is a tragedy. I don't know if I can continue talking to you.*

Eva rolled her eyes, hoping her mother wasn't paying too much attention to her reaction. Eva glanced up, but she was still staring, transfixed, at the screen, and Eva realized she had no idea what was happening in the movie. She was sure she'd never seen that character before.

Oops.

Oh well. There was nothing she could do about it now—she wasn't going to ask her mother to rewind, unwilling to risk being asked what had Eva so distracted.

I never took you for a movie snob, Eva typed, accepting she still wouldn't be able to contribute to a conversation about *Star Wars* in the future and tuning out the sound of dueling lightsabers.

It's a classic.

Eva bit back a scoff. *No, a classic is something like Gone with the Wind.*

Ah, you like boring movies. Gotcha.

It's not boring!

It's like four hours long.

We're going to have to agree to disagree.

I agree you have terrible taste in movies, yes.

Eva snorted, trying to fight the smile pulling at the edges of her lips. Despite her reservations, she couldn't deny Molly made her feel happier than she had in a long time.

She hoped like hell it didn't come back to bite her on the ass.

Eva was happy to see Carly in attendance at her next science club.

It would give Eva an opportunity to raise the issues Lily had brought to her the other day, a chance to dig down to the root of the issue and find out if Carly needed some extra help and support.

"Welcome, everyone," Eva said, once most of the seats in her class were filled. "I've got a couple of activities planned for you today. As you can tell from the microscopes around the room, we'll be diving into cell biology today. First things first—do we have anyone in here who's squeamish at the sight of blood?" A few pairs of wide eyes stared back at her, but no one raised their hand. "How about any vegetarians or vegans?" Two hands shot into the air, and Eva nodded.

"Today you're going to be making blood smears. These are used to look for abnormalities in blood cells. If you're interested in working in a pathology lab in a hospital, this will be something you'll be carrying out frequently. Now, I didn't want to try and get permission slips to let you stab your own fingers for your own blood, so I've gotten some sheep's blood for you to use, instead. If that's going to be a problem for anyone"—her gaze flickered to the two who had raised their hands—"then let me know, and we can find something else for you to do."

Neither of them came forward after she'd given out the instruction sheets, so Eva let them loose, trying her best to ignore the squeals of disgust as she handed out small vials of blood to each pair.

"The sheet says a drop, Mo," Eva said when she saw one microscope slide dripping onto her desk. "How many did you put on? Ten? Clean it up. Now."

Mo scurried off, and Eva was glad to see they seemed to be the only group who couldn't follow the simple instructions.

Eva watched upturned noses turn into fascination when they looked down the microscope lens, some of them identifying the different types of cells without her assistance. It was what she loved the most about teaching—taking something seemingly foreign and making it accessible, watching interest bloom across their faces, feeding into the insatiable curiosity that a lot of kids held.

Eva wished she could do more lab work in her regular lessons, but the syllabus—and her budget—didn't allow it.

"Who can tell me the different types of white blood cells?" Eva said, once they'd all taken turns viewing the slides they'd made. Carly's was the first hand in the air.

"Lymphocytes, monocytes, neutrophils, eosinophils and basophils," she said, without hesitation, and this was the girl Eva was used to, one brimming with enthusiasm and knowledge, not one who was unfocused and apathetic. At least, Eva mused, it meant there was hope. Carly was still in there, somewhere. Eva just needed to find a way to help Lily bring her out.

Eva kept Carly behind once she'd wrapped up.

"Did you enjoy that?" Eva said, though she already knew the answer—there was a spark in Carly's eyes she hadn't seen since her biology classes last year.

"Yeah."

"So, tell me, then—what's going on in your chemistry class?"

Carly's face darkened. "What do you mean?"

"Don't play dumb with me." Eva leaned back in her desk chair, her gaze trained on Carly's face. "Teachers talk sometimes. I know you're struggling. What I don't know is why." Carly had always seemed herself in homeroom, but Eva knew that didn't mean everything was fine. She was no stranger to putting on a brave face to fool everyone else into thinking you were okay. "Talk to me. Is it something at home? Something in school? An issue with Miss Cross in particular?"

Carly stayed silent, and Eva sighed. No matter—Carly might be stubborn, but so was Eva. She could wait her out.

Eventually, an answer came.

"It's not Miss Cross. She's…way too peppy and tries too hard, but she's not a bad teacher."

Eva's lips twitched at the description of Lily.

"And everything's fine at home. My mom's boyfriend is still around, but he's growing on me. There's still time for him to pack up and leave like all the others do"—vulnerability flashed across Carly's face—"but there's nothing wrong."

"What is it, then?" Eva didn't believe for a second Carly would stop trying for no reason.

"I just…I don't get it." Carly ran a frustrated hand through her hair. "Biology was easy—and it was interesting—but chemistry is—it's boring and it's complicated and I feel like if I zone out for even one second than I'm completely lost. Sometimes it's like Miss Cross is speaking a foreign language, and I know she'd help me if I asked but it's been so long that it almost feels like it's too late." The words came out quickly, like they'd been building for a while. "And then what if she does spend time helping me and I still can't do it? What if I don't ever get it? At least if I don't try—"

"Then if you fail it's not because your best isn't good enough." Eva watched Carly's cheeks flush, shoulders sinking as she hunched in on herself, and sighed. "Do you still want to be a veterinarian?"

Carly's lip trembled. "Yeah, but I know I'm not good enough."

"Don't ever say something like that again," Eva said, voice so sharp Carly's head snapped up. "You are good enough. No matter what. And if you're willing to try, I know Miss Cross will help you get the chemistry grade you need. I know you're worried, but believe me when I say she won't give up on you." Eva might not have the highest opinion of Lily as a person, but she'd proven to be annoyingly determined when it came to trying to get Eva to like her. Eva saw no reason why she wouldn't apply that same determination to Carly's education. Lily hadn't had to come to Eva about Carly, after all. She could've let Carly flounder, flunk out of her class, but instead Lily had swallowed her pride and asked Eva for help.

Eva had a new-found respect for the woman.

"Okay." Carly fiddled with the strap of the bag on her shoulder, jaw set. "I'll go and talk to her."

"Do you want me to come with you?"

"No, it's okay. I should do this on my own." Carly slouched toward the door, and Eva watched her go, hoping she'd helped.

Eva's phone buzzed, drawing her attention. A message from Molly awaited her.

What's your favorite season?

Eva wondered if Molly had a list of questions stashed away somewhere. She seemed to have a new one each day. Yesterday had been about Eva's favorite book, the day before that her best vacation spot, before that, her earliest childhood memory.

Each time, she'd answered honestly. It was unlike Eva to offer up parts of herself—any part, no matter how innocuous—willingly, feeding Molly tidbits about her life. But then, maybe it wasn't so surprising. Since moving, her mother was the only person Eva had to talk to. It was nice to have someone else, much as Eva liked to insist she was fine on her own. It was easier for her to open up, too, when she was talking to a phone screen.

Winter, Eva typed, without thinking, and the dots appeared straight away. Realizing her mistake, she was quick to write a follow-up. *Don't you dare make another Frozen joke.*

The dots disappeared, then re-appeared.

You know me so well.

Eva felt a flutter of something in her chest. Did she? Certainly, Molly knew Eva better than most of the people around her, but that wasn't difficult. It was strange to think the same might be true in reverse. Did Molly have a hard time trusting, too?

Eva could ask, but that strayed into territory they'd yet to touch upon. Their conversations were light-hearted, fun, steering well clear of anything remotely serious. Which was part of the appeal, Eva supposed. This way, it was less real.

What's yours?

Fall. I like the color of the trees. The way they change. Plus, Halloween is awesome. I like scaring any kids that come knocking.

Me too. Much to her mother's disapproval. There was another thing to add to the ever-growing list she and Molly had in common.

Her phone buzzed again, but this time, it wasn't a message from Molly. It was a new like on her profile, and Eva quickly swiped the notification away, uninterested. She'd delete the app entirely if she had Molly's number, but she hadn't been brave enough to ask yet.

It felt too much like crossing a line, and Eva didn't want to ruin things. She liked talking to Molly too much, liked having another friend—a rarity, for her—and didn't want to do anything that might scare her away.

Which was dumb. She was getting too attached. Eva chastised herself as she slid her phone back into her pocket. She needed to stop overthinking.

If only it were so easy.

Lily blinked in surprise when Carly appeared in her doorway.

"Can I talk to you?"

"Of course, come in." Lily hadn't expected Eva to work her magic so soon. "What can I help you with?"

Carly shuffled to the front of Lily's room and paused, shifting from one foot to the other as she weighed up what she wanted to say. "I know I didn't do so great on the last exam. Or on anything else recently."

Lily waited for the rest of what Carly had to say, knowing it must have taken a lot for her to seek Lily out. She didn't want to push or shatter Carly's confidence.

"I know I've said I'm fine whenever you've asked, but…" Carly paused to take a deep breath. "I lied. Truth is, I don't get anything you've said for the last few weeks. Chemistry's hard." Carly glanced up, meeting Lily's gaze for the first time, vulnerability written across her face. "Did you…did you mean it when you said you'd help me?"

"Of course I did, Carly. I want you to succeed."

Carly nodded. "Okay. So could I come see you after school some days?"

"Would that help you?"

Carly's face creased into a frown, like she wasn't used to being asked what she wanted. "I-I think so."

"Okay. We can start tomorrow afternoon, if you like."

"Thanks, Miss Cross." Carly's gaze fell back to her shoes. "I really appreciate it."

"You don't have to thank me, Carly. I'm just doing my job."

From the look on Carly's face as she slipped through Lily's door, Lily suspected her fellow teachers might not be as willing to go above and beyond for the kids they taught.

The thought broke her heart.

Lily began to put some materials together that might help Carly's understanding. Their current topic—structure and principles of matter—wasn't the most complex they'd be covering over the course of the year, but it was an important one, forming the basis for the rest of the course.

A shadow fell over Lily, and somehow she wasn't surprised to see Eva when she looked away from her laptop screen.

"Carly come to see you?"

Lily hid a smile. It seemed Eva did have a caring side, after all—even if she did try hard to hide it.

"She did. I'm going to start offering her extra help after school."

"Good."

"Thank you," Lily said, before Eva had the chance to turn on her heel and stalk away, "for your help."

"I didn't do it for you."

"Right." There was the Eva that Lily knew so well. "Still."

Eva gave a curt nod, and Lily turned away when her laptop pinged with an e-mail notification, her good mood falling away as she read the subject line.

Great. Another complaint about the GSA.

"I thought only I brought that expression out of you."

Lily jumped at the sound of Eva's voice. She hadn't realized Eva was still there.

"You and asshole parents."

"What've you done? Had the audacity to give one of their little darlings a detention? Taught them Earth isn't flat and evolution is, in fact, real?" Eva arched an eyebrow, leaning against Lily's doorframe and looking like she belonged there.

"No. Dared to start a GSA." Lily pressed her fingers to her temples. "They've been coming in all week. People aren't happy."

"Fuck what other people think," Eva said. "You're doing something important for the kids. And they can't stop you from meeting."

"I know, but it doesn't make reading their e-mails any easier." Lily deleted most of them as soon as they came in, but she'd still seen enough things to make her wince.

"Forward the e-mails to me if you like—eviscerating some homophobes would be a lovely stress reliever."

"Offering to help me out twice in one day?" Lily leaned back in her chair, smile playing around the edges of her lips. "Wow. Are you feeling okay?"

Eva glared, but it didn't wipe away Lily's smile.

"I'm growing on you, aren't I?"

"You are doing no such thing." Eva drew herself up to her full height, her voice haughty as she retreated down the hall without another word.

Lily's grin widened. "I so am."

Chapter 10

Carly frowned at the problem in front of her, and Lily held her breath.

After almost two weeks of after-school tutoring, Lily was hoping she'd finally managed to drill the complexities of bonding and intramolecular forces into Carly's head.

It wasn't an easy concept to grasp, and Lily tried not to lean too far over Carly's shoulder as she lifted pen to paper to finish the diagram showing the electron structure in a molecule of ozone.

"Is this right?" Carly hesitantly pushed the paper over toward Lily. Lily had learned over the past few days that though Carly exuded an air of confidence, it was merely for show. Beneath her tough exterior she was fragile—quick to blame herself when things went wrong, and Lily had been trying her best to build her up wherever possible.

"Yes, Carly, that's perfect. Well done."

Carly's beaming smile made all of Lily's efforts feel worth it.

"I'm going to give you some more problems to take home," Lily said, producing a booklet she'd put together last night. "It covers the things we've just gone over as well as some other topics from our last few classes. It'll help me figure out what we need to focus on, and what you're doing well on."

"Okay." Carly tucked the booklet into her backpack. "I'll do it tonight."

"There's no rush." The last thing Lily wanted was for Carly to neglect her other classes in favor of chemistry. "By next Monday will be fine."

"Thanks, Miss Cross."

"You don't need to keep thanking me, Carly."

Carly ducked her head. "Sorry."

"Or apologizing." Lily had noticed her doing that a lot. "Now get yourself out of here, you've done enough work for today."

"See ya tomorrow." Carly shuffled toward the door, and Lily watched her go. She'd settled at her desk to tackle the handful of e-mails she'd gotten at the end of the day when her door creaked open again.

Eva stood in the hallway; it must be one of those rare days she stayed late.

"I just saw Carly leaving," Eva said, leaning against the doorframe. "How is she getting on?"

Lily couldn't help but smile—she loved seeing this softer side to Eva. Not that Lily would ever dare say as much to her face. She valued her life. "She's doing great. Already coming on leaps and bounds in just two weeks."

"You think you'll be able to get her the passing grade she needs?"

"As long as she's willing to put in the work." Which, from what Lily had seen over the past two weeks, Carly was.

Eva nodded. "Good." Eva's mouth opened and closed a few times like she was struggling to think of something to say. "I wanted to thank you for what you're doing for her. A lot of others wouldn't have been so willing to help."

"Wow." Lily was sure her shock showed on her face. "Did you just give me a compliment? Did that physically pain you? I guess there is a first time for everything."

A signature Eva Thomas glare graced Eva's face. "And a last."

Lily grinned. Yeah—she was growing on Eva. That had almost sounded fond.

And Lily had to admit that Eva was starting to grow on Lily, too. She was starting to see through the cracks in Eva's armor, the uncaring façade she portrayed to the rest of the world...and Lily liked what she saw; liked Eva's ferocity when it wasn't directed at her—when it was devoted to her students, to doing what was best for them—liked her quick wit, even if it was usually trying to take Lily down a peg or two.

Lily told herself, as she watched Eva stalk away, that it wasn't a problem. That starting to like Eva wouldn't set her on a dangerous path where someone—most likely herself—would get hurt.

It was fine.

"Miss Cross, did you know it's National Coming Out day today?" Denny Marshall's voice rang across Lily's classroom. Lily didn't like the smug look on his face one bit.

She had a feeling today was the day Denny would push things too far.

"I don't see how that's relevant to the task at hand," Lily said, not wanting to humor him.

Not that he let that stop him.

"It's not, but I wanted to take this opportunity to make an announcement."

One of Denny's friends snickered, and Lily had the feeling she was going to be handing out a detention before the class was done.

"I have chosen to identify...as a table."

Several laughs echoed around the room, but it was Jude's reaction that captured Lily's attention. His back was ramrod straight, his jaw clenched tight, and Lily knew this must be difficult for him.

"Do you think that's funny?" Lily tore her gaze away from Jude and back to Denny—she didn't want to give anything away, her voice icy. It wasn't a tone she used often, and while to her, the warning beneath it was clear, the smile on Denny's face didn't drop.

"No, I take my identity very seriously. From now on, I'd like to be referred to as Mahogany, and—"

"Outside," Lily said, not interested in letting him finish. "Now."

He blinked at her, and Lily clenched her jaw.

"Is selective deafness a new part of your identity?" Lily heard someone suck in a sharp breath. "Have your legs turned to wood and no longer work?" This class had driven her up the wall a dozen times this semester, but she'd never been angrier. "Get. Out. Don't make me repeat it a third time."

He did, though it was with a scoff, the door slamming shut behind him. The rest of the class stared after Denny, their eyes wide.

"Get back to work!" Lily said, and they did so in silence for the first time since she'd started teaching them.

Jude stared at her in shock, and Lily wondered, with an ache in her chest, if this was the first time a teacher had stopped that kind of conversation in its tracks. She hoped not, but she also knew the two girls who had called Macie a dyke had barely been punished at all. Lily thought of David telling her a GSA "wasn't an acceptable use of school resources" and felt her blood boil.

Attitudes at this school needed to change and, no matter how small a difference she could make, Lily was going to do something about it.

When she'd managed to calm down, she went into the hall and found Denny sulking outside her door.

"That kind of behavior is unacceptable," Lily said, trying to keep her voice from shaking. "And I won't tolerate it in my classroom." She knew she could say more, but she'd wasted enough of her lesson on him already. "Here." She handed him the detention slip she'd just filled out. "You'll be spending an hour after school with me tonight."

"But I've got football practice."

"Should've thought about that before you opened your mouth, shouldn't you?"

"But—"

"But nothing," Lily said, cutting him off. She knew his type—the school jock who thought they were above punishment because they belonged to a team. "Don't turn up, and it'll be a weeks' worth. See what Coach thinks about that."

Denny scowled, but he didn't argue, taking the detention slip and slouching back into her classroom.

Thankfully, the remaining fifteen minutes of the lesson passed without incident.

I'm having a shitty day at work, Lily typed, once her final class of the day had rushed out the door. *Cheer me up?*

Elsa's messages were fast becoming the highlight of her day, and Lily thought it would be just the pick-me-up she needed.

Sea otters hold hands when they sleep.

Animal facts? Oh my God, are you a secret nerd? That is otterly adorable.

…Puns? Really?

Lily was still smiling when she knocked on Mei's door.

Mei sat behind her desk and pulled out her earbuds when she saw Lily. "Hey. I hear you've had an eventful day. Tore Denny Marshall a new one."

"How do you know that?"

"Everyone was talking about it at lunch. Apparently you're scary," she said, and Lily laughed. "I don't see it myself, but it must mean I've not managed to piss you off yet."

"There's still time."

"Don't get on the wrong side of you—got it," Mei said, chuckling. "You keeping him for detention?"

"That's what I wanted to talk to you about. I was so mad at him I forgot what day it was—could he sit in here? I've got a GSA meeting in my room."

"Sure." Mei didn't hesitate, and Lily felt a swell of gratitude.

"Thank you. I'll bring you a pack of Twizzlers tomorrow as payment for putting up with him for an hour."

"Payment I will gladly accept."

"I'll bring him in when he gets here." Or should that be *if*? Lily wasn't convinced he'd turn up at all.

Lily had lost all hope by the time she'd ushered the last of the GSA kids into her classroom with the promise she'd join them soon. Macie launched into business as Lily hovered by the door, only half-listening.

"As we all know, today is National Coming Out day. We didn't decide to do a school wide event, but—"

Lily tuned her out as Denny came into view, slouching down the hall toward her.

"Sorry I'm late. I had to explain to Coach why I wouldn't be at practice." His lip curled, and Lily hoped it had been an unpleasant conversation.

"You can stay an extra five minutes," she said, and Denny didn't argue. "Come on. You'll be sitting with Miss Chen."

"Take a seat," Mei said, with as much as cheer as she could manage. Lily rolled her eyes when he threw himself into the chair closest to the door. He pulled out a textbook, and Lily shook her head.

"Actually, Denny, I have a research project for you." Lily handed him a tablet. "I want you to look into the statistics around LGBTQIA+ youth and incidences of mental health issues and suicide. I want you to think about why they might be at an increased risk of both of those things. Think about what you, as a—presumably, but feel free to correct me—white heterosexual cisgender young man, may have done to contribute to those feelings. And what you can do better in future."

Lily crossed over to Mei's desk.

"Damn, woman. I see the scary side of you now."

"Let me know if he's any trouble. I'll come back at the end. You want a coffee or anything?"

"Nah, I'm good." Mei tapped the half-full mug sitting beside her laptop. "If I have another there's no way I'll sleep tonight."

Lily returned to her own classroom to find the conversation had moved onto other topics.

"Perfect timing, Miss Cross. We're talking about how we can give back to the community. We were thinking about having a bake sale to raise money for an LGBTQIA+ charity."

"That's a wonderful idea." Lily knew many of the teachers, at least, would be more than happy to donate in exchange for sweet treats.

"But what charity would we choose?" Mark said.

"How about The Trevor Project?" Kelly suggested, and a few of the other kids nodded.

"Or GLSEN," Sara said.

"There are a few local ones, too," Lily said. They'd been on her radar for a while. "I know there's one that offers mental health support to LGBTQIA+ kids, another one helping homeless youth. And a few others, too."

Mark frowned. "How are we supposed to pick?"

"Who says you have to choose one?" Lily said. "You could split the money between a few. Or you could have a different charity each month and come up with different ways to fundraise for them. Maybe get some other students involved."

"I like that." Macie tapped a pencil against her lips. "We could do a sponsored walk or run. Or a rummage sale." Excited at the prospect of having a new idea, they brainstormed among themselves, and Lily was only too happy to let them.

With a tentative date for the bake sale penciled in and ideas for another few other fundraisers, they left Lily's room at 4 p.m. still chattering away.

"Thank you," Jude said before he joined the others. "For earlier."

"You don't need to thank me, Jude. I did what anyone should have done. And I can assure you he's down the hall being made to think about what he said."

Jude nodded, and Lily followed him out, hoping Denny had behaved himself.

"He was quiet as a mouse," Mei said, when Lily asked.

His head was still bent over the tablet, and Lily checked the time. "You can go now, Denny." She hoped, as Denny got to his feet, that he'd learned his lesson.

"I-I'm sorry, Miss Cross," Denny said, once he'd handed her back the tablet, his head bowed. It could be with insincerity, but Lily hoped it was contrition. "I didn't realize."

"A lot of people don't. You never know what someone might be struggling with behind the scenes. What could push them over the edge. A little kindness goes a long way."

"I'll do better," he said, and Lily hoped he meant it.

"Off you go. I don't want to see you back here again."

Denny nodded before scurrying away, and Lily let out a sigh. She knew it wasn't entirely his fault. This behavior was learned, and it was her role, as an educator, to expose the kids she taught to different points of view.

It was one of the parts of the job she enjoyed the most—the fact she got to make a difference, no matter how small, in someone's life. That she might leave an imprint, be remembered as a positive influence, somewhere later down the line.

"All right?" Mei said, and Lily nodded.

"Glad it's nearly home time."

"Speak for yourself. I still have ten term papers on the origin of the universe left to grade." Mei waved the stack of papers sitting on her desk. "I've already had to read one talking about it being God's creation. Give me strength."

Lily gave her a pat on the shoulder. "Then I'll leave you to it. Thanks again. I'll put those Twizzlers on your desk tomorrow morning."

"I might still be here. Keeled over. Dead of boredom."

Lily was still laughing when she returned to her own classroom, where she found a notification waiting for her.

Cheered up yet?

A little. Lily sat at her desk to type the reply. She had work she ought to be doing but talking to Elsa took priority.

Good. Can't have you being upset on a holiday.

A holiday?

It's National Coming Out Day, isn't it? You seem like the type to celebrate.

What gives you that impression? Lily was curious what conclusions Elsa had drawn about her over the past few weeks they'd been talking.

I don't know. You're easily excitable. And I've seen the pride flag in your window on a few of your photos.

Lily grinned. She couldn't argue with that. *True. But it's not a holiday I feel like celebrating.*

Had a bad coming out experience?

Something like that, Lily typed, shuddering at the memory of being shunned by the other kids at school. *I struggled with my sexuality when I was younger. I mustered up the courage to tell my best friend, and she outed me to the whole school.*

Shit.

Yeah. It wasn't fun. Lily didn't know what she would have done if not for Daisy threatening anyone who dared so much look in Lily's direction with a sneer. *I went back into the closet for a long time.*

I don't blame you. Were your parents okay with it?

When I eventually told them, yeah. Lily remembered bringing her first serious girlfriend home from college, her stomach in knots, only for her parents to accept them both with open arms. *Were yours?*

To be honest, I think my mother knew before I did. Elsa had never mentioned a father, and Lily got the impression he wasn't in the picture. She hadn't pried about the reasons why though, trusting Elsa would tell her if she wanted Lily to know. *She used to strategically place things around the house that let me know she was okay with gay people.*

How long was that happening before you told her?

About a year. I wanted to see how far she'd push it. When my bedroom was overflowing with LGBTQIA+ books and movies—and we'd watched Ellen coming out fifty times on her show—I decided to put her out of her misery.

Lily laughed, setting her phone aside and logging into her laptop. Her day might not have gotten off to the best start, but she was in a much better mood now, and she knew she had Elsa to thank for it.

"I'd like a word, Aaron." Eva raised her voice to be heard over the sound of rustling bags and stools being tucked under benches, her AP class eager to escape and start their weekend.

Other than Aaron, one lingered, and Eva sent Tiffany a withering look as she hovered in the doorway. "I don't recall asking for you to stay too, Tiffany. I won't keep him for long. I'm sure the two of you can manage being separated for five minutes."

Though based on the way Eva had seen them canoodling at lunch times, it might be a stretch.

Aaron approached her desk with his bag slung over his shoulder. "Have I done something wrong?"

"No. But I've noticed your grades slipping these past few weeks." A few fluctuations throughout the year were to be expected, but not a dip to this extent. "Is everything okay? Are you struggling with the workload?"

"No." He fiddled with the strap of his bag. "Nothing like that."

"Then what's the problem?"

"My mom had a new baby. She cries a lot, y'know? Makes it hard to concentrate on homework."

"I see." Eva glanced at Aaron's face, searching for bags under his eyes. "Are you getting enough sleep?"

"When I don't it's my fault for staying up late playing video games."

"And you're not expected to help look after the baby, are you?"

Aaron shook his head. "It's just the crying, Dr. Thomas, I swear. I'll try and do better next time."

"All right." Eva made a mental note to keep a closer eye on him in the next few weeks. "But if you need any extra help, you can come and see me after school."

"Okay. Thank you."

She dismissed him with a nod and made her way across the hall to Alisha's room. The meeting was already in full swing, and Eva slid as quietly as she could into her usual seat.

"I met with the school board earlier this week," Alisha said. "They're pleased with the work we're doing and are starting to put together the timetable for next year. If there are any changes to the syllabus anyone would like to make, come and talk to me in the next few weeks. And if anyone has any suggestions for more electives we could offer as a department, I'd love to hear them."

"How about forensics?" Lily said. Her enthusiasm for her craft had yet to be beaten out of her by her punishing schedule. "We ran that at my previous school and the kids loved it."

"Do you think you could put together a syllabus for it?"

"Sure."

"Excellent. It'll be easier to sell—and to split the teaching hours—if it has a good mix of biology and chemistry in it," Alisha said, and Eva fought back a groan, knowing what was coming next. "If you could run it by Eva and make sure it has a healthy mix that would be great."

It seemed she'd be helping Lily Cross out yet again.

Eva didn't expect it to be quite so soon, surprised when Lily knocked on her door a few minutes after the meeting ended.

"Is, um, now a good time to talk about the forensics syllabus?" Lily looked like she'd rather be anywhere else in the world.

Eva shared the sentiment.

"Aren't you eager to be running off to the bar with the rest of the department?"

Lily shrugged. "They'll still be there when we're done."

"Very well." Eva waved her inside. "As long as I can be out of here by half past." Eva had to take her mother to a neurologist appointment. "What did you have in mind?"

Lily approached Eva's desk. "I printed off the one from my old school. I thought we could use that as a starting point."

Eva held out a hand, and Lily passed her the piece of paper. "You can sit down, you know. I won't bite."

"Could've fooled me," Lily said, and Eva felt her lips twitch into a smirk. At least Lily seemed to be learning it was wise to keep her distance.

It had only taken her three months.

The legs of the stool she chose screeched as she dragged it to Eva's desk, and Eva tried not to let the racket distract her from the syllabus in front of her. One that would not be taught if she were in charge of the school. "This is weak."

"Why?"

"It's convoluted. You could fit this whole thing into half the time, and a single semester, which would make it easier to teach. And these labs... the kids could come up with better ones than this." Eva glanced at Lily, expecting some pushback, and was surprised when Lily merely nodded.

"Okay. What do you suggest?"

"Cutting these lessons entirely." Eva grabbed her trusty green pen and slashed through a few words. "Glass analysis? Talk about boring."

"I liked teaching it." Lily sounded affronted, and did she really expect Eva not to pounce on an opportunity like that?

"Well, that's hardly surprising."

"Because I'm boring, right?"

"You said it."

"You are such an asshole." Lily muttered it under her breath, and Eva was so surprised she huffed out a laugh.

No one had ever been brave enough to say that to her face before.

"Yes, I know. But I'm an asshole who knows what I'm doing," Eva said, striking forensic entomology from the list as well, because she didn't want any bugs being dissected in her classroom. "You don't have to listen to my suggestions, though."

"I want your input. But you could be nicer about it."

"If you came in here expecting niceness, Lily, you're even more naïve than I thought." Eva glanced up. "Do you have any bright ideas?"

"I was thinking of adding some drugs lessons."

"As in 'don't take them or you might end up dead'?"

Lily rolled her eyes. "No. As in: 'Here are some—fake, obviously—drug samples, show me which one is cocaine. There are indicators and tests you can use.' Shouldn't be too hard to set up."

"Huh. That's not a bad idea."

"You don't have to look so surprised. Sometimes other people do know what they're talking about. I used to work in pharma. Which you'd know if you'd ever bothered getting to know me."

"Don't take it personally—I haven't bothered getting to know anyone else, either."

"So I'm not special?" Lily pressed a hand to her chest. "You wound me."

Lily's tone was almost teasing, and Eva shouldn't be enjoying having someone to banter with. Lily was special in that regard—she was the only one who'd ever dared fire back at Lily.

"You can't get rid of blood spatter," Lily said, leaning forward to see what Eva was doing. "That's not boring."

"No, but it's messy." Eva shuddered at the thought of red paint splattered across the white walls of her classroom.

"The kids love it."

"Fine. But if I'm the one teaching it, you'll be the one cleaning up my room afterwards."

"Wait, you think I'll still be here next year? What happened to 'I'll be surprised if you last the week?'" Lily's imitation of Eva's voice made her eyes roll.

"Well, you're still here, aren't you? I suppose you're stubborn enough to stick around."

"If only to annoy you."

Eva shook her head, trying to focus on her notes and not the pair of twinkling eyes beside her. Goddammit. Lily was starting to get under Eva's skin—and not just in an annoying kind of way. In a maybe-you're-not-so-bad-to-have-around kind of way.

Which was unacceptable. "Here you go." Eva returned the piece of paper to Lily, her handwriting scrawled all over the front of it. "I trust you can type this up yourself?"

"I'm sure I can manage." Lily plucked it from Eva's grip. "Thank you."

"Yeah, yeah. Don't get used to it."

"I think your cat wants to murder me." Daisy eyed Hades warily from where she sat, poised on top of Lily's refrigerator like a queen sitting on her throne, green eyes watching their every move.

"I wouldn't worry. She looks like that all the time," Lily said, spreading flour generously over the countertop and glaring up at the cat. "And don't you dare jump in the middle of this."

Hades had done it before, streaking her black fur with white, treading it all over the house before Lily had managed to catch up with her and wrangle her into the bathtub.

The scratches had taken weeks to fade.

Lily rolled out a thin sheet of the dough she'd made earlier. "What are these cookies for again?"

"My mommie's group. It's my turn to bake."

"And you couldn't go to the store because…?"

Daisy looked appalled. "I can't give them store-bought, Lily. I'd be kicked out."

"Seriously?"

"Yes."

"But getting your sister to bake them for you is allowed?"

"If they don't find out about it, yes."

Lily snorted. "Right, of course." It had worked out well—the bake sale for the GSA was on Monday, so Lily had already been planning on spending the day baking. She just needed to double up her batches. "You could help, you know."

"And ruin your good work?"

Lily tossed Daisy one of her cookie cutters. "If you can ruin it using one of those, I'll be impressed."

Daisy mumbled something under her breath, but she stepped up to the counter. Lily left Daisy to the cookies as she began to gather the ingredients for her famous red velvet cupcakes, which Daisy had also requested.

"Thank you, by the way," Daisy said, once the first batch of cookies were baking. "I know there are other things you'd rather be doing on a Saturday."

"I don't mind." It was preferable to work, that was for sure. "Could you check the recipe on my phone? I can't remember how much of everything I need."

"Sure. It's one and a half cups of—wait a second. Who is QueenElsa35?"

Lily froze with her hand outstretched toward the flour. "What?"

"She's sent you a message. On CuteMeet. You know, a dating app that you seem to be using even though you swore you weren't interested in dating?"

Lily swallowed as Daisy leveled her with a piercing stare.

"Let's see what she has to say, shall we?"

"No!" Lily tried to grab her phone, but her sister was nimble, pirouetting away like a ballerina.

"Jesus Christ, Lily. You've been talking for weeks!" Daisy's eyes widened, her thumb scrolling, no doubt through their message thread.

It distracted Daisy long enough for Lily to wrestle her phone back, but she knew the damage was already done.

"It's nothing, okay?"

"Nothing? All those messages aren't nothing. Why didn't you tell me you were seeing someone?"

"Because I'm not. We're friends."

"Friends don't send a thousand messages on a dating app."

"Well, we do."

"Okay, then. What's your friend's name? Age? Occupation?"

"I...don't know."

Daisy blinked at the side of her head. "What do you mean, you don't know?"

Lily shrugged. "We made a deal when we started talking to keep things vague. To not say anything that would make us identifiable."

"Why?"

"So we could get to know one another without any preconceived expectations."

"That is weird as fuck."

Lily snorted. She could see Daisy's point, though; it was weird she knew Elsa's favorite meal and her preferred vacation spots, and not her name, but it was working. And Lily liked the ease of it. Liked knowing there was someone on the other end of the phone who wanted to talk to her—and not just to send her sexually explicit messages or offers for a threesome like most of the others in her inbox. She liked asking Elsa questions—both serious and random—just to see what she'd say. To add to the picture Lily was building of her in her mind.

"Have you spoken to anyone else on there?"

"No." Lily hadn't so much as scrolled through another profile in weeks.

"Even though it's a dating app," Daisy said. "You know, to find people to date?"

"Yes, I know, but...I don't know if I need that right now. I only downloaded it to see what's out there. I like talking to her. And that's enough for me, for now."

Daisy didn't look convinced.

"Are you ever going to meet up with her?"

"I dunno." Lily turned her attention back to her cupcakes, opening the recipe on her phone and resisting the itching curiosity to see what Elsa had messaged her, knowing she'd have Daisy's eyes on her the whole time. "Probably not."

"And you're okay with that?"

"Yeah," Lily said, and she meant it. She knew Daisy didn't understand, but Lily didn't need her to. "I am."

"But don't you want to—"

"Enough." Lily waved a wooden spoon toward her. "I don't expect you to get it, but I'm done talking about this." Lily narrowed her eyes when

Daisy opened her mouth to argue. "If you carry on then no baked goods for you."

"All right, all right. Sorry for snooping." It was an afterthought, but it was still an apology. Only so Lily would continue to help her out, but she'd take it.

"Just don't do it again."

"I won't."

"Hand me the whisk."

Chapter 11

TIME PASSED, THE LEAVES ON the trees outside of Lily's classroom window turning hues of orange and red before falling to the ground. Each day the air grew colder, a smattering of snow falling more often than not as Christmas approached, and with it, the prospect of a few days off.

Lily needed it. Her workload seemed to be increasing with each passing day, and she felt close to burning out. She had exams to grade over the break—and was particularly interested in seeing how Carly had done on her first exam since Lily had started tutoring her—but at least she could do that at home in her pajamas.

When the bell rang for her last class on the final Friday of the semester, Lily didn't know who was more relieved—her or her students.

They all scampered away, free for the holidays, and Lily breathed out a long sigh, leaning back in her chair and kicking her feet up on her desk. She tilted her head to look at the equations she'd scribbled on the board before giving up with teaching and letting her class talk among themselves for the last ten minutes.

"Long day?"

Lily spun her chair around to see Mei in the doorway. "Long semester."

"Yeah, the first one's always rough." Mei hopped onto the front row of desks. She didn't look tired in the slightest, which Lily thought was hardly fair. "On the bright side, we have two weeks off."

"Only after this stupid staff Christmas party."

"Eh, it's not too bad as long as you keep drinking."

"Is it long?"

"Few hours."

Lily groaned. "All I want to do is go home and sleep."

"There's time for that later."

"What if when I go home to change, I don't come back?"

"Unfortunately, attendance is considered to be mandatory."

"David's not going to fire me if I don't turn up, is he?" Not that she should be giving David a reason. Lily was already in his bad books, after all.

"No, but you would get a stern talking to, I believe. Come on, it's not so bad. The first three drinks are free." Mei had far too much enthusiasm. "It'll be over before you know it."

Lily grumbled, but she knew she had no choice. Their usual Friday drinks had been canceled because of it, so she went straight home to get herself ready for the night ahead.

She complained about it to Elsa, touching up her make-up in between exchanging messages.

Must be a popular night for Christmas parties—mine is tonight too.

Maybe we'll run into one another. Not that Lily would have the slightest idea. As well as she felt she knew Elsa by now, she wasn't delusional enough to think she'd be able to pick her out in a crowd.

Unless she loudly insulted *Gone with the Wind*, anyway.

We could've already run into one another. We wouldn't know.

True. Elsa could be the cute cashier at the grocery store, the barista at the coffee shop, even the mechanic Daisy kept bringing up whenever they saw one another.

Do you think we ever will? Meet in person, I mean?

Lily didn't know why she asked it, why she risked breaking the spell. They'd both been so careful to avoid anything too personal, and there Lily was, blowing it wide open.

I don't know. I look forward to these messages. What if we meet in person and we hate each other?

Lily didn't think that was likely. Sure, sometimes Elsa could be brash and cutting, but there was an underlying humor there, a sense of vulnerability driving her responses.

I guess, Lily typed, biting on her bottom lip. *No sense ruining a good thing, right?*

Right. Although...

The pause made Lily's curiosity burn.
Although? Lily waited with bated breath for a response.

It's not quite meeting up, and you can say no, but could I have your number? Then I won't have to keep opening this app when I want to talk to you.

It echoed the same sentiment Lily had been feeling, lately. She didn't need the app—didn't use it except for a messaging app, and there were easier ways to do that. She just hadn't wanted to ask.
Sure. So long as you don't use it to stalk me. Lily typed a string of numbers at the end, and a moment later her phone buzzed with a new message from an unknown number.

Thank you.

Lily couldn't hide her smile, and knew she'd be in a good mood all night—and then she swore when she caught a glimpse of the time. She'd gotten distracted, and her ride would be there any minute.

She dressed in a hurry. The e-mail had stated that formal wear was required, so Lily donned a red dress for the occasion. It wasn't too clingy, the extra padding on her stomach and around her hips hidden by the silken material. It did show off her best assets, though, the scoop neck revealing just enough cleavage to be appropriate for a work function. She even slipped on a rare pair of heels, barely recognizing herself when she glanced in the mirror.

Her phone dinged to tell Lily her Uber had arrived as she was running a brush through her hair.

The Uber pulled to a stop at six fifty-six, meaning she was precisely four minutes early.

Through the windows of the bar the school had booked for the night, Lily could see groups of teachers, raucous laughter spilling out onto the street when someone opened the door.

Mei, Alisha and Brandon were standing on the sidewalk waiting for her, shivering even though they wore thick jackets. Lily wondered if Alisha was regretting her offer for the department to go inside as a group.

"Have you been here long?" Lily said as she joined them, and Mei shook her head.

"A few minutes. I hope the others hurry their asses up. Oh, here comes the wicked witch, so it's only Andrew left."

"Behave," Alisha hissed, elbowing Mei in the side, and Lily turned to see Eva crossing the street to join them. Lily's breath caught at the sight of her. Sure, she'd noticed Eva's attractiveness before. But she'd only ever seen her in skirts or pantsuits, every inch the professional.

But, tonight, Eva wore a dress the color of sapphires, a slit in the skirt that stopped an inch or two above Eva's knee. It was off-the-shoulder, her open jacket revealing an expanse of smooth skin, the delicate points of her collarbones, and Lily's throat went dry. She forced her gaze away, hoping Eva hadn't noticed her scrutiny.

Lily told herself she was just caught off-guard, not having expected Eva to turn up. As much as Mei insisted tonight was mandatory, a part of Lily had wondered if that applied to Eva. She didn't seem the type to enjoy any kind of social activity with the people she worked with, and yet, there she was.

Looking devastating.

"Hi, Eva," Alisha said when Eva paused beside her. "Glad to see you made it."

"Did I have a choice?"

126

"No." Alisha sounded cheerful. "None of us did."

Eva sighed, leaning her shoulder against the brick wall behind her. Was she going to spend the whole evening with them? Lily hadn't considered it, but where else would Eva go? She didn't seem like the type to have friends in other departments.

They'd never spent time together in the presence of other people, Lily realized. Would they still argue if they had witnesses? Or would Eva be different, especially if Alisha was around?

Someone nudged her, and Lily turned to find Mei looking at her, head tilted to one side. "You okay?"

"Yeah, why?"

"I dunno. You look off."

"I'm fine." Lily forced a smile, and Andrew's arrival saved her from any further questions as Alisha ushered them all inside.

The bar had been split into two sections—tables on one side and a makeshift dance floor on the other, and Lily knew where she'd be spending most of her night. The sound of laughter and idle chatter washed over her as they stepped inside. Alisha claimed one of the larger tables before making a beeline for the bar.

"I'll get your first drink," Mei said, throwing her jacket over the back of one of the chairs. "Gin and tonic?"

Lily sat in the chair next to Mei's and nodded. "Yes, please."

Too late, Lily realized Andrew and Brandon had followed Alisha, leaving her and Eva alone. She sat watching Lily, drumming manicured nails on the table and looking like a goddess.

"Are you, uhm,"—Lily cleared her throat when the words came out in a croak—"not getting a drink?" Eva didn't seem like the type to be able to get through the night sober.

"I'll wait until the line's died down." Eva shrugged out of her jacket, leaving so much skin on display that Lily swallowed, her throat feeling tight.

"You look nice."

Why had she said that? When had she lost all control of her brain? What was wrong with her?

Eva arched an eyebrow, gray eyes meeting Lily's, and she hoped Eva couldn't tell what she was thinking. "You look acceptable."

Lily snorted. "Gee, thanks." She needed to keep Eva talking, because the insults might uncloud her mind. "Though I guess that's a compliment, coming from you."

"You can interpret it that way if you like."

Lily breathed out a sigh of relief when Mei dropped into the seat beside her and handed over a large glass. "I asked him to put in a generous amount of gin," Mei said, sipping from her daiquiri. "You're welcome."

"Thank you." Lily relaxed once she was surrounded by the others—it almost felt like a normal Friday night at the bar. Almost, because though she was quiet, sipping from a martini, Eva was there. Lily felt her presence even when absorbed in conversation with Mei and Andrew.

The tap of metal on glass echoed over the sound of chatter, and everyone turned toward the stage at the rear of the dance floor, where David Blake was holding a microphone.

"Karaoke!" Someone shouted, resulting in a few chuckles around the room.

"No one wants to hear that, trust me," David said, his laugh grating on Lily's nerves. "I won't talk for long, because I know the only reason you're all here is for the free booze."

"Damn straight!" Another voice called, and David's smile widened.

"It sounds like some of you have already well and truly started the party. First, I want to thank each and every one of you for your hard work this semester. It's always a challenge to come back from the summer break and start all over again. We've made great progress these last few months—"

"I've got a fun drinking game for you," Mei said, leaning close to speak into Lily's ear. "Take a sip every time he says the words 'progress' or 'thanks'; I bet you'll have finished your gin by the time he's done."

"But he said it would be short."

"He says that every year, and every year it's a lie."

Sure enough, by the time he wrapped up, Lily's drink was nearly gone.

"Told you," Mei said, setting her empty glass on the table. "Every time."

"I guess it's my turn to get this round," Lily said, draining the last of her gin. "Does anyone else want a refill?"

When they all shook their heads, Lily rose to her feet. Her knees wobbled, and she should have eaten something more than toast before she came out, but at least getting drunk wouldn't be expensive.

Sure enough, by the time she was on her fourth gin and tonic, everything was fuzzy around the edges. Mei dragged her to dance to the awful music the DJ played, but Lily was drunk enough not to care, her inhibitions lowered and enjoying herself more than she thought she would.

"I'm going to go get some air," she said to Mei after the fifth song, sweat beading at her brow.

"Hurry back—I'm not done with you yet."

Eva slipped out without anyone noticing.

In fact, the only person who seemed to have noticed her all night was Lily Cross, her gaze flitting to Eva whenever there was a lull in conversation. Eva hadn't missed the way it had tracked over her skin, lingering at the swell of her breasts, growing more brazen with every drink she emptied.

It was a fabulous dress, so Eva couldn't exactly blame her.

And Eva had found her own gaze lingering more than once. Out of her usual frumpy wardrobe and in a gorgeous red dress with a dangerously low neckline, Lily had captured Eva's attention.

Eva had stopped drinking after her third martini, blaming the alcohol for the way she kept being drawn to the sway of Lily's hips on the dance floor.

Maybe it had been too long since she got laid. The words sounded suspiciously like Kate, and Eva shook her head.

The air outside the bar was cold, and Eva zipped her jacket up to her chin as she opened the Uber app on her phone. "Fifteen-minute wait time?" Eva said, her breath fogging in the air. "Unbelievable." It must be a busy Friday night. She could go back inside, where she'd be warm at least, but the thought of spending another moment around her colleagues was unpleasant.

She'd rather freeze.

The door opened behind her, the sound of voices and music drifting out onto the otherwise quiet street, and Eva mentally steeled herself in case whoever it was attempted to strike up a conversation with her.

Lily Cross stumbled into view, and Eva sighed

Of course.

Her cheeks were flushed, sweat sticking her hair to the back of her neck. Lily looked shocked to see her, coming to a stop leaning against the coarse brick wall of the bar, gooseflesh rising on her skin.

"Are you leaving?"

"I've made an appearance and gotten my free drinks," Eva said. "That's more than enough."

"Are you not having fun?"

Eva scoffed. "This is nowhere near my idea of fun."

Lily moved closer, pausing a few steps away, shrouded in darkness out of reach of the streetlights dotted around the block. "I bet your idea of fun is going to the opera."

"It's certainly not that." Eva jerked her head toward the bar. "Though you look like you were enjoying yourself."

"You noticed?"

"No," Eva said, too quickly, and Lily's lips twitched. "I try my best not to notice you at all." That was too honest.

"Why?"

"Because you're annoying."

Lily grinned. "That the best you can come up with? You're losing your touch."

"How dare you."

Eva expected Lily to duck back into the bar, but she seemed rooted to the spot, looking at Eva with unfocused eyes.

At least Eva wasn't the only one who wasn't sober.

"Everyone else steers well clear of me," Eva said, tilting her head to one side. "Everyone else is scared of me, but not you. Why?"

It was the most annoying thing about Lily. The thing that set Eva off.

"I dunno. Cause you're not scary?"

Eva's eyes narrowed, and Lily's smile widened.

"And because it's fun to wind you up."

"You don't find me scary?" Eva drifted closer without thinking. She expected Lily to retreat, to back down, to scuttle back into the bar where Eva didn't have to think about her anymore.

But she didn't.

Instead, Lily straightened her spine and set her jaw, leaning her head against the wall behind her and looking Eva in the eye. The challenge in her gaze was clear—I'm not afraid of you—and Eva hated the way it made her heart pound.

No one else would ever dare, and wasn't that part of the draw? Wasn't that why Eva couldn't stay away? Equal parts fascination and dislike had led her here, walking a dangerous tightrope, swaying in the breeze.

Eva didn't stop moving until she was mere inches away, perfume and sweat hitting her nose.

"How about now?"

"You're intimidating," Lily said, voice low, rough, affected by Eva's proximity. "But you're not scary."

Eva could smell the gin on Lily's breath, see her pulse pounding at the base of her neck. Was it with fear, after all? Or was it with something else entirely?

Eva thought of Lily's eyes, drifting her way all night. Thought of the double-take she'd done, when she'd gotten her first glimpse of Eva's dress. The way she was looking to Eva's painted lips, her eyes dark and unfocused.

"Hmm."

Eva took stock of their positioning; of the heat she could feel radiating off the woman before her. She should walk away. She should wrestle back her self-control, turn on her heel and never look back, because—

"What—what are you doing?" Lily said, her breathing ragged, Eva swaying ever closer.

"Honestly?" Eva's voice was low—she couldn't deny she was affected by this, her skin aflame, losing all sense of rationality every time Lily's gaze flickered to her mouth. "I have no idea."

Eva shouldn't be entertaining this. It was dangerous; they were only a few feet from the entrance of the bar, and anyone could walk out and see them.

Eva didn't move away.

She wondered what was going through Lily's head. She wondered who would crack first.

Eva expected Lily to shove her away and retreat in a storm of fury. A slap wouldn't have been remiss, considering Eva's complete disregard for personal space.

What she did not expect was for Lily to surge forward.

She paused, lips mere millimeters from Eva's, breath hot on her mouth, and Eva knew she was asking for permission, giving Eva an out if she decided this was a step too far in whatever little game they'd been playing for the last four months.

It was an out Eva knew she should take.

Eva pressed closer, instead.

The kiss wasn't soft, it wasn't chaste—it was hot and furious, their teeth clacking together before they readjusted, Lily's tongue curling against her own.

Surprisingly, Lily was a fantastic kisser—something else Eva could add to the 'unexpected things about Lily Cross' list—her lips leaving Eva breathless and aching. Eva splayed her hands against the wall on either side of Lily's head, so she didn't give in to the temptation to reach out and touch, refusing to indicate it wasn't just morbid curiosity, letting this continue—refusing to show that a traitorous part of her wanted Lily.

Lily had no such self-control, wrapping one hand around Eva's waist as the other fell to the slit of her dress. She scraped her nails over bare skin, and Eva nipped at her bottom lip in response. Eva leaned closer, pressing a thigh between Lily's legs and trying not to groan when her hips rocked against her.

God, what was she doing?

This wasn't like her.

So why couldn't Eva stop?

It was the screech of wheels against tarmac that brought them back to Earth. Eva wrenched herself away from Lily like she'd been burned, her heart pounding. Lily looked at her, chest flushed and heaving with the force of her breaths, staring at Eva like she'd never seen her before.

Eva's Uber pulled up to the curb, the window sliding down. "One of you Eva?"

Why couldn't they have gotten there five minutes ago? Eva ran a shaky hand through her hair. Then she wouldn't be in this mess.

"Yes." Eva was relieved her voice was steady. Steadier than she felt, her knees weak as she stumbled toward the car. Toward safety. Toward the end of whatever the fuck that lapse in judgment had been.

Blame it on the alcohol.

"Wait!" Lily's call stopped Eva as she was reaching for the handle of the rear door. Against her better judgment, she looked back; Lily was exactly where she'd left her. "That's it? You're just going to walk away? Pretend it never happened?"

"That's exactly what I'm going to do," Eva said, wrenching open the door. "And you should, too."

Eva had just managed to get her heart rate back to normal as she slid her key into her front door.

Her mother was still awake, a movie playing on the TV, and Eva bent down to say hello to the sleepy Spaniel that trotted over to greet her.

"It's early," her mother said with a tut, eyeing Eva in disapproval. "I thought you'd stay out longer. Have fun with your friends."

"I told you I wouldn't be out late."

"Still. Did you have a good night, at least?"

Eva tried not to think about Lily Cross's dark eyes, the heat of her mouth, the imprint of her fingers on the bare skin of Eva's thigh. "It was all right. I'm going to shower and get to bed. Don't stay up too late."

Eva bent down to kiss the top of her mother's head before retreating up the stairs with Franklin in tow. He curled up in his bed beside her desk as Eva grabbed her pajamas from the foot of her own. A glance in the mirror as she waited for the water to heat up revealed her cheeks were still flushed, her eyes wild, and Eva knew, as she stepped beneath the spray, that she was slick between her thighs.

Eva felt like she'd been betrayed by her own body, and she ignored the ache as she washed the scent of Lily's perfume from her skin. She wished she could wash away the memories as easily, wished she'd never been weak enough to let it happen in the first place.

What had she been thinking?

She wasn't thinking, clearly. Eva knew she should've stayed away from Lily, and look what had happened! Stupid.

Come January, Eva would keep Lily at arm's length, lest things get even more out of hand.

At least she had two weeks reprieve.

All Eva had to do was stop thinking about Lily, and everything would be just fine.

Gritting her teeth, Eva tried to push the thoughts away as she climbed beneath her sheets. She tossed and turned for an hour before giving up on sleep entirely, reaching for the phone on her nightstand.

As Eva often did when she felt down, she gravitated toward her message thread with Molly. The stab of guilt was unexpected—she hadn't done anything wrong tonight. Hadn't made any kind of commitment to Molly. Had brushed her off, in fact, earlier that night, by declining to meet up face-to-face.

Eva shouldn't feel any kind of way about using her to forget about Lily. If they were friends—real friends—her unfortunate mistake would be something Eva would tell her, that they'd laugh about, that Molly would tease her with for the foreseeable future.

But Eva couldn't tell her. Couldn't admit to the weakness that had overtaken her. How could Eva explain kissing someone she claimed to dislike?

Eva couldn't even explain it to herself.

Hope you had a good night, Eva tapped instead, sending it to the number Molly had given her earlier. It was a long shot—Molly was probably still out enjoying herself. She could even be tangled up with someone beneath the mistletoe. Eva knew she had no right for the thought to bother her, especially considering where her lips had been a few short hours before. No right, and yet her stomach twisted with dread. If Molly found someone else, would she stop talking to Eva?

Annoyed, Eva tossed her phone back onto her bedside table. That had been meant to make her feel better, not worse.

It was just the alcohol, she told herself, rolling onto her side and closing her eyes, willing herself to believe it.

She wouldn't feel any of this in the morning.

Chapter 12

Lily woke with a killer hangover.

She reached blindly for her phone to check the time and groaned when the screen remained black. She'd neglected to put it on charge the night before.

Plugging it in, she wandered downstairs, in need of some water for her painfully dry throat. Lily had fuzzy memories of the previous night—too many drinks, a lot of dodgy dancing, some questionable choices on the karaoke machine at the bar they'd gone to once the staff party had wound down—and no idea how Mei had ended up passed out on her couch.

"Must've been a crazy night," Lily said to herself, filling a glass to the brim and hoping it might ward off the pounding behind her eyes.

And then she had a flash of memory from earlier in the evening—Eva, pressed close, Eva, with her mouth on Lily's—and the glass slipped from Lily's grip, shattering on the kitchen floor.

An inhuman groan came from the direction of the couch. "You know, if you wanted to wake me up, Lily, you just had to poke me. No need to start throwing things." Mei appeared in the doorway a moment later, her hair sticking up in all different directions. She glanced at Lily's face. "You okay?"

Lily was far from okay.

Lily was spiraling, Lily was remembering Eva. Outside of the bar, the challenge in Eva's eyes as she'd invaded Lily's space—how Lily hadn't been able to let it go, instead rearing up and kissing Eva, hard.

Oh, no. No, no, no, this couldn't be happening. How could she have been so stupid? She and Eva had been getting to a good place, and now it would be ruined.

"You look like you've seen a ghost," Mei said, oblivious to Lily's inner turmoil. "Did you forget you let me crash here? It was your idea. Save money on the Uber fare."

Lily needed to focus. She could freak out later, when she was alone. There was no way in hell she could tell Mei what had happened. "Yeah, no, I remember." Vaguely, anyway. "I'm good. Just clumsy."

Lily swept up the pieces of broken glass before Hades got any stuck in her paws. As if summoned by the commotion, she appeared as Lily was tipping the last few fragments into the garbage.

"I didn't know you had a cat!" Mei looked overjoyed, stretching out a hand for Hades to sniff. "What a cutie."

"Only when she wants something." A pointed meow was sent in her direction, and Lily tipped some kibble into her bowl.

"What's her name?"

"Hades."

"For a girl?"

"Well, I got her when she was a scrawny rescue kitten, and they told me she was a boy. I was always losing her underneath things—the couch, the kitchen cupboards, even the floorboards once. Seeing as Hades is the God of the underworld, I thought it fit. By the time I found out she was a girl, the name had already stuck."

"I love it."

"Want something to eat? Nothing cures a hangover like something greasy."

"Count me in." Mei hopped onto one of the countertops as Lily reached for a frying pan, rubbing a hand against the back of her neck.

"Sleep funny?" Lily said. "I have a guest room, you know. You didn't have to stay on the couch."

"Drunk me heard you say that and decided going up the stairs was far too much effort."

Lily snorted, the smell of frying bacon filling the room. "How drunk were we?"

"Hammered. Luckily, Alisha had just as many drinks, so don't worry. You didn't make a fool out of yourself."

Lily thought of Eva's tongue licking into her mouth and wasn't so sure about that.

Having Mei in her space was nice. It was a step of their friendship they'd yet to make—hanging out with one another without work giving them an excuse—and it was one Lily was happy to take. She was glad she'd met Mei, glad she was starting to build something of a life for herself here, something separate from her family, something that was just hers.

After they'd eaten, food and coffee soaking up any lingering alcohol in her system, Lily drove Mei home, surprised to find she only lived a few blocks away.

"You should come by one day," Mei said, before she got out of the car. "I'll cook you dinner to repay you for letting me drool on your couch."

"Sounds good," Lily said around a laugh. "Have a good Christmas."

"You too." Mei waved, and Lily waited for her to get inside before returning home.

A shower was the next thing on her agenda—Lily was sure she smelled terrible—but she was distracted by her phone, abandoned on her bed. A text waited for her when it eventually turned on, and Lily scoffed when she read it.

She wouldn't classify her night as good by any stretch of the imagination. While she'd had fun with Mei and the others, it was overshadowed by her idiocy, but she didn't want to talk about it with Elsa.

It offered a welcome distraction, though.

I got very drunk. It was messy.

Elsa had replied by the time Lily had gotten out of the shower, feeling refreshed and clad in her favorite Christmas pajamas. While she'd been working, she hadn't been in the festive spirit, her house bare of the decorations usually adjourning every visible surface.

Something she was going to remedy today.

She needed a distraction. If Lily kept busy, she'd stop thinking about how Eva had felt pressed against her.

Are you regretting it this morning?

A little. Some aspects more than others. *But I'm already feeling better.*
Lily tucked her phone into the pocket of her pants—one of the reasons she loved those pajamas so much—and busied herself with sorting through the boxes she'd gotten down from the attic the previous weekend.

She'd had good intentions until she'd let herself get distracted with work.

Got anything exciting planned for the day? Or are you sleeping it off?

I'm decorating, Lily replied, snapping a photo of the bare Christmas tree tucked into the corner of her living room. *I'm willing to take bets on how long it lasts before Hades tears it down.*

Five minutes?

Likely. Are your decorations already up? Elsa seemed like someone who'd be prepared. Less scattered than Lily, who would lose her head if it wasn't attached to her body.

We've just taken them down. Hanukah ended a few days ago.

You're Jewish? Lily hadn't realized, but how could she if Elsa had never mentioned it before?

My mother is. I stopped following religion many years ago, but I celebrate the holidays with her.

Makes sense. I guess I do that, too. I'm not a Christian, but I celebrate Christmas.

I think it stopped being a religious holiday a long time ago, Elsa replied. *Commercialization and all that. You can't go to the store without hearing three million Christmas songs.*

Why do I get the feeling you wouldn't celebrate it even if your mother wasn't Jewish? Lily didn't want to call Elsa a Grinch, but she had a feeling it would be a fitting description.

Because I wouldn't. But I bet your house looks like Santa's grotto.

Guilty. Lily couldn't help it. She loved the holidays: the decorations, the music, the movies. Loved spending time with her family—especially this year, with Emma to spoil. She'd already booked out a day to take her to see Santa at the mall.

Send me a picture when you're done. I'll rate it on a scale from one to horrific.

Lily laughed, setting her phone aside and kneeling on the floor. She had Christmas lights to untangle, ornaments and tinsel to place, and she wasn't going to let herself get distracted again.

Christmas meant nothing more to Eva than a blissful two-week vacation.

Angela spent Hanukah with the Thomases, so they were invited for Christmas dinner—an offer Eva declined. Spending hours with Angela, her husband and their extended family sounded like hell on earth, but Eva was only too happy to drop her mother off. The prospect of a day with the house to herself was too great to ignore.

It meant Eva could do something she hadn't done for ages, something she enjoyed whenever she needed to quiet her mind: clean.

And God, did Eva need to quiet her mind. Never mind the ghosts of Christmas past, present and future—Eva was being haunted by the ghost of Lily Cross.

Despite Eva's best efforts, that kiss still weighed on her mind. Lily had even been in her dreams every night.

The house would be spotless by the time Eva went to pick her mother up. Was it the best way to spend a Saturday? Not by most people's standards, but to Eva, it was a catharsis little else could bring her.

Especially without her mother trying to help—purely because she felt like she should be doing something—and only getting in the way.

"Sorry, buddy," Eva said to Franklin when she pulled out the carpet cleaner. He hated it even more than he hated the vacuum. "I'll take you out for a long walk later to make up for it."

He scampered away to hide upstairs, and Eva put herself to work, gaining a deep sense of satisfaction every time she had to change the water, the carpets in every room a shade lighter once she was finished.

By the time she'd mopped the kitchen floor until it was sparkling, Eva was sweating despite the dusting of snow on the lawn outside.

She checked her phone when she paused for a drink of water and was surprised to see a text from Molly.

Though it was rare they went a day without talking anymore, she knew Molly was spending the day with her family and hadn't expected a reply to the Merry Christmas she'd sent earlier that morning.

I've been questioned four times about why I haven't brought anyone to dinner. Why is it any of their business?

Eva chuckled at Molly's words. Ah, the pitfalls of family functions. It was times like these Eva was grateful her own family was small.

Because families are nosy? Eva suggested, wondering whether she should tackle the kitchen countertops or the bathrooms next.

Is yours?

Not much family to speak of. A father who walked away and never looked back. A mother with a strained relationship with her parents choosing a fresh start somewhere new. *It's just me and my mother. But yes, she is nosy. Asks me at least once a week if I've met anyone new. Tells me I need to put myself out there more.*

Why don't you?

Eva considered the question as she started scrubbing the marble counters. She blamed the endorphins for making her answer so honest.

I think part of me is scared of getting hurt.

Had your heart broken too many times?

Only once. Victoria was the only woman Eva had ever truly let close. Eva let her mind drift, remembering winter breaks spent wrapped up in one another, mixing the traditions of two families into one. *But it's not an experience I want to repeat.*

So you're never going to open up to anyone again? If it were from anyone else, Eva would have bristled at the question, reading judgment between the lines. But Molly wasn't like that.

Maybe when the right person comes along. Not that Eva thought that was ever likely to happen. She'd have to let it, and showing vulnerability had never been her strong suit. *What about you? Why are you still single?*

Turning the question around was safest. Even with Molly, Eva had her limits to what she was willing to reveal.

No one will put up with me.

Eva narrowed her eyes, because she'd given a real, raw answer, and Molly was palming her off with something vague. Annoyed, Eva put her phone aside and went back to scrubbing, more fiercely than before.

Her phone buzzed again, making her pause.

No, that's not true. To be honest, I find dating exhausting. Getting to know someone, opening up to them, trying to see if you'd be a good fit only to discover, in the end, it doesn't work and having to start all over again. I thought I'd finally found someone, when I met my ex, and then it turned out she'd been cheating on me for almost the whole relationship. I only found out after we'd bought a place together. And pretty much all my friends—or I thought they were my friends—knew but didn't tell me. They let me think I was losing my mind. When we broke up, I couldn't handle being around any of them anymore. I ended up moving halfway across the country. Kinda hard to summon the will to start again after that.

Eva blinked. Well, she'd wanted honesty, and Molly had certainly given it to her. She received another message.

Sorry. That was a lot.

It's okay. You can tell me anything. The message felt too heavy, but Eva pressed send anyway. *I'm sorry that happened to you.*

Thanks. I think part of my problem is I keep finding myself attracted to unattainable people, too. That way I can't get hurt, because it'll never happen, you know?

I do. Wasn't that what Eva was doing right then with Molly? The only reason she told Molly half the things she did was because it felt less real, hiding behind a screen.

We make quite the pair, don't we?

They could, perhaps, in another life. They could, perhaps, manage to make a go of things, if only Eva were to take a leap. The foundations were there—Molly was kind, and attentive, and a bit of a dork but in an endearing way Eva liked to make fun of.

She didn't want to ruin things. She didn't want to—in Molly's words—"have to start all over again".

Better to have this, than nothing at all.

Lily loved her family, but her limit on social interaction had been reached somewhere around the fourth round of charades, watching her mother attempt to act out *Magic Mike*.

She escaped outside for a breath of fresh air—and spluttered when she inhaled a mouthful of cigarette smoke.

"Shit. Sorry, Lil." Jack, her youngest cousin, quickly stamped it out with the heel of his boot. "I didn't think anyone would come out here."

"You're smoking now?"

He offered her a sheepish look from beneath his wild curls. "Not often. Please don't tell my mom."

"Hey, you're nineteen now." Which she couldn't believe. She could still remember him being in diapers. "It's none of my business what you get up to." She wished he'd choose a less deadly vice, but it wasn't her job to parent him.

"Thanks. You need to escape, too?"

"Just for a minute." Lily buried her hands deep into the pockets of her jacket and leaned against the wall. "They're...a lot." Lily turned to face him. "Your mom's going to kill you when she gets a whiff of your clothes."

Jack produced a bottle of aftershave from his pocket, and Lily laughed, breath fogging the air.

"Have you got mouthwash, too?"

"I'm not an amateur, Lil."

She shook her head. "How's college?"

"Good. How's being back here?"

Lily shrugged. "It's not so bad. Nice being able to see everyone again."

"Is it?" Jack said, as a loud peal of laughter carried through to the yard.

"Uh-huh." She loved her family, eccentric though they may be. Lily's phone buzzed in her pocket, and she wondered what Elsa was asking her now.

I have a charade for you, Lily read, in response to her complaining about what the night had devolved into. *The Shawshank Redemption.*

They couldn't get the Sixth Sense, Lily typed back. *I think that's out of their league.*

"Have you got a secret girlfriend or something?" Jack said, and Lily glanced away from her phone to find him watching her closely.

"What? No. Why would you ask that?"

"Because you've had that same dopey smile on your face whenever you've looked at your phone today," Jack said, and Lily wondered when he'd become so observant. She'd seen him playing on his Switch for half the day. "You can tell me. We can be secret buddies."

"Sorry to disappoint, but I don't have a secret girlfriend."

"Who is it, then?" He gestured toward her phone, and Lily slipped it back into her pocket. First Daisy, and now Jack? Elsa was right—family was nosy. At least her mom hadn't picked up on it. Lily would never hear the end of it if she ever did.

"A friend."

"I don't look that happy whenever my friends text me."

"When did you become such a smart ass?"

"Puberty," Jack said, his grin cheeky, and Lily rolled her eyes.

The door to the yard slid open and Lily groaned, hoping their peace wasn't about to be disturbed. She turned, but it was only Daisy, closing it behind her as she came to join them.

"Is this where all the cool kids are hanging out?"

"I don't think I've ever been described as cool in my life," Lily said.

"Speak for yourself." Jack looked affronted. "Has anyone noticed we've gone?"

"Nope. They're all in a world of their own." Daisy situated herself between Lily and Jack. "How long are you in town for, Jack?"

"Heading back to Philly in time for New Year."

Daisy turned toward Lily. "Ooh, New Year. How are we celebrating this year? We should go out for it, Lily. I'll find you someone to kiss at midnight."

Lily could think of nothing worse. Clubs and bars were always packed to heaving, sweaty strangers grinding everywhere she looked.

"No, thank you. I've already made one bad kissing mistake this holiday—I don't need to add another to the list." Lily said it without thinking, and only realized what she'd said when Daisy turned to her with wide eyes, looking like Christmas had come again.

"What? Who have you been kissing?"

"I knew you had a secret girlfriend," Jack said, triumphant, and Lily wanted to go and grab the shovel leaning against the side of the garage and dig herself a hole to hide in.

"Secret girlfriend?" Daisy looked between the two of them. "What?"

Lily groaned. "I don't have a secret girlfriend."

"But you've been kissing someone."

"Now seems like a good time for me to bow out," Jack said, looking delighted. "See ya back inside." He ducked into the kitchen, and Lily stared after him longingly.

"Details."

"It was nothing, okay? I made out with someone when I went out for the work Christmas thing." Lily knew she wouldn't get away with brushing Daisy off, but she didn't have to tell her all the details, either. She sure as hell wasn't going to say it was someone from work.

She'd never hear the end of it.

"It was dumb and it was a mistake and I'd rather forget about it, all right?"

"Touchy!" Daisy blinked at her, eyes dark in the moonlight. "Was it that bad?"

Lily tried not to think about how it was the best kiss she'd had in her entire life.

"Awful."

Awful, because she'd yet to stop thinking about it. Awful, because she had no idea how she could possibly look Eva in the eye once school started up again. Awful, because she'd been so stupid, and she wished she could take it back.

"So why not go out on New Year and make some better memories?" Daisy said, wiggling her eyebrows, and Lily sighed, stepping toward the kitchen door—somehow, her family's antics seemed preferable to Daisy's third degree.

"Not going to happen."

As much as Eva enjoyed being off work, it didn't take long for her to be climbing the walls.

She'd never been good at being idle. Being a professor had been great for that, because even when she'd finished grading papers and prepping lectures, she had meetings with her grad students, grants to write, projects to design and research to do. Her mind never truly shut off, and while she knew some of her colleagues had struggled to cope, Eva had reveled in it.

Now, within the first week of her vacation, Eva had: cleaned the entire house from top to bottom (twice); caught up with all her grading; planned her lessons for the first month back; figured out what activities she'd be doing in her next two science and STEM club sessions; and finished all the little niggling departmental jobs Alisha had assigned her.

She still had a week left, and Eva was bored out of her mind. The dinging of her phone was a welcome distraction while she waited for the bread she'd spent the better part of the morning making to bake.

Got anything exciting planned for today?

Unlike Eva, Molly seemed to be enjoying her time away from work. Whenever Eva asked, she was out with family or friends—she'd never mentioned being bored once.

Might go for a long run later, Eva replied. She needed something to fill the day—she'd been up for five hours and it wasn't even noon yet.

You do understand that the purpose of a vacation is to relax, right?

I do, Eva typed, smile pulling at the edges of her lips. *But I've never been good at that.*

Well, then let me help. Why don't we watch a movie together later?

Eva frowned at her screen. How would that work, when they'd agreed not to meet up? She asked, curious what Molly was thinking.

You have Netflix, right? We can choose something on there. Both press play at the same time. Text our opinions to one another.

Not something Eva ever would have thought of doing. It was rare for her to sit down and watch a movie. She only did it with her mother because she knew it made her happy, and because it was nice for them to spend time together.

All right, Eva wrote, because it wasn't like she had anything else planned for the day. *But we're not watching Star Wars.*

I still can't believe you didn't like it.

It's not my kind of movie.

Because things actually happen?

Eva replied with a middle finger.

I'll pick something I think you'll like.

Why can't I pick? From what Eva knew of her and Molly, their tastes couldn't be more different.

Because it was my idea. You can pick next time.

Eva liked the thought of their being a next time. *I'll be free in half an hour,* Eva replied, after checking the timer on her phone. *Let me know when you want to start.*

Two hours later, Eva was doing something unheard of—sliding into her bed in the middle of the afternoon with her laptop balanced on her knees, not wanting to disturb her mother's marathon on the TV downstairs.

Are you in position?

Eva opened Netflix and tapped on the search button. *Yes. What am I putting on?*

The Devil Wears Prada.

Eva was intrigued. *What makes you think I'll like it?*

I think Miranda Priestly will remind you of someone. It would have also been an apt username for you.

We'll see about that.

Though Meryl Streep's Miranda had barely been on the screen for ten seconds and Eva could see why Molly had said it. People scrambled to tidy the office before she arrived, and scattered around her in the lobby, and Eva smiled—the kids did the same whenever she walked down the hall.

There was a woman she could admire.

Okay, Eva typed. *You may have a point.*

I knew it. I can't believe you've never seen this before.

Eva couldn't either, and she snorted when Emily Blunt's character made a despairing comment about Anne Hathaway's fashion sense. She had to agree—the skirt did belong in a convention.

Are you into fashion? Molly asked.

I'm not particularly into designer clothing, but I'll pay a lot for a brand I know will last a long time. Are you?

Not at all.

Somehow, Eva wasn't at all surprised. *You're an Andy, aren't you?*

Absolutely.

Eva smiled, relaxing back into her pillows, and enjoying herself far more than she thought she would.

Chapter 13

LILY DREADED THE FIRST DAY back at school. Not even Elsa's *Have a good day at work!* text could alleviate the panic churning through her gut at the thought of seeing Eva again.

Lily could still remember the heat of her touch, the taste of her skin. It crept in at the most inopportune of moments, along with a heady sense of regret, because what had she been thinking? She'd only been in the job for a few months, planned on staying long-term, and she could have ruined it all for a drunken hook-up.

Lily had never done something so stupid—and vowed never to do something as stupid ever again, nervous anticipation sparking along her skin as she shouldered open the door to the science hallway.

The lights weren't on in Eva's room, and Lily breathed a sigh of relief as she made her way to the teacher's lounge. Mei and Alisha were already inside and offered a welcome distraction.

"Morning, Lily," they chorused.

Lily decided to make some coffee—she needed a pick-me-up—putting her lunch in the fridge while she waited for it to brew.

"Did you manage to have a good break?" Alisha looked like she'd had a relaxing one, an easy smile on her mouth as she sipped from her own mug of coffee.

"I did."

Behind Alisha, the door opened, and Lily swallowed when she saw Eva stride inside. She paused, for a fraction of a second, when she saw Lily before she looked away.

What was she doing in here?

Eva hardly ever came in during the day. She wasn't holding a mug, so she couldn't want a drink. She wasn't approaching the fridge, so she mustn't want something to eat. Was Eva there just to torture her?

Lily supposed it would be on brand.

"I hope you weren't too hungover after the Christmas party," Alisha said, not noticing the way Lily's mind was spinning out of control.

Of course, Eva had to wear a skirt today. Her legs were covered by pantyhose, but still. Lily could remember running her fingers over Eva's thigh, could remember that thigh pressing against her center, and—

"Oh, we were both a mess on Saturday," Mei said. "You should've seen the state of us."

"You went home together?" Alisha said.

"Lily kindly loaned me her couch for the night."

"I don't think there was much kindness to it," Lily said, forcing herself to contribute to the conversation, to look away from Eva. "How long did it take to work the kinks out of your neck?"

"I think one's still there." Mei rolled her head for emphasis, and Lily forced a laugh.

"Alisha?" Eva had apparently had enough of their idle chit-chat. "Could I have a word?"

"Sorry, Eva, of course. I trust you had a relaxing vacation?"

Lily glanced toward her as Alisha led her out into the hall, but Eva's face didn't change. She seemed determined to ignore Lily altogether. Lily hadn't realized "pretend it never happened" was code for "pretend Lily didn't exist".

And Lily knew it was for the best. She didn't want the rest of the department to know about their tête-à-tête—but hell, it still stung, to have the woman who had kissed her senseless less than two weeks ago snub her completely.

It shouldn't have surprised her. Lily knew what kind of person Eva was. She didn't exactly go to great lengths to hide her true colors. It should be a relief, this indifference, yet Lily found herself thinking of Eva's long legs, the slope of her neck, the noise she'd made when Lily had rocked against her, and Jesus, that was not helping.

Lily cleared her throat, grabbing her forgotten-about coffee, and realized she hadn't heard a word Mei had said since Eva had left the room. Fuck.

She needed to shake this off before her first class of the day. At least Lily would be starting with some good news—Carly had scored the second-highest mark in Lily's honors class on their last exam, and Lily couldn't wait to see Carly's face when she told her.

"Before I forget," Alisha said at the start of their first department meeting of the semester. "We've been asked who we want to send as department representatives on the D.C. trip this summer. Eva, I assume you'd like to go?"

"Please." Eva tried not to scowl when she saw Lily glance over at her in shock. No doubt Lily was wondering why Eva would volunteer to spend her time chaperoning forty teenagers. Which was fair—it didn't exactly seem like something Eva would like to do. But it meant a trip back to the city she'd called home for so many years, and the chance to catch up with people she hadn't seen in too long. "We should be able to have full use of the labs at Georgetown again. I'll double-check with my former colleagues."

"Excellent. Anyone else want to take the second spot?"

They hadn't the last two years, leaving it for Alisha, and Eva doubted it would change now.

"Lily?" Alisha said, and Eva tensed. "It's a nice break. We take them around the Smithsonian. Might even be able to get them into the chemistry department if Eva can manage it."

Christ, Eva hadn't considered Lily. Had been trying her hardest to not think of her at all. But surely, she wouldn't say yes. Not after everything. Lily's gaze flickered once again to Eva, settling on her face, and Eva ground her teeth.

"I don't know if I feel ready for that," Lily said, after what felt like an age. "Maybe next year?"

"All right. I'll go along then." Alisha made a note on the sheet of paper in front of her, and Eva breathed a sigh of relief.

Eva could still feel Lily's gaze on her face, and not even a poisonous glare could get her to look away.

It drove Eva wild, because didn't Lily know how much harder she was making this? Eva couldn't think straight with those blue eyes resting on her. Eyes that seemed to see too much, things Eva didn't want to show—things only Lily seemed to bring out of her.

Lily barely looked away from Eva for the remainder of the meeting. It had Eva cornering Lily in her classroom—the first time they'd spoken since Eva had slipped out of her grip in a cloud of shame—once the meeting was over, filled with a reckless kind of anger. "Will you stop it?"

"Stop what?" Lily said, like she was oblivious, like her eyes hadn't been following Eva around all damn week.

"Stop staring. If I'd have known you were incapable of any semblance of self-control, I never would have—" Eva cut herself off abruptly, unwilling to verbalize it. Not here, when she never knew who might be close by, listening in.

"Never would have what?" Lily's spine straightened, and there was that spark, present again, that challenge in blue eyes that had gotten them into this mess in the first place. "Kissed me?"

Eva felt her lip curl, and she resisted the urge to glance over her shoulder.

"Have you forgotten you were a willing participant?"

"A severe lapse in judgment," Eva said, her teeth gritted. "Something that will never happen again."

"Oh, gee, how will I ever cope?" Lily raised a hand to her chest. "I'm not that desperate."

"Then why can't you keep your eyes off me?"

"You noticed?" Lily skirted around the edge of her desk, stopping so close Eva could feel the heat of her. They stared at one another, both breathing heavily, and Eva's mind flashed back to the last time they'd been this close. To the heat of Lily's breath on her lips, to the feeling of her mouth, moving against her own. "Have you been staring, too?"

Eva ground her teeth. "Of course not."

"I think you have." Lily's voice was low, and Eva felt her traitorous heart beating fast in her chest. "I think you—"

"Stop it," Eva growled, because she couldn't stand to hear another word.

"What are you so afraid of?" Lily swayed closer, and did she know how dangerous the game she was playing was? "Feeling something?"

Eva's lip curled, but before she could say anything, there was a light knock on the door, and they both sprang apart.

"You read—oh." Mei paused in the doorway, brows drawing close as she looked between the two of them. "Sorry. I'll meet you at the bar?"

"I'm coming now." Lily seized her bag and breezed past Eva without another word, and Eva stared after her, jaw clenched, furious that Lily had had the last word.

Her mood was improved only by the ding of her phone an hour later.

Thank God it's the weekend.

Eva echoed the sentiment. *Long week?* Hers certainly had been. She felt like she'd lived a lifetime in the last seven days. Five more months until the end of the year. If Eva could make it that long without either kissing or killing Lily she'd count it as a victory.

The longest. Movie this weekend?

Sure. My turn to pick this time, though.

I'll prepare myself to be bored out of my mind.

Eva laughed, already thinking of what classics she could expose Molly to in order to change her opinion before the weekend was through.

"Thanks for helping me out today." Her father accepted the towel Lily handed him when he emerged from beneath the SUV with a busted engine. "I appreciate it."

"I don't know if helping is the right word, but you're welcome." Lily wasn't as useful as his fellow mechanics, but she supposed she was better than nothing. She leaned against the side of the car as her father rummaged through his toolbox, smothering a yawn with the back of her hand.

"Tired already? Don't you get up earlier than this for school?"

"Yes, but not on a Saturday." Lily took a sip from her thermos of coffee, willing the caffeine to get to work soon. "Luckily, I love you enough to sacrifice my weekend lie in for you."

"My hero."

Lily stuck her tongue out at him. A bell jingled, and Lily turned toward the door leading to the office.

"That'll be the auto inspection we're expecting."

"I'll go and book them in."

"Thanks, love."

Lily nearly turned and retreated to the workshop when she stepped into the office and found Eva resting her hands on top of the desk. Her bored expression morphed into shock when her eyes met Lily's. She even dressed well for a visit to the mechanic. The white sweater looked cashmere, and the tailored pants clung to her legs. Lily swallowed her embarrassment at being seen in her sweatpants and an oversized, stained T-shirt.

"Are you fucking kidding me?"

Lily was thinking the same. After the way they'd left things the day before, Lily hadn't expected to speak to Eva again for another week, at least.

"That's not a nice way to greet the person you're about to give your car keys to," Lily said, reaching for the pen tucked behind her ear.

"I know teaching doesn't pay well, but surely it's not bad enough to need a part-time job."

"It's not." Lily tapped the award sitting proudly on the desk, the name Cross Auto Repair written above Mechanic of the Year. "It's my family's business."

"Of course it is."

Lily couldn't believe her luck. Someone above had it out for her. "My dad said you're here for an auto inspection?"

"That's right."

"Can I take your registration please?" She'd already scrawled Eva's name onto the form, printing the registration carefully beside it as Eva read it out. "And your phone number so we can let you know when it's ready?"

"I'll come and wait in here after I've run some errands, if that's all right."

Lily bit her tongue before she said no, wondering if Eva would be so reluctant to give her number if Lily hadn't been the one asking. "Suit yourself. Keys?"

Eva handed them over. "It's parked out front. Try not to scratch it."

Lily was still muttering under her breath when she returned to the workshop.

"You okay?" Her father said when he got a look at her face.

"I'm fine. Do you want me to bring this car around?"

"Sure. Park it in bay two, please."

Even without the Mercedes tag on the keyring, Lily would have been able to identify Eva's car. Three were in the lot—Lily's Corolla, a beat-up Subaru, and the sleek silver Mercedes that flashed when Lily clicked the key. It had a rack on the roof, and Lily wondered, as she slid behind the wheel, if it was a modification for Eva's mother.

She was unsurprised to find the inside of the car immaculately clean, not a wrapper or water bottle in sight. Classical music played through the speakers when the engine purred to life. Putting the car into reverse, Lily checked her mirrors three times before releasing the handbrake.

She tossed the keys to her dad once she'd successfully parked it in the workshop, and he caught them with practiced ease, tucking them into his pocket.

"Would you mind going out front? There's a few admin tasks that need doing. Orders, filing, things like that."

"Things you find too boring, you mean?" Lily knew he much preferred the hands-on aspect of the job.

He grinned and bumped her shoulder with his own. "Too right. But let me know if you need a hand."

"Like you'd know how to help. Do you even know how to use a computer?"

"I've come a long way since you were last here. I can make a spreadsheet now. Anna taught me."

"So you can teach a dinosaur new tricks."

He flicked his greasy towel toward her, and Lily leapt out of the way. "I hope you don't speak to your usual boss that way."

Alisha would find it funny. "I know you can take it." Lily pressed a kiss to his cheek before returning to the office. Much to her relief, it was empty, but she knew it wasn't likely to last for long.

Sure enough, the bell jingled half an hour later, signifying Eva's return. She glanced once at Lily before taking the furthest seat she possibly could, and Lily tried to ignore her as she concentrated on ordering twenty tires from their usual supplier. Her dad would kill her if she got the wrong ones.

A phone rang, and Lily tried not to listen as Eva answered it.

"Hi, Angela."

Okay, she didn't try very hard. Who the hell was Angela? Did Eva, the self-professed loner, actually have friends?

"Is everything all ri—what?"

The note of panic in Eva's voice made Lily look away from the computer screen, because she'd never heard her sound like that before. Her face was pale, the fingers of Eva's hand shaking where they held the phone to her ear.

"Is she conscious? Have you called an ambulance?"

Jesus. Was it her mom?

Eva was shaking her head, beginning to shove the papers she'd been grading into her bag with one hand. "No, no, that's okay. I didn't realize Tom was with you, if he can drive her to the hospital that's fine. I'll meet you there as soon as I can." Eva hung up the phone, her eyes wild as she turned to Lily. "How much longer do you think my car will be?"

"Uhm." Lily glanced through the window toward the workshop. Her dad was bent over the engine of Eva's Mercedes. "I can ask, but I think it'll be a while. It usually takes an hour or two, and he's on his own this morning."

"No matter. I'll call an Uber." Eva was already scrolling on her phone.

"I can drive you to the hospital. Save you from having to wait."

Extending the offer in light of everything was madness, but Eva was frantic, and Lily wasn't going to leave her stranded. She'd make the offer to any other customer. It didn't have to mean anything.

Eva's head jerked away from her phone, her gaze meeting Lily's, disbelief written across her face. "You would?"

Lily shrugged. "Sure. It's not too far from here."

"I—thank you."

"Let me just go tell my dad," Lily said, logging off the computer and pushing herself away from the desk, "and we can go."

A plastic water bottle hit the side of Eva's foot as Lily pulled her Corolla out of its parking space.

"Sorry about the mess." Lily looked sheepish, ducking her head and hiding her flaming cheeks behind her hair. "I wasn't expecting company."

Eva waved a hand, because the fine layer of dust on the dashboard was the least of her worries. She could still hear Angela's frantic voice in her ear—"your mother's had a fall, I think she hit her head, and her ankle doesn't look good"—adrenaline making her heart pound, and Eva wished Lily would put her damn foot down.

A distraction. Eva needed a distraction so she didn't think about head injuries or surgeries or long-term complications or—

"I've seen your desk," Eva said, glancing at Lily out of the corner of her eye. "This doesn't come as much of a surprise."

"My desk isn't that messy."

"It is compared to mine."

"Anyone's would be a mess compared to yours. You do know a desk is for storing things, right? The world won't end if there's one piece of paper not in a drawer."

This, Eva could do, this easy kind of back-and-forth banter only Lily seemed to be able to illicit. Eva felt the tremble in her hands lessen as Lily pulled onto the highway. "There's nothing wrong with order. With having everything in its rightful place, if the alternative is chaos."

"Is that what you think I am?" Lily's gaze darted toward Eva before back to the road. "Chaos?"

Okay, maybe this hadn't been such a good idea after all.

"I think you're a lot of things," Eva said instead. "A giant pain in my ass, for one."

"You know, I don't get what I've done to make you hate me." Lily's hands were tight on the steering wheel, her knuckles flashing white. "So I got in your way on my first day and then tried to talk to you at lunch. Is that really all I did wrong?"

Eva sighed, watching the trees flash by the window and wondering if she should have waited for an Uber after all. She and Lily never had done well in enclosed spaces, and there was no option for Eva to escape unless she wanted to ruin her sweater by rolling out of the passenger door and onto the road.

But Lily was doing her a favor, even after Eva had been horrible to her earlier in the week, so maybe she owed her a sliver of honesty.

"You didn't do anything wrong," Eva said, refusing to take her eyes from the window. "I'd have acted the same with anyone else."

"You don't, though. You don't argue with anyone else. You don't—"

"Kiss anyone else outside bars at Christmas parties?" Eva supplied.

"So, why me?"

Now, there was a question Eva wished she had the answer to. "I don't know. Maybe because no one else has ever bitten back before. Not the way you do."

"Oh, so you can give it but you can't take it?"

"Something like that."

Lily was quiet for a while, the only sound the terrible pop song on the radio. Eva would never understand how people could listen to that noise.

"We could get along, you know, you and I." Lily looked straight ahead, her jaw clenched like she was wondering if this was such a good idea. "If you'd let it happen."

"I'm not so sure about that."

"But aren't you tired of all this back and forth, arguing all the time?"

"No. It keeps me on my toes." It kept Lily from getting too close; kept Eva from doing something she couldn't take back. "But I suppose it's not exactly professional."

"Right. So how about a truce."

"A truce?" Eva pursed her lips, mulling it over. "Are you going to be less irritating?"

"Only if you're less annoying."

Eva huffed out a laugh. "I'm not confident how long it'll last, but… I suppose there's no harm in trying."

Lily let out her breath, relief on her face, and Eva wondered, as Lily pulled into the hospital parking lot, whether things would really feel different come Monday morning.

"Thank you," Eva said, her fingers curled around the door handle. "You didn't have to do this, and I...I do appreciate it."

"It wasn't any trouble. I hope your mom's okay. It is your mom, right?"

Eva had to force herself not to bristle at the question, her automatic response being to shut Lily down. "Yes. She had a fall. Hopefully not too serious, but I guess I'll find out soon. I'll come by and pick my car up when I can."

"Don't worry about it, my dad said we can hold it for as long as you need."

"Thank you." Eva slipped from the car, already lifting her phone to her ear. She didn't watch Lily drive away. "I'm here," she said when Angela answered. "Where are you?"

"Still in the ER," Angela said, and Eva hurried toward the door. It wasn't difficult to find them inside—they were tucked into a corner, Angela's wheelchair beside her mother's and Tom sitting on one of the plastic chairs beside them.

"Mom, are you okay?" Eva fell to her knees in front of her, taking her mother's hands and peering at her face. She was pale, a trickle of blood on her brow from where she must have hit her head, and Eva could see from a glance her ankle had swollen to nearly twice the size.

"I'm fine." She smiled, but it was weak, and Eva knew she was putting on a brave face. "There's no need for all this fuss."

"Yes, there is. What happened?"

"I was trying to get into the stair lift. Thought my legs were behaving themselves today so I stood up, but they buckled. Went over my ankle and hit my head on the wall."

Eva groaned. "Mom, you need to be more careful. What if Angela hadn't been there? What if you were knocked unconscious and I didn't get back for hours?" Eva thought of her mother lying sprawled at the bottom of the stairs and felt sick.

"Don't you go blaming yourself for this," her mother said, voice stern. "Accidents happen."

"But I should have been there." Wasn't that why she'd moved back here? To stop things like this happening? To make her mother safer?

"You can't watch me twenty-four-seven, Eva. If you did, neither one of us would survive it."

Eva knew it was an attempt to make her laugh, but she couldn't smile, not with her stomach roiling.

"I'm going to be fine." Her mother touched gentle fingers to Eva's cheek. "It'll take more than a wall to kill me off."

"Don't joke about that." Eva's voice was sharper than she intended, but she couldn't bear the thought of no longer having her mother around.

"I'm not going anywhere. You, however, could go and get me a coffee if you want to make yourself useful."

"I don't think that's a good idea. What if they need to operate on your ankle?"

"Please, there's nothing wrong with it."

"It's doubled in size."

"Maybe I just have a lot of water retention today."

Eva shook her head, but at least her mother's ability to joke about it meant it might not be as serious as Eva feared. She rose to her feet and took a seat beside Tom. "Thank you for bringing her here. You two don't have to wait—it could be a while."

Tom shook his head. "Nonsense. We're not going anywhere until we know she's going to be okay. Besides, you'll need a ride back into town, won't you? Or is your car all finished?"

"No. I got a ride here."

"Then it's settled."

Flooded with gratitude, Eva squeezed his arm and blinked away tears. She was so used to it being her and her mother against the world—knowing they weren't alone, that there was someone there to lend a helping hand, meant more than she could ever possibly say.

Eva thought of Lily, offering to help despite the way Eva had treated her since the night of the Christmas party, and felt something twist inside her chest. Eva wasn't used to people treating her that way, to reaching out when she was in need. And she knew that was her own fault—what she wanted, even, from the way she acted, her attitude toward everyone around her. But not Lily.

Never Lily.

When would she stop surprising Eva? When would Lily react like everyone else did? When would Eva push her so far she'd never come back?

It was a miracle Eva hadn't already.

Eva thought of Lily's warm blue eyes, the softness of her voice in the car, and swallowed down the flame that flickered to life in her long-dormant heart. No. This wasn't happening. Eva shook her head; this was merely a gut reaction to what had happened to her mother, to how lonely Eva would be without her.

Lily didn't mean anything to her.

And she never would.

Chapter 14

Lily did a double-take when she found Eva in the teacher's lounge on Monday afternoon. She'd expected her to rush home the second her classes were done, but apparently not before she made a phone call, a faint note of exasperation in her voice.

Lily forced her gaze away from taking in the sight of her charcoal pencil skirt tight over her ass as she leaned over the counter, because if she was caught ogling Eva, it might fracture the tentative truce between them before it had even had a chance to get started.

Lily went to the coffee machine. The phone clattered back onto the hook as Lily was filling her mug. Eva heaved a frustrated sigh, and Lily turned toward her.

"Everything okay?"

"Parents are the worst part of this job."

Something else they agreed on. "I guess you didn't have to deal with that at Georgetown."

"No." Eva pinched the bridge of her nose. "If they spent even half of the amount of time they spend complaining actually parenting their children, then they wouldn't misbehave to the point of needing a detention."

"Yeah, but entitled parents want us to do the parenting on top of everything else we do for their kids." Lily took a sip of her coffee and noted the bags under Eva's eyes. "How's your mom?"

Lily had been relieved of lending a helping hand by the arrival of Anna before Eva had returned to pick up her car. The last time Lily had seen Eva, she'd been racing toward the door to the ER.

"As best as she can be, all things considered. She had a broken ankle but no concussion."

"Is it a bad break?"

"No, but she'll be in a cast for six weeks. At least she's already used to using a wheelchair, so it shouldn't hamper her too much. I wanted to thank you again for taking me to her." It looked like it physically pained Eva to say it, and Lily tried not to grin.

"Don't worry about it. I'm glad she's okay."

"Me too," Eva said quietly, her relief clear to see on her face. "I'd better be getting back to her. Make sure she's not caused any more damage while I've been here."

"See you tomorrow." As the door shut behind her, Lily marveled at the fact they'd just managed some civility. If she could forget they'd kissed at the Christmas party, maybe things between them could almost be friendly.

Shaking her head, Lily followed Eva out. Outside of her classroom, a small group of kids awaited her. Lily had extended her tutoring sessions from just Carly after noticing a few of her other students struggling as the content got harder.

Carly still came, even though her grades—and her confidence—had improved. She smiled at Lily as she ushered them inside.

"Is there anything in particular you'd like to go over today?" Lily said, setting her mug of coffee on her desk as the seats on her front row were filled.

Amanda raised their hand. "Calculating molar mass."

"And Avogadro's number," said Ben.

"Okay." Lily turned to the board. "Let me know as soon as something doesn't make sense."

Over the next ten minutes, Lily covered the board in notes and equations, six heads bobbing in unison whenever she asked if they were okay. Afterwards, Lily set them off on some problems, and smiled when she noticed Carly leaning over to help Amanda with a question.

One of Lily's favorite things was seeing someone who was struggling begin to succeed, and she hoped, as she assured both Carly and Amanda the answer they'd come to was right, that Carly no longer dreaded Lily's class.

And knew that there was at least one other teacher in the school who was rooting for her.

A light knock sounded on Lily's door, and ten pairs of eyes turned toward it.

Their GSA group had grown, and Lily looked forward to Thursdays, to seeing what bright and beautiful ideas they came up with. Were they about to have a new member? Lily called "Come in!" when the door didn't open.

She nearly fell off her chair when Denny Marshall stepped inside.

"What are you doing here?" Jude's eyes narrowed when he saw Denny, and Lily didn't blame him. Denny had been well-behaved since his detention, but Lily knew old wounds didn't heal easily—and who knew how he was in his other classes? What snide remarks had been left unchecked by Lily's colleagues?

"I'm interested in joining now the football season's over." Denny scratched at the back of his neck, his eyes on the floor, and Lily wondered if he was regretting his decision.

A surprising decision, to be sure. Had her research task had a long-standing effect on him? Lily hoped there was nothing insidious at play.

"Why?" Jude wasn't the only one who looked confused. Denny, it seemed, had quite the reputation with most of the GSA members.

"I want to help. Spread the word, or whatever. You don't have to be gay to join, do you?" Denny turned defensive, and Lily wondered if he'd been naïve enough to think there wouldn't be any pushback. "Doesn't it stand for gay-straight alliance?"

Denny willingly doing his own research? Unheard of. Lily wished he could apply the same drive in her class—he might be well-behaved, but despite being in her honors class he was still her laziest student by far.

"It does, but we don't have to accept everyone," Macie said, glancing toward Jude. "And we have more than one reason not to accept you."

"Yeah, I know. Look, I know I've been a dick." He glanced toward Lily. "Sorry."

She waved him off—he was right, after all.

"But when I was in detention with Miss Cross, she opened my eyes to a lot of things I'd never thought about. How much stuff you all go through. How hurtful words can be. And I know I can't take back all the shitty— sorry again—things I've done, but maybe I can help make up for them."

"I think it's something we need to discuss," Macie said, speaking slowly, and several of her peers nodded in agreement.

"I'll wait outside." Denny hiked the strap of his bag further up his shoulder and stepped back into the hall.

Jude turned to Lily with wide eyes. "What did you do to him?"

"I gave him a research project. Had him look into the high rates of mental illness and suicide in the LGBTQIA+ community. I thought it would be a fitting punishment. After all, homophobia and transphobia have their roots in ignorance. I didn't expect it to have this kind of effect, though." Denny had made no indication of his change of heart in her lessons.

"Do we think he's genuine?" Macie said.

"He seems it." Hannah twirled a piece of hair around their index finger. "But it's a risk if he's not. This is our safe space. If he goes running his mouth, it could be bad for some of us." They glanced at Jude. "What do you think?"

"I don't know. I feel like we shouldn't discriminate, but at the same time…" Jude's eyes flickered to Lily. "Do you think he's changed?"

"I think he looked contrite by the time I was through with him." Lily didn't think Denny was much of an actor. "If you decide to let him in, I can have a word with him if you like. Stress there will be strong repercussions should he cause any of you trouble."

"I'm happy with that," Jude said, and several of the others nodded.

"All right. I'll go and tell him." Denny was waiting down the hall. "They're happy for you to join, but there are a few conditions.

"First of all, whatever is mentioned in the group doesn't leave this room. While it might be public knowledge to some, you don't talk about who's in the group with other people. If I hear so much as a whisper you've broken either of those, you'll be in detention every night with me for the rest of the year."

"I won't, I swear."

"The last one—and this an important one—it isn't their job to educate you, or to tell you how to do better. That's something you need to figure out for yourself."

"Okay."

Lily held Denny's gaze, checking one last time for some sign of deceit. Finding none, she stepped aside to let him into her classroom. Several of the kids gave him a wary look as he dropped onto a seat near the back of the room.

It took a while for conversation to pick up again. When Denny seemed content to listen, the others grew in confidence until it was like a normal Thursday afternoon.

"LGBTQIA+ history month is coming up," Macie said, while Lily was using the time to check through her e-mails.

Four of them were excuses from her students for why they were unable to do this week's homework. Only one seemed valid—she'd be handing out detentions again.

"I thought it might be fun for us to do a session where we each choose a person from history to do a presentation on." Macie's gaze flickered to Denny. "Maybe we could all learn something."

"We could make posters, too," said Kelly. "Hang them up around school."

"You could write an article for the school newspaper." Denny swallowed when everyone turned to look at him. "I know some of the seniors who run it. I wouldn't be able to write it." He ran a hand through his hair, his smile wry. "But I could talk to them about it. I doubt they'd say no."

"Thanks, Denny. That's a good idea." Macie looked as surprised to say it as Lily had been to hear the suggestion come from him in the first place. "Maybe we could have a regular column."

"We could ask them to put in the details for the rummage sale at the end of the month, too," Hannah said. "The more people we get to come, the more profit we'll make."

They chatted among themselves for the remainder of the session, and Lily was glad to see a smile on Denny's face when he left the room.

There was a matching one on her face, too.

It was good to feel like she was making a difference.

Eva slung her bag over her shoulder and locked the door to her classroom. Her papers were safely tucked inside, ready for another night of grading sitting in front of the TV with her mother.

She was halfway down the hall when she heard the sound of breaking glass.

"Motherfucker."

The curse echoed through the hallway, and Eva paused beside Lily's open door.

"I didn't know that word was in your vocabulary," Eva said, and Lily glanced up. She was hunched over at the back of the room cradling a bloodied hand, broken pieces of a conical flask scattered around her feet.

"Are you all right?" Eva said when she studied Lily's face more closely. She was pale, swaying in place where she crouched.

"Been better." Lily shifted to lean against the cupboard behind her.

"Let me see." Eva strode forward, picking her way through the glass in her black ankle boots and extending a hand toward Lily.

"I'm okay."

"You're not. You're white as a ghost."

"I'm not too good with blood." Lily refused to look at her hand, instead keeping her gaze on Eva's face.

"What do you do once a month?"

"Power through."

Eva huffed out a laugh before reaching again for Lily's hands. Lily winced when Eva uncurled her fingers to reveal the cut: about an inch long, the slice ran down the center of her left palm. "It's deep," Eva said, and she grabbed some paper towels from by the sink and pressed them to Lily's palm to try and stem the bleeding. "Come on, there's a first aid kit in the teacher's lounge."

"You don't have to help."

Eva wondered if it was instinct, to resist Eva's offer. To dig in her heels, so she could lick her wounds in private.

Eva supposed she'd feel that way if their positions were reversed. But Lily had helped her at the weekend, and it was her turn to return the favor.

"What are you going to do if I don't? You can't even look at it."

"I could manage."

"Don't be so stubborn." Eva gave Lily her best no-nonsense look, and Lily sighed before following her out of the room. "Keep putting pressure on it. Raise it above your head."

"Wouldn't have thought you were first aid trained," Lily said, but she did as she was told as Eva pulled the first aid kit out of a cabinet beneath the sink and set it on the table.

"Are you trying to say I'm not the caring type?" Eva raised an eyebrow, and Lily chuckled. "I didn't do it for the school," she said, not looking Lily in the eye as she wrapped her fingers around the soft skin of her wrist, bending her head to examine the extent of the injury. "They don't even know. I don't want them sending kids to my room to stick a Band-Aid on a papercut." Eva shuddered at the thought. "I did it for my mother. In case she ever needed it."

"So you are the caring type," Lily said, and Eva's fingers twitched, just barely resisting the temptation to poke her.

"Only for her," Eva said, and when she glanced up she found Lily's gaze on her, their faces mere inches apart. Eva swallowed, not realizing they were so close—close enough for Eva to be able to smell her shampoo, to see the delicate curve of her cheekbones, the flutter of her eyelashes as she winced when Eva swiped an antiseptic wipe across the wound.

Lily cleared her throat, and Eva looked away, fingers shaking as she reached for a bandage.

"It must be hard."

"It's not a round-the-clock job. She's independent. In fact if you asked her, she'd say she doesn't need me at all."

"Still. You've given up a lot."

"And I'd do it all over again," Eva said without hesitation, ripping off a piece of tape with her teeth to secure the bandage in place. "There. Now we're even."

"We don't have to keep score, you know." Lily sounded amused. "That's not what friends do."

"Friends?" Eva couldn't hide the disbelief, and Lily grinned, some color coming back to her cheeks. "Let's not get too carried away."

"Friends, colleagues, casual acquaintances. I'll take you not wanting to murder me when we pass one another in the hall." Lily stretched out her hand, looking at Eva's handiwork.

"I don't think it needs stitches," Eva said, "but if it bleeds through, you should think about getting it checked out by a professional."

"Yes, doctor. Hey, that still works." Lily smiled at her own joke, and Eva rolled her eyes.

"Has the blood loss gone to your head?"

"Possibly." Lily reached for the box of cookies on the table. Eva shook her head when Lily offered it to her. "What was your doctorate on?"

"I specialized in targeting receptor signaling pathways as a potential treatment for cancer," Eva said, the words rolling off her tongue.

"Oh yeah? Which pathways? p53? Notch? RAS?"

Eva blinked—she hadn't expected Lily to have the slightest clue what she was talking about—and Lily grinned at the look on her face.

"Not as dumb as I look," Lily said, and Eva threw a pointed glance at the bandage wrapped around her hand. "Uncalled for."

Eva felt her lips twitch into a smirk. "How did you know all of those?"

"Used to work in pharma, remember? I was part of a few projects targeting cell signaling."

"I'm guessing you didn't enjoy it." Eva leaned against the kitchen counter, realizing it was the first time she'd ever inquired about any of her fellow teacher's lives.

"I liked the research well enough. Not so much the rest of it. I'm curious, though," Lily said, and Eva braced herself. "What do you think I did before teaching?"

"Modeled for the Gap?"

"You think I could be a model?"

"That's what you took from that?" Eva shook her head. "I think you need to sort your priorities out."

"My priorities are fine, thank you." Lily was smiling, her hand seemingly forgotten.

Who would've thought they could banter like this without wanting to kill one another?

"I should be getting home." Eva re-packed the first aid kit with efficiency before tucking it back into the cabinet. "Try not to injure yourself again."

"It almost sounds like you care."

"I merely don't want you to take up any more of my time," Eva said, but she knew it lacked its usual bite.

Happy Valentine's Day. Molly's message was accompanied by a gif of a bouquet of roses, and Eva shook her head.

Valentine's Day is even more commercialized and contrived than Christmas, Eva replied. *It's not a real holiday.*

Wow. Someone didn't get any presents this morning.

Eva hadn't received a Valentine's Day present ever. *I just don't see the point in it. Surely, if you're in a relationship with someone you should show them you love them every day. Not once a year when the price of flowers and chocolates go up three-fold.*

"Eva! You're not watching!" The indignant voice sounded from a few feet away, and Eva glanced up from her phone to find a four-year-old glaring at her from the top of the tallest slide on the playground.

Babysitting hadn't been on Eva's agenda for the morning, but when Angela's grandkids had spied Eva dropping her mother off at Angela's house, she'd been roped into helping. Alison and Sam loved her—because she didn't fuss over them like everyone else—and not even Eva was immune to the twins' puppy-dog eyes.

Eva watched Alison fly down the slide, whooping with glee, before turning her attention back to Molly.

Sometimes it's nice to have an excuse to spoil someone.

Why do you need an excuse?

I didn't have you pegged as a hopeless romantic.

Eva snorted. *That's a bit of a stretch. My ex certainly wouldn't say so.*

Rough breakup?

Nothing like yours, Eva typed, remembering Molly's cheating ex. *But it hurt all the same. I had to move away from where we lived due to circumstances outside of my control. I thought she'd come with me, but she refused. She promised we'd still be able to make it work long-distance, but... turned out she was good at breaking promises as well as hearts.*

Eva couldn't remember the last time she'd willingly talked so openly about Victoria. She'd used to refuse, the wounds still feeling raw, but two years later, with the weak winter sun on her face and the sound of giggling children all around her, it didn't ache as much as it used to.

Her loss. You deserve better than that.

Eva swallowed, the words hitting harder than she expected. *And so do you. Someone who will buy you stupidly expensive flowers and chocolates. And not just once a year.*

I'll settle for picking up something heart-shaped in the sales tomorrow morning, Molly replied, and Eva chuckled.

A tiny hand tugged on the bottom of her jacket, and Eva found Sam staring up at her with hopeful green eyes. "Will you push me on the swings?"

"Come on, then." Eva slipped her phone into her pocket and let him drag her over to them, leaving Alison chattering to Angela and her mother with a speed only little kids seemed to be able to manage.

Chapter 15

THE NIGHT OF THE WINTER Formal arrived, and in light of her and Eva's new-found civility, Lily found she wasn't dreading it as much as she thought she would.

Not that she was looking forward to it. A night spent chaperoning rowdy teenagers wasn't high on Lily's agenda, but at least she wouldn't be on edge the whole time, braced for attack.

Lily arrived at the country club chosen to hold the event early. A few other cars were in the parking lot, and she noticed Eva's Mercedes among them. She walked into the large function room where the last-minute preparations were being made by the planning committee. Drapes hung from the ceiling, and snowflakes were dotted around the room. Spring colors might have been more appropriate, considering it was nearly March—why they were holding Winter Formal so late in the year, Lily didn't know—but she had to admit the white and blue hues looked beautiful.

Eva was tucked away in a corner, her dress a deep purple. It wasn't as clingy as the one she'd worn to the Christmas party—thank God—but she still looked breath-taking, and Lily averted her gaze.

She was grateful for the distraction of the students arriving, music from the DJ pulsing through the room, because it stopped her attention from wandering to Eva.

Most of the attendees were juniors, but Lily spotted a few familiar faces. Mark and Hannah from the GSA waved when they saw her, and a couple of her students had been brought along as dates.

Lily glanced at her watch and groaned when she saw barely an hour had passed. No one would miss her if she ducked out for a breather, would they? A quick round of messages with Elsa would perk her up, and then she'd be ready to take on the rest of the night.

The club was a maze, and Lily found herself on a balcony overlooking the golf course, the lights of the suburbs visible in the distance.

Somehow, she wasn't surprised to find someone else already there, their hands splayed across the wrought-iron railing.

Eva turned at the sound of Lily's heels hitting the concrete floor.

"Hiding from someone?" Eva leaned her back against the railing. "Or looking for me?"

This was a bad idea, Lily thought as she stepped closer, a shiver running through her as the night air hit the bare skin of her arms. "Why would I be looking for you?"

"I don't know. You always seem to be around, don't you?"

"What can I say? I live to annoy you."

"So it seems. Are you not having fun?" Eva looked more relaxed than usual, her eyes dark in the moonlight.

"Watching teenagers awkwardly slow dance? Love it."

Eva's lips curled, and Lily pressed a hand to her chest.

"Oh my God, I didn't know you could smile."

"Don't ruin the moment," Eva said, without missing a beat. Like this, shrouded in darkness, her face open and unguarded, it was so hard for Lily to deny the attraction igniting in the pit of her stomach.

Wrong, Lily thought, as she drifted closer. Wrong to feel that way for Eva. To think of her like that. She shouldn't want Eva.

But then, maybe that was part of the draw. Knowing it was wrong. Knowing it could end in nothing short of disaster. Lily had trust issues a mile long, and what better person to want than someone who would never want her back? Who could never hurt Lily, because she wore her intentions on her sleeve like some people wore their heart, someone who had walls even higher than Lily's, so high they were impossible to scale?

"Why are you looking at me like that?" Eva tilted her head to one side, and Lily blinked—she was staring, lost in her own self-realization, and she hoped her cheeks didn't burn red in the moonlight.

"Sorry. Miles away."

"Everything okay?"

"Are you feeling okay? You sound concerned."

Eva rolled her eyes. "I could insult you, if you like. I wouldn't have to dig deep. That dress is…" She trailed off, her gaze taking Lily in, and Lily felt the heat of it like a physical touch. "Interesting."

"Is that the best you can come up with? You're losing your touch." Lily found herself gravitating closer, until her hip was leaning against the railing beside her. "I think you like it."

"I don't like a thing about you." Eva said it like a reflex, and Lily tried not to grin.

"See, I think you do," Lily said, her voice light. "And that's what you can't stand."

Eva's expression turned thoughtful. "Are you sure you're in the right career? You might prefer being a therapist. Or teaching psychology."

"I don't think I'd be good at that." Lily rested her arms on the balcony railing and tried to ignore the heat she could feel radiating from Eva as she glanced up at the sky. It was a cloudless night, and the stars glittered above. "It's too subjective. I like chemistry because it's certain. You add an acid to an alkali and you know they make a salt and water. You know if you add a catalyst it speeds up the rate of reaction. But people—people are hard to understand. People don't make sense, and they rarely do what you expect them to. They're messy and unpredictable and that—that's terrifying."

Eva tilted her head, studying Lily closely. "I agree, but isn't that what keeps things interesting? Life would be boring if we all went around behaving the exact same way."

"Maybe you're right. God, imagine a world full of yous." Lily shuddered, and Eva's eyes narrowed into slits. "You'd fight to the death until there was only one left standing."

"Imagine a world full of yous," Eva countered, her lip curled in distaste. "Everything all sunshine and rainbows. Talk about boring."

"I suppose everything needs a counterbalance. Acid and alkali. Bitter and sweet."

"Are you saying we neutralize one another?" Eva quirked an eyebrow. "That we should mix and see what happens?" Amusement underlined the words, but a dark look flickered in Eva's eyes, and Lily wondered if she was remembering the last time that had happened.

Remembering Lily's tongue stroking against hers, Lily's hands on her skin, and Lily burned with the memory of it, especially now, with Eva so close, her perfume invading her senses.

"I don't know." Lily barely recognized her own voice, low and breathy, lost in the gray of Eva's eyes.

They stood on a precipice, one they kept finding themselves returning to, no matter what they tried.

Maybe they needed to try something new.

"Maybe we should try."

Eva's eyebrows twitched upwards, but her gaze dropped to Lily's lips. "I don't think that's a good idea."

"Neither do I." It was a terrible idea, in fact. The worst she'd ever had, yet—there was a part of her that still wanted it. Which was absurd. Lily's heart was beating so fast, it was a wonder Eva couldn't hear it, her throat tight and her mouth dry, anticipation humming beneath the surface of her skin.

"But we can't keep ending up like this." Lily couldn't stand it.

"No. I suppose you're right."

"So, scientifically speaking," Lily said, gaze falling to Eva's lips. "We should try an alternative approach."

God, what was she doing? Something stupid, something reckless, something completely unlike her.

Eva took a breath, and Lily waited. Was she about to agree? Was she about to scoff in Lily's face, turn on her heel and insist this was all a giant joke? Was she—?

Eva leaned forward and kissed her.

This is the worst idea she'd ever had, Eva thought, as she dragged Lily over to a darkened corner of the balcony and pressed her bodily against the wall.

A terrible idea, as a thigh slipped between Eva's legs and a tongue licked into her mouth, Lily's skin soft and warm beneath her searching fingertips, but Eva didn't know how to stop now she'd started.

Eva pressed closer, and Lily shifted her hands to Eva's ass, digging her nails in to pull Eva into a slow grind that set her whole body alight.

Lily lifted one of her legs, resting her foot against the wall, pressing her thigh firmly against Eva's center. The friction had Eva's eyes rolling, and she dropped one of her hands to Lily's other thigh, slipping her fingers beneath the silken material of Lily's dress to rake across her skin.

The last time they'd kissed, Eva hadn't allowed herself to touch Lily, because in her head that made it more real, felt like admitting defeat, that Eva wanted her, but the rock of her hips had already given the game away, so Eva didn't hold herself back anymore.

Eva settled her other hand on Lily's chest, cupping one of her full breasts, a groan echoing into her mouth and a nipple stiffening beneath her palm. Lily arched into her, and Eva could feel slick heat against her thigh, wondered how quickly Lily would fall apart when Eva slid her fingers between her legs.

"Sh-should we not... Fuck!" Lily snapped her jaw shut when Eva trailed her lips over it, tongue slipping free to taste the skin of her neck. "Should we not move this elsewhere?"

"I'm good with here."

"What if—God—someone comes looking for us?"

"They won't." Not for Eva, anyway. Eva doubted anyone had noticed she'd disappeared.

"But—"

Eva sighed, nipping her teeth at Lily's skin to try and shut her up. She needed Lily to stop talking, she decided, dragging her lips down her neck. Lily moaned when Eva flickered her tongue against the throbbing pulse in Lily's neck, and that was a sound Eva wouldn't mind hearing again.

Dangerous, this feeling. Dangerous, the way Lily clutched at her, groaning when Eva's fingers teased a nipple through the thin material of Lily's dress. Dangerous, and heady, and oh-so-wrong, the sound of the music pulsing all around them.

What would happen if the door opened and they were discovered?

Stupid, Eva thought, her lips on Lily's neck as she slid her hand down Lily's stomach. Reckless.

And yet worth it. To finally quiet the roiling feeling inside her chest whenever she looked Lily's way was its own form of vindication.

Eva raised her head. Lily's was tilted back against the wall, her lips parted to draw in ragged breaths, her eyes dark and her pupils blown wide.

Lily's eyelashes fluttered when Eva rucked up the skirt of her dress and pushed soaked cotton aside. She spread her legs for Eva's searching fingers, and Eva found Lily slick and aching.

She was so wet, Eva's fingers sliding through her folds, and at the first swipe of her clit Lily's hips jerked, her hands tangling in Eva's hair. Eva loved nothing more than having a woman at her mercy, but knew she didn't have time to tease.

Knew they shouldn't be doing this in the first place—certainly not there.

Eva pressed two fingers inside oh so easily, and when she added a third, Lily breathed out a curse. Eva took in the sight of her—head back, eyes screwed shut, lips parted, eyeliner smudged and sweat sticking her hair to her brow—and knew it would be burned into her memory for years to come.

Eva worked Lily up with broad strokes, letting Lily pull her into a kiss that turned messy as she circled Lily's clit with her thumb. Lily's whole body tensed when she came, her hands tight in Eva's hair, pulsing around Eva's fingers.

Eva knew she should slip away, once Lily had stopped quaking. Should come to her senses, excuse herself to the bathroom with the promise of never speaking of it again, but when Lily reached for her with her hands, Eva didn't bat them away.

This had been building for months, and Eva didn't know how she could possibly pull away.

Lily surged forward and switched their positions, pressing Eva against the wall and her mouth to Eva's neck. Her teeth scraped across Eva's skin as her hands slid over Eva's hips. Lily wasted no time in diving her fingers beneath the skirt of Eva's dress, and Eva wondered if the urgency was because of where they were, or because Lily thought Eva might push her away at any moment.

But Eva didn't know how to summon the will, not with Lily cupping her through damp lace, palm of her hand grinding against Eva's clit. Fuck, that felt better than it ought to, Eva's teeth clamping around her bottom lip to smother a moan.

She felt Lily smile against her neck, lips pressing open-mouthed kisses to her skin as Lily tugged Eva's underwear aside, the pads of her fingers exploring slick skin.

Teasing touches turned deliberate, Eva's knees trembling when two fingers pressed inside her, Lily's thumb settling at her clit, teeth working at her neck and making her head spin.

Eva splayed one hand against Lily's back as her hips rocked into Lily's touch, her other cupping a full breast, thumb flicking over Lily's nipple.

"Fuck," Lily whispered into Eva's skin, driving deeper. Eva's heart thundered in her ears, her breathing ragged. Lily's fingers curled and her thumb circled faster and...goddammit, Lily wasn't supposed to be so good at this...the breath was knocked from Eva's lungs when she came, Lily coaxing her through the aftershocks as her vision went white.

"This is not how I thought this night would go," Lily said as Eva tried to catch her breath.

Eva agreed wholeheartedly, tilting her head back and admiring the glow of the stars above. "Me either."

God, what had she done? All those weeks of trying to keep Lily at arm's length, of not letting her get too close ruined in a single moment of surrender.

How could they carry on as usual now that Eva had felt Lily fall apart in her arms? How could Eva stop herself falling if all it took for her walls to collapse was Lily stepping close?

Eva stiffened in Lily's arms, feeling like she was suffocating with the press of Lily's body against her own.

"It was fun, though, right?"

Eva noted the quiver of vulnerability in Lily's voice, the uncertain look in her eyes when Eva looked down, and Eva swallowed, her throat feeling tight. "Yes. Could you not tell?" Eva raised an eyebrow, and Lily's breath puffed against her collarbone when she chuckled.

Lily's eyes were bright in the darkness, her smile glittering like the stars above, and Eva pushed down any feelings of warmth the sight flooded through her chest.

"We should head back," Eva said, because the longer they stayed, the more likely someone would notice they were missing. "Before anyone comes looking."

"Right." Lily stepped back, running a trembling hand over the skirt of her dress and smoothing it back into place. "I'll go first. See you out there."

Lily glanced back at Eva before she slipped through the door, taking one last look. Eva watched Lily go, her heartbeat ringing loud in her ears, wondering what the hell she was supposed to do now.

Lily wished she could possess even a modicum of Eva's composure as she watched Eva from across the room. Aside from a few flyaway strands of hair, and a flush high on her cheekbones, not a trace of what had transpired lingered on her skin.

But Lily…

Lily couldn't stop thinking about Eva rocking her hips against Lily's hand and digging her nails into Lily's skin.

God, this night couldn't end soon enough. Because if her eyes kept meeting Eva's over the heads of the student body dancing between them, Lily was going to wrap a hand around her wrist and drag her back to that balcony.

It was a relief when the dance wound down, kids getting picked up, no doubt off to some after party or another Lily would pretend not to hear the details about at school on Monday.

Once the last of the students had been herded from the room, the teachers were quick to follow. Lily ended up walking out beside Eva, their shoulders brushing with every step. Lily should say something, shouldn't she? Something to shatter the oppressive silence between them.

"I—" Lily paused, Eva's screensaver lighting up as she checked the time. The photo should have been innocuous. Lots of people had animals as their backgrounds. Lily's had been Hades for as long as she'd had her. "You have a dog?"

"What?" Eva turned to her with a frown, but Lily had her gaze focused on Eva's hands, on the brown eyes of a black Spaniel, a red collar fixed around its neck.

A dog she'd seen before.

Dozens of times.

"Yes. Why?"

"What's his name?" Lily said, voice a whisper. She already knew.

"Why are you being so—"

"Eva." Lily stepped closer. "What's his name?"

"Franklin."

Eva stared at Lily like she'd grown a second head, and Lily was spiraling, Lily was panicking, Lily was realizing the woman she'd been talking to for the past few months—the woman who might know her better than anyone else in the world—was the one standing in front of her now.

Oh, God, she was going to be sick.

"Why does it matter?"

Lily shouldn't tell her. Lily should take this secret, lock it away, and take it to the grave. But was it fair to hide it? Christ, Eva was going to kill her. Her body would never be found.

"Franklin," Lily said, her voice sounding very far away. "Springer Spaniel. Black. Likes long runs in the park, terrified of the vacuum cleaner."

It could still be a coincidence, Lily thought out of sheer desperation.

"How…how did you know that. You can't know that."

Lily reached for her own phone and searched for the message thread with shaking fingers. "I do. Because you've told me all about him," Lily said, turning her screen around to show a photo Elsa had sent the night before, of Franklin sprawled out on the end of her bed.

Lily waited for Eva to accept the truth, watched Eva's nose scrunch, watched her brain work, her eyes darken with denial. "You're Molly?"

"And you're Elsa."

Eva shook her head violently. "No. That can't be. I won't have it."

"Except it can." Lily thought of all the things she'd filed away about Elsa, things that, looking at Eva now, she could see reflected back at her. *I don't trust easily. I don't have many friends. I find it hard to open up to people. I don't mind my job, but I don't love it—and I can't stand the people I work with.*

Of course, Elsa was also things Eva was decidedly not—like warm and funny and vulnerable when she felt like opening up. Although hadn't Lily seen a hint of that in Eva, too? Through the cracks in her walls?

"All this time—it's been you." Elsa. Eva. Molly. Lily.

"No." Eva seemed to be in a heavy state of denial, and Lily didn't blame her. What a betrayal this must feel like, to expose so much in the safety of anonymity only to discover the person you confided in was someone you saw every day. "No, you're not Molly. This is some kind of cruel joke."

"MollyCule13," Lily said, and Eva flinched. "Molecule, because I teach chemistry. Thirteen, because that's my birthday. I—"

"Stop it." Eva's voice was low and pained. "Just stop."

"But—"

"No!"

Lily reached for her, but Eva stepped away. "I need to go."

Eva fled before Lily could stop her, sliding behind the wheel of her Mercedes and peeling out of the parking lot. Lily stared after her, shivering in the cold, tears burning on her cheeks, unable to believe what had just happened.

Eva had to pick her mother up from Angela and Tom's, and the drive passed in a blur. She had no idea how she managed to make it there in one piece with how her mind was spinning. Molly and Lily simply couldn't be the same person. How could they be?

No. Somehow, Lily had gotten hold of her phone and found out about Molly. Somehow, that seemed more likely than the possibility the person on the other end of the line was Lily Cross.

As Eva pulled into Angela's driveway, she took a moment to check her reflection in the rearview mirror. She'd put herself back together after her and Lily's balcony tryst, her lipstick freshly re-applied and her hair straightened, but it wasn't the after-effects of that encounter Eva was worried about hiding.

No, it was the wild look of panic in her eyes, the flush of anger on her cheeks, the tension radiating off her in waves.

What had she done? Bad enough, Eva had caved into…whatever it was growing between Lily and her. They'd well and truly fanned the flames, an ember building into a fully-fledged blaze, and Eva needed to smother it before it was the death of them both.

And now Lily was the person she'd been enjoying getting to know? The person whose texts had brightened up her days? If Eva had been worried about letting Lily too close before, it was nothing compared to how she felt now.

The air in the car felt too thick, like she was breathing in quicksand; Eva had never had a panic attack before but this must be what it felt like. She curled her hands around the steering wheel until her knuckles flashed white, trying to get herself under control.

Eva took a breath and got out of the car, forcing her emotions down deep—she'd deal with them later. For now, she needed to pretend everything was fine.

"Come on in, Eva," Tom said when Eva knocked on the door of the bungalow. He sat in the living room with a bottle of beer, a soccer game playing on the TV. "They're in the kitchen."

"Thanks." Eva ventured further into the house, and found her mother and Angela huddled around the kitchen table doing a jigsaw puzzle.

"Did you have a good night?" Her mother said, and Eva struggled not to wince.

"It was a school dance, Mom."

"Still. No reason not to enjoy yourself."

Oh, if only she knew. "How was your night?"

"Just wonderful. We made chilli."

"There's plenty left over if you'd like some, Eva," Angela said. "We weren't sure if you'd have eaten."

"I haven't, actually." Though the thought of food made Eva's stomach churn.

Angela wheeled herself over to the refrigerator and retrieved a full Tupperware box. "There's some cookies, too."

"You don't have to—"

Angela waved off her protests. "Nonsense. Here you are." She handed Eva the two containers; sometimes it was like having two mothers fussing over her.

Eva picked up her mother's bag from the floor. "You ready to go?"

"Okay."

When they arrived home, Eva was quick to excuse herself to the shower, eager to wash the night away. But before she stepped into the bathroom, Eva couldn't resist picking up her phone, chest feeling tight as she opened the message thread.

Please tell me you had a nice boring night in, she typed, with tears stinging at her eyes. *Please.*

There was still hope, Eva thought, waiting for a reply as the shower warmed up.

Until it buzzed.

I can't do that, Eva.

Eva. Not Elsa. She gripped the phone so tight it was a wonder it didn't snap and had to resist the urge to throw the damn thing at the wall.

Breathing heavily, she stepped beneath the searing hot water. Once out, Eva stared at her reflection in the mirror, taking in the haunted look in her eyes.

How could she face Lily on Monday morning after everything between them had changed, shifted off-center, into uncharted waters? Lily was going to want to talk about it, wasn't she? Or worse—ask Eva what it meant, when she didn't even know the answer to that herself.

Eva groaned, tipping forward to rest her forehead against the cool glass and closing her eyes. All she did know was that she needed to put a stop to things before they went any further. Eva was already too close to the edge—another step and she'd fall over it completely.

And that was unacceptable. Eva remembered the pain of Victoria leaving her, remembered her vow that she'd never let anyone put her in a position to be hurt again—and tried not to think about the way Lily had clutched at her, about how Molly's texts had made her feel.

Tonight had been a mistake, from start to finish, and Eva couldn't let it happen again.

Not if she wanted to keep her heart intact.

Chapter 16

As she strode down the hall, Eva thought that if she didn't look at Lily's room, she could pretend Lily didn't exist.

Eva had had to take her mother to the hospital to check how her ankle was healing. It meant she'd bought herself an extra hour where she didn't have to set eyes on the woman she'd been unable to stop thinking about all weekend.

The consequence was that someone had to cover her first class. And who better than the only science teacher with a free period first thing on a Monday?

Eva knew to expect it, but she was wholly unprepared for the sight of Lily sitting behind her own desk as the last of the stragglers of Eva's freshman basics class packed up their things.

Lily looked awkward and out of place, her laptop balanced precariously close to the edge of the desk, as though she was afraid to take up too much room. And maybe she was—Eva wasn't exactly the most welcoming of people to those who invaded her space.

The board was covered in Lily's messy scrawl explaining the levels of organization, and Eva supposed she should be glad they'd had a teacher who knew what she was talking about.

"I trust they weren't too much trouble," Eva said, announcing her presence. She tried to keep her tone gruff, tried not to be too overly familiar, not like the last time they'd laid eyes on one another and Eva had turned tail and run, the memory of Lily's kiss fresh in her mind.

"N-no." Lily cleared her throat. "They were fine." She was staring, her eyes drinking in Eva's face, a tremble in her lip. Lily wasn't going to cry, was she?

Eva stared at a spot to the left of Lily's head to avoid meeting her gaze. "May I have my desk back?"

"Oh, right! Of course." Lily scrambled to her feet, and Eva gritted her teeth when she knocked a pile of papers over in her haste to get out of Eva's way. "Shoot, sorry, I'll—"

"It's all right," Eva said, waving her off as she bent to attempt to pick them up. "I'll get them."

Eva expected Lily to leave, to scamper away back to the safety of her own classroom. But when Eva looked up, Lily was still hovering at the end of her desk.

"What do you want?"

"I just—is everything okay? When Alisha said you weren't in this morning, I…well. I guess I worried you were avoiding me."

Eva knew Lily was only concerned. That she cared about her—though if the concern was more for Eva or Elsa, she couldn't say.

"If you must know," Eva said, her words clipped, "I had to take my mother to a hospital appointment—not that it's any of your business."

"Oh." Lily blinked, mouth opening and closing as she searched for what she wanted to say. "Is she okay?"

"She's fine." Unlike Eva. Her head felt like it was spinning whenever she glanced Lily's way. She was barely holding herself together and wished Lily wouldn't linger.

"Good. That's good. Can we…can we talk? Please?"

Eva let out a long breath. "I don't think that's necessary."

Lily scoffed. "Seriously?"

"Yes."

"Come on, Eva. We need to talk about this."

"We need to do no such thing."

"But—"

"Okay." Eva raised her head, setting her jaw and meeting Lily's gaze, knowing if she didn't put a stop to this—if she didn't set a clear boundary—things would only get worse. It was for the best, to end things now, before they ever truly begun. Better to halt whatever it was blooming between them before someone got hurt. "You want to talk? The other night was a mistake. I don't want to be your friend, I don't want to be your lover, I don't want us to be anything other than colleagues, and really would appreciate it if you refrained from talking to me or meddling in my affairs from now on."

Lily spluttered, her eyes widening. "Meddling in your affairs?"

"Will that be a problem?"

Lily stared at Eva, a flush on her cheeks and her hands clenched into tight fists. "Is that what you want?"

"Yes." *No. I don't know.*

Lily sighed, her shoulders dropping in defeat. "Fine. I won't bother you again." She turned on her heel and strode from the room, slamming the door behind her, and Eva let out her breath.

It was what she'd wanted, but why did she feel so empty?

Eva dropped into her chair and held her head in her hands. She could feel a migraine building—she'd hardly slept over the weekend, and it was catching up with her now. She should've gone to make herself coffee.

Then maybe she could have avoided Lily for longer.

But not forever, Eva supposed. It was a conversation that needed to happen sooner rather than later.

A tentative knock sounded on the door, and Eva glanced up to see one of her AP students peering through the glass.

"Dr. Thomas? Class started five minutes ago."

Shit. Eva hadn't noticed the time. Had there been students in the hall when Lily had stormed out? Would the rumor mill be swirling? Eva wondered what they'd come up with. Sure, kids could be creative—but the truth was so unlikely she doubted they'd ever even think of it.

"Sorry. Come on in."

In all her years of teaching, Eva had never once shown weakness in front of a class. She was determined today would be no exception, though it took gargantuan effort to rise from her seat as her class took theirs.

"Today we'll be continuing our journey into the wonders of cell division. Cohl, can you remind me how many pairs of chromosomes are in a mammalian cell?"

Chatter buzzed around the room in the closing stages of the class, but Lily didn't have the heart to tell the kids to be quiet. They'd done the work, so what was the harm in letting them have five minutes at the end of the day to relax? Five minutes where she didn't have to concentrate? Where she could stare at her laptop screen like it held all the answers in the world, while trying not to tear her hair out.

"I don't want to be your friend, I don't want to be your lover," echoed in Lily's mind on a loop, and she dug her nails into the palms of her hands. This weekend without Elsa's messages had been hard enough, but to know no more were coming? Maybe it was naïve to think it would keep happening, that Eva could allow herself to open up, knowing Lily was on the other end of the line—but it still stung.

Lily had lost a friend, and that hurt, no matter who had been behind the screen. Didn't it show she and Eva weren't that different? That they could get along, if they allowed themselves to? It explained the draw they had to one another. There was something there, and it was impossible to deny it.

But Eva was trying to. Wouldn't allow a friendship or romance to flourish, because Molly being Lily made it real in a way neither of them had been prepared for.

The bell rang, and Lily let her students go with a wave of her hand, promising herself she'd be a better teacher tomorrow. Lily knew she hadn't been at her best, bumbling through the day with a numbness in her chest, feeling like she'd lost so much in the blink of an eye.

A knock sounded at her door, and Lily resisted the urge to hide under her desk, sure she was one conversation away from an emotional breakdown.

Mei popped her head into her classroom, a mug in one hand and a pack of cookies in the other.

"What's this?"

"Looked like you were having a shitty day." Mei dropped both onto Lily's desk. "Figured you could use these."

Lily was touched. She knew she'd been crappy company all day, barely saying a word at lunch after spending a truly horrific forty-five minutes in the school cafeteria refusing to turn her head too far in case it put Eva in her direct line of sight.

At her last job, she'd been cordial with her colleagues, but they hadn't been particularly friendly. They hadn't hung out together outside of work, and they wouldn't have ever brought her a treat to cheer up—because they wouldn't have noticed anything was wrong in the first place.

"You're amazing."

"I know." Mei grinned and perched on a nearby desk, swinging her legs back and forth. "We haven't known each other for that long, but I hope you know you can come and talk to me about anything. I'm a good listener... even if easily distracted."

"Thanks." Lily took a sip of coffee, made exactly how she liked it. "I... had a rough weekend." She wanted to give Mei enough details to stop her worrying, but knew she couldn't tell her the full story.

Lily had a feeling Eva wouldn't take that well.

"But I'll be all right."

"How was the dance Friday?"

Lily tried not to wince. If not for that stupid dance, none of this would have happened. She'd be sending a dumb text to Elsa right now. She wouldn't remember what Eva sounded like when she came.

"Boring." Lily hoped Mei believed the lie. She needed to change the subject. "How was your weekend? How are things with James?"

"Good, and amazing. I'm meeting his daughter next weekend."

"Ooh, that's a big step. How old is she?"

"Six."

"That's a good age. Old enough for them to hold a conversation, but not so old they'll start talking back," Lily said, and Mei laughed at her assessment. "You nervous?"

"Terrified."

"But you're good with kids. You were an elementary school teacher, weren't you?"

"Yeah, but it's been a while."

"Still, I'm sure you'll do great. Are you taking her somewhere nice?"

"The zoo. Giraffes are her favorite."

"If you're finding it hard to win her over, buy her a stuffed giraffe."

"Bribery?" Mei's brows twitched. "I like the way you think."

Lily laughed, already feeling better. Mei lingered a while longer, engaging her with idle chit-chat, and Lily appreciated it to no end. She had work to do—as always—but she knew she wouldn't be able to concentrate on it here.

Lily gathered her things before slipping out of her classroom. As she locked the door, she couldn't help but glance down the hall. Eva's room was dark.

Had she been off her game today, too? Was she hurting as much as Lily was? Had her fingers been itching to pick up the phone, to take back what she'd said earlier, and see if they could salvage something?

Lily shook her head. It didn't matter. Eva had drawn a line in the sand, set a clear boundary, and Lily was going to stick to it.

No matter how much it might hurt.

When Eva's phone rang late on Wednesday night, she was scared to look at her caller ID.

She was scared of it being Lily, scared of what Eva would do if it was—would she answer? Would she break? Would she tell Lily how much she'd missed her messages over the past few days? How hard it had been to walk past Lily in the hall and pretend she didn't notice her at all?

Eva breathed a sigh of relief when she saw Kate's name flashing across her screen.

"Thought you weren't going to answer," Kate said when Eva picked up. "This a bad time?"

Every time was a bad time since Eva had found out that Molly was Lily. "No. Just catching up on some grading."

"Do you ever stop working?"

"Doesn't feel like it, sometimes." Eva stretched her arms above her head and leaned back in her desk chair. "How are you? How are things with Dan?"

Kate sucked in a breath. "We…we're getting a divorce."

"Shit, Kate, I'm so sorry."

"Me too." Her voice was sad, and Eva wished she could be there to offer some comfort. "But it wasn't working. I think all couple's therapy did was make us realize that. He moved back in with his parents last week."

"How are you holding up?"

"Not too bad. It helps that it's been building for a while. And I've been keeping busy. I've got a full teaching schedule this semester."

Eva's busiest semester had always been in the fall, guiding freshmen through foundations of biology. She'd been chosen for the job as the most no-nonsense of the department—she could weed out those who weren't serious about the subject, and nurture the ones who were—but her favorite classes had been those in junior or senior year. Eva liked the smaller groups, liked diving into the details of cell division and cancer biology, liked sharing the knowledge she'd cultivated over the years.

"I'm mentoring three students in the RISE program, too."

"I bet they're keeping you busy." Eva had loved the program, which gave students their first taste of a real research project in their final year, but it had been exhausting. They were like babies when they walked into the lab for the first time, terrified of touching any of the expensive equipment, but they made up for it with enthusiasm and a willingness to learn—even if they did need to be near-constantly supervised.

Kate groaned. "Don't. One of them broke the centrifuge the other day. We've had to shell out a grand for a new one."

"What did they do?"

"Fuck knows. But they aren't allowed to touch the new one unless someone else is around."

"It's going well, then?"

"Oh, swimmingly. So long as none of them want a job working in a laboratory ever again."

Eva snorted, bending down to scratch Franklin under the chin when he pressed a cold nose to her knee.

"How are things with you?"

A question Eva didn't want to answer. "More of the same. Teaching is keeping me busy."

"Too busy to chat up eligible women on a certain dating app I forced you to download?"

Eva tensed. She'd been hoping Kate might have forgotten all about it. "I deleted it." Not a lie. It had been off her phone for weeks, and she wasn't planning on ever re-downloading it.

It had caused her enough trouble.

Where would Eva be, if Kate hadn't meddled? Eva supposed she couldn't blame her for all of it. She'd fucked Lily not knowing she was Molly. But what would have happened in that parking lot if Lily hadn't seen her screensaver?

"Did you at least talk to someone before you deleted it?"

"I did."

Kate sucked in a breath. "And?"

"It didn't end well." Something of an understatement. "But that's not a story for now." It would only spill out of her when she was very, very drunk.

"Well, how about you tell me when you come and see me at Georgetown in May?" Kate said, and Eva's lips curved into a smile.

"We can have the labs?"

"You can have the labs. Full access on the Wednesday you requested. In chemistry, too."

Not for the first time, Eva was glad it was Alisha accompanying her, and not Lily. "Perfect." Eva already had some ideas of what she could do to spark the interest of the kids they were taking along with them.

"So you can sneak away one night and tell me all about your love-life woes."

"Sounds like a plan." Eva was looking forward to her reward for making it through another year of teaching. It was the perfect thing to kick-off her summer—returning to her roots and catching up with those she'd missed.

"I'll let you get back to work," Kate said. "I just wanted to give you the news."

"You know you don't have to have an excuse to call though, right? If you ever need anything, I'm here."

"Hey, now," Kate said, and Eva could hear the smile in her voice. "Don't you go soft on me. I won't be able to cope."

"Fuck off."

Kate laughed. "Much better. I'll speak to you soon."

"Take care." Eva hung up and set her phone aside. At least she had something good looming on the horizon. A welcome break from life at Greenfield, and some much-needed distance from Lily Cross.

Eva just needed to make it there first.

Three more months. Three more months, and Eva could try and put this whole unfortunate thing behind her.

Chapter 17

Lily walked into the teacher's lounge smothering a yawn with the back of her hand. She had a parent to call, their number scrawled on the Post-it Note stuck to the back of her notebook. Speaking to parents or guardians was a necessary part of the job, but it wasn't Lily's favorite—especially when the parents had requested it. More often than not, they wanted to pick a fight, because there was simply no way their precious little darling could have done something wrong.

Sighing, Lily picked up the receiver of the phone—there was no way she was calling a problematic father on her cell—and punched in the number.

"Hello?"

"Hi, is that Mr. Kane?"

"Speaking."

"This is Miss Cross calling from Greenfield High. I received an e-mail saying you wanted to talk to me?"

"Ah, yes." Mr. Kane sounded like Lily had expected from the tone of the e-mail—haughty. "About Kayden's report card. His grades in chemistry are low."

A fact Lily knew full well, considering she'd been the one to fill it out. "Yes, they are. We've moved onto a new topic, and—"

"What are you going to do about it?" Mr. Kane asked, cutting her off, and Lily gritted her teeth.

Her job? She'd had too long a week for this. How was it only Wednesday? "Kayden is struggling with the math part of class. I've offered him help, and the opportunity to come and see me after school for extra tutoring, neither of which he seems to be interested in."

Kayden wasn't interested in much, in truth—unless it was dicking around with his friends or trying to flirt with the girl sitting behind him.

"That's unacceptable."

"I agree," Lily said, and Mr. Kane let out a huff. "But there's not much I can do if he won't accept my help."

The lounge door opened, and Lily smiled as Mei stepped inside, a box of Pop-Tarts tucked under her arm.

"All right?" Mei mouthed.

Lily mimed lifting a gun to her temple, and Mei snorted.

"You should be doing more," Mr. Kane argued. "Make it more engaging for him. He's a smart kid."

"He is." Lily wouldn't dream of saying a student wasn't. "But he refuses to apply himself. As I've said, I'm more than happy to run sessions after school, but I can't force him to turn up. Maybe you could have a word with him about it. Ask him why he's chosen not to." Before he started accusing Lily of doing a shitty job.

"Very well."

"Is there anything else I can help you with?"

"No, thank you." He hung up, and Lily rolled her eyes as she let the phone clatter back onto the hook.

"Why do parents always want to blame us for their kids doing badly, when it's the kids who can't be bothered to make the effort? What do they want me to do? Spoon-feed them the answers?"

"Obviously." Mei fished a Pop-Tart out of the toaster. "It's never the kids fault. Who was it?"

"Kayden Kane's dad."

Mei winced. "Oh, yeah. You're not the first to have a run-in with him. Pop-Tart?" Mei shook the box at her. "Proven to fix even the worst of days."

"Are they?"

Mei shrugged. "Works for me."

"I'm guessing you're having a rough day, too, then?"

"I had to keep my whole class behind for fifteen minutes because they wouldn't stop messing around, and I have mid-terms to grade and finals papers to write."

"So, in short: yes."

Mei put another Pop-Tart into the toaster for good measure.

"And don't remind me about finals papers. I don't even know where to start." Lily hadn't been entrusted to do it when she'd been training.

"I can help you," Mei said. "Show you where to find questions."

"Thanks." Lily was about to ask something else when the door opened once more, but the words died in her throat when Eva strode into view.

Eva's eyes landed on her, and Lily swallowed, wondering if the room felt like it had gone ten degrees colder to anyone else. She half-expected Eva to turn around and walk back out, but she glanced at Mei and seemed to steel herself, grabbing an apple and a bottle of water from inside the refrigerator before retreating.

It had been weeks since Winter Formal, weeks of no contact, weeks of complete avoidance except where necessary, and still, Lily felt like she was breathing in quicksand whenever they saw one another.

"Okay," Mei said, glancing between Lily and the closed door. "I've bitten my tongue for long enough. What the hell is going on between you two?"

Lily let out an indignant squeak. "What? Nothing."

"Something. There's a weird vibe whenever you're around each other. And that day I walked in on you arguing? You looked like you couldn't decide whether you wanted to rip her throat out or her clothes off."

Lily cleared her throat, feeling her cheeks burn, mortified Mei was right. She'd never wanted things with Eva to spill out beyond the walls of her classroom, but there Mei was, staring at her expectantly.

"So, tell me," Mei said, eyes on Lily's face. "Do you like her?"

"Uhm, have you met Eva?" The Eva she showed at work, anyway. The one behind closed doors was a different persona entirely.

"Uhm, have you ever heard of avoiding the question?"

"I don't like her." Lily pushed away the traitorous voice in her head that screamed that was a lie. "And there's nothing there."

Mei looked like she was itching to press, eyes narrowing as they took in Lily's expression. Lily prayed Mei wouldn't. Mei might be her closest friend in town, and she hated lying to her, but the alternative… it didn't bear thinking about.

"If you say so," Mei said eventually, shoulders lifting in a shrug, and Lily breathed a sigh of relief. "Sure you don't want a Pop-Tart? Last chance."

"No, thank you."

"Your loss."

Lily left Mei to it, retreating down the hall. Eva's classroom door was staunchly closed, and Lily averted her gaze, wishing it didn't make her chest ache.

The last of Lily's honors class were barely out the door before Alisha came speeding through it, something wild in her eyes.

"Are you okay?" In the eight months she'd been at Greenfield, she'd never seen Alisha look rattled.

"I've had better days. My father's been rushed to the hospital. Suspected stroke."

"Shit, I'm sorry. What do you need?"

"You're free next period, right?"

"I am." Lily had been planning on making a start on writing her finals exam, but Alisha's emergency took priority.

"How do you feel about taking my AP class?"

"Whatever you need," Lily said, already gathering her laptop and her diary.

"Thank you. You don't have to teach them the lesson. I've got a bunch of worksheets they can do. Just offer them a hand if they're struggling on a question."

"Okay." She'd yet to be trusted with the AP class, but Lily figured this could be a good start. If she wanted to take the class next year, she needed to prove to Alisha she could handle it—Lily just wished the opportunity had come under better circumstances.

Alisha fell into step beside Lily as they walked down the hall. "Thank you, Lily. You're a lifesaver. The worksheets are on my desk, along with a seating plan. Will you be all right letting them in? I need to tell Eva she's going to be in charge of things for the next few days."

A prospect Eva would no doubt relish.

"No problem. Do you need help with any of your other classes?" Lily knew how difficult it was to be absent as a teacher. It was often more work than coming in, and it was why Lily hadn't missed a day yet, even when she'd woken up feeling like death—and Alisha must be desperate to be on her way.

"I think they've got a substitute coming after lunch, but if you could find some work for my chemistry classes, that would be great."

"Just let me know where you're up to and leave it with me."

Alisha squeezed her elbow as they arrived at her door. "Thank you, Lily." She continued down the hall to Eva's room.

Lily stepped into Alisha's classroom, earning herself a few curious looks from the students lined up outside.

It took her a moment to locate the worksheets Alisha had mentioned, the surface of her desk strewn with pieces of paper and textbooks. She thought of the last time she'd covered a class—Eva's, the Monday after Winter Formal. Her desk couldn't have been more different: immaculate, in a way Lily knew she'd never be able to emulate. Everything in its rightful place.

It was always weird to teach in a different classroom. Things were kept in different places, which made Lily feel off-balance, no matter how minor. At least in Alisha's room, Lily wouldn't be terrified of making a mess, wouldn't try to make herself as small as possible, not wanting to make a lasting impression in what felt like enemy territory.

She was being ridiculous. Lily set her laptop down and located the promised seating plan. Satisfied, she crossed over to the door and waved the students inside.

"I'm Miss Cross, and I'll be covering Mrs. Woods's class today," Lily said, as they settled into their usual seats. "Can you take one of these and pass the rest along, please?" Lily handed the worksheet to someone on the first row—Penelope, according to the seating plan—who volunteered, and the class fell quiet as they got on with their work.

Alisha ducked inside a few moments later and handed her a piece of paper. "I've written down all the lessons they should be doing today and tomorrow. Let Eva know what you find? She'll be the one meeting the substitute."

Lily made sure to keep her face even, knowing they had an audience, but boy, was she regretting her offer. Still, it qualified Eva's condition—it would be a conversation about work. Nothing more.

"Will do. Now go," Lily said, because she could see Alisha hesitating. "I promise the place won't fall apart without you."

Alisha did, though not without warning her class to behave. Lily watched her go before turning her attention to the paper she'd been handed. Alisha taught AP chemistry eight times a week, and general chemistry five times a week.

It was easy enough to find work for the general class—they were at the same point as Lily's, and she'd already planned out her lessons for the week. The AP class wasn't as simple. The syllabus was unfamiliar, but a quick look told Lily they still had one topic to cover before they were done. With their exams fast approaching, it would be a tight squeeze to finish it all if Alisha was going to be out for more than a week or two.

A hand raised at the front of the class, the student situated in a wheelchair, and Lily looked away from her laptop screen to glance at the seating plan. "Yes, Shanice?"

"Can you help with this question please, Miss Cross?"

Lily sure hoped so, and she climbed to her feet. "What's the problem?"

"I'm not sure if I've calculated molarity right."

Lily breathed a sigh of relief—she could do molarity in her sleep.

A handful of other students asked her questions as the class progressed, and Lily found herself relaxing further with each one. By the end of the period, the board was scrawled with notes and explanations, and she was hopeful they'd all managed to learn something.

Her good mood plummeted, though, when the bell rang. Lily steeled herself for an encounter with Eva—her first, alone, since that fateful Monday morning. There was no avoiding it, though.

It was for Alisha, Lily told herself, as she knocked on the door. She was being a good person.

"What is it?" Eva called, and Lily realized, as she stepped inside, that Eva hadn't glanced up to see who was there. She frowned at her computer screen, eyes hidden behind the frames of her glasses, and Lily wondered if she was struggling to cope with all the extra work that had been dumped in her lap.

Lily cleared her throat, and Eva turned her head, her jaw clenching when she realized it was Lily who had come to call. "I sorted the work for Alisha's chemistry classes for the week," Lily said, and it was a miracle she could form words under the weight of Eva's gaze, directed at her for the first time in two months. "I printed everything the sub will need for today."

Lily willed her legs to move, to propel her forward, to set the papers down on the corner of Eva's pristine desk.

"Thank you."

Lily blinked in surprise—she'd half-expected Eva to watch her go without uttering a word. Eva yanked off her glasses and rubbed her eyes, and Lily took the opportunity to drink in the sight of her in a way she hadn't allowed herself to in weeks. Eva looked exhausted, but Lily doubted it was just from today. The bags under her eyes indicated many sleepless nights—was Eva losing sleep because of her?

Wishful thinking, maybe.

"Alisha and I were talking before she left," Eva said, discarding her glasses on her desk. "We're not sure how long she'll be gone for. Might be a few days, might be longer, depending on how things look. If it is going to be a while, we were hoping you could take her AP class and get a sub to cover yours. What do you think about that?"

Lily wondered if she had a choice. Would Eva take the chance to wield the authority she'd been given? No matter—Lily had been thinking the same thing earlier, anyway.

"I'm okay with that." It would mean extra work, having to set something for her own classes when she had to be in with Alisha's, but if it would help, she was willing. No one could ever say Lily wasn't a team player.

"Great. I'll be in touch once I know more."

There was a note of finality in Eva's voice, but Lily hesitated. They'd managed to have a civil conversation—was there any way to bridge the gap between them? To turn things around? Get back to the way things were?

She'd take animosity over silence at this point.

Eva looked up, meeting her gaze, but Lily didn't know what she could possibly say. She didn't know how to fix this—and she knew Eva did not want her to try.

So, Lily turned on her heel and left, shutting the door behind her.

Alisha had been gone for two weeks, and Eva felt like she was barely staying afloat.

She didn't know how Alisha managed to do so much—keep supplies in stock, fill orders, manage the budget, deal with behavior issues, attend meetings with the school board, and a dozen of other things Eva had always taken for granted—without breaking a sweat.

It didn't help that spring was always a busy time for Eva anyway. She had to prepare her AP students for their exams, write finals for her other classes, and keep on top of everything she usually did.

Spring, with the end of the school year looming on the horizon, was also the time Greenfield High conducted its teacher evaluations. Alisha's job, usually—but with her out of action for the foreseeable future, it had fallen onto Eva's to-do list, instead.

Which was how she found herself sitting in the rear of Lily Cross's classroom, back ramrod straight and a notebook balanced on her knee. It was, as Eva watched Lily wring her hands together at the front of the room, the first time she'd regretted taking on the role of second in department.

Bad enough, having to see Lily every day. Bad enough, having to check in on the progress of Alisha's AP classes. Eva was forced to spend the following forty-five minutes observing a lesson on titrations, when she'd rather be anywhere else in the world.

Lily, for her part, looked just as uncomfortable. She hadn't said a word since Eva had taken a seat, though her gaze darted over every few seconds as she waited for her students to arrive.

Eva was probably supposed to coddle or reassure her, but she'd done neither, stealing into the room with a sharp nod and a "pretend I'm not even here" like Lily would ever be able to manage it.

How could she, when there was so much history between them? History Eva was trying hard to smother, even though it lingered, heavy in the air between them.

Eva recognized a few faces; they were a good bunch of kids, and Eva suspected Alisha had chosen this class for Lily's evaluation on purpose, wanting to give her an easier ride.

Lily cleared her throat, and Eva noticed a tremble in her hands as she straightened some papers at the edge of her desk. It was the moment of truth: would Lily be able to shake it off? Or would she crumble beneath the weight of Eva's gaze?

"Last lesson we talked about the theory behind titration. Today you'll be doing it for yourselves, but first—who can give me one of the four categories of titration? Yes, Macie."

"Acid-base."

The answer made Eva think of that night on the balcony, of Lily's speech about chemistry—and everything that had happened afterwards.

Eva set her jaw, trying to shake it off. She had a job to do, and it wasn't to sit reminiscing on the past.

On things that could never happen again.

"Perfect." Lily's smile was warm, and Eva watched some of the tension in her shoulders melt away. "Can anyone give me another? Luke."

"Precipitation."

"Excellent."

Lily's confidence grew by the second, and she kept her gaze determinedly away from Eva. Which suited Eva fine—it was easier to observe someone who was pretending they didn't know they were being watched.

Eva had never particularly enjoyed chemistry—too much theory about bonds and molecules she hadn't cared enough to memorize—but if she'd had a teacher like Lily, she might have gotten a better grade.

Her chemistry teacher had been monotonous and boring, droning on and on and oblivious to his students' eyes glazing over, but Lily was his antithesis.

Pacing at the front of the room, Lily's hands were constantly in motion as she talked, firing off more questions and rewarding those with the best answers. She was good, made it clear she cared about her kids, and Eva didn't think there was a thing she could fault her on.

When the class moved on to the practical element, Lily took the opportunity to walk between the benches, checking everyone knew what they were doing, and Eva was left staring at her.

Staring, and trying not to remember what her skin felt like beneath her fingertips; what her mouth felt like, pressed against Eva's neck. Easy to brush aside when she was pretending Lily didn't exist, but not as she watched her stride around her classroom with an air of authority Eva had never seen on her before. Like she belonged, in a way she'd never seemed to when she was in Eva's space.

Here, seeing Lily in her element, Eva saw for the first time some of Molly in her. The way she shut down a smart-ass remark from a kid with a sarcastic comment of her own. The way she patiently walked through a set of equations step by step with a student who was struggling.

It was jarring, to say the least. Eva had been trying hard to think of them as different people, to deny she'd felt something for the woman she claimed to despise, but Lily and Molly were one and the same, and it was plain for her to see.

Worst of all—it made Eva miss Molly. She'd been doing so well at not thinking about it, at squashing any feelings that threatened to come to life, but Eva couldn't deny her nights were lonely without Molly's messages. Sometimes, when Eva was bored, or if something interesting happened in her day, Eva's fingers reached for her phone like it was a force of habit, hovering over Molly's name before Eva remembered herself.

Eva wondered what might have been, had she and Lily met under different circumstances. Could they have ever been friends? Or would their perception have always been forever tainted by a bad start, by Eva's standoffish attitude?

She didn't know, and she never would.

Eva only knew this: whatever she had felt, once upon a time, she wouldn't allow herself to feel again.

Lily tapped her pen so hard against the page it was a wonder she didn't tear a hole through it, her whole body on high alert.

She'd survived a lesson observation—one of the least pleasant, in her opinion, parts of the job—with Eva. Survived the rest of the day, stressing about how it had gone, too. Lily just had to endure the meeting that came after it, and then she could forget all about it.

The one-on-one meeting, with no students to serve as a distraction for her attention. Just her and Eva alone in a room together.

Would they manage to survive it intact?

It was up for debate.

When Eva strode into Lily's room, she left the door open a crack and sat as far away as physically possible.

Eva's face was drawn, more bags under her eyes, and Lily surmised she still wasn't sleeping. Lily remembered Elsa telling her she never slept well, that she rarely got more than five or six hours.

Lily wondered how many Eva was getting now. Was she up late, staring at the phone like Lily sometimes did, wondering what would happen if she cracked and sent a message?

But no, she always told herself. Eva had been clear, and Lily wasn't going to break first, no matter how much she might want to.

"I'll make it quick," Eva said, once she'd settled into her seat. She kept her gaze focused on the desk, seemingly unwilling to look Lily in the eye. "You did well today."

Lily tried not to look too pleased, tried not to preen at what she knew was a rarely-offered compliment. Impressing Eva was no mean feat, and Lily was happy that—despite all their history—Eva thought she was good at her job.

"You made the lesson engaging and offered support to everyone who needed it." It sounded like Eva was reading from a script, and Lily wondered what was written on the paper she was staring at so intently. "It looks like you've settled in here well."

Apart from with Eva, Lily added in her mind, knowing that was the one area where she was lacking. With everyone else, Lily already felt like part of the furniture, like she'd been there an age, like she fit, but with Eva...with Eva she felt off-kilter, unbalanced, and never more so than when she was right there but refusing to look at her.

"I don't see any areas for concern," Eva continued. "And I'll be saying as much to Alisha when she returns." Eva glanced away from her notes, but still didn't look Lily in the eye. "Is there anything else you wanted to discuss?"

Nothing Eva wanted her to. Lily bit down on her bottom lip so she didn't say the words aloud. "That's it?" Lily said, instead, because she was under the impression these things usually lasted longer. Mei had been in with Eva for half an hour the previous day—she knew, because Mei had complained about it for another ten minutes to Lily after Eva had departed.

"What more would you like?" Eva arched an eyebrow, and Lily saw a flicker of the woman she was used to in the straightening of her spine. "A commendation?"

"It just feels short, considering it's my first full year."

"If you're suggesting I'm allowing our personal issues to interfere with work—"

"I didn't say anything about that, but if you're thinking it, maybe it's a sign of a guilty conscience."

The sound of Eva's jaw clacking shut was loud enough to echo through the room. Lily was surprised steam wasn't coming out of her ears.

Frustration flooded through Lily. "Can we act like adults about this?"

"I thought we were."

Lily scoffed. "You haven't looked at me once since you came in here."

Eva's eyes fluttered closed, and the papers she held between her fingers trembled. "I can't," Eva said, her voice deathly quiet, raw and open in a way Lily had never heard before. "I can't look at you."

"Why?"

"You know why." Eva's voice cracked, and Lily watched her chest expand as she took a deep breath. "We're not talking about this." She pushed herself to her feet and gathered up her things. "You should be proud of what you did today."

"Wait—"

Eva was halfway through the door before Lily could blink, but Lily moved quickly to stand in her way, attempting to get her to stay, to get her to talk, because if they could have one honest conversation, then maybe they could fix this.

"Get out of my way, Lily." Eva sounded as tired as she looked. "Please. I just want to be left alone."

It stung more than it should, but it had its intended effect, Lily stepping aside to leave a clear path to the door. Eva strode away, heels clicking on the floor. One step forward, two steps back.

Lily threw herself onto her desk chair and buried her head in her hands.

Summer could not come soon enough.

Chapter 18

Lily was manning a table at the GSA's bake sale—the second of the year, after the first had done so well—when Alisha approached with a warm smile.

Lily knew she was back but hadn't seen her yet, as Alisha had been busy catching up on what she'd missed in her month away. She looked worn, her eyes tired, but God, was it a relief to see her.

"Hey." Lily beckoned her behind the craft table. "How are you?"

Alisha tilted her head. "So-so."

"Your dad?" Lily kept an eye out for any potential customers swooping in for the last of her brownies.

"Out of intensive care," Alisha said. "But he's not been allowed to come home yet. He's having a lot of mobility issues. They're not sure if he'll ever fully recover."

"Oh, Alisha, I'm so sorry." Lily curled a hand around Alisha's forearm, though she knew the words did little. "Are you sure you want to be back here?"

"Honestly, I was going stir crazy being stuck in that hospital," Alisha said. "And I've been doing some work at home for the past few days. It's a relief to have something to keep my mind busy."

"That makes sense." Lily didn't do well when she was idle.

"How have things been while I've been gone?"

"Fine. I managed to finish the last topic with your AP class." Just about. Lily hoped what she'd done with them was up to Alisha's standards.

"Yeah, I just had them. They gave you a glowing review."

Lily felt a flutter of relief. They were a good class—smart, unafraid to ask questions to make her think, which was one of the best parts of the job—but covering for another teacher was never easy, especially when that teacher was beloved.

"How would you feel about continuing to take them on your free period once a week? They'll just be going over everything they've been taught, but I can't think of a much better way to get you ready to have the class next year."

"I'd like that." Lily's smile threatened to take over her whole face. "If you're sure you're okay with it." Lily didn't want to steal Alisha's classes from her, no matter how much she might enjoy it.

"I'm okay with anything that involves less work for me," Alisha said. "I'm swimming in it at the minute."

"If there's anything else I can do to help, let me know."

"You might regret saying that, because there was something I wanted to ask you."

Lily waited, sure whatever it was, she'd be quick to agree. But then:

"As I'm sure you know, the D.C. trip is fast approaching."

She didn't, actually. In fact, Lily had forgotten about it—a throwaway comment, in a department meeting months ago. Lily remembered being surprised Eva wanted to go, before realizing a return to Georgetown on the school's dime was probably her idea of heaven.

"With my dad being in the hospital—and the amount of care he's going to need when he's out—I don't feel entirely comfortable going away for the week."

Lily's stomach plummeted, because she knew where this was going: Washington D.C., a group of rowdy teenagers—and Eva.

"I was wondering if you'd be willing to take my place. I know you were worried about not feeling ready, but they're good kids. And a couple of sophomores are going so you might know them. It's a great opportunity, and it's not all chaperoning—it can be fun, too. There's a lot of downtime."

That's exactly what Lily was worried about. "I—I don't know. Wouldn't Mei or Andrew be a better choice?" Anyone. Anyone other than Lily.

"I could ask them," Alisha said, but her lips were pursed, and Lily could tell she didn't like the idea. "But I think you'll be a better fit. We've already got the chemistry labs booked for the day there—I'm sure you'd do an even better job than I would, of showing them what the subject has to offer."

Lily had never been good at disappointing people. Especially people in a position of authority. She hated it. And with Alisha looking at her with hopeful eyes, asking her for a favor, Lily knew she should say no. Knew Eva might murder her if she didn't.

But Lily didn't know how to.

"O-okay."

Alisha beamed so wide it was almost worth it. "Thank you, Lily. I don't know what I'd have done without you these last few weeks. I'm so glad you're part of our department."

Warmth flooded Lily's chest—it was nice to feel like she belonged, that she was doing some good—but a chill crept in once Alisha had excused herself and left Lily alone.

Lily thought of a week with Eva and felt her stomach churn in knots. God, what would Eva say when she found out? She'd be furious. Lily gulped, and forced a smile when someone approached the table.

"Could I have two brownies and a muffin, please?"

"Of course you can. That's five dollars altogether." Lily exchanged the treats for the cash, tucking the bill into the lockbox with the rest of the money she'd collected. They were doing well, and Lily knew that this month's charity—Project Fierce—would do a lot of good with the funds they'd raised.

At least she'd done one good thing today.

The bell for the end of the period rang, and Lily swapped places with Macie and Sara, who carried boxes filled to the brim with cakes to replenish their supply.

"Are you two okay setting up?" Lily said, glancing at her watch. She had a class to teach in three minutes.

"Yep. Thanks, Miss Cross. We'll let you know how much we made on Thursday!"

Lily hurried off, weaving through the busy halls of the main building and arriving at her classroom—if slightly out of breath—right on time.

She caught a glimpse of Eva at the other end of the hall just before she stepped inside. She looked relaxed, so Alisha must not have given her the good news yet.

Lily didn't want to be around when she did find out.

But it couldn't be that bad, right? It wasn't like they'd be alone. They might not even have to spend that long together.

It'd be fine.

Knuckles rapped gently on her door, and Eva was unsurprised to see Alisha standing there.

"Sorry." Alisha looked weary as she leaned against the door frame. "I wanted to catch you this morning, but I haven't stopped all day. Have you got time for a quick meeting?"

"Of course." Eva set aside the papers she'd been grading and motioned for Alisha to take a seat. "Long day?"

"Part of me is regretting coming back," Alisha said, all but collapsing into a seat on Eva's front bench. "But it's nice to have a distraction."

"Still no change in your dad?" They'd been in frequent contact while Alisha had been off. Eva had wanted to make sure she was keeping on top of everything she was supposed to.

"Not really. They're not sure if he'll ever be able to walk again."

Eva cast her mind back two years to when she and her mother had heard those words for the first time. She remembered the uncertainty, the worry, the panic over what would happen next, how they would possibly adapt, now their lives had been irrevocably changed.

She'd had no one to lean on for support at the time. Eva hadn't wanted to put the burden on her mother, not when she was busy mourning the loss of the life she was used to. It wouldn't have been fair, so she'd shouldered it herself.

Eva had made it a habit not to reveal her personal life at work, and in two years, she'd never—willingly—broken that rule. But she decided, looking into Alisha's tired eyes, this would be a worthy exception.

"My mother's in a wheelchair," Eva said, focusing her gaze on the papers on her desk so she didn't have to see Alisha's surprise. "Has been for two years now. She has MS, so it's not the same—she still has some mobility when she's having a good spell. But I know how difficult it can be."

"I had no idea."

"No one does. If you ever need any advice or support, I'd be happy to lend a helping hand."

"Thank you, Eva." Alisha's voice swelled with gratitude. "Is that why you left Georgetown?"

"Yes." Eva glanced away from her notes and tried not to shrink beneath the weight of Alisha's gaze. This was why she didn't tell people. They looked at her differently. Like they felt sorry for her. Like they understood her.

She hated it.

"I'd appreciate it if you kept that information to yourself."

"I will," Alisha said, and Eva had no reason to doubt her sincerity.

Eva cleared her throat, eager to change the subject. "Now. What do you want to talk about first?"

"God, where to start?" Alisha glanced down at the notebook in her hands. "Shall we go through the performance reviews?"

"Sure." Eva grabbed the relevant papers from her desk and joined Alisha at the front of her room.

"I'll have to arrange yours at some point, too."

"Just let me know when." They didn't faze her. They were better than the evaluations she'd used to have as a professor—those were student surveys, and eighteen-to-twenty-one year-olds were a lot harsher than a fellow professional.

"We'll start with Lily's."

Eva obliged. At least she'd get the most unpleasant one out of the way first.

By the time they'd finished—moving on to finals papers, report cards, AP exam entries and arrangements, any budgetary changes and the minutes from all the meetings Eva had attended in Alisha's absence—nearly two hours had passed, and Alisha winced when she glanced at the clock.

"So much for making visitors hours today."

"I'm sorry. I didn't realize it'd take so long."

"Oh, it's fine. I needed to know what I'd missed. And Darius will have gone to see him. Not that he's too self-aware at the minute." Alisha smothered a yawn with the back of her hand. "Before I go, there's one more thing. Because things are touch-and-go, I won't be coming on the D.C. trip this year."

That made sense. Eva would do the same if she were in Alisha's place. In fact, it was something of a relief—she liked Alisha just fine, but spending the week in relative solitude would suit her, too.

"But I've asked Lily to go in my place," Alisha said, and Eva felt her relief turn to dread, felt her brain go fuzzy, felt her blood freeze in her veins. "You'll look after her, won't you?"

Eva barely heard the question, mind too busy spiraling, because she and Alisha were supposed to be sharing a room, and that meant she and Lily would be sharing a room, and if that wasn't a recipe for disaster, Eva didn't know what was.

"Is that okay?" Alisha said, and Eva blinked. Alisha was looking at her strangely, a furrow between her brows.

"I…" Eva desperately searched for a polite way to say, "Fuck, no!" when it seemed the deal had already been struck.

"Eva?" Alisha pressed, and Eva tried not to laugh.

No, but she could hardly say that to Alisha. It had been too long since she'd spoken and Alisha was still waiting for a response, staring at her with concern written across her face, so Eva forced a smile. "Yes, that's fine."

Fine, like her insides didn't feel like they were twisted into a tight coil. Fine, like Alisha hadn't just done the equivalent of detonating a bomb on her. Fine, like the thing she'd been looking forward to for weeks wouldn't be tainted by the essence of the woman she was trying so hard to escape.

"Excellent. Well, I'd better go." Alisha's chair squeaked over the floor as she pushed it beneath the desk. "Thank you, again, for everything." Alisha touched her fingers to Eva's shoulder, but Eva barely felt it.

Barely registered Alisha leaving, either, remaining where she was for a long time, a scream trapped in her throat.

Chapter 19

Lily pulled into the school parking lot at 2 p.m. on Sunday afternoon with her stomach roiling. She'd barely slept the previous night, panicking at what the next few days might bring.

A handful of students were dotted around the lot, their chatter carried by the wind. Summer fever had well and truly set in—it was the last week of school, the long vacation almost upon them—and Lily wished she could share in their excitement.

She stepped out of her car and joined the other teachers, relieved to see a few faces she recognized. Obviously, there was Eva, a sleek black suitcase propped against her legs and her phone in her hand. She knew the harried-looking woman with a stack of papers in her hand was Daphne, one of the assistant principals. And then there was Paige, one of the English teachers Lily shared her lunch duty with, who welcomed her with a warm smile.

Daphne did a quick headcount, and then handed out the papers she held. "Here's the agenda for the week," she said. "We've split the kids into four groups—A to D. Two members of staff with each group, so choose a buddy at your own peril."

Lily glanced at the schedule. The trip to Georgetown wasn't until Wednesday, looming over her like a guillotine.

Around her, people were buddying up, and Lily felt panic bloom in her chest, because no one was going to choose Eva, and if no one also chose Lily they'd be stuck together all week.

It was bad enough that they were sharing a room. When Alisha had revealed that little tidbit of information, Lily had wished more than ever she'd refused to go.

"Want to be my buddy?" Paige came to her rescue, and Lily hoped her sigh of relief wasn't too audible.

"Sure." Lily could use someone to cling on to for the week.

"Any preference on a group?"

Lily searched the page, trying to figure out which one had the more interesting activities. Most were the same—all the kids would be visiting the Capitol, the Lincoln memorial and Georgetown before the week was done—but there were a few unique activities, too. Lily would much prefer a trip to the Smithsonian over an art gallery. "A?"

"Sounds good. I'm not too bothered either way—I've done it all before. Is this your first school trip?"

"Is it that obvious?"

"You do look like a fish out of water," Paige said, laughing. "But you'll soon settle in."

Would she? Lily's gaze flitted to Eva. She appeared to be paired with Daphne, and Lily wondered if either of them were happy about it.

Lily didn't think she'd feel settled at all, not when she knew who would be sleeping beside her when they arrived in the capital. She hoped to God they had separate beds—sharing a double was the last thing either of them needed.

The arrival of the bus served as a distraction, and they gathered the kids into their groups. Hannah from the GSA was in A with her, so at least Lily knew one of her charges, and Lily had a feeling she'd soon learn the others. They all seemed to be the chatty type.

Carly was the only other student she recognized. She hovered near Eva, clutching her bag close to her chest and looking as out of place as Lily felt. Lily was glad to see her there—Carly was one of the kids who would benefit the most, and she deserved it after working so hard throughout the year.

Wrangling all forty kids onto the coach was a mammoth task, and Lily wondered, as they began to drive toward O'Hare, what exactly she'd signed herself up for.

Stress, Lily decided, as she tried not to lose a teenager in the departures lounge. Ten years off her lifetime, as she herded them onto the plane. She'd never been a fan of flying—being crammed into the seats, breathing the same stale air, the turbulence. The only part Lily did like was hitting the runway on the other side and knowing it was over, but today even that carried a pointed edge, because she knew what awaited her.

Which was: clearing security, baggage claim, and another bus ride taking them toward the glittering city lights of the nation's capital. And to Lily's doom.

At least the sights were beautiful, the Washington Monument standing tall in the distance. Their hotel was a convention center in Penn Quarter, a stone's throw away from the White House, though they reached it faster than she'd like.

By the time a room key had been pressed into her hand, Lily was exhausted. A combination of her sleepless night and the stress of the day had her feet dragging over to the elevator.

"You okay?" Paige said as she pressed the button for the fourth floor.

"Tired."

"I don't think you're the only one." Paige glanced toward the handful of kids crammed into the elevator with them, some of their earlier enthusiasm dimmed. "I think I'll grab something from the hotel bar to eat, if you want to join me?"

It beat eating alone, so Lily nodded. "What about the kids?"

"So long as they're back in their rooms by nine, they're allowed to do what they want," Paige said, and Lily followed her out onto the fourth floor. "I'll meet you back here in an hour?"

"Sounds good." Lily could use some time to relax. Maybe she'd have a shower to wash the stench of traveling from her skin.

At least if Lily was sequestered in the bathroom, she wouldn't have to face Eva.

Their rooms were spread over two floors, and Lily made sure all the kids on hers—four to a room—were safely inside before she turned to room 443. Her own personal hell for the week.

Not that she was being dramatic, or anything.

Lily opened the door to find Eva already in there, her suitcase in the middle of one of the two queen-size beds.

"You can have the room tonight," Eva said, barely looking at Lily as she tossed her jacket onto the unclaimed bed. "I'll be out late."

Lily supposed that shouldn't be surprising. Eva had, after all, used to live here. The hotel wasn't too far from Georgetown—maybe she was going out to visit her old haunts. Maybe she had people out here, though the thought of Eva having anyone resembling a friend was hard for Lily to believe.

Lily wasn't going to complain, though, able to breathe easier once the door had shut behind her.

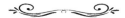

"I need a drink," Eva said, when Kate opened her front door.

Kate glanced at Eva's face as she ushered her inside. "Christ, you look terrible. Are you okay?"

"I'm fine." Eva shrugged out of her coat and hung it up beside the door.

Kate shot a look that said she didn't believe her.

"I've just opened a bottle of wine, but I think you're in need of something stronger."

Eva followed Kate down the hall toward her kitchen, the wooden floorboards creaking underfoot. She noticed the picture frames that used to line the wall had been removed, Kate stripping away the reminders of a marriage no longer viable.

Two wine glasses—one full and one empty—sat on the black granite counter of Kate's kitchen, but Kate's attention was on her extensive liquor collection, her hands settled on her hips.

"Martini with enough gin to knock a lesser woman unconscious?" Kate said.

"Please." Eva heard a meow, and glanced down to find Kate's tortoiseshell cat, Penny, winding around her calves.

"She's missed you," Kate said, when Eva bent down to scratch behind her ears. "And Franklin. She has no one to play with anymore."

"You should get her a puppy."

Kate laughed as she poured a generous helping of gin into a glass. "I do not have the patience to potty train a puppy." She added vermouth and an olive before pushing the glass over the counter to Eva. "Have you eaten?"

"No." Eva had been in too much of a rush to get out of her hotel room. She eyed the full glass in her hand after taking a sip that nearly made her eyes water. "I should before I finish this, though."

"Wouldn't want to be hungover on your trip tomorrow," Kate said, her eyes twinkling. "What would the kids say?"

"They wouldn't dare say anything," Eva said, and Kate grinned.

"I'd love to sit in on one of your classes. I bet they're scared shitless of you."

"You've seen me teach before." Not often, but Kate had sometimes sat in on a lecture or two.

"Yeah, but not teenagers."

"Some of them are better behaved than college kids. At least no one cracks open a red bull mid-way through a class."

"Hey, don't knock it 'til you've tried it. Red bulls have gotten me through many a late night of grading." Kate took a sip of her wine. "Want to order takeout?"

Eva eyed the stack of pizza boxes and empty containers from their favorite Chinese place on the counter and raised an eyebrow. "How much takeout have you eaten in the last few weeks?"

Kate grumbled. "You know Dan did all the cooking. I hate it. Especially after a day at work."

"I'll make something."

"You don't have to."

"I don't mind. You know I like cooking. Think of it as payment for the martini." Eva opened the nearest cupboard and peered inside. "When was the last time you went shopping?"

"Um… two weeks ago?"

"Honestly, Kate. How did you survive when you were single?"

"I had roommates."

Eva shook her head in exasperation. She managed to cobble together enough ingredients to make a simple pasta dish; it wasn't her best work, but it was edible, and at least it would soak up some of the martini she drank with it.

"So," Kate said, once they'd finished eating, eyeing Eva across the dining table. "I believe you have a story for me."

Eva was impressed she'd managed to wait this long to ask. "I need a refill first," Eva said, shaking her now-empty glass. "I can't do this sober."

"Must be a bad story," Kate said, swiping the glass from between Eva's fingers.

"It's not a good one." Eva gathered up their plates and dumped them in the sink as Kate topped her drink up. They retired to the living room, curling up on opposite ends of the couch. Penny leapt into Eva's lap the second she'd sat down.

"She never sits on me," Kate said, looking forlorn as Eva scratched under her chin. "The traitor."

Eva chuckled as Penny purred like an engine.

"Right, come on." Kate nudged Eva's thigh with a socked foot. "Spill the details of your dating app disaster."

"A disaster that's entirely your fault," Eva said, still not sure she'd forgiven Kate for downloading the damn thing in the first place. "I should've deleted it right away."

"But you didn't." Kate looked entirely too smug. "Because you wanted to meet someone on it."

"I wanted nothing of the sort."

"Then why did you keep it?"

"Because someone messaged me, and I was intrigued." Lily's first message felt like a lifetime ago. So simple, and yet it had worked. Eva thought of the awful pick-up lines that had followed and stopped a smile by taking a sip of her drink.

"Okay, so you started talking. What happened? Did they ask you for nudes? A threesome? Start sexting?"

Eva made a face. "No." Thankfully. How much deeper would her mortification run if anything like that had happened? "We both agreed we weren't looking for anything, and to stay as friends, and it was…nice."

Nice was something of an understatement—but Kate didn't need to know that. She'd think Eva had gone soft.

"So, what happened?" Patience had never been one of Kate's strong suits.

Eva sighed. "There's a woman at work," she said, watching confusion cross Kate's features. "She's on this trip, actually. She's…" Eva searched for the right words. How did she even begin to describe her nine months of history with Lily Cross? "She's my complete opposite, in every way. We got off on the wrong foot, and she's been stepping on every single one of my nerves since."

Another understatement.

"The woman I was talking to on the app… there were some things we didn't mention. Our real names, where we lived, our jobs."

Kate's eyes widened. "It was her?"

"It was her. She saw my screensaver one night." Eva was going to keep the details of what else had happened that night close to her chest—there were some secrets that never needed to be spilled. "Recognized Franklin from the dating profile."

"Shit."

Eva took a gulp of her martini. "Yeah."

Kate observed Eva over the rim of her wineglass. "But isn't this a good thing?"

"How on Earth is it a good thing?"

"Because you found someone you like. Someone who lives—"

"I do not like her."

"But you did." Kate tilted her head to one side. "On the app."

"As a friend."

"Huh."

Eva was starting to regret opening her mouth. "What?"

"Nothing. But it's odd, this bothering you so much, if she was just a friend."

Eva's jaw clenched. This was why she didn't tell people things. Because they tried to read her, tried to interfere, and—

"Please stop looking at me like you want to kill me," Kate said, the corners of her mouth twitching. "That doesn't work on me, remember? I'm immune."

"You're about to be something else." Eva muttered the words into her glass.

"Touched a nerve, have I? Look, I'm just saying," Kate added, in response to Eva's pointed glare. "You must've had something good going with her if you kept talking to her. Why does that have to change now you know who she really is?"

"Because it does. Because it's different now. Because I never would have opened up like I did if I knew I was talking to her."

"But you already have opened up to her," Kate said, draining the last of her wine. "So what's the harm in carrying on?"

"I didn't come to you for logic," Eva said, blaming the gin for the whine in her voice. "I came to you to complain."

Kate laughed. "All right. Complain away."

"I don't want to talk about her anymore. It's bad enough she's waiting for me back at the hotel."

"Waiting for you?"

"We're sharing a room."

"Are you serious?"

"Why would I joke about something like that?" Eva wished she was. Hell, she'd rather share a room with Daphne—who was genetically incapable of shutting up—than Lily.

"Wow. Well, you're welcome to the guest room here tonight if you want."

"Really?"

Kate shrugged. "Why not? It's not like Dan is using it anymore."

Eva would have to set an early alarm so she could sneak back in unseen, but it would be doable. Preferable, even, to lose a few hours of sleep if it meant she wouldn't have a fraught night tossing and turning with Lily mere inches away.

"Thank you."

"No need to thank me. The company will be nice."

Eva saw a flicker of sadness in Kate's eyes. "Are you struggling?"

"It's not so bad. The quiet is the hardest part. Having someone else around. I talk to Penny more often than I care to admit."

"Well, she is a good listener." Eva glanced at the cat in her lap, stretched out on her back with all four legs in the air.

"Refill?" Kate nodded toward Eva's glass as she climbed to her feet.

"I shouldn't." Eva could already feel a pleasant buzz sinking into her skin.

"But you'll drink it if I make one," Kate said, plucking the glass from Eva's hand as she passed.

"You're a bad influence!" Eva called over her shoulder.

"Please. You love it."

Eva shook her head, giving Penny another scratch on the chin as she waited for Kate to return.

It was nice to feel like she was home.

Lily couldn't sleep.

And she could make excuses—that the bed was too soft, that the curtains in the hotel room didn't do a good enough job of blocking out the light, that it was too loud being next to a main road when she was used to the quiet of the suburbs—but she'd be lying.

Lily couldn't sleep because the bed beside hers remained empty.

Eva's suitcase still lay on top of untouched covers. Whenever Lily looked—at midnight; at 2 a.m.; at 4 a.m.—she was confronted with the same sight.

Nothing.

Where was she? Eva said she'd be out late, but not all night. Had something happened? Should Lily be worried? Or was this Eva's way of staying out of her way?

Did Eva have an ex-girlfriend out there, in the city, whose bed she was crawling into?

Lily shouldn't care. It shouldn't bother her. She didn't have a right to know. Yet, every time Lily glanced across the room, it felt like a knife was being jabbed between her ribs.

Lily just needed to stop thinking about Eva, and for the love of God, she needed to go to sleep.

But when the hotel room door clicked open at 6 a.m., Lily was still awake.

She closed her eyes, not wanting Eva to know, opening them to sneak a peek as Eva ruffled through her suitcase. Her clothes were the same ones she'd left in, and Lily wondered if the creases on the skirt were from spending a night discarded on a bedroom floor.

Lily clenched her jaw and rolled over, staring at a spot on the wall, instead. She listened as Eva shut the bathroom door, the shower starting up a moment later. Washing a sense of regret off her skin?

Groaning, Lily rubbed at her eyes. What would Eva say if she knew Lily had been up the whole night because of her?

This trip was a mistake. One Lily wished she hadn't made, but it was too late for her to do anything about it now.

Eva stuck around long enough to shower and change, but this time, Lily didn't breathe easier when she was gone.

Any attempts to snatch a few more minutes of sleep were futile, so she dragged herself out of bed and dressed in a sluggish haze before going down to the lobby for breakfast.

Much to her surprise, Lily wasn't the first one there. Three of her fellow teachers—including Paige, who waved as Lily walked into the hotel restaurant—sat at one of the tables, a few of the kids dotted around the others.

She wasn't particularly hungry, but with a full day ahead of her, Lily knew she should eat something from the buffet breakfast. She settled on eggs on toast, with a mug of black coffee to go with it.

"Didn't sleep well?" Paige said, when Lily dropped into the seat beside her.

Lily hid a yawn behind the rim of her coffee mug. "It's hard to sleep when I don't have the dulcet tones of my hangry cat lulling me to sleep." Hades would be hounding Lily's parents for her breakfast as she spoke. "Excited for the Capitol trip?"

"I've done it so many times I could take the tour myself."

"Maybe you could earn some extra cash as a guide while you're here."

"If I thought I could get away with it, believe me, I would."

Lily grinned, feeling more human by the time she'd finished eating. She gave up her seat to one of the stragglers—Mr. Jones, one of the history teachers—and walked with Paige into the lobby.

She regretted it when she saw Eva leaning against a pillar, a paper cup of coffee clutched in her hands. Lily didn't blame her—the hotel coffee was lacking.

Once again, Lily wondered where she'd been. Was Eva going to do that every night? Stay out late and come back in the early hours of the morning? Surely not. But Lily wouldn't put it past her. If there was one thing Eva was good at, it was avoidance tactics.

"You all right?" Paige asked, and Lily blinked, realizing she'd been staring at Eva.

"Fine. Just mentally preparing myself for the rest of the day." Which she'd better do. All the kids were going on the Capitol tour, which meant she'd still be spending the day with Eva despite their different groups.

"You'll love it," Paige said. "I promise to make my tour much more interesting than the regular one."

Lily chuckled, relieved she had someone to chat to over the coming days, because Eva obviously wasn't going to talk to her. Lily had a feeling Eva wasn't going to be giving her much of anything.

As they gathered the kids into groups to do a headcount, Lily tried to pretend it didn't sting.

219

Chapter 20

AFTER THE CAPITOL TRIP, IT was surprisingly easy to avoid Eva.

Their groups didn't overlap, so Lily only saw Eva in their room, which was a rarity in itself. She still had no idea where Eva was spending her time—knew it wasn't her business—and Eva hadn't spent the night in the room once, always sneaking back in at around 6 a.m.

Lily had gotten used to it, she was sleeping better, and she was managing to enjoy herself, despite the trip to Georgetown fast approaching. She'd made good friends with the other teachers, and it was fun to learn more about the kids. They kept her entertained with random questions and interesting stories, and Lily was looking forward to teaching some of them in her AP class next year.

Lily had never gone on a trip when she'd been a high schooler, and it felt a bit like reliving her youth, in the best kind of way.

So she was in a good mood, the morning of the Georgetown trip. Eva seemed to be, too, smiling at something Carly was saying as they waited for the bus to arrive. Lily wondered if she was looking forward to visiting her old stomping grounds.

It wasn't lost on Lily that this could be an opportunity to learn more about Eva. Had Eva been a different person when she'd lived here? Had moving away from her dream job made her bitter and withdrawn, or had she always been that way? Would there be anyone waiting to greet her at the department? Did she still have friends there?

All things Lily itched to know, to chip more away from the enigma that was Eva Thomas.

"Excited for today?" Paige said.

Lily nodded. "It'll be nice to get into a proper lab." She didn't miss much about her old job, but getting to play around with fancy equipment was on the list. "I bet you're not, though." Lily knew she wouldn't enjoy an English lecture.

"Correct. But at least I won't have to do much. I can let my eyes glaze over while you and Eva go on about DNA, or something."

"DNA or something?" Lily grinned. "Is that the extent of your scientific knowledge?"

"Yes. I failed science miserably in high school. I don't know how you do it."

"Maybe you didn't have the right teachers."

"Possibly. But don't be offended if I don't understand a word you say today."

"Noted," Lily said, still smiling when the bus pulled up outside the hotel.

Daphne called everyone to order. "Okay, kids. Let's have group A on first. Look alive, people! It's not even that early."

No, but Lily suspected the excitement of the trip was beginning to wear off on what was to be the final full day. Plus, she knew a college visit wasn't as fun as a museum or the various landmarks they'd seen over the last few days.

Still, Lily was going to try and make it as interesting as possible for them.

But she needed to get through Eva's lab first.

Lily had gone to college at NYU, its buildings scattered across the city. In contrast, Georgetown sat on one campus, and Lily admired its old-school architecture as they approached.

"Beautiful, isn't it?" Paige said. The building they pulled up beside looked like it should be part of a cathedral. Fitting, Lily supposed, for a Jesuit university.

"Gorgeous. A much better view than Greenfield."

"That wouldn't be hard. I don't think we've had a remodel since it was built sixty years ago."

Lily chuckled, because she had to agree. The science labs were painfully outdated. She was sure the labs here would make her insanely jealous.

"I'll let you take the lead today, Dr. Thomas," Daphne said once they'd all disembarked, and Eva stepped to the front of the group.

She looked happy, Lily realized, not listening to a word Eva said as she outlined what they'd be doing for the day. Freer than Lily had ever seen her, and Lily had to brace herself.

She had a feeling it was going to be a long day.

Eva had forgotten how good it felt to step back into a lab.

She'd been given access to her old teaching lab for the morning, and she reveled in the familiarity as she booted up the computer and slipped on a pristine white lab coat.

The activity she'd chosen for the morning—a DNA fingerprinting activity to solve a fake crime—wasn't the most interesting, but it let the kids use a wide variety of equipment Greenfield couldn't afford to buy, and they always liked the fun of a mystery to solve.

None of the kids looked at home behind the lab benches, arranged in pairs and perched on plastic stools. Some pulled nervously at the collar of their lab coats, while the more curious ones examined the equipment set out in trays in front of them.

The other members of staff hovered around the edges of the room. They looked just as out of place—none more so than Lily, who appeared to be trying her hardest to ignore Eva completely.

"Good morning, everyone," Eva said, the room falling silent as soon as she opened her mouth. "I've brought you all here to show you what kind of thing you might be doing if you decide to take biology as your major in college. Today you're going to solve a murder for me using a combination of PCR and gel electrophoresis."

A few heads perked up at "murder", but Eva had lost them again by "electrophoresis". No matter. She'd make forensic experts out of them before the day was done.

"Can someone tell me what PCR stands for?" Several hands rose into the air, and Eva deliberately avoided the handful of students who were in her current AP class. "Yes, Carly."

"Polymerase chain reaction."

"Thank you. And what do we use it for?" Eva glanced around the group. "Frankie."

"It amplifies small sections of DNA."

"And why do we think that might be useful in the context of a murder investigation?" That seemed to stump them, and Eva waited a few seconds until one brave soul raised their hand. "Hannah."

"Because you might only have a small amount left at the crime scene?"

"That's right. Now, if you look in your trays of equipment, you'll see that you have samples from the crime scene and three suspects. By the end of this session, you're going to be able to tell me which of the three suspects is guilty and why. I have here"—Eva waved a stack of papers—"step-by-step instructions of how you're going to do that. I'll give you ten minutes to read it over before we begin. Feel free to discuss it in groups, and to ask me any questions you might have."

Eva returned to the front of the lab once she'd handed out the sheets, enjoying the babble of chatter that filled the room. She'd missed this, the spark of interest, the joy of doing something new.

Behind her, the lab doors opened, and Eva turned, smiling when she saw one of her former grad students strolling toward her.

"Hey, Dr. T."

"Matthew! What are you doing here?"

"Heard you were in town," he said, pausing by Eva's desk. "Had to drop by. Thought I'd offer my assistance, if you wanted it. Help you whip these kids into shape."

"You're more than welcome to join us." It would run smoother if there were two people present who are familiar with all the equipment. "How are things going?"

"All right." Matthew tucked his hands into the pocket of his lab coat. The sleeves were stained and in desperate need of dry-cleaning—Eva never would have let them get to that point if she were still his supervisor. "Carter reckons I've got another six months of experiments left, and then think I can start writing up."

"Things still going okay with him?"

"Yeah. Though he's not as tough as you." Matthew grinned at her. "I was wondering if I could hit you up when I'm preparing for my defense? If I can face up to your questions, the real thing will be a breeze."

Eva smirked, remembering the handful of thesis defenses she'd done during her tenure at Georgetown. All but one had cried. "Of course you can. And if I can do anything else to help, let me know." He'd been one of her brightest students, nurtured from when he was in her undergraduate program, and she had no doubt he'd go on to do great things.

"I will. Is this what you're doing today?" He reached for one of the spare protocols Eva had handed out, brushing shaggy brown hair from his eyes with his other hand. "You should do a prize for who gets the best gel at the end of it."

Eva raised an eyebrow. "Is a career in teaching on the horizon for you?"

"Nah. But I know what would've motivated me when I was their age."

"Please. The only motivation you needed was to be better than everyone else." It was one of the reasons she'd been drawn to Matthew—he had a drive to succeed and a thirst for knowledge that rivaled Eva's own.

"You might have a point there."

"I usually do," Eva said, before turning back to the class. "Your ten minutes are up. Does anyone have questions?" No one seemed willing to ask one in front of their peers. "Off you go, then. If you do need any help, feel free to ask either Matthew or I as we're walking by."

The bustle of lab work sounded all around her, and Eva sighed in contentment. It was good to be back.

Lily thought Eva had been her element when she'd shadowed her science club, but that was nothing compared to seeing her now, strutting around the Georgetown lab like she owned the place.

Lily supposed she might have, once upon a time. She must have spent many hours walking between groups of kids frowning in concentration as they used an automatic pipette for the first time.

Eva looked perfectly at ease, laughing at something the young researcher—Matthew—standing beside her was saying.

There was a familiarity there, an ease to the way they spoke that reminded Lily of the way Eva was with Carly. He must have meant something to her when she'd been a professor here.

It was weird, catching a glimpse into this side of Eva's life. She'd thought she knew a lot about Eva, but Lily still felt like she'd barely scratched the surface. Lily wanted to dive deeper, wanted to understand, fully, what made Eva tick.

The three-hour lab flew by with Eva as her test subject, and when a group of undergrads turned up to give the kids a tour of the campus, it gave the teachers a much-needed reprieve.

"Want to come for a walk?" Paige said as they followed the kids out of the lab. "I know a few nice spots, and it's a lovely day."

It was, the sun beating through the windows in the hallway they found themselves in, but Lily had other ideas. "Maybe later? I want to have a look at the chemistry lab for this afternoon. Familiarize myself with it before I have forty kids staring at me."

"Makes sense. I'll catch up with you later, then?"

"Sure." Lily waved her off before pulling out the map she'd been handed earlier that morning.

"Are you all right?" A voice asked, and Lily turned to see a redhead standing a few feet away. A lanyard hung around her neck with Staff printed on it in white letters. The badge dangling from the end of it read Dr. Acazee. "You look lost. Are you from the school trip?"

"Is it that obvious?" Lily tucked the map away and held out a hand. "Lily Cross. I'm supposed to be taking a chemistry lab this afternoon, and I wanted to make sure I don't get lost."

"Ah, I see." Dr. Acazee's grip was firm as she shook Lily's hand. "You do know there's a woman you work with who could tell you, right?" She glanced through the glass windows looking into the lab, toward where Eva stood talking to Matthew within. "Eva used to work here."

"I know, but she, uhm, doesn't like me." Something of an understatement, but still more than this stranger needed to know.

"Don't take it personally," Dr. Acazee said cheerfully. "She feels that way about most people."

Lily huffed out a laugh.

"Chem is upstairs. Come on, I'll show you."

"Thanks, but I wouldn't want to put you out—"

"Nonsense. I need to go up there anyway." She headed for the stairwell, and Lily fell into step beside her.

"Are you a professor here?"

"Oh, where are my manners?" Dr. Acazee turned to offer Lily her hand. "Kate. And yes, in virology. Have been for the past seven years."

"So you know Eva?"

"I do."

Lily glanced at Kate out of the corner of her eye, trying to figure out if it was a good or bad relationship as Kate pushed open a set of wide double doors. "What was she like? When she worked here?"

Lily knew she shouldn't ask—that if it got back to Eva, she'd be furious—but she couldn't help it. There she was, being presented with an opportunity to learn more about Eva from someone who had known her years ago, and Lily couldn't let it slip through her fingertips.

Kate didn't answer at first. She swiped her badge against a keypad beside a heavyset door. "This is the lab you'll be in today," she said, pushing open the door and ushering Lily inside.

The space could easily fit a hundred students, the benches glowing white in the sunlight and already filled with the equipment Lily had requested.

"And she was a lot of things," Kate continued, her gaze settling on Lily's face. "Haughty. Private. Quiet." Nothing new. "But she's got a brilliant mind. It's a shame we lost her, though those kids at your school are lucky to have her."

"Yeah," Lily said, her voice soft as she looked around the space. "They are."

"I don't think I'm allowed to leave you in here unsupervised." Kate looked apologetic. "But at least you won't get lost trying to find it."

"Thank you." Lily took one last look before stepping back into the hall, the door clicking shut behind her.

"Know your way out?"

"I think so."

"Hope your session goes okay."

"Thanks." Lily made her way back to the stairwell as Kate disappeared down the hall, some of her nervous energy dissipating with every step. The sun was shining, and she had an hour to kill—time to find Paige, eat lunch, and then blow the kids minds with advanced chemistry.

Eva paused on the way to Kate's office, staring at a closed door that had once belonged to her.

Her name plaque had been stripped away, but no new one lay in its place, and Eva tried the handle.

It was unlocked, the inside bare aside from the chair and desk, her old desktop gathering dust on top of it. Eva sighed, knowing that in another life, if things were different, she'd be sitting behind that desk right now.

Nostalgia was one hell of a drug, but Eva knew this time of year was busy. If she were still a professor, she'd be drowning under a pile of grading and preparing for the upcoming semester, while as a teacher, things were starting to wind down.

Eva didn't begrudge her mother a thing, but she couldn't deny that she missed this place more than she could say.

Tearing herself away, Eva retreated further down the hall and knocked lightly on Kate's ajar door.

"Intruder alert," Kate said, lips curving into a smile when she glanced away from her computer. "I told them to change the locks. Shouldn't you be out having lunch with the people you work with?"

Eva wrinkled her nose and sat in the chair on the other side of Kate's desk. "No, thank you."

"You're so antisocial."

"I'm being sociable right now."

"Yeah, with someone who lives seven hundred miles away."

"All the more reason for me to be here," Eva said, crossing one leg over the other. "I'm leaving tomorrow, remember? I've got to take advantage of the time we've got left. Especially as you're abandoning me tonight."

Something Eva wasn't looking forward to. She'd have to be creative to avoid Lily that evening. Although the teachers usually had a get-together on the last night—maybe Lily would go to that, offering Eva a reprieve.

Kate rolled her eyes. "Having dinner with my sister is hardly abandoning you. And don't pretend you usually spend this much time with me—last year I barely saw you."

"Is it a crime to want to spend time with my newly-divorced friend?"

"Ouch." Kate pressed a hand to her chest. "We both know that has nothing to do with why you're acting like my shadow. It's because you're avoiding that pretty blonde thing."

"I am not—wait." Eva frowned. "I never told you she was blonde."

Kate pursed her lips. "Didn't you? My mistake. Must have assumed."

Eva narrowed her eyes; she could always tell when Kate was lying. "What did you do?"

"Nothing!"

"Kate…"

"Okay, fine. I ran into her earlier."

"Ran into her," Eva said, her voice flat. "By accident, I'm sure."

"Quite," Kate said, her smile innocent.

"I can't believe you." Eva could, though—it was exactly the kind of thing Kate would pull.

"Like you wouldn't have done the same thing."

"I would never involve myself in your business."

"Please. Yes, you would. And don't give me that," Kate said, when Eva glowered. "Anyway, our chat was…enlightening. She seemed very interested in you."

Eva was immediately on edge. "What about me? If you mentioned anything, Kate, I swear to—"

"Oh, calm down. I did nothing of the sort."

"I don't believe you."

"Ask her, if you like. Although considering you seem to be avoiding her…"

Eva ground her teeth. "And what's wrong with avoiding her?"

"Come on, Eva. You must have had some sort of connection or you wouldn't be this rattled. So she got to see the real you through the app. Why is that such a bad thing?"

"I already told you."

"No, you gave me excuses."

"It just wouldn't work, okay? She's annoying, she's naïve, she's far too soft, she has the dress sense of a teenager, she—"

"I think she's good for you," Kate said, and Eva's mouth dropped open in shock.

"Did you not hear a word I just said?"

"Oh, I did. But I think the lady doth protest too much. After all, you got along talking just fine online, didn't you? That has to mean something."

"It means nothing." The words came out more vicious than Eva intended.

"If she means nothing to you, why are you so worked up about it? Why are you avoiding going back to your hotel room?"

"I didn't realize that was a crime."

"It's not. The crime is not exploring something that might be wonderful because—"

Eva shook her head. "There is nothing wonderful about Lily and I together. We can barely be alone without it devolving into a screaming match—how is that healthy?"

"If you put that tension to other uses, then maybe—"

"We already tried that," Eva said, without thinking, and Kate's eyes widened.

"I'm sorry, what?"

Fuck. Eva hadn't meant to expose that little secret.

"You've had sex with her?" Kate pressed, pouncing on Eva's weakness. "When?"

Eva sighed. "Months ago. Just before I found out she was the one I'd been talking to all along."

"You left that out the other night. Seems like a big part of the story." Kate leaned forward in her chair. "If you don't like her as much as you claim, why did you have sex with her?"

Eva rubbed a hand over her face, knowing it was a question she couldn't answer. "I knew I shouldn't have come here."

"But you did, because I'm your only friend. Look, I think you wouldn't be crazy to give it a chance. What's the worst that could happen?"

"Office romances are never a good idea."

"So, you break up, and you go back to avoiding her. Like you are now, but you get a few months of decent sex out of it."

"I don't think so."

"You should consider it, at least. She seems nice."

Nice. That was a good way to sum Lily up. Too nice for Eva. Too nice and too meek, and yet, she showed that sliver of steel whenever they argued. That spark of something that held Eva's attention.

But it didn't matter—Eva wasn't going to listen to what Kate said. She only had to make it through one more night, then two more days at school, and a Lily-free summer would spread out before her.

By the time they started back again in September, Eva would be over all of it.

Chapter 21

"You made drugs, Miss Cross?" Frankie's eyes widened at the admission, and Lily regretted being so blasé in reference to her former job.

Lily was quick to clarify. "Pharmaceutical drugs. Like aspirin."

"That's cool." Frankie, along with a few of the other kids, had lingered in the lobby to ask her questions about the afternoon. "How?"

"Short answer: chemistry. Long answer: with a lot of research, chemical synthesis and engineering. Not to mention what happens after you've developed a product. It takes years for one to be approved—if they ever are at all."

"And you can do that with a chemistry major?" Alison, one of the other students asked, and Lily nodded.

"You can do all sorts of things with a chemistry major. Forensics, chemical engineering, pharmacology. Not to mention things like sales, scientific writing or journalism."

Frankie's mouth opened, but Daphne spoke before he could ask anything else. "I think that's enough questions for Miss Cross, don't you? It's your last night here. Go and enjoy your freedom."

A whole evening—so long as they were back by nine—stretched out before them, and the kids hurried off with a quick good-bye.

"You were great today, Lily," Paige said, following Lily to the elevators. "You even taught me a few things."

"Thanks." Lily's cheeks felt warm, buoyed by the praise and from the afternoon, having the luxury of Georgetown's chemistry department at her disposal. If only Lily could get a bigger equipment budget at Greenfield. She'd be unstoppable.

"Coming to drinks tonight?" Paige said.

Lily nodded. The alternative was staying in the room, alone, so she may as well spend her time surrounded by others and drinking margaritas in the hotel lobby.

"Great. We're meeting at six, so I'll see you in an hour."

Lily retreated to her room for a much-needed shower, relieved to find it empty. She hadn't seen where Eva had disappeared off to when they'd arrived back at the hotel—too busy being swarmed by curious students—but clearly, she still had better places to be.

Lily took her time getting ready, not bothered if she was a few minutes late to meet the others. In hindsight, she should have gotten changed in the bathroom—she was, after all, not the only person with a key to the room—but Lily hadn't seen Eva this side of midnight all week, so she figured it would be safe enough.

Such complacency was a mistake, it turned out, when she heard the sound of the door clicking open.

Half-naked, Lily scrambled for the dress she'd left on the bed to cover herself—but not before Eva got an eyeful.

"For fuck's sake, Lily!" Eva whirled around to face the door, and Lily wriggled into the dress, cheeks blazing hot.

"Sorry! I didn't think you'd be coming back." Lily smoothed down the skirt with trembling hands. "You can turn around now. I'm decent."

Eva did, her own cheeks pink, and Lily thought about the way Eva's shocked gaze had lingered for just a second too long on Lily's breasts.

"Decent is up for debate," Eva said, shrugging out of her jacket and tossing it on the bed. The blouse she was wearing beneath it had two buttons undone, gaping open to reveal a tempting expanse of smooth skin Lily could remember pressing her tongue against.

"What's that supposed to mean? There's nothing wrong with this dress." It was one of the nicest ones she owned, tight and blue, bought for a wedding a couple of years before.

"Are you going to a nightclub?"

"What business is it of yours?" Lily folded her arms across her chest. "I haven't asked where you've been every night."

Eva arched an eyebrow, and Lily tried not to grind her teeth. Why had she said that? She didn't want Eva to think she cared.

"Jealous?" Eva's mouth curved into a smirk, and Lily wanted to wipe it from her face.

"Don't flatter yourself."

"So you don't want to know where I've been?"

"What's it to me?" Lily shrugged. "You've made it perfectly clear you want nothing to do with me. Although you're the one that keeps breaking the rules. You told me never to talk to you again, and yet here you are, striking up another conversation. Why is that, do you think? Do you miss me?"

Lily was treading dangerous water and she knew it. Eva's eyes flashed as she took a step toward Lily, her hands clenched into fists by her sides.

"I don't think about you at all."

"Liar." Eva must, for this trip to have bothered her so much. Eva must, to be doing everything she possibly could to avoid being alone with Lily—to avoid a difficult conversation like this where there was no escape, where she was trapped, where she was forced to confront all of the things they'd both been trying their best to ignore.

And, like a wild, cornered animal, Eva was preparing to fight back, preparing to spit fire, preparing to tear Lily to shreds. But Lily could take it. It wouldn't be the first time Eva had tried, after all.

"I bet you think about me all the time."

Lily knew she couldn't stop thinking about Eva. What Eva was doing, who she was with, whether she'd reply if Lily picked up the phone, or delete it without even reading the message.

"Now who's flattering herself?"

"Who's avoiding the question?" Lily fired back, watching Eva's lip curl.

"Why are you like this?" Frustration laced Eva's every word. "What do I have to do to get you to leave me alone?"

"I have been," Lily said, affronted. "Unless you still think my presence here on this trip was all part of some big conspiracy. You're the one who can't seem to help wanting to have the last word."

Eva glowered, and Lily knew it was because she was right. Lily had no desire to chase someone who wasn't interested, no matter how much she might want Eva's veneer to crack.

"So I should be asking you—why can't you leave me alone?"

Part of her asked the question because she knew it would piss Eva off, but a part of her also wanted to know the answer. Lily didn't think she'd get one, but Eva paused, head tilted to one side, studying Lily like she was a particularly stubborn problem.

Which, Lily supposed, she was.

"I wish I knew," Eva said, her voice unusually soft. "If I did, then I could stop—" Eva cut herself off, and Lily desperately wanted to know what she was going to say.

"Stop what?" Lily took a daring step closer. "Talk to me, Eva."

"I can't."

"But you did. Just because you didn't know it was me, it doesn't change anything—"

"It changes everything! You think I'd have told you half those things if I'd have known it was you?" Eva's eyes were blazing. This had been a long time coming. Maybe this confrontation was what they'd needed all along. They'd never talked about what happened and how they felt, not properly—maybe if they cleared the air, everything would be all right.

"I think you'd rather saw off your own hand than tell me anything remotely personal," Lily said, hoping it might make Eva crack a smile.

She didn't.

"But I can't pretend you're a stranger knowing everything I do about you. We could be friends." Could be more, Lily thought, remembering Eva pressing her against a wall, Eva's mouth hot on her neck.

"I don't need a friend."

"That's not what you said. "I could use a few more of those." That's what you told me."

Eva ground her teeth together at her own words being thrown back in her face.

"Would it be so awful?" Lily couldn't keep the note of pleading from her voice.

"Yes."

"Why? Because people might start to think of you as human?"

"No. Because you're already too close."

Lily smiled in spite of herself. "I don't feel it." It felt like there was a chasm between them, Lily suspended on a tightrope high above it, desperately trying to keep her balance as she walked toward the other side. "Why are you so scared to let someone in?"

"I'm not scared of anything. Certainly not you."

But when Lily took a step forward, Eva retreated.

"Why would you even want to be friends after everything I put you through?"

A good question. One Lily had asked herself a dozen times. "Because…I like you, Eva. Sure, you're brash and guarded and you can be harsh sometimes, but you're also smart and strong and funny, when you want to be. You care about people—even if you pretend you don't. Look at what you gave up." Lily gestured around them with her hands. "I saw you today. You looked at home. Happier than I've ever seen you. But when your mom needed you, you dropped everything—left your life—for her."

Lily was making some assumptions, but she was pretty sure they were accurate based on the way a muscle in Eva's cheek twitched.

"You have a big heart, for someone who doesn't want others to think she has one."

Lily expected a rebuff. Lily expected Eva to spit poison.

What she did not expect:

Eva, stepping closer.

Eva, cupping Lily's jaw in her hand.

Eva, with her gaze focused on Lily's lips, saying "Why is kissing you the only thing I can think about right now?"

And Lily didn't know, but God was she glad. "Would it make you feel better if you knew the feeling was mutual?"

Eva answered by kissing her senseless, and oh—maybe Lily should have confronted Eva a lot sooner, if this was going to be the result.

Lily let Eva back her into the wall, her hands falling to the curve of Eva's hips as a firm thigh fell between her own.

Was it healthy, to allow this distraction, when they might have finally been getting somewhere? Was it healthy, to fall into one another like this, when the last time it had ended in such disaster?

No, but Lily didn't know how to pull away. Not with Eva pressing close, not with her own fingers plucking open the buttons of Eva's blouse, exploring the skin revealed when it was gaping open.

Last time hadn't been like this—it had been quick, frantic with the risk of discovery, clothes rucked up instead of being discarded—but Lily planned to take full advantage of the change in circumstances.

The night stretched out in front of them, and before it was done, Lily was going to have mapped every inch of Eva's skin with lips and teeth and tongue, was going to have her begging, aching, was going to make sure this encounter wouldn't be so easily brushed aside.

To her own detriment as well, maybe, Lily thought, as she ran her hands over the lace of Eva's bra, Eva's groan echoing in her mouth when Lily squeezed. But she'd gladly take the consequence, if Eva would arch into her again, if Eva would drag her lips down the column of her neck, teeth nipping at Lily's skin.

Lily pushed herself away from the wall, steering Eva toward the bed. She half-expected Eva to fight her, to want to stay in control, but she went willingly, Lily straddling her hips once Eva was sitting on the mattress.

Eva reached for the zipper of Lily's dress with her fingers and tugged until it pooled at her waist, her bra discarded onto the floor a moment later. Lily shivered, the air cool against her bare skin, but it was soon chased away by the heat of Eva's hands. Eva cupped her breasts and dragged her thumbs over Lily's nipples.

Lily tangled her hands in Eva's hair as Eva ducked her head, taking a nipple between her teeth, her tongue teasing. Lily swore, rocking her hips against Eva's stomach, wondering what that tongue would feel like elsewhere.

Lily shoved Eva's blouse down her shoulders, desperate to be skin-on-skin. Why had they wasted so much time? They could have been doing this for months—should have been doing this for months—driving out any animosity between them with heated kisses and deliberate touches.

Lily unhooked Eva's bra and tugged it off, pressing on her shoulders until Eva was on her back with Lily hovering above her, setting her mouth on her skin. She found a spot on Eva's neck that made her breath tremble when Lily traced it with her tongue, discovered Eva's nails would bite into her hips if Lily scraped her teeth over her collarbones.

A knock sounded on the door and Lily froze, her lips pressed against the side of one of Eva's breasts and her heart thundering in her ears.

"Lily?" Paige's voice sounded through the wood, and Lily cursed—she'd forgotten about drinks.

"Ignore it," Eva said, her voice ragged, her hands splayed at the small of Lily's back.

"Just checking you're all right," Paige continued. "We were supposed to meet half an hour ago."

"I'm fine, Paige!" Lily called over her shoulder, ignoring Eva's glare as she pushed herself off her lap. Lily let her dress fall to the floor and shrugged into the oversized shirt she slept in.

"Sorry," Lily said, running a hand through her hair and opening the door a crack, blocking any view into the room with her body, conscious of Eva, topless, within. "I should've texted you. I'm feeling a headache coming on—I think I might have an early night."

"Oh, okay." Paige looked disappointed. "Are you sure you're all right? You look flushed."

Flushed, from the heat of Eva's mouth, her lips kiss-swollen and her chest heaving. Lily cleared her throat, praying Paige remained oblivious. "I'm good."

For a moment, Lily thought Paige was going to press, to linger, but then she nodded and took a step back. "Okay. I'll see you in the morning."

"Have a good night!" Lily said, her voice strained, and she collapsed against the door to close it once Paige had gone.

That was close. What would Paige and the others say, if they knew why Lily had blown them off?

They'd understand, Lily decided, if they could see Eva now: her eyes dark and wild, her hair mussed from Lily's fingers, her chest bare, breasts rising and falling with every shallow breath.

"We should talk about this," Lily said, able to think more clearly without her hands on Eva's skin.

Not that Lily was unaffected, her gaze skittering over the planes of Eva's stomach as she pushed herself up on her elbows.

"Do you think that's a good idea?"

"None of this is."

"Finally," Eva said, lips curving into a smirk. "Something we agree on."

"I think we agree on a lot of things." It was a bad idea, to sway closer. A bad idea, to retrace her footsteps, to hover in front of Eva on the bed, just out of reach. "But you don't like to admit it."

Eva didn't move, looking up at Lily through her lashes. "I don't like to admit many things when it comes to you," Eva said, her voice soft, and Lily's breath caught, because that might be the most honest thing Eva had ever said to her.

"Like what?"

Eva shook her head, and Lily knew, as Eva pushed herself upright, that was all the honesty Lily was going to get from Eva that night. And she could push, she could press, she could send Eva skittering away, back behind her walls, or—

Lily could let Eva curl her hands around Lily's thighs and tug her closer. Lily could let Eva's mouth cover her own in a hot slide. Lily could let her hands fall to the zipper of Eva's slacks and tug them down her legs, sink to her knees and spread Eva's thighs as she settled between them.

They should talk about this, Lily thought, as Eva fisted her hands in Lily's hair when she licked a broad stripe along Eva's sex. But this was its own kind of surrender.

They had tomorrow, to ruin it with words. They had tomorrow, to weigh themselves down with regret.

But here and now, with Eva scratching her nails over Lily's scalp, with Eva rocking her hips against Lily's mouth, with Eva's taste—rich and sweet—exploding on her tongue, the only sound Lily needed to hear was Eva moaning her name.

Eva stared at the ceiling, the soft sound of Lily's breathing filling her ears.

Eva was a poor sleeper at the best of times—never mind when she'd spent the better part of the night wrapped around someone she wasn't supposed to like, no matter how many orgasms she might have gotten out of it. Lily seemed to have no such qualms— she'd passed out over two hours before and slept soundly since.

Eva sighed, rolling onto her side and studying Lily's face in the darkness, knowing she only had herself to blame. She was the one that had started this. Why was kissing Lily Cross a temptation Eva couldn't seem to resist?

Why did she keep finding herself unable to move away when Lily stepped close?

Eva knew why, a voice—sounding suspiciously like Kate's—whispered in her head. It was because she was drawn to Lily. Because she did like Lily, in spite of everything.

Eva clenched her jaw. This exact situation was what she'd been afraid of when she'd found out Lily would be coming to D.C. The slip of her tenuous self-control, the sheer disaster of her and Lily alone together. The heady descent into madness, the slow dissolution of her sky-high walls, gone with an arch of Lily's hips against her own.

Eva couldn't lie there for another second. Not with her mind so restless. Eva rolled out of the bed and landed lightly on her feet, not wanting to wake Lily. She was supposed to be meeting Kate for breakfast, but she had two hours until then. Loitering around the streets while she waited wasn't an appealing proposition, so she passed the time in the hotel's gym, instead.

After an hour on the treadmill and a shower—in the gym, her desire to not wake Lily overriding her distaste at using a public shower—she dressed and slipped back into the room to pack her things. It was time to meet Kate.

Eva took her case with her, dropping her room key at reception on the way out, and trying not to feel a twinge of guilt at leaving Lily behind. Would Lily be angry, when she woke up alone? Or would she be relieved?

The café she and Kate had chosen for breakfast was a block away from the hotel, and Eva found Kate already there waiting for her.

"Rough night?" Kate's eyebrows raised when she got a look at Eva's face.

"It was fine." Eva had already talked about Lily too much—she wasn't about to tell Kate what had happened last night. She'd never hear the bloody end of it.

"Lily around?"

"No." Eva kept her face neutral as she slid into a booth. "I don't know where she was."

"That's a shame," Kate said, picking up a menu. "I was hoping for fireworks. Maybe for the two of you to finally have a proper conversation."

"Sorry to disappoint." Eva hid her face behind her own menu in a bid to escape Kate's roving eyes. "But no conversation is going to happen."

Eva had seen to that, distracting Lily with heated kisses. Talking was unnecessary. Talking would involve acknowledging there was something between them, and Eva had only just been able to accept that in the safety of her own mind.

Eva was not ready to say any of this out loud to anyone. Herself, Lily, or her best friend.

"How was your night?" Eva said, once she'd ordered her eggs benedict. "Your sister okay?"

"She's good. Says she's going to start coming to visit more often. I think she thinks I'm lonely."

"You are lonely."

"Still." Kate made a face. "I don't want anyone else to know that."

"But it's okay if I do?"

"Sure. You're the loneliest person I've ever met."

Eva swallowed. The words shouldn't sting—they were true—yet they didn't sit right in her chest.

"And you're doing fine, right?" Kate said, looking imploringly at Eva over the rim of her coffee mug.

Was she? Months ago, Eva wouldn't have hesitated. She liked her life the way it was—no distractions, no complications. No feelings. But Eva couldn't deny those few months talking to Molly—Lily—she'd been happy. That it was nice to have someone to speak to at the end of the day, whether it be to complain, to laugh, to lighten up an otherwise dreary day.

And then there was Lily herself, bursting onto the scene and making Eva's life more interesting. Challenging Eva, every step of the way, rising up to meet every single one of Eva's barbs, and seeing things in Eva few others had ever bothered to stick around long enough to find out.

"Of course," Eva said, but the words sounded flat to her own ears. What was wrong with her? One night with Lily and she was a wreck.

Except it wasn't one night, was it?

It was months of conversation, of laying herself bare. Months of learning everything there was to know about Lily—from her earliest childhood memory to the reason she was still single. They were connected in all of the ways that mattered, in all of the ways Eva had been trying to deny since she found out who Molly really was.

"Isn't this a good thing?" Kate had said, when Eva had spilled the whole sorry tale. "A good thing, to find someone you get along with so well?"

Except they didn't in person, unless they were fighting or fucking.

Which was the crux of the problem, wasn't it?

And Eva knew that was squarely her fault. From the get-go, she'd been determined to keep Lily at arm's length—by any means necessary. She was the one who kept lashing out in sheer desperation, terrified of letting Lily get too close.

But Eva didn't know how to do anything else. Didn't know how to put the pieces together the right way, merge the online persona into real life to finish the puzzle and open up in a way she'd never dared to before.

Eva didn't even know if she could.

"You've only got a couple of days left at school when you get back, right?" Kate's voice tore Eva out of her thoughts.

"Last day is Monday." An institute day, free of any students, where Eva could lock herself in her room and do the last few things she needed before the summer. "And then nothing until August."

The Lily-free summer she'd wanted—except Eva hadn't made it there unscathed. She'd had to go and complicate things the night before, caught in Lily's eyes. In Lily's words, "You have a big heart, for someone who doesn't want anyone else to think she has one."

Lily saw through Eva, in a way no one else had ever tried.

Just a few more days. Just a few more days, and then Eva didn't have to see Lily, and she could forget all about her.

Chapter 22

"DON'T TAKE THIS THE WRONG way," Paige said when Lily slunk into the lobby five minutes before they were due to leave. "But you don't look like you had a good night."

Lily tried not to be bitter. She had had a great night—at least until she'd woken up alone. Not that she had been surprised. Eva didn't seem like the type to stick around the morning after. Slipping out under cover of darkness was probably her MO.

Eva was nowhere to be seen, and Lily wondered if she wasn't the only one leaving things until the last minute.

"I didn't sleep well," Lily lied, because she couldn't bear the mortification of telling Paige about just what, exactly, she'd been up to all night. "I can't wait to be back in my own bed."

Away from Eva

Eva didn't look Lily's way once as the kids were rounded up in the lobby, and Lily sighed. She closed her eyes, and remembered the taste of Eva on her tongue, the feeling of her hands, clutching Lily's back as her hips arched.

Lily thought it had been bad after the Winter Formal, but now she knew exactly what Eva looked like beneath her pencil skirts and crisp blouses, and she didn't possibly know how she could look her in the eye ever again.

"We should talk about this," Lily had said, and it was like watching a shutter go down behind Eva's eyes. She'd let it go but she'd meant it, too—they couldn't go on like this.

Not anymore.

Lily couldn't exactly accost Eva on the bus ride to the airport with so many ears around. Unless...

Lily glanced at her phone, an—admittedly risky—idea forming in her mind. She waited until they were on the bus to put it into action, when Paige was distracted by another teacher as Lily typed.

I meant what I said last night. We need to talk.

Her thumb hovered over the send button before pressing down.

Eva sat three rows in front of her, and Lily watched as she shifted in her seat to fish her phone out of her pocket. She turned around to glare at Lily when she read the message on her screen.

If looks could kill, Lily would be a mere puddle.

I told you to delete my number.

Well, I didn't. Obviously. *And I wouldn't have had to use it if you weren't so determined to avoid me.*

I'm not avoiding you.

Lily scoffed. *Oh, please. What time did you sneak out of the room? Five? Six?*

Lily could no longer see Eva's face, but the movement of her shoulders suggested she jabbed angrily at the phone of her screen as she replied. Well, let her be angry—just like Lily had been waking up alone.

There was no sneaking anywhere. It's not my fault you're a heavy sleeper.

Only when properly worn out, but Lily would never tell Eva that. Her ego didn't need feeding. *You could've woken me up. Just admit you didn't want to see me.*

Of course I didn't want to see you. Happy?

Lily ground her teeth. How did she manage to be just as infuriating over text? She scrolled through their earlier messages, struggling to believe she was speaking to the same person.

You can't avoid me forever, Eva.

I can try.

Lily nearly threw her phone out of the bus window.
Paige noticed her distress. "You okay?"
Lily forced a smile. "Fine."

All I want is a conversation.

And all I want is to be left alone.

You could stop replying, Lily suggested, but she knew Eva wouldn't. She'd want the last word. *You have to admit there's something between us.*

No, I don't. Last night was a mistake.

Maybe, but it was also part of a pattern. Once is an accident, twice could be a lapse in judgment, but three times? Only two of their kisses had led to more, but Lily knew they wouldn't be there if not for the one that had started everything at Christmas. The catalyst for everything that had come after. *That has to mean something.*

What does it mean to you?

That I can't keep pretending I don't feel anything for you.

Too honest? Maybe, but Lily was tired of games, tired of hiding. If she wanted Eva to open up, it was only fair for Lily to return the favor. And it was much easier to do that staring at a screen than it was looking Eva in the eye. A few months before, Lily wouldn't have hesitated to tell Elsa anything. If Lily could convince herself to feel the same way now, knowing who was on the other end of the phone, it might be the solution to solving this whole mess.

At least Lily was leaving the ball in Eva's court, now. If Eva was honest in return, maybe they could build something. If she wasn't…maybe it was time for Lily to re-download the dating app and try and put her attention elsewhere.

Lily's message bounced around the inside of Eva's skull like a screensaver all the way through airport security and the painfully long walk through the terminal to their gate.

I can't keep pretending I don't feel anything for you.

It was still there, emblazoned on Eva's eyelids, when she sat on the plane and closed her eyes, tilting her head back against the seat.

Eva hadn't replied, because how could she? She didn't know how to put her jumbled thoughts into words. Hadn't expected such brazen honesty from Lily, but perhaps she should have. The woman was always surprising her.

That had to mean something.

Eva opened her eyes, gaze seeking out the woman never far from her mind. Lily was a few rows in front, only the top of her head visible.

It meant Eva couldn't deny the draw she felt toward Lily. The fascination. Lily was right—there was something there—but Eva had no idea what to do about it.

It was easier, to admit the words in the safety of her own mind. Safer, than typing them on her phone and sending them into the void.

Vulnerability didn't come easy—it never had. Better to shroud herself in privacy, in mystery, than let someone in—because then they couldn't leave. No one could walk away, no one could hurt her if they couldn't get close enough.

But Lily hadn't left. Lily hadn't given up on her, no matter how hard Eva had tried to push her away.

"You have a big heart," Lily had said, in spite of Eva doing everything she possibly could to try and prove she didn't.

And wasn't that one of the reasons Eva found her so infuriating? Because Lily refused to be kept at bay; because she questioned Eva; because, no matter what Eva threw at her, Lily took it in her stride.

Because Lily was still trying to reach out, even after everything. Even when it would have been so much easier to let it go.

"I think she's good for you," Kate had said, and Eva hadn't wanted to believe her. But as the plane touched down on the tarmac at O'Hare, Eva wondered if Kate might be right.

By the time they'd all collected their suitcases and everyone had been counted onto the bus, Eva had come to a decision. She was tired. Not just because of her sleepless night—the whole year had been exhausting, a war of attrition with Lily she no longer wanted to fight. Eva wanted peace, if not harmony. An end to the battles they'd been engaging in ever since Eva had first laid eyes on Lily outside her classroom door.

Eva pulled out her phone.

You're right. I can't avoid you forever. I can't ignore what's between us forever, much as I might be trying to.

Pressing send before she could second-guess herself, Eva waited with bated breath for a reply. Lily sat a few rows behind her, so she couldn't see her reaction—or if she had realized there was a message at all.

Eva stared out of the window, watching fields flash by, her leg bouncing against the floor. She shouldn't have said anything. She should have let it go. She shouldn't have put herself out there like that, should have—

In her lap, her phone buzzed.

And what is between us? Because after last night, I don't think we'd make very good friends.

Friends with benefits, maybe. But Eva didn't think that was a good fit.

I don't know. It's inexplicable. Inexplicable, the way Lily had wormed her way in close. Inexplicable, how Eva's stomach twisted whenever their eyes met. Inexplicable, how Lily had managed to flip her whole life upside down in just a few short months.

245

It's not. It's simple, really.

Eva frowned at her phone. *How so?*

It's chemistry.

Eva scoffed. It was the first time she'd seen a hint of Molly in Lily's messages today. *Really? Clichés are as bad as puns.*

Even if it's the truth?

Technically, it's biology. Hormones are on the syllabus.

And hormones are what? Chemicals. Which cause a chemical reaction. Ergo, it's chemistry.

Eva shook her head. It shouldn't be this easy, to fall back into things. Shouldn't have her smiling like a teenager with their first crush. Not when everything was so muddled. *What are we doing?*

What we do best, Lily replied. *Skirting around the issue. Isn't that what got us into this mess in the first place?*

Yes, with arguments and kisses and distractions—anything to avoid how they really felt. *We should talk.*

Funny, I suggested that about four hours ago.

I had to come to that conclusion on my own. I'm stubborn.

Yeah, as a mule.

Brakes screeched as the bus pulled to a stop, and Eva glanced away from her phone, shocked to see they'd arrived back at Greenfield. The school day had ended over an hour ago, the only cars still left in the lot belonging to teachers or kids with after-school clubs.

"I hope everyone had a good trip," Daphne said, before letting them disembark. "And you've all managed to learn something."

Eva certainly had, turning her head to find Lily looking right at her. More than she thought she could.

"Off you go, then. Have a good summer, if I don't see you beforehand." Daphne stepped aside to let the kids past.

Eva got to her feet once the aisle was clear of teenagers, following the other teachers out onto the parking lot. Lily stood nearby, Paige bidding her good-bye, and Eva pulled out her phone to call an Uber.

"Where's your car?"

Eva turned to find Lily by her elbow. "You think I'd leave my Mercedes parked here for nearly a week?"

"My car was perfectly fine."

Eva glanced toward Lily's beat-up Corolla. "Your car isn't one many people would want to steal."

"Ouch." Lily placed a hand over her heart. "That hurts. Now I'm not going to offer you a ride."

"You were going to offer me a ride?"

Lily shrugged. "Sure. I'm driving that way anyway—I need to pick up Hades from my parents. But if you'd prefer an Uber, then by all means…"

Lily's eyes settled on her face, and Eva swallowed. She'd said they needed to talk, but she hadn't expected it to be right then.

"I…okay." What was the harm, when Eva was already this far down the rabbit hole? "Seeing as you didn't kill me last time."

"I am an excellent driver." Lily dragged her suitcase over to her car, and Eva eyed the dent in the rear bumper with a critical eye.

"Are you?"

"That was not my fault," Lily said, noticing the path of Eva's gaze.

"Hmm."

Lily opened the trunk and turned expectantly toward Eva. Glancing at her suitcase, Eva knew this was her last chance to back out, to put a stop to this thing between them once and for all.

She lifted the case into the trunk and walked around to the passenger door of Lily's car. A few feet away, some of the kids and teachers from the trip were gathered, but as she slipped inside, Eva didn't care what they thought.

Lily was the only one who mattered, and, suddenly, admitting it didn't feel like defeat. Instead, it felt like comfort, like a warm embrace, like the start of something new.

Chapter 23

LILY KEPT SNEAKING GLANCES OVER at Eva, unable to believe she was sitting in her passenger seat.

"You cleaned," Eva said, buckling her seatbelt as Lily pulled out of her parking spot. "I didn't know that was possible."

"I'm not a slob, you know. I'm just not a neat-freak like you."

"Please, I've seen your bathroom counters. They're a mess."

"So there's not a single product left out in your bathroom?" Lily didn't try to hide her smile. "Actually, I bet there's not. Do you have a filing system? Oh! And a label-maker?" Lily snuck a glance at Eva out of the corner of her eye—the clenched jaw and sour look on her face gave her away. "You totally have a label-maker."

"Like I told you before—there's nothing wrong with having everything in its place."

"Because you hate chaos," Lily remembered, and Eva nodded. "You never answered me last time. Is that what you think I am?"

"Chaotic is certainly a good description of the way you make me feel."

Lily tightened her hands on the steering wheel, because she never thought she'd get this. Never thought she and Eva would ever be able to have an honest conversation, to break down the barriers separating them, and talk the way they should have done a long time ago.

How much time might they have saved? How much pain, if they'd have been ready to lay it all on the line sooner?

"Chaotic in a good way?"

"In an...unfamiliar way. I told you I didn't want to get hurt again."

Lily remembered the drunken conversation at Christmas, annoyed by her family's pressing.

"That makes it hard for me to open up to people. Talking to you—as Molly—felt safer, somehow. Easier to be open and honest if you don't have to look someone in the eye. If there's no expectation."

Eva's gaze was focused on her lap, her fingers playing with a loose thread on the sleeve of her sweater.

"When I found out it was you—I felt betrayed, though I had no right to. You hadn't done anything wrong. But it made things real in a way I was utterly unprepared for. Especially after we'd just…" Eva trailed off, and Lily thought of a balcony, of heated kisses and wandering hands. "I was scared. Scared of it meaning something. There you were, the woman I'd been enjoying getting to know, not so out of reach after all."

Eva took a deep breath, and Lily knew this must be hard for her.

"I pushed you away because I couldn't handle it. Because I didn't want to admit I was starting to feel something for you. Because I wasn't ready for something serious. And honestly, I still don't know if I am, or if I can be the person you want me to be, but I can't keep doing what we're doing. It's exhausting."

"Yeah, it is." Lily felt like she'd lived a lifetime in the past few months. "And I don't want you to be something you're not, Eva. I know the real you, remember? That's the person I want. The one you showed me. The one you keep showing me, though you try so hard not to."

Eva glanced up. "You want me?"

It could be teasing. It could be flirtatious, but there was no smirk on Eva's face, only vulnerability. Insecurity wasn't something Lily would have ever expected to see on Eva, and it made her realize how serious this was for her. How much Eva was trying.

"Yes, I do." It was the first time she'd ever said it aloud, but it felt right. Lily was tired of denying it. And if Eva couldn't handle it…well. Better to rip the Band-Aid off now.

"But what if it doesn't work? What if we're too different?"

"Then at least we know we gave it a real shot. At least we'll know for sure. Isn't it better to have that closure than to keep wondering what might have been?"

"I suppose you're right."

"Oh, my God," Lily said, with enough force that it had Eva's head jerking toward her. "You think I'm right about something? This is a truly historic moment. Quick, write down the date."

Eva smacked her in the shoulder, and Lily grinned.

"You're going to have to direct me as we get closer," Lily said when she pulled off the freeway.

"I'm surprised you haven't already figured out where I live."

"What do you take me for, some kind of stalker?"

"It felt like it, in the beginning."

"As we've already discussed," Lily said, relaxing now they'd steered to a less serious topic. "It's not my fault you moved to my hometown."

"Did you like it? Growing up?"

Lily shrugged. "It was all right. I already told you I had a rough time at school with a few of the other kids. I was glad to get out, but I don't mind visiting."

"You don't live there?"

"I live right by Greenfield. I love my family, but a little distance is nice, too. How about you? Do you like it? It must be weird to go from D.C. to here."

"It is, but I don't mind it. I like the quiet."

Lily had hated that when she'd been younger, but, older and wiser, she could see the appeal it would have. "When did your mom move here?"

"As soon as I left for college. She'd been desperate to for years—too many bad memories of my father in our hometown—but she didn't want to uproot me."

Eva always spoke fondly of her mother, and it was a relationship Lily was fascinated by. "Has she been staying alone while you've been in D.C.?"

"No, she's been with a friend. I'm supposed to go and pick her up later."

"And Franklin?"

"He went with her. He wouldn't cope in kennels—he's much too needy."

Lily grinned. She wouldn't believe Eva was capable of taking care of something needy had she not seen it with her own eyes.

"It's left up here," Eva said, when they got to the outskirts of High Grove. "Straight across the stop sign and then the next right. It's the last house before the bend in the road."

250

Lily pulled up outside a two-story townhouse with a blue door, and Eva's Mercedes parked in the driveway. She couldn't hide a flutter of disappointment at reaching their destination—she'd been having fun talking the way she and Eva had used to over text.

"Thank you," Eva said, hesitating with her fingers on the door handle. "Would you like to come in?"

"I'd like that." Hades could wait another hour, and Lily felt like there were still so many things left unsaid.

Lily waited while Eva retrieved her suitcase from the trunk, its wheels crunching over gravel as she followed Eva to the front door. When it opened, Lily heard the sound of a TV within, and a black blur darted down the hallway to launch at Eva's legs.

Lily frowned. "I thought you said—" She cut herself off when she heard the squeak of wheels on wooden floorboards, Eva's mother appearing in a doorway further down the hall. Her eyes widened when she saw Lily.

"Mom, what are you doing here?"

Lily didn't think she was imagining the faint note of panic in Eva's voice.

"I thought I was supposed to pick you up from Angela's later." Eva set aside her suitcase to rub the head of the Spaniel standing on his hind legs, his front paws scrabbling for purchase on her bare legs.

"I can see that," Eva's mom said, her eyes still on Lily's face. "Tom finished work early. He offered to give me a ride back to save you a trip."

"You could've texted to let me know."

"And ruin the surprise? Oh, no. Are you not going to introduce me to your friend?"

Lily watched Eva's jaw clench. This was clearly a scenario neither of them had been prepared for when Eva had invited her inside.

"Mom, this is Lily. Lily, my mom."

"N-nice to meet you, Ms. Thomas." Lily couldn't keep the tremble out of her voice. They had the same eyes, Eva and her mother, though right now, Eva's weren't the ones Lily found the most intimidating.

"Oh, that makes me sound old. Please, call me Eleanor." Eleanor turned back to Eva. "Are you not going to invite her in? Don't leave the poor woman hovering in the doorway. That's rude."

"Actually, I should get going," Lily said, because she felt like she'd stumbled into a weird family dynamic. Eva and her mother were glaring at one another, having a silent conversation Lily wasn't privy to, and things with Eva were far too delicate for her to want to risk ruining it by meeting the parents. "Leave you guys to it."

"Don't go on my account," Eleanor said. "Come in. Stay for dinner. I've made brisket—there'll be plenty left over."

"I..." Lily turned to Eva, searching for some hint of what she was supposed to say. Should Lily make up some kind of emergency, insist she leave? Lily didn't think she was as good at conveying what she meant as the two Thomases.

"You can stay," Eva said, her voice soft. "If you want."

And Lily wasn't going to turn down an offer like that. Not to see Eva in her natural environment, with the woman who meant so much to her.

No way in hell.

"Okay."

"You've been keeping secrets from me."

Eva glanced toward the open kitchen door, praying Lily couldn't overhear from where Eva had left her in the living room. "I don't know what you're talking about, Mom."

"I never forget a face, you know. That's the woman we saw in the grocery store months ago. The one from work."

Eva took a deep breath. How had this situation spiraled so far out of her control? This morning she'd woken beside Lily, determined it was a mistake she needed to put behind her, and now, just a few hours later, the woman was in her home, about to have dinner with Eva and her mother.

All because Eva had asked—wanted—Lily to stay. And what better way to show Lily she was serious about this than inviting her into the lion's den?

Not that Eva had expected her mother to be inside the house. That was a surprise she could have done without. She and Lily hadn't properly talked about what they were doing yet, and she was going to get the third degree.

"Yes, she's from work. She kindly agreed to give me a ride back here, and I invited her inside for a drink as a thank you. That's all."

"Hmm."

Eva felt her mom's gaze on the side of her face as she filled a glass with some lemonade. "What?"

"It doesn't sound like something you'd do."

Because it wasn't, but Eva wished her mother wouldn't point that out. "I can't believe you invited her for dinner."

"It's the polite thing to do."

"Polite has nothing to do with it. You want to be nosy—"

"I wouldn't have to be nosy if you'd just tell me things."

"You're not entitled to know everything about my li—"

"Oh, so there is something to know?" Her mother raised an eyebrow, and Eva heaved a sigh.

"No. Do you need help with dinner?"

"It's all handled." Her mother rolled up her sleeves and wheeled to the stove. "You go. Talk to your friend." With the emphasis she put on the word she may as well have been wiggling her eyebrows, and Eva ground her teeth, snatching the glass of lemonade from the counter.

Lily was sitting on the couch. She had one of Franklin's toys in her hand, the other end in his mouth, his tail wagging as he tried to pull it free.

"I'm so sorry," Eva said, closing the living room door behind her. "I didn't know she'd be here. Or that she'd extend a dinner invitation."

"It's okay. Unexpected, but okay." Lily released Franklin's toy to accept the glass of lemonade from Eva. He dropped it at her feet and sat waiting for it to be thrown, his tail swishing across the wooden floor. "He's even cuter in person," Lily said, kicking the toy to the other side of the room. Franklin scurried after it.

"Yes, he is." Eva sat beside Lily on the couch, and Franklin took it as an invitation, leaping into Eva's lap with his toy in his mouth. "I suppose we have you to thank for all of this, don't we?" Eva rubbed the top of his head. "What if I'd have had something else as my profile picture?"

"Depends what it was. You said your friend set up the profile for you, right? What picture would you have used if you did it yourself?"

"I wouldn't have ever set it up myself," Eva said, scratching behind Franklin's ears. "So I don't know."

"Well, I'm glad you did," Lily said, her voice quiet, her gaze on the glass in her hands.

"Me too." It was getting easier to admit things, now Eva had opened the floodgates. Where would they be, if not for the app? Would things be different? Would they have gone their separate ways after Winter Formal, agreeing to never speak of it again, or would it have progressed to something more, quicker than they'd managed?

Eva wasn't sure, but she didn't think she'd change a thing. How could she, when Molly had meant so much? How could they have ever had something meaningful, if Eva didn't feel like she could share all the deepest parts of herself?

"Do you want to get dinner tomorrow night?" Eva said, tongue feeling heavy in her mouth. "Without my mother there to act as a nosy chaperone?"

"Like...as a date?" Lily's eyes were wide and hopeful, and Eva's heart felt like it did a somersault in her chest.

"Yes. I...I feel like we started this all wrong." Or backwards—they'd seen each other naked, but they'd yet to share a meal. "And I know I've done a lot wrong, so I'd like to start fresh. Do things properly."

"I'd like that." Lily shuffled closer on the couch, her gaze flitting down to Eva's lips, and Eva leaned forward, meeting her in the middle.

It was brief, chaste, a world away from the fiery kisses they'd exchanged the night before, but no less perfect, filled with the promise of what was to come.

"As long as I can choose the restaurant," Lily said, her breath on Eva's lips. "You're bound to pick somewhere pretentious."

Eva huffed out a laugh, lost to another kiss.

"So, you two work together?" Eleanor asked, eyeing Lily from across the table.

Lily swallowed her bite of brisket before replying. "That's right. I started teaching at the school this year." Though Lily felt like she'd been at Greenfield for a lifetime. She thought back to her first day, to feeling out of place, to running into Eva and wondering what she'd gotten herself in to.

Now, everything was different. Lily felt like she belonged, and she was sitting in Eva's home, their thighs pressed together beneath the table, elbows brushing every time Lily lifted her fork to her mouth.

How far they'd come.

"And you like it?"

"I do." More than ever. Lily glanced at the side of Eva's head, still barely able to believe the turn the last twenty-four hours had taken.

"What do you teach?"

Lily wondered if she was going to be quizzed for the entirety of dinner. "Chemistry."

"I wasn't good at that at school. Nor biology, to be honest with you. How Eva got to be so smart with mine and her father's genes to work with I'll never know." Eleanor's gaze flickered to Eva, pride written all over her face. "She's the first doctor in the family, you know."

"Mother," Eva said through gritted teeth, and Lily bit back a smile.

Was she embarrassed? Lily wasn't sure. It didn't seem like a feeling Eva would have much experience with—but then, she supposed they were both feeling out of their depth tonight.

"What?" Eleanor looked affronted. "I'm allowed to show you off."

"I wish you wouldn't." Eva reached for the glass of red wine sitting in front of her and took a hefty sip. "How was your week with Angela and Tom?"

Eleanor waved a hand. "Fine, fine. Franklin had a visit from their grandkids, so he had fun with them. I trust you had a good time in D.C., Eva?"

Lily tried not to blush as Eleanor glanced toward her daughter, lowering her own gaze to her plate.

"I did."

"And you, Lily? Have you been before?"

"I hadn't, actually."

Eva looked appalled. "You didn't have a trip there when you were in high school?"

"I didn't go. But I enjoyed it. It was enlightening." Lily grinned when Eva narrowed her eyes at her. "I can see why Eva likes it so much." When no more questions were immediately forthcoming, Lily took the opportunity to eat several more bites of brisket. "This is amazing, Eleanor," Lily said, the meat practically melting on her tongue. "Thank you."

"No need to thank me," Eleanor said, though she seemed buoyed by the praise. "It's not every day Eva brings someone home."

"Mother," Eva hissed again, shooting one of her signature glares at her mother across the table.

"What? You haven't." Eleanor observed the two of them, her chin resting on her steepled hands, finding them much more interesting than dinner. "So, tell me. How long have the two of you been dating?"

Lily nearly choked on a piece of carrot, her eyes streaming as she reached for her glass of water. She wished she'd asked for something stronger.

Eva looked stricken. "We are not...there's no...I don't..." Eva turned toward Lily as though expecting her to jump in. Lily merely shrugged, because it was up to Eva how much she revealed.

Eleanor cleared her throat, an eyebrow raised, and yeah, Lily could see where Eva got it from. Her mom was intimidating.

"Fine." Eva heaved a sigh and then curled the fingers of her left hand around the back of Lily's right where it rested on the table. "It's new. Hours-old new. Certainly not at the point where I'd be bringing her home to meet you, but here we are. Happy?"

There was a challenge in Eva's gaze, her skin soft as her thumb brushed the back of Lily's knuckles.

"As long as you are, dear," Eleanor said, her voice so tender Lily felt like she shouldn't be listening. "That's all I've ever wanted."

"I am," Eva said, just as softly, a tremble in her fingers as she refused to look Lily in the eye, like she was afraid it would send her skittering away.

If anything, it was the opposite. All Lily had ever wanted was honesty, was openness, and now Eva was willing to offer it, she only felt herself falling harder. Lily could let herself fall harder, without second-guessing herself, without hating every moment of it, because she knew Eva wanted her back.

"I am, too," Lily said, smiling when Eva's head jerked around to meet her gaze, willing Eva to believe her.

Eleanor clapped her hands together, making Lily jump. "Good. Now, Lily, tell me more about yourself. Are you from around here? Do you have a big family? How long have you been teaching?"

The rest of dinner passed in a blur of questions and answers, and Eva's eyes were apologetic as she led Lily to the door once they were done.

"I'm sorry."

"It's fine. Sweet, even. And don't worry—I'll spare you the cross-examination by my parents for a while yet." Lily grinned when relief passed over Eva's face. "I'll see you tomorrow."

Eva nodded, leaning down to capture Lily's lips in a kiss that left her breathless. What she'd give to let Eva fist a hand in her shirt and drag her upstairs—but they couldn't. Lily had a cat to pick up, and there were some things Lily wanted to do to Eva she didn't want her mother overhearing.

Lily pulled away with no small sense of regret, mouth going dry at the dark look in Eva's eyes. Seeing Eva at school the next day and not being able to kiss her was going to be torture.

Chapter 24

"YOU LOOK HAPPY," MEI SAID, when Lily walked into the teacher's lounge. "Good trip? Or are you just glad to be back?"

Lily hadn't thought her good mood would be so apparent, though the high from dinner at Eva's place last night—as intimidating as her mom had been—had yet to wear off. God, Lily wasn't glowing, was she? Eva would kill her if she let the cat out of the bag before they'd had a chance to get started.

"Both," Lily said, reaching for her coffee mug and keeping her voice light. "D.C. was fun, but it's good to be back."

"Things weren't weird with Eva?" Mei regarded Lily closely as she switched on the coffee machine.

Lily played dumb, trying not to think about the long kiss good-bye Eva had planted on her before she left. "Why would things be weird with Eva?"

"I told you. You guys have a weird vibe. Can't be fun, to be stuck with someone you don't like for so long."

Lily shrugged, and hoped she was a convincing liar. "I didn't see her that much. We were in separate groups. Did I miss anything fun while I was gone?" Changing the subject seemed like a safe bet.

"Nope, it's been boring as ever. I hate the last week of school. No one wants to be here, and you can tell."

"Does that include you?"

Mei grinned. "Obviously. I don't want to be here at the best of times, never mind at the start of summer."

"Two more days," Lily said, because she was counting down, too—especially knowing what the summer would entail.

Three months of Eva, the two of them figuring out if there was space for the other in their lives, if they could exist together as something more than colleagues—and enemies. Lily knew it wouldn't be easy—they'd both made getting to that stage as difficult as possible—but she was sure the long and arduous journey would be worth it, in the end.

"Monday afternoon can't come quick enough," Mei said. "At least today is our last day of kids. Though institute days are boring as fuck."

Lily snorted, because she was right—the schedule for Monday promised a day of meetings and team-building exercises Lily would rather do without.

"Still, drinks tonight can be an early celebration."

Lily froze, having forgotten what day it was. She'd been so overjoyed by Eva asking her on a date Lily hadn't realized she already had other plans.

"Or not?" Mei said, noticing the look on Lily's face.

"I can't. I…I have a date."

Mei's eyes lit up. "You do? Tell me everything."

"Um." Lily stalled for time, because there was no way in hell she was going to tell Mei everything—not that she'd have time to even if she wanted to. Lessons started in less than five minutes, and she'd need at least an hour. "Do you remember that person I told you I was talking to the night of the Homecoming game?" Not the full truth, but not a lie either—which Lily hoped would make it more convincing. "We're finally going out."

"Oh, my God! I'm so happy for you. You'll have to tell me all about it on Monday." The first bell rang before Lily could agree, and Mei sighed. "Better get to it. We're going to the funfair at lunch, right? I want to kick your ass at some games."

Lily grinned. "We'll see about that. Thanks for helping the kids with it while I wasn't here, by the way." Lily had been there to lend a hand setting up the craft tables in the school courtyard that morning, but Mei had handled a lot in the past few days.

"No problem. It was fun."

They left the teacher's lounge together, and Lily noticed Eva's door opening out of the corner of her eye. Lily allowed herself one brief glance to admire the curve of her ass in the black pencil skirt.

Lily had a full day of teaching, starting with her honors class.

"I got you something, Miss Cross," Carly said at the end of the period, approaching Lily's desk with her head ducked as the rest of the kids rushed out the door. "To say thank you for everything you've done for me."

Carly handed over a wrapped box, and Lily tried not to let herself be overcome with emotion as she slid a nail beneath the paper.

Inside was a mug, much like the one she already owned, except instead of her name spelled out using elements of the periodic table, it said Best Chemistry Teacher.

"It's not much," Carly said, staring at her hands, "and some of the symbols are made up, but I...I thought you might like it."

"I love it," Lily said, her throat tight. "Thank you, Carly." It meant so much; a reminder Lily had made a difference to someone. "And well done, for all the work you've done this year. I know it wasn't easy, but you passed with flying colors."

"Thanks, Miss Cross."

"Have a good summer."

"You too." Carly ducked out of the door, smile on her face, and Lily set the mug carefully on her desk.

The rest of the morning passed in a blur. The kids were excited about their summer, and Lily was happy, after they'd gotten through all the activities she'd prepared for the lesson, to let them chat about their plans.

Mei appeared in her doorway at lunch, the sleeves of her blouse rolled up to her elbows. She cracked her knuckles. "You're going down, Cross."

"Keep on dreaming, Chen."

They followed the sound of excited chatter out to the courtyard. Macie and Sara waved shyly at Lily from the bean bag toss stall, and Hannah was manning the balloon pop game. Lily was impressed by the turnout, students milling around in small groups vying to win a prize. All had been donated, either by students, staff, or even some friendly local businesses willing to lend the GSA a helping hand.

"Oh, my God," Mei said, fingers clutching at Lily's elbow to get her attention. "I know what we're doing first."

Lily turned to see what she was looking at and felt her jaw drop. They'd managed to source a dunk tank, and who was climbing up the steps?

Eva.

She slipped off her blazer as she reached the top, folding it delicately and placing her glasses and shoes on top before taking the seat suspended high above the water.

"She replied to my e-mail asking for volunteers but I thought she was joking." Mei looked overjoyed. "I can't believe this. Let's go."

Lily let Mei drag her over. While she was distracted handing Mark a five-dollar bill, Lily leaned against the side of the tank.

"What the hell are you doing?"

"Raising money for a good cause," Eva said, looking at ease, poised and regal with her legs crossed. "I figured there's a few people in this school who would relish the opportunity to dunk me."

"I don't know," Lily said. "They might be too scared of you."

"I think they'll manage to overcome their fears. The seniors, especially, seeing as they'll never see me again. And the staff certainly seem eager." Eva's gaze flickered to where Mei was getting a feel for the ball.

"But...you'll get wet."

"I think that's the point." Eva's lips curved into a smirk, and Lily wanted to kiss it from her mouth. "You're not worried about me, are you? It's only water."

Worried about staring when Eva's clothes were plastered to her body, maybe. "No. It just...doesn't seem very you."

"Maybe not. But I'm doing this thing where I try new things."

Eva's gaze was soft, open in that way Lily was starting to love, and she felt her heart beat faster in her chest.

"We have our first contender," Mark said, and Lily stepped back as Mei positioned herself behind the black cross taped to the floor. "You get three shots, Miss Chen."

"I'll only need one," Mei said, already drawing her arm back.

Eva snorted, her arms folding across her chest. How did she look so comfortable? "Please. I suspect you'll need at least ten." And how could Eva taunt the person about to try and knock her from her perch?

Though perhaps Lily should give Eva credit, because it seemed to rile Mei up—so much so that when she threw the first ball, hard, it missed the target by some distance.

"You can do better than that, surely," Eva said, and Mei scowled as she marched forward to retrieve the ball.

Her other two attempts were unsuccessful, her face thunderous as she handed the ball back to Mark.

"Come on," Lily said, knocking Mei's shoulder with her own. "Let's go and play something else."

"Do you not want a try?" Mei seemed surprised. "I would've thought you'd be all over this."

Lily glanced back at Eva. It might be satisfying to wipe that smug look from her face, but Lily wasn't willing to jeopardize their blooming relationship because of it.

Eva had no such qualms.

"Come on, Miss Cross," Eva said, the challenge in her eyes unmistakable. "Let's see what you can do. It's for a good cause, remember?"

"All right." Lily dug a hand in her pocket for her wallet and handed the cash over to Mark. "But here's a little-known fact about me. I was a pitcher on my high school and college softball team."

Still, Eva looked unfazed. And her smugness grew as Lily threw her first ball, missing the target by a couple of inches. But at least now she knew how heavy it was—and what angle she needed to throw it at to hit the button.

"Are you sure about that?" Eva called as Lily retrieved the ball. "Because it looks like—"

Lily didn't wait until Eva had finished before aiming her second throw. It hid dead center, and Lily watched Eva's expression morph into one of surprise before she disappeared into the water.

"I suppose I deserved that," Eva said when she re-appeared, and if Lily had thought that skirt looked sinful before, it was nothing compared to it now. It was molded to her thighs, her blue blouse clinging to her skin, outlining the definition of her abs, and Lily ached to trace that same path with her tongue. "Well done."

Eva looked amused more than anything, running a hand through her hair to slick it back against her head as she re-took her seat. "Does anyone else think they have what it takes?"

A line had formed behind Lily, and she stepped out of their way. Mei clapped her on the shoulder. "Nice. I bet that felt good."

"Yeah." Though not for the reasons Mei was thinking. "What's next?"

After her final class of the day had skipped from her room, Lily returned to the courtyard to help the kids dismantle what was left of the funfair. Once they were done, they retreated to Lily's classroom to count the money they'd raised and reflect on the year they'd had.

Lily looked around the room once they were all inside, happy that their little group had grown from seven to seventeen in the span of just a few months.

It was a relief, considering the administration's reticence to start up the club in the first place, that they'd managed to do so well...which Lily was only too happy to tell them all once the meeting was nearly over.

"I'm so proud of each and every one of you," Lily said, trying not to get emotional for the second time that day, "and everything you've achieved this year. It's been a privilege getting to know you all, and I'm so grateful you trusted me to be your advisor. You've managed to raise nearly two thousand dollars over the past few months for all kinds of worthy causes, not to mention raise awareness of the issues the LGBTQIA+ community face across the school. I feel like we've barely gotten started, and now summer's here, but I know when we come back in the fall we're going to pick things back up again. I can't wait to see what the next year has in store for all of you."

"Thanks, Miss Cross." Macie was misty-eyed in the front row. "We wanted to thank you for everything you've done for us, too. We wouldn't have a club if not for you. We got these for you."

Macie, Sara, Hannah and Jude approached her desk, each of them holding a candle.

"These are from one of the charities we donated to," Sara said. "All the proceeds go toward their projects to help LGBTQIA+ youth."

"Thanks." Lily didn't make a habit of hugging her students, but she figured this called for an exception. "You have a good summer, okay? And I'll see you all in August, hopefully with some new ideas."

Her classroom felt too quiet when they were gone. The GSA was the highlight of her week, and she'd miss seeing them all over the summer.

Lily was gathering her things when someone knocked on her door. She glanced up, knowing she was alone in the department—Eva had left to go and get ready for their night, and the others had gone to the bar over an hour ago—and found David Blake standing in the hall.

"Got a minute?"

Lily glanced at her watch. A minute, maybe. If she wasn't out the door in five, she'd be pushing it to pick Eva up on time.

"Sure." What had she done now?

"I wanted to apologize," David said, digging his hands into the pockets of his jacket. "What you've done for the kids over the past few months, and the amount of money you've managed to raise... I was wrong to try and stand in your way."

"Oh." Lily blinked, hoping her surprise wasn't obvious on her face. This was the last thing she'd expected. While David hadn't made any further comments about the GSA since their initial frosty exchange, he hadn't exactly been eager to involve himself in their activities the way some of the other teachers had. "Thanks."

"Keep up the good work," David said, ducking out with a nod, and Lily waited a few seconds before she followed, a spring in her step as she made her way to the parking lot.

The butterflies she'd been keeping at bay all day erupted as Lily arrived home. She'd purposefully not given herself long to get ready, knowing she'd only overthink if her mind was left idle.

How could she not, after everything she and Eva had been through? What if Eva had changed her mind? What if dinner was a disaster, and they realized they wouldn't work together? What if this was all a giant mistake?

Lily took a deep breath, concentrating on touching up her make-up. There was no point worrying until after they'd been on the date.

On her bed, Lily's phone buzzed, and she smiled when she saw Eva's— she'd finally changed it from Elsa the night before—name on the screen.

Am I allowed to know where we're going yet?

I told you—it's a surprise.

I hate surprises.

I know. Lily smiled, stepping into her dress. *I'll be leaving in five minutes, so I should be at your house by seven.*

My mother will have a field day when she sees your car. She hasn't shut up about you since you left last night.

Lily's smile widened. *I made a good impression, then?*

You are the first woman I've brought home to her in three years, so... it's a low bar.

You can say yes, you know. It won't kill you.

It might.

Laughing, Lily slid her phone into her bag and hurried down the stairs. She tipped some kibble into Hades' bowl and scratched the top of her head. "I'll be back later. Don't get into any trouble while I'm gone." Hades meowed in response, and Lily headed for the front door.

The drive to Eva's house shouldn't be familiar to her already, but Lily found it with no trouble and pulled to a stop outside. The door opened before Lily had the chance to reach for her phone, and she waved to Eleanor, visible through the doorway as Eva walked down the drive.

Lily's breath caught at the sight of her. Eva wore the same dress from Winter Formal, and Lily swallowed, vividly remembering what the material of that dress had felt like beneath her fingertips.

"You're evil," Lily said, when she got in the car, and Eva's lips curved into a wicked smirk.

"What? You told me to wear a nice dress."

"Not that dress."

"It's lucky."

"It's something," Lily muttered. "Are you trying to kill me?"

"No." Eva's eyes found hers, gray and smoldering. "Because I have a lot of plans for you, and none of them involve you dying before I'm through with you."

Lily swallowed, her throat feeling tight, the air feeling so thick it was hard to breathe. "Why are we going to a restaurant and not my empty house right now?"

"Because we're supposed to be doing this properly," Eva said, her gaze fixed on Lily's lips.

"What's wrong with a little impropriety?"

"Dinner," Eva said, though the way her tongue swept along her bottom lip was utterly sinful. "And then you can drive me back to your place for as much impropriety as you want."

Lily nodded, tearing her gaze away from Eva's mouth and stepping on the gas. The woman was going to be the death of her, Lily was sure, but oh, what a sweet way to go.

The Italian restaurant was a twenty-minute drive from High Grove, nestled between a cocktail bar and a dry-cleaners.

"I hope this is okay," Lily said, wringing her hands after she'd put the car into park. "I've been here a few times. It's a family-run place, but they do great pizzas and—"

"Lily." Eva cut off her rambling and settled a hand high on Lily's thigh. "Breathe. You don't have to impress me, you know."

"I don't?"

"Of course you don't. You could take me to a food truck on the side of the highway if you wanted."

"All right, then." Lily reached for the ignition, a grin stretching across her mouth. "I think I saw a taco truck on the way—"

"Let's not be too hasty," Eva said. "We're already here."

Lily's grin widened, but she let her hand fall back to her lap. "I'm sorry. I'm just nervous, I guess. I haven't been on a first date in three years."

"How do you think I feel? I haven't been on one in five."

"I'm terrified of messing this up."

"Honestly? Me too." Eva met Lily's gaze. "But…we can't go into this second-guessing ourselves, or putting too much pressure on it, because here's the thing: we are going to mess up. Relationships are messy at their core. And I don't know if you and I are going to be strong enough to weather the storm, but I…I want to try."

"Me too." Lily leaned over the center console to risk smearing Eva's lipstick.

Eva let herself get lost in the kiss for a long moment. "We should go inside," Eva said when they parted, both breathing heavily. "Before we get too carried away."

It was hard not to feel smug at the dazed look in Lily's eyes. Lily shook her head as if to clear it before reaching for the door handle, and when she slipped her hand into Eva's once they were outside, Eva didn't pull away.

Only half of the tables in the restaurant were full, and they were led to a booth in the back corner. The red leather creaked as Eva sat down, Lily's face illuminated by the flickering candles set in the middle of the wide table.

Eva glanced over the menu. "What do you recommend?"

"The ravioli is good. That's your favorite, right?"

It had been an offhand comment in a conversation months ago, but then, Eva supposed she shouldn't be too touched Lily had remembered, seeing as she was sure she knew what Lily would be ordering. "And yours is ham and pepperoni pizza."

Sometimes, Eva struggled to remember that Lily and Molly were the same person. But it was getting easier, the more time they spent together, to put together the pieces in her mind and merge them into one.

"Do you want wine? I think they do half bottles."

Eva shook her head. "I want to remember every second of this night." She lowered her voice. "Especially everything that happens after we get out of here."

Lily's swallow was audible, her cheeks turning pink, and Eva chuckled. It was so easy to make her squirm.

Eva's gaze settled on Lily's face once their server had taken their orders. "How much did you make from the funfair?"

"Nine hundred," Lily said with pride.

"Wow. Well done."

"Thanks. Though I suppose I should be thanking you—how many people tried to dunk you?"

"Hmm…at least thirty. Only four were successful, though." It had been a better outcome than Eva was expecting.

"Sorry."

"Don't be. It was all in the spirit of good fun. Besides, I think you made Mei's year." Eva had never seen their colleague so overjoyed. And speaking of Mei... "Does she know about us?"

Lily was quick to shake her head.

"It's okay if she does. I know you two are close."

"We are, but I haven't told her anything. I didn't think you'd want me airing our dirty laundry in the department."

Eva supposed that might be for the best. If Mei did know, she would've probably marched into Eva's classroom and threatened her.

"She knows I'm on a date tonight," Lily said. "But I didn't tell her it was you."

Who did Mei think it was with? Were there other women Lily had been speaking to, women Mei was privy to but Eva wasn't? Had she ever spoken to anyone else on the app? Eva knew she didn't have a right to feel jealous about any of it, but she couldn't stop it sparking to life in her gut.

"Well, I suppose I did, in a way." Lily smiled, and Eva quirked an eyebrow. "Mei was the one who told me about CuteMeet. She asked me, once, if I'd met anyone on it, and I told her about Elsa. Never mentioned the rest of it, though."

"I see." Eva dreaded to think what the reaction from their co-workers would be when they did find out, but...that was a worry for a different day. For now, she had Lily sitting opposite her in a beautiful green dress, and she was the only one who mattered.

Dinner was a mixture of delicious food and light conversation, Eva laughing more than she could remember doing in a long time. She'd feared it would be difficult, or awkward, that the two of them simply couldn't fit together if they weren't fighting, but...it was easy, now she'd let down the last of her walls.

"Shall we get out of here?" Lily said, almost the second the check was placed on their table. Eagerness was written across her face, and Eva felt giddy as Lily took her hand and dragged her out to the car.

The night stretched out before them, and this time, when they fell into one another, there would be no frantic rush, there would be no need for distraction, there would be no sinking feeling of regret.

There would be only tender touches, heated kisses and greedy hands, Eva mapping out every inch of Lily's skin in a way she'd never dared allow herself before.

They had a long, winding road ahead of them, damage they needed to repair, wounds they needed to heal, but Eva knew, as Lily smiled at her from the driver's seat, that it would be worth it.

Epilogue

Eva pushed herself faster, her breathing turning labored as her feet pounded against the sidewalk. It was eight o'clock, but the day was already warm, the mid-August air humid, and Eva sighed in relief when she turned the corner onto her street.

She heard the quiet sound of voices when she opened the front door, and Franklin raced into the kitchen as soon as Eva had unclipped his leash.

Eva kicked off her shoes and followed him down the hall, smiling at the sight that greeted her. Lily stood at the stove, a spatula in hand ready to flip the pancake sizzling in the pan. She wore one of Eva's old Georgetown shirts and a pair of pajama shorts that hugged her curves.

Eva's mother sat at the kitchen table, a mug of coffee in her hands and the puzzle section of the newspaper spread out in front of her.

"Are you two doing the crossword again?" Eva said, making a beeline for the refrigerator and a cold bottle of water.

"Always," Lily said. "You'll never guess what ten down was."

"What?" Eva leaned against the counter and smirked when she caught Lily's gaze lingering on Eva's abs, left bare by her sports bra.

"Eleanor?" Lily flipped a pancake with ease and added it to the large stack of them already on a plate.

"Idina Menzel voiced this character in *Frozen*," her mother said, and Eva nearly choked on her water. "Lily helped me out on that one."

"I'll bet. She is a big Elsa fan, after all."

Lily shrugged. "She's okay."

Eva narrowed her eyes, but Lily just grinned. After three months together, Lily was immune to Eva's glares.

"Only okay?"

"She's no Ariel."

Eva shook her head. "I don't know. You have the audacity to insult me when you're in my house, wearing my clothes, eating my food—"

"Making your food, you mean?" Lily countered, adding the last pancake to the stack and turning off the burner. "Unless you don't want any of these."

Lily waved the plate toward Eva, and her traitorous stomach rumbled. Eva was a good cook, but Lily's talents when it came to sweet treats were unrivaled. Eva had been going out on extra runs to compensate for the increased calorie intake.

"I won't turn them down."

Lily laughed as she set the plate on the table.

"Thank you for breakfast, Lily," her mother said, and Eva wasn't sure who appreciated Lily's presence in their life more. Lily and her mother got along like a house on fire—often banding together against Eva, but Eva didn't mind. She was happier than she could ever remember being, and she knew it was all down to the woman sitting beside her.

"Not a problem," Lily said. "I thought I'd better take advantage of our last quiet morning."

Tomorrow, the school year began again. At least they had two institute days to ease them into it, but Eva wasn't looking forward to it. Usually she was desperate to get back to her classroom, boredom taking hold in the long break, but she'd enjoyed her summer with Lily more than she'd ever thought possible.

A part of Eva was scared to go back to work. She and Lily had been existing in a bubble for the past three months, splitting their time between Lily's place and High Grove, and Eva didn't want it to pop once the real world crept in. Eva worried about making time for one another when their schedules were a mess, and while she wasn't worried about their colleagues finding out, she did worry about what they might say to Lily. Would they try to talk her out of it? Not that she'd listen. Lily was almost as stubborn as Eva, and she hadn't given Eva a single reason to doubt she wanted to be with her.

Old wounds healed slowly, but Eva finally felt like she was in a good place and she didn't want anything to jeopardize that.

"Have you got anything nice planned for the day?" Her mother broke Eva out of her thoughts.

"Shopping," Eva said around a mouthful of fluffy pancake. "Seeing as somebody is woefully unprepared for the coming year."

"Well, we can't all be as anal as you when it comes to organization, can we?" Lily's eyes were bright in the early morning light. "Have you got your label-maker ready?"

"Yes, to label you with a warning—highly irritating."

"Oh, you two." Eva's mother shook her head. "Never a dull moment when you're together."

Right on cue, a commotion erupted in the corner of the kitchen. Franklin—who had been sleeping soundly, exhausted after their run—leapt up with a yelp as a streak of black fur made a beeline for his bed.

Franklin's claws skittered on the linoleum floor as he scrambled to his feet, racing under the table to hide behind Eva's legs as Hades perched in the center of the dog bed and licked delicately at one of her paws.

"You big baby," Eva said, stretching a hand down to scratch the top of Franklin's head. "You're three times the size of her."

Big brown eyes blinked up at her.

"Oh, look at his face." Lily leaned over to give Franklin a pat of her own. "I'm sorry I keep bringing her here to terrorize you."

"Please, she's harmless. He just needs to stand up for himself." Which he wouldn't, because he was too soft.

"They need some time to warm up to one another," her mother said, and Eva thought of her and Lily, and how far they'd come in a year.

"That sounds familiar," Lily said, a smile playing around the edges of her mouth, and Eva knew she was thinking the same. "He'll grow on her eventually."

"Wear her down, more like."

Lily knocked Eva's shoulder with her own, and Eva smiled, settling a hand on Lily's thigh beneath the table. She was going to miss mornings like this, the three of them doing the crossword with nowhere else to be.

High Grove hadn't ever felt like home, but now, with Lily, Eva felt content, could imagine a future there in a way she never had before. And it had only been three months, but it was long enough for Eva to know one thing: Lily was a part of her life she never wanted to be without.

"You said you need a few things, Lily." Eva, weighed down by several bags, complained as Lily led them out of the stationery store.

"I didn't specify how many 'a few' was."

Eva glared, and Lily leaned on her toes to press a kiss to her cheek. "Come on, I'll buy you a coffee to make up for it."

Eva was still grumbling when Lily pulled open the door of the coffeehouse.

"You can go back to my place if you want. I'll be—"

"No. Fucking. Way."

Lily whirled around at the unexpected interruption and swallowed when she came face-to-face with a wide-eyed Mei.

"What are you two doing together?" Mei's eyebrows creased into a frown as she looked between Lily and Eva. This was not the Wednesday afternoon Lily had expected.

"Uhm..." Lily's mind went blank.

Lily hadn't seen Mei much over the summer, but when they had met up Mei had been eager to hear all about Lily's new girlfriend.

A girlfriend Lily had neglected to mention was Eva.

And it wasn't like she wanted to keep it a secret. Lily wasn't ashamed of Eva. But she hadn't known how Mei would react, and she and Eva hadn't really talked about being open about their relationship at work, and—

"Lily?" Mei was still waiting for an answer, and Lily knew Eva was letting her take the lead.

"We're together because we are together," Lily said, reaching down to slip her fingers through Eva's. "Eva is the woman I've been seeing."

"I knew it!" Mei's voice was loud enough to draw the attention of the people sitting at the nearby tables. "I said there was something there and you denied it! I can't believe you lied to me. Actually..." Mei glanced toward Eva. "Maybe I can."

"I'm going to order," Eva said, because they were next in line. "Caramel macchiato?"

"I'm supposed to be paying."

"It's fine." Eva waved her off, and Lily wondered if she just wanted an escape. "Do you want anything, Mei?"

Mei looked at Eva like she'd grown a second head. "No, thank you." She waited for Eva to walk away before adding: "I don't trust you not to poison it."

Lily elbowed Mei sharply in the side. "Stop it."

"I'm sorry, have you suffered a blow to the head?"

"No." Lily took Mei's arm and steered her to a table at the back of the coffeehouse. "Look, I'm sorry I lied, okay? I didn't want to say anything until I knew what was going on between us, and then…then I didn't know how to tell you."

"How the hell did this start?"

"I didn't lie about that." Lily might not have been forthcoming with all the details, but she'd used some of the truth when Mei had asked her how things were going. "We did start messaging on CuteMeet, and I had no idea who she was. At the same time, in real life… we annoyed each other, but there was a spark we couldn't ignore, too. So when we found out we'd already been talking it just made sense to try and make a go of it." An abridged version of events, perhaps, but Mei didn't need to know every detail.

"It was the D.C. trip, wasn't it?" Mei shook her head. "I knew there was a reason you looked so happy when you got back." Mei glanced toward Eva where she waited for their coffees. "And are you? Happy with her?"

Lily answered without hesitation. "Yeah, I am. I know based on what you've seen of her it doesn't make sense, but…we're good together. We balance each other out." The summer months had been some of the best of Lily's life.

"Oh, God." Mei scrunched her nose. "You're in love with her, aren't you?"

"What?" Lily squeaked, because that was a step she and Eva had yet to take.

"It's written all over your face."

Lily looked at Eva again, who had now collected their coffees and waited a few feet away, not wanting to infringe on Mei and Lily's conversation. Eva still had Lily's bags slung over her arm, her hair and her blouse rumpled from Lily's wandering hands before they'd left the house, and when their eyes met, Lily felt her heart beat faster in her chest and knew Mei was right.

"She's not the person she pretends to be," Lily said, instead of admitting it.

"I'll have to take your word for it." Mei didn't look convinced. "But... if she makes you happy, and she treats you right, who am I to say you shouldn't be together?"

Lily could've kissed her.

"Does this mean she's going to start coming to after-works drinks?" Mei looked terrified of the prospect, and Lily laughed.

"Let's not get carried away." Lily couldn't see Eva settling across from the others with a martini, but then, Eva had done a lot of things this summer that surprised her. "You could stay for a coffee though, if you wanted."

"I'm actually late to meet James," she said. "I only came in here because when I saw you with her I couldn't believe my eyes. Tomorrow's going to be weird."

"It won't be."

"It will. I'll know you've seen Eva naked."

Lily laughed. "I'll spare you the details of how many times."

"Thank you." Mei pulled her into a hug. "I'll see you in the morning. And don't worry—your secret is safe with me."

Mei ducked out the door, and Eva approached the second she was gone. "Everything okay?"

"Everything's fine." Lily accepted the coffee cup Eva handed her with a smile. Her heart jolted as their fingers brushed, and she marveled at the effect Eva still had on her three months in.

"What did she have to say? Nothing good, I bet." Eva's lips curved downwards, and Lily could see a storm building behind her eyes, knew she still worried something was going to tear them apart, that Lily would decide the two of them together was a mistake and walk away.

But Lily wasn't going anywhere. She'd had her doubts, in the beginning—how could she not, after all they'd been through? But Eva had let her in, had shown Lily they could work together, and now Lily couldn't imagine a life that didn't have Eva in it.

"Why are you looking at me like that?" Eva asked, her frown deepening by the second.

"Because I…" Was a coffeehouse the best place for this conversation? No, but Lily was tired of waiting. She and Eva had done too much of it already. "I love you."

Surprise flickered across Eva's face, but her frown morphed into a smile as she curved her free hand around Lily's waist. "You do?"

"I do."

Eva ducked her head to press a soft kiss to Lily's lips. "I love you, too," Eva murmured against Lily's mouth, and she sighed when Lily kissed her again. "Now, can we please leave? I'm losing circulation in my arms, and I don't know how well I'd be able to teach next week if they fall off."

Lily laughed and let Eva tug her toward the door, knowing that whatever the next school year brought, she'd be facing it with Eva by her side.

Other Books from Ylva Publishing

www.ylva-publishing.com

Never Say Never

Rachael Sommers

ISBN: 978-3-96324-429-2

Length: 220 pages (75,000 words)

Ambitious Camila might have lost her marriage but she doesn't need love to build a TV empire and raise her young son. What she does need is a nanny.

Enter Emily—bright, naive, and new to New York City. Emily is everything Camila is not and that's not all that's unsettling.

Surely she can't be falling for the nanny?

An age-gap, opposites-attract lesbian romance with a puddle of melted ice queen.

Coming Home

Lois Cloarec Hart

ISBN: 978-3-95533-064-4

Length: 371 pages (104,000 words)

Rob, a charismatic ex-fighter pilot severely disabled with MS, has been steadfastly cared for by his wife, Jan, for many years. Quite by accident one day, Terry, a young writer/postal carrier, enters their lives and turns it upside down.

A triangle with a twist, *Coming Home* is the story of three good people caught up in an impossible situation

The Music and the Mirror
Lola Keeley

ISBN: 978-3-96324-014-0
Length: 311 pages (120,000 words)

Anna is the newest member of an elite ballet company. Her first class almost ruins her career before it begins. She must face down jealousy, sabotage, and injury to pour everything into opening night and prove she has what it takes. In the process, Anna discovers that she and the daring, beautiful Victoria have a lot more than ballet in common.

Lost for Words
Andrea Bramhall

ISBN: 978-3-96324-062-1
Length: 300 pages (104,000 words)

Massage therapist Sasha's meddlesome mother and best friend conspire to shake up her mundane existence by entering her into a scriptwriting contest. She's not entirely sure how she feels about the life-upending chaos that ensues, which includes meeting an attractive, perfectionist film producer.

A bittersweet lesbian romantic comedy about the fun of never knowing what life will bring.

About Rachael Sommers

Rachael Sommers was born and raised in the North-West of England, where she began writing at the age of thirteen, and has been unable to stop since. A biology graduate, she currently works in education and constantly dreams of travelling the world. In her spare time, she enjoys horse riding, board games, escape rooms and, of, course, reading.

CONNECT WITH RACHAEL
Website: www.rachaelsommers.com
E-Mail: rachaelsommersauthor@gmail.com

Chemistry
© 2022 by Rachael Sommers

ISBN: 978-3-96324-679-1

Available in e-book and paperback formats.

Published by Ylva Publishing, legal entity of Ylva Verlag, e.Kfr.

Ylva Verlag, e.Kfr.
Owner: Astrid Ohletz
Am Kirschgarten 2
65830 Kriftel
Germany

www.ylva-publishing.com

First edition: 2022

Credits
Edited by C.S. Conrad and Sheena Billet
Cover Design and Print Layout by Streetlight Graphics

Printed in Great Britain
by Amazon

85158200R00171